I0716052

Penn & Ava

Penn & Ava

a novel

SUSAN VICTORIA BECHER

Pen & Publish
Saint Louis, Missouri

Published by Pen & Publish, LLC, USA

www.PenandPublish.com
info@PenandPublish.com

Saint Louis, Missouri
(314) 827-6567

ISBN: 978-1-956897-43-2

Library of Congress Control Number: 2024938411

Printed on acid-free paper.

Cover artwork by Julia Whitney Barnes
"Nocturnal Nature (Hibiscus, Goldenrod, Poppies, Cosmos, Pollinators, etc)"
www.juliawhitneybarnes.com

To everyone who loves me for the person I really am.
May we all become a safe place for others.

♥

part one

Slowly fade
into vastness

Reach out
to find
more of the same

You see me
in the shadows
of monotony

It's you who
teaches me
it's okay

To not be okay

chapter one

Ava tucked a strand of hair behind her ear as Leona's shrieking laughter filled the open-concept first floor. She glanced over at the group of guys in the corner of Trish's living room, hoping Lukas would look her way, just once. Ava leaned further into the kitchen island's marble countertop and searched his face for any sign of interest. Tonight, he was too busy rehashing last night's soccer game to notice her subtle flirtation.

The party felt stale, a repeat of the same people and the same progression. Freshmen girls huddled together in the middle of the room, clutching red plastic solo cups to their overly padded breasts. They twirled their hair in unison, eyes scanning the room for their latest crush.

Boys from the football team drifted up from the basement, filling the room with the thick scent of weed and cheap beer. Liam parted from the pack and made his way over to their small circle. He reached his meaty hand into a near-empty bag of chips sitting in the middle of the island. Ava winced as he shoved fistfuls of crumbs into his mouth. As attractive as he had gotten this year, she still found his eating habits repulsive.

Ava wasn't all that interested in Liam or Lukas, but she needed a new way to pass the time. She had begun to feel so numb, nothing could break through the dense fog of unwavering monotony. She'd spent the start of the school year partying as usual with Leona and Trish, but the thrill was fading fast. She felt she might be fading away in some sense as well.

Breaking up with Lukas last week hadn't gone as smoothly as Ava planned. When she pulled him into the trees on the edge of Westwood High's track to say it was over, he merely shrugged. It was then she realized Lukas cared less about her than she cared about him. It stung more than the breakup itself. She thought tonight if she could lure him back to her, prove to him she was worthy of his attention, then maybe, this time, she'd feel something.

"Uh, hello? Ava?" Leona asked, waving her sharp black fingernails in Ava's face. "We've asked you the same question three times. Are you trying to get back with Lukas?"

"N-no. What do you think I am, desperate?" Ava replied, trying her best to sound incredulous.

Though Leona and Trish were smart enough not to answer, Ava caught them locking eyes and smirking. They'd been doing this a lot lately, not bothering to hide it from her anymore. Before, she had found this behavior endearing, a way to feel bonded to them. Now she found herself queasy in their presence.

Ava set her aluminum can softly down on the island, murmuring that she needed some air. She slipped in and out of acquaintances, nodding slightly to acknowledge them but not enough to welcome conversation. The sliding glass door on the side of the house led to an empty patio filled with bare furniture, stripped of cushions now that fall was ending. She'd committed to memory all the quiet places Trish's giant home had to offer. This one was her favorite. In the past, she would have invited a boy out here, but tonight, the only company she wanted to entertain was her own.

Shivering, she squatted down on the concrete step. She cursed out loud for not bringing the jacket she'd glanced at on the coat rack back at home. Her need to show an extra inch of stomach overpowered the basic human need for warmth, yet again. As overbearing as her older sister was, if Jacklyn were here, she would've made sure Ava grabbed it. Instead, Ava wrapped her arms around her bare skin.

The night sky was dark and clear, allowing the stars to shine as they were meant to. A sliver of the moon was visible amidst the treetops. For the briefest moment, she felt she belonged to something much larger than herself. It was a fleeting relief from the underwhelming reality playing out behind her. Once she stepped back inside, she'd go back to feeling utterly replaceable, entirely forgettable. Yet the comforting glow of the evening light was not enough to heal whatever it was within her that ached.

She shifted her weight back into her hands. A crisp breeze washed over her, chilling her to the bone. The familiar scent of damp, decaying leaves met her nose, and with it, she breathed in memories of Halloweens past. Ava always dressed up in a mini-version of Jacklyn's costume, their little brother Mac trailing close behind as a cute prop.

Ava wished she could sit frozen to the ground forever as the door slid on its track behind her. Warm air rushed across her back. Leona's sickly sweet perfume invaded her reverie, causing her forehead to wrinkle in disgust.

"What the *hell* are you doing?" Leona asked, her shrill voice cutting through Ava's short-lived peace. "It's freezing. Get in here. Liam is asking about you!"

Ava turned to stare at her friend's shapely calf below her plum-colored miniskirt.

"Well, are you coming or not? Don't expect me to stand here waiting forever," Leona complained. Ava lifted her gaze upward, but Leona was too captivated by her phone to notice. The bluish glow illuminated Leona's large brown doe-eyes.

"Why are you so obsessed with getting me together with Liam?" Ava asked, more to capture Leona's attention than she cared to know. Leona blinked a couple of times, then tossed glorious waves of dark hair over her shoulder.

"He's super-hot, Ava. *Obviously.* And single. Plus, you need to move on from Lukas. Liam is perfect for you, trust me."

"*Perfectly Neanderthal,*" Ava muttered under her breath as she stood and heaved a loud sigh. Leona turned and flicked her hair behind her, hitting Ava across the chin. Ava usually kept a wide berth around Leona for this very reason.

As Ava made her way back to the kitchen, she spotted Liam on the cognac leather sectional. At over 6′4″, he took up a third of the sofa all on his own. He had one arm draped loosely on the back of the seat cushions and a long muscular leg propped up on the glass coffee table. Lukas noticed Ava checking Liam out. In response, Lukas stretched his arm around the sophomore who now joined him in the corner. Ava noticed the sophomore's cleavage was remarkable, without a trace of padding involved. She crossed her arms over her small chest, uncomfortable admitting she judged other girls too much by their cup size.

When Liam glanced her way, Ava gave a small half-wave. He raised an eyebrow, too cool to lift his arm, or meaty hand, to greet her. She debated whether she should pursue him or not. She wasn't entirely sure if it mattered either way. She could easily coax him up to a bedroom upstairs, initiate some sort of fling, and let it entertain her until it didn't anymore.

She studied him, homing in on his sharp jawline, which had emerged from what were chubby cheeks this past summer. Though his jawline was admirable, it was his vibrant salmon shorts that caused her to second-guess this plan. When Liam's gaze rested on the girl's ass in front of him, Ava's mind was made up.

She poured the rest of her beer down the sink. When she turned around, she watched Leona and Trish clink their shot glasses together and drink them down without her. It was clear they didn't care whether she participated or not in the evening's festivities. A familiar jolt shot through her stomach. She'd known since Jacklyn left she'd been on the edge of this friendship. But tonight, in her sobered state, she knew "the edge" was generous. They hardly tolerated her anymore.

As this realization hit her, Ava edged toward the front door. She ducked around classmates, tugging at her regrettably short sweater. When she reached the entryway, she paused, questioning whether she was allowed to leave without Leona's permission.

Ava jumped, startled, as a girl to her left stumbled into her, beer slopping onto the tile floor. Ava steadied her, glancing back to make sure Trish and Leona were still preoccupied. Giggles descended from the upstairs landing. Ava looked up to find the freshman girls she saw earlier in the evening gathered. They reminded her of vultures circling their prey.

"Are those your friends?" Ava asked the unsteady girl, now clutching her arm. The girl looked up, dazed. It was astonishing how young she appeared under her ill-matching foundation and dark eyeliner. "Do you want a ride home?"

"Oh, she's *fine*. We're training her on how to get properly wasted," a pretty freshman answered from above. She leaned her long, lean torso further over the railing to peer down at Ava. "We only invited her because we got stuck in a group project together. She practically begged to come." The other girls tittered, watching in awe as their friend spoke to an upperclassman. "You're Jacklyn Pierson's sister, aren't you?"

Ava's skin felt as though it had been set on fire. She bit her lower lip, heard her heart pounding in her ears.

"Why don't you leave with me?" Ava asked the girl who still clung to her. "You don't have to stay here."

The girl's face contorted as if Ava had said something highly offensive. Then, she ripped her arm away, her solo cup flying onto the sandstone floor, splattering those nearby.

"I'm fine! Where's that hot guy? The one on the football team? My friends say he's into me."

Ava looked up at the gathered trio, now doubled over in laughter as their classmate slipped on her beer trail. She wanted to follow the girl as she stumbled away but knew it was pointless. These parties wouldn't be successful if there weren't someone to laugh at. She would know; it was usually her, Trish, and Leona doing the laughing.

With one last look, Ava spotted Trish and Leona disappearing into the basement. She made her escape, rushing out the door and jogging down the long stone walkway. Her high wedged heels carried her as fast as they could up the block. She exhaled in elation at the sight of her Jeep sparkling under a streetlight.

Ava hopped in and started the ignition, shaking from the cold. Loud techno beats boomed from the speakers. She smacked the volume knob to turn it off and reached into the back floorboard to grab her bright red fleece blanket to lay across her lap.

Driving miles under the speed limit, she shivered on the short drive home. Pulling into her driveway, she turned the headlights off, letting the car idle. She planted her elbows on the steering wheel, creating a shelf with her hands to rest her chin. She imagined her garage door transforming into a magic portal that would transport her far away from Westwood. She even thought she might cry but knew that was ridiculous. Nobody cried in the Pierson house. Especially not in the driveway where the whole neighborhood could see.

Slumping back into her driver seat, Ava turned the car off then slipped inside her house. The glow of the TV danced across the walls of the living room to her right. Tiptoeing into the foyer, she found it was Mac in front of the screen, his skinny frame engulfed by their gigantic sectional.

"You're home early. Everything okay?" Mac asked, pausing his video game. The question tugged at her, activating emotions she could no longer suppress now that she'd crossed the threshold of her home. Nodding quickly, she raced up the polished white marble staircase to her bedroom.

Ava sighed in relief as she threw herself face down onto her bed. She pulled hangers and clothes out from under her and tossed them onto the floor. Rolling onto her back to stare at the ceiling, she hoped it was all just a bad case of PMS. Her phone vibrated at the foot of her bed. She kicked her purse to the floor, knowing she'd soon face endless questioning about what was wrong with her tonight.

Rolling onto her side, Ava curled into a tight ball. She wrapped her arms around her torso and held herself until a single tear released itself across the bridge of her nose and onto the soft pink comforter below her cheek. She wanted to make it stop, but nothing could prevent her forbidden emotions from surfacing. The dam had broken.

With one muffled sob, Ava's tears fell in quick succession. Her chest heaved from the crushing weight of forces she couldn't name. Then with closed eyes and her arms still wrapped around her, Ava cried herself to sleep.

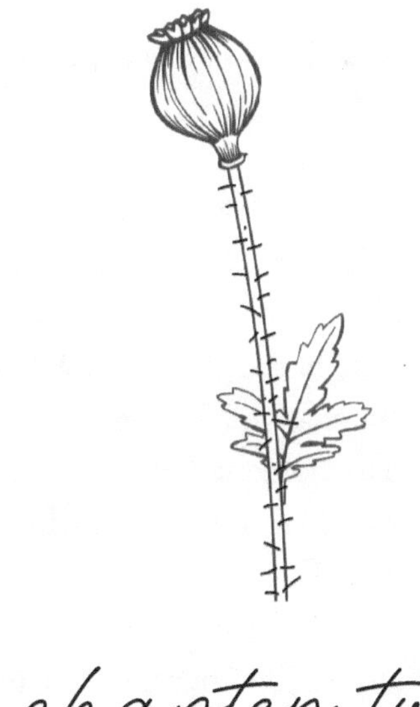

chapter two

Ava cherished the hours she spent on Sunday tangled up in her covers, alone. Her phone was still dead, protecting her from the outside world. The only company she kept was her black and white cat, Olivia, who curled in the nook of her knees, not once questioning her lack of mobility.

On Monday morning, Ava woke to a harsh chink of sunlight streaming through her blinds. She winced and rolled over, wishing the weekend would stretch one day longer.

"Shit," she gasped at the sound of her brother moving in the hallway. She scrambled out of bed to open her laptop to check the time. There was less than half an hour left to get to school before the tardy bell rang. With a bolt of panic, she scrambled down the hall to the bathroom, passing Mac on the way.

"Slow down, Sis. What's the hurry?" Mac asked, ruffling his hair in the hallway mirror. Ava was too busy splashing water on her face to answer. He shrugged and turned back toward his bedroom, dressed in faded jeans much too short for him. Ava couldn't believe how much he'd grown over the summer or how much he was beginning to resemble their father.

"Can you take the bus today?" Ava asked, spitting her final rinse into the sink.

"I guess. If I go now, I can still make it," Mac answered, eyeing her greasy hair suspiciously. "Are you sick or something?"

"No, don't worry about it. Take the bus or hitch a ride after school, too, okay? I've got practice today."

"*I know.* I always find a way home after school. You sure you're okay?"

"Yeah, yeah. I really gotta change and get out of here. I'm fine," Ava persisted, waving him off. Mac took one last concerned look before slinging his backpack over his shoulder. He headed down the stairs as Ava slammed the bathroom door shut.

Ava dabbed aggressively at her face with a washcloth. She tried to get rid of the leftover mascara residue beneath her puffy eyes. Fumbling through the cabinets, she found an old bottle of Jacklyn's dry shampoo and sprayed it onto her locks. Cursing, she threw her hair into a high ponytail, hoping to hide the whole disaster.

Time was not on her side as she shimmied on yoga pants and an over-sized gray long-sleeve tee. She ravaged her closet, tossing aside heels until she found a pair of forgotten sneakers hidden under a mound of t-shirts. Ava pictured Leona's face at the sight of her wearing white high-tops but didn't have time to change. She shuddered in the mirror at the zit forming on her chin before racing downstairs to the kitchen.

Her mother sat perched on a stool next to the spotless black marble countertop. She didn't look up from her computer as Ava grabbed a banana from a bowl near the sink.

"I've got practice today, but I'll be home in time for dinner," Ava said as she jogged to the front door. Mrs. Pierson held up a finger, signaling she was in the middle of working on a critical case. Ava danced in place, checking the clock on the stove. When Mrs. Pierson finally raised her head, Ava couldn't help but notice her hair was swept into a flawless updo.

"I won't be home until late tonight, and your father is still in the city. Make sure your brother eats something," Mrs. Pierson said, grimacing at Ava's outfit before returning to her screen.

Ava nodded, then sprinted out to her car and slammed the key into the ignition. She whipped into the parking lot with minutes left to spare, then scaled three flights of steps to the entrance of Westwood High. She hustled down the main hallway, arriving inside the doorway of Algebra 2/Trig as the bell rang.

Panting, she slid into the front desk in the row closest to the door, careful to avoid eye contact with Trish, who sat at the back of the class. The minute-hand of the clock moved painfully slow through the lesson on polynomial division.

After what felt like months, the class ended, sending Ava rocketing into the hallway. She ran down a small flight of stairs to the safety of her AP English class. Leona, Trish, and anyone with an ounce of popularity wouldn't be caught dead there. Ava still couldn't figure out how the school counselor had convinced her to take it.

Ava settled into a seat near the wall of windows overlooking the soccer field. She hardly noticed as classmates filled in around her. When the bell rang, she glanced up to find Mrs. Papayanni scribbling on the whiteboard. The chunky streak of gray that curled around the left side of her face was extra endearing this morning.

"All right, settle down, settle down! Mr. Reuben, please find your seat! Ms. Davis, please put your phone away," Mrs. Papayanni demanded, pausing for the students to quiet down. "Who can tell me what's next on our syllabus?"

Ava rubbed her lips together, averting eye contact as much as the other students. Then a hand shot up in the seat next to her.

"Yes, Mr. Abrams?"

"Since we completed *Fences* by August Wilson last week, we'll start *Death of a Salesman*," the boy said. "It's a play written in 1948 by American playwright Arthur Miller, produced in 1959. It will be the last play we study before we move into poetry."

"Exactly, right!" Mrs. Papayanni exclaimed, ignoring the loud groans issuing from around the room.

A subtle smirk appeared on the boy's face next to her as he leaned forward in his seat. He shook out his hands, preparing to take in Mrs. Papayanni's assignment. Ava widened her eyes and quickly looked away, afraid he might try to talk to her.

"You will be dividing into pairs for one of my favorite projects of the semester!" Mrs. Papayanni said. The boy beside her looked like he might start drooling in anticipation. Mrs. Papayanni continued, "Your assignment is to recreate the stage production of *Death of a Salesman*. From set to costume to lighting design, from actors to venue choice, you'll want to research every aspect of what goes into creating a successful play." A murmur grew loud throughout the classroom. "I'm trusting you to choose your partner wisely."

Ava looked up from her desk, mortified. Though she'd lived in Westwood her entire life, she hadn't spoken to a single person in this class. Everyone around her was already pairing off. Her heart began to race in her chest. She stared down at her hands, afraid to look up and find that no one wanted to partner with her.

A voice like an electric current shocked her back to the present.

"Hey, I don't know your name. Do you want to be my partner? Honestly, you might have to be my partner. Pardon me?" The boy who had answered Mrs. Papayanni's question leaned over the sidebar of his desk. He moved his arms frantically to get her attention.

"*Ava*," she whispered, horrified.

"I'm sorry. I didn't catch that?"

Ava turned in her seat, scared to meet his jarring direct stare. His head was cocked at a sharp angle, tight curls springing in opposing directions.

"A-A-Ava. *My name*. It's Ava."

"Oh, Ava. Great. Great! I'm Penn Abrams. Partners?" he asked, his voice several decibels louder than necessary. He stuck out the same hand she was annoyed by moments before.

Ava hoped he wouldn't notice her sweaty palms from the mild panic attack she was experiencing. As they grasped hands, Ava looked down at a large vein running the length of his forearm. Then, looking back up into Penn's face, she saw his eyes were a rare hazel color, almost bronze. They seemed ablaze as sunlight streamed through the windows beside her.

"You can let go now!" Penn said, smiling. "That's how handshakes work. You don't have to hold on!"

Ava jerked her hand back and faked a laugh. She noticed Penn jiggling his right leg rapidly. His excitement for this project seemed to be growing stronger by the minute.

"So, *Death of a Salesman*, hunh? Sounds like a real uplifting piece of work," Ava said, attempting a joke.

"It's actually an incredibly compelling play. I saw it at the college my mom works at. Their theater department put it on this last spring," Penn said, mistaking Ava's politeness for interest as he moved his arms around emphatically. "The main character, Willy, grapples with his identity, questioning what's real and what's not, reliving the past while coming to terms with the present all while his sons. . . . Well, I don't want to give the best parts of it away!"

Ava gave a polite half-smile, hoping SparkNotes would give her enough detail to get through this project without ever touching the book.

"We can read through it together!" Penn nearly shouted. "You can be Linda. Or gosh, no, that's sexist. You can be whoever you want, and I can be Linda! Oh, that would be so interesting."

Ava held up a hand to stop him. A monumental headache was beginning to form behind her eyes.

"I can read the book, play, whatever on my own. Okay? I won't make you do this whole project by yourself if that's what you're worried about," Ava said, offended.

"Of course, of course, you can! My apologies, Ava. I get carried away sometimes. I have no doubt you'll contribute wonderful ideas to this project," he said, sitting back in his seat. Ava was grateful he wasn't entirely arrogant.

"So, are you new here too? It doesn't seem like you know many people here either," he said.

Ava knew it was an innocent question. She knew Penn had no idea she was born in Westwood. But it didn't stop every emotion Ava felt over the past few months from fighting its way to the surface. Though she tried her best to bite them back, hot tears slid aggressively down her cheeks. She turned to the soccer field and brought her sleeves to her face, hoping she could block Penn from seeing her. She attempted to gather herself together as he grew silent, but her tears fell faster.

After a few moments, she peeked over at him, assuming he was looking around for a new partner. But instead, he was writing in what looked like some kind of day planner. He stopped moving his pen when he noticed her eyes on him.

"Hey, I didn't mean to upset you," Penn whispered.

Ava swore under her breath. She rarely cried in public, especially not because of something as silly as this.

"I am very sorry for anything I said to offend you," he continued. "It was not my intention to hurt you. I hope I can do better to communicate with you going forward." Penn leaned in closer so no one around could hear him. "I transferred here last spring, and it's been difficult to make friends. I was curious, that's all. Clearly, I touched a nerve, and I truly am sorry."

For some strange reason, his apology caused more tears to form. Penn noticed and stood up. Ava hoped it wasn't to touch her; it would only make it worse. Instead, he walked to the corner of the room to grab a box of tissues. He slid the box onto her desk and stood with his back facing the rest of the class. Ava blew her nose and wiped her face. She found she didn't mind his standing close to her. He smelled like a strange mixture between fresh laundry soap and the inside of a library book.

"God, I am so sorry. You must think I'm ridiculous," Ava started.

"You don't have to apologize for having feelings," Penn said as if these were the most natural words in the world.

She nodded, stunned, a large lump stuck in her throat. Penn sat back down in his seat and pulled his planner close to him. He gave her a few more minutes before returning to business as usual.

"I want to give you time to read the play before I get ahead of myself here. We have our blocked period on Wednesday, and tomorrow we can start a simple outline. Does Wednesday give you enough time to read the first act?"

Ava nodded eagerly, thinking she might read the stupid thing now that he'd been so kind to her.

"I think we should block out time during the week to get together. I don't think we'll be able to do everything we need to during class. Does that sound okay? You can stop me at any point if this is too demanding."

Ava cleared her throat and tried her best to look astute. "No, it uh, it sounds good. I have volleyball practice every day after school except Friday, and a game or two on weeknights, but aside from that, I should be able to make it work."

Penn turned back to his planner, flicking to the following week. The page was as color-coded and meticulously planned as the last.

"What about Saturday evenings? Around eight?" Penn asked, glancing over to see Ava's eyebrows raised high.

"Wait, that's weird, isn't it? Saturday night. Yes. That's weird. Sorry! How about Sunday afternoon? Four p.m.?"

Ava stifled a laugh but felt her mood lift ever so slightly.

"Well, my planner, as in my phone, is dead right now, but I'm sure Sunday will work fine," she said. She had a feeling her Sundays would no longer need to be reserved for hangover recovery.

"Perfect! I have it in here," Penn said as he scribbled it down then snapped his planner shut. She couldn't help but notice how peculiar he was compared to other boys she knew.

"Is your entire life scheduled down to the minute?" Ava asked.

"Look, when you have a mom like mine, you've got to be on a schedule," Penn said, chuckling.

"Control freak?" Ava asked, thinking of her father.

"No, actually, the complete opposite! My mom is an Art Instructor over at Everton Community College. And an artist she is, down to her very core. Without me, I doubt she'd remember to show up for work."

Ava wasn't sure if she'd met an artist in real life. The bell rang before Ava could ask Penn more about her.

"Well, Ava, it was lovely to meet you," Penn said, smiling as he gathered his things into a worn leather shoulder bag. Ava thought the word lovely was a bit of a stretch. "I'll see you tomorrow?"

Ava smiled in return, staying seated as she surveyed Penn's wiry frame walk confidently from the room. She thought he could easily be mistaken for a Teaching Assistant, with his plain navy button-down, dress slacks, and brown oxfords.

She took her time in leaving the classroom, replaying the last hour in her mind. For the past sixteen years, she was raised to believe emotions were a weakness. As a result, she considered herself a master at stuffing them down, tucking them away, hiding them in places she hoped she'd never find. Never had anyone, before Penn, told her it was okay to feel them.

As Ava rose from her seat, her shoulders relaxed, her jaw unclenched. Something unfurled in her chest, strengthening her as she stepped outside the classroom. Instead of running to her next class, she squared her shoulders and headed in the opposite direction.

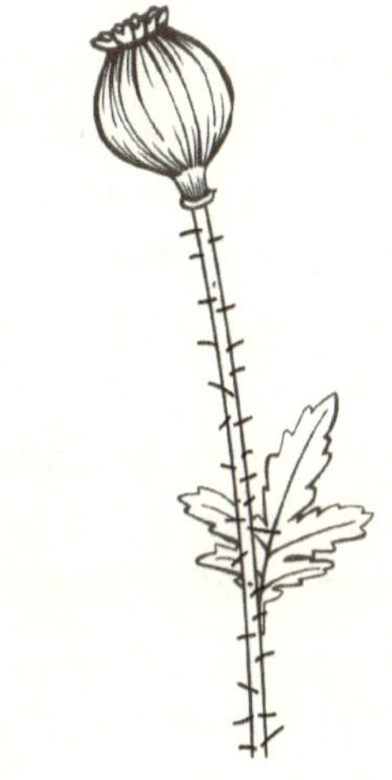

chapter three

Ava rounded the corner to the senior locker bay. Trish and Leona were right where she thought they'd be, huddled together in the far-left corner of the room. Leona was reapplying her lipstick in Trish's small locker mirror. Liam, along with a few other seniors on the football team, hovered around, laughing obnoxiously. Ava cleared her throat as she made her way to stand in front of Trish.

"Holy shit, Ava! Where did you come from?" Trish gasped; her glittery pink nails clutched to her chest.

Leona whipped around to meet Ava with a seething glare. "Oh. It's *you*. Have you decided to stop creeping around the school to avoid us?" she asked, popping her merlot-shaded lips.

The newly discovered confidence Ava unearthed in Mrs. Papayanni's classroom evaporated. Under the scrutinizing stare of Leona, and the trace of confusion left on Trish's face, Ava questioned why she chose to leave the party at all on Saturday night. She took a step back from both girls, right into the pack of senior boys now throwing a water bottle overhead.

"I, um, I . . . ," Ava faltered, stumbling away from the impromptu football practice. Leona looked over at Trish, then burst into laughter.

"This is just so sad, Ava," Leona said, tossing her hair behind her with extra emphasis. "You realize you have no friends besides us, now that your sister left, right? And the way you've been acting lately, it's almost desperate. Lukas is with someone way prettier than you now, and Liam was only interested in you because I talked you up. You know he's actually into *me*, right?"

Ava felt the blood drain from her extremities. She stood there, shock slung across her face, as Leona's nasty smirk grew into a horrific smile. Trish continued to lean against the lockers, straightening and releasing the same strand of dark curly hair.

Leona elbowed Trish sharply in the side of her pastel purple sweater. "Are you going to back me up or not? You've agreed with me for weeks now," Leona demanded. Trish released her hair but refused to look directly at Ava.

"Yeah," Trish said, barely above a whisper. "You seem off. Since Jacklyn left, it doesn't feel like you want to be around us anymore."

Ava attempted to form a response, but Leona's words played on a loop in her mind. Finally, the warning bell rang out from the intercom above them. Ava's mouth was half open as Leona slammed the locker shut. Leona stepped forward to close the gap between them, so close Ava could smell her spearmint gum.

"*Off* is a generous way to put it," Leona sneered. "You're impossible to be around. You never were as much fun as your sister, but Jesus! I never realized you have zero personality. Also, a quick tip now that I won't be lying to boys about your 'great sense of humor' anymore: you might want to dab at the oil glistening off your forehead. Whoever said you can pull off the no-makeup look—they lied."

Leona pushed by, knocking Ava's shoulder as she passed. Trish hesitated, now looking at Ava's throat.

"Ava," Trish began.

"We don't have time for her shit today, Trish! Let's go!" Leona yelled, her voice amplifying across the locker bay, causing everyone to stare in their direction.

"See you at volleyball practice later, okay?" Trish whispered, rushing away.

Ava didn't move, even after the final bell rang. Instead, she stood rooted to the spot, staring at the space Leona and Trish just abandoned. She knew she should get to class, but she was still fighting against the paralysis driven by Leona's remarks. The bay grew quiet as teachers began to shut their doors, leaving Ava alone in the silence.

Ava's eyes fell on Jacklyn's old locker in the opposite corner. She walked over and leaned against it, then slid to the floor. With her head hung low, a memory sparked at the sight of her high-tops. Almost two years had passed since Aunt Brene bought them for her.

"Those are great shoes, aren't they?" Aunt Brene asked, shielding the sun from her eyes as they strolled together in downtown Pittsburgh. Ava shrugged, watching with longing as the girl wearing them passed her by.

"Let's get you a pair!" shouted Aunt Brene, skipping in the direction of a shoe shop.

"Oh, I can't wear something like that," Ava responded, sauntering behind her aunt.

Aunt Brene stopped in her tracks. "Why not?"

"Because they aren't—"

"Oh, you're worried what people will think!"

"Well, yeah, and I can't pull off something like that."

"Of course, you can," Aunt Brene said, taking Ava's arm in her own. "Look, Ava, you can spend your life caring what everyone else thinks. Or you can avoid a midlife crisis like the rest of us and care more about what you think. I know I'm a lame adult whose opinion doesn't matter, but I do believe you'd look phenomenal in those shoes. Now, what do *you* think?"

Ava landed back in the present moment, tugging at her laces, still bright white from lack of wear. That was the last time she saw her Aunt Brene before her mother decided not to speak to her anymore. Ava wished she knew what happened between them.

Heavy footsteps echoed off the empty walls in the hallway. Ava jumped up and ran down the steps toward her most trusted shortcut. As she sprinted through the library, it wasn't the kind words Penn said or Aunt Brene's encouragement that carried her feet to marketing class. It was the same small voice she heard on Saturday night: her own.

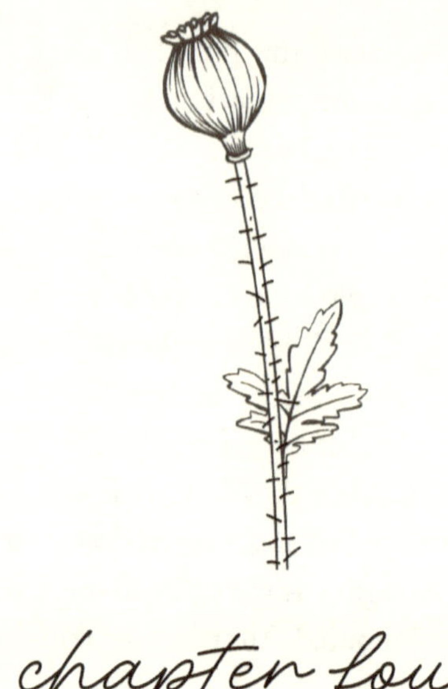

chapter four

Ava managed to get through the rest of the morning without another run-in with Leona or Trish. It wasn't until lunch rolled around that her stomach began to churn, and not from hunger. She took her time walking to the lunchroom, her underarms pooling with sweat. No matter which way she entered to buy her lunch, she'd have to walk right by their usual table.

Escape options were illuminating themselves as she drew closer to the cafeteria. Ava thought a toilet stall might work, though it wasn't the most sanitary of options. Or there was her car to run to, but there was always the risk of getting caught. She wracked her brain for anyone else she could sit with, but everyone she knew sat with Leona and Trish.

Ava hesitated outside the lunchroom door. She wrung her clammy hands as a few latecomers passed around her. Mr. Tully, the school principal, was approaching at a fast pace. At the sight of him, Ava threw the door open and rushed inside. His awkward questions were more than she could handle on this never-ending nightmare of a Monday.

Inside the lunchroom, she found her usual lunch table abandoned. Ava looked to the left and spotted everyone through the windows, eating outside. She breathed out a sigh of relief and headed toward the food line at the front of the room.

"Ava?" A voice rang out behind her. She looked around, trying to locate the source.

"Hey, Ava! Over here!" the voice yelled again. Ava looked back to her right, and there, in a booth on the far wall, sat Penn, arms waving in the air. She ditched the line and walked closer to find him sitting with a book propped open on his shoulder bag.

"I didn't know you had this lunch hour!" he shouted, though she was now right in front of his booth.

"Is it okay if I sit here?" Ava asked, looking around to see if anyone was joining him.

"Well, I usually have loads of friends who join me. *Tons.* You wouldn't even be able to find me in the sea of them. But for today, I will make an exception," he said. Ava sank into the seat opposite him, too exhausted to decipher if he was joking. Penn scooted his open lunch sack in her direction.

"Here, take some of this food. I can't let you go back to that lunch line. My ma always overpacks anyway. She can't remember to set her alarm in the morning, but she always makes sure my lunch bag is stuffed."

Ava's stomach growled at the sight of fresh produce. It was much more appealing than the brown slop sitting on the trays around her.

"Are you sure?" she asked as she plucked out a red pepper before he could answer. Penn laughed and set his book down on the seat beside him. He let her pick over his lunch before setting his determined eyes on her.

"Ava, I know I don't ask the most sensitive questions, but can I ask you something serious?" he asked as Ava shoved a cherry tomato into her mouth. She looked up at him, her face scrunched, afraid of what he might say.

"Is everyone at this school an asshole?"

Ava nearly spat the half-eaten tomato onto the table. She held a hand up to her mouth to hide her reaction.

"I mean, not you, of course. Not that you've shown yet anyways. But man, I've been at this school since March and haven't managed to make a single friend. Unless you count the teaching staff," Penn trailed off before registering Ava's worried expression and corrected himself. "Which I definitely, *definitely* don't. I even joined the cross-country team hoping for something! I think I pissed them all off because I outran them during my tryout. Is it me they hate, or are they like this in general?"

She looked outside the windows at Trish and Leona, both preoccupied with their phones. Lukas's new girlfriend draped herself prettily across his lap as Liam, on the other side of the bench, emptied the contents of a bag of Doritos into his mouth.

"I don't know," Ava answered, staring outside. Penn's words suddenly felt like a balm on the wound Leona had ripped open. "I guess I never really thought about it like that until maybe recently." She paused, looking back to Penn, who angled his head slightly, contemplating her words. "I think, maybe, I'd like to become less of an asshole."

Penn burst into laughter, then nodded his head in approval. "I believe that's the most we can hope to become in this life: less of an asshole!"

The lunch hour flew by as Penn picked Ava's brain about the quirks of Westwood High. His bronze eyes focused intensely on her as if she were the most captivating subject he'd studied in years. Whenever she touched on something particularly interesting, Penn responded energetically, hands conducting in the air, encouraging her to go on. He tugged at his curls whenever he couldn't quite get his point across.

When the bell rang out, they couldn't believe it. Ava and Penn continued to talk nonstop as they exited the cafeteria, unaware of anything going on around them.

"Wow," Leona said, sidling up next to Ava, a smile already playing on her lips. "It looks like you wasted no time finding a guy who doesn't mind sleeping with the ugly Pierson sister."

Ava wished Leona would have slapped her across the face rather than say these words in front of Penn. Her face flushed as Penn looked across her to see who had spoken. She tried to talk but once again found her words had run back into their hiding places. Only a bubbling of anger rose in her throat. Ava tried to speed up, but Penn's arm shot out in front of her.

"Hi! I'm Penn," he said to Leona. Leona looked at his outstretched hand in disgust. Penn waggled his fingers in response. "May I ask what your name is?"

Leona scowled, flipping her hair across Trish's anxious face.

"I shouldn't have to introduce myself to you, whoever *you* are. If you were anyone worth knowing, you wouldn't have to ask," Leona said, causing Penn to withdraw his hand to his chest.

"It's Leona," squeaked Trish. Leona jerked her head around, shocked that Trish would speak up without permission.

"Thank you!" Penn said, smiling at Trish. "Le-on-a, that's a nice name. Were you named after Leona Florentino by chance?"

Leona looked at him as though he were certifiably insane.

"No, I guess not. She's an incredible poet, though, in case you were wondering. You should check out her stuff," Penn continued, not bothered by Leona's death stare. "Well, Leona, I just want to say one thing before we have to, unfortunately, part ways."

Leona sized him up, full of disdain. This didn't stop Penn. In fact, Penn's smile grew even brighter.

"I'm not sure what your story is, or what made you say such a thing to my friend, Ava, here. And I do think, someday soon, she will find a way to say this to you, but it's not okay to take your shit out on people. Not on her, or me, or on this nice girl here who told me what your name is. We've all got our stuff to deal with. Yours isn't superior."

Ava stared at Penn in awe, wondering if he realized how unpopular he was about to become. She peered closer at his face, investigating whether an eighty-year-old man inhabited his teenage body. Ava was far too scared to look over at Leona, who could melt her to the floor with one savage expression.

The four of them continued down the hallway, silenced by Penn's pronouncement.

"Welp, I'm right here!" Penn said, gently squeezing Ava's shoulder as he slipped into the classroom on the left. Ava looked over to find Leona's face wiped blank of the judgment it usually possessed. Trish, however, had the slightest trace of a smile on her glossy lips.

Without speaking a single word or tossing her hair, Leona cut to the stairway on the right. Trish hesitated, then followed Leona down the stairs at a further distance than usual.

Ava shook her head in disbelief. She stood still, students racing by. A boy apologized as he bumped into her shoulder, nearly knocking the books out of her arms. She caught the book on top of her stack in midair. Confused, she steadied an unfamiliar copy of *Death of a Salesman*. Ava flipped it open to a random page with her free hand. Scrawled in the margins was vaguely familiar, cramped handwriting.

She smiled to herself as it dawned on her who it belonged to, a particularly full day-planner rising to the surface of her mind. Then, hating herself for thinking it, she ran her fingers across the page, hoping Penn meant it when he called her his friend.

chapter five

The rest of Ava's evening was spent curled up in her bed with Olivia, reading Penn's copy of *Death of a Salesman*. She cringed each time Willy spoke down to Linda and swore loudly at Biff and Happy whenever they bragged about the many women they'd slept with. Penn's side commentary was both hilarious and insightful, keeping her up well past midnight. She fought droopy eyelids until she finished the book, her eyes closing as the curtains fell on the final page.

After a suspiciously uneventful Tuesday, Wednesday arrived with the promise of an entire block period with Penn. Ava found it difficult to fight back her excitement. She wanted to pinch herself as she entered English class, smiling as she found Penn in the seat next to hers, already scribbling furiously in his planner.

"Find some plans for this Saturday night?" Ava asked as she sat down. Penn jumped, so enthralled with his schedule, he didn't notice her walk into class.

"If watching a documentary on Marsden Hartley with my mom is considered plans, then yes, I am fully booked," he said, the bell ringing before Ava could ask who in the hell that was.

"Mr. Reuben, PLEASE find your seat!" Mrs. Papayanni demanded wearily from the top of the classroom. She paused, placing her hands on her hips as she waited for him to stop flirting. "I hope today will be quite productive for all of you. I'll give you these block periods through the next month to continue to work on and finish your project, but that doesn't mean I don't expect you to spend time working on them outside of class."

Mrs. Papayanni wore a deep teal scarf this morning, far outside her neutral color range. Ava wondered what inspired the accessorizing as she looked down at her colorless apparel.

"Our other class periods will focus on discussing elements of literature, beginning with character. For homework, I'd like you to pick one character from the play and keep them in mind for Friday's class. Then we'll walk through a series of questions to learn more about the character's arc, motivations, strengths, flaws, etcetera. Now," she said, clapping her hands together. "Let's get to work!"

"So, Ava, I was thinking along the same lines as Mrs. Papayanni," Penn said, turning to her. "I thought if we dive deeper into the characters today, we could start outlining some important pieces of our project. It should help us when it comes to choosing actors and costume design. What do you think?"

Ava found herself nearly as excited to start on the project as Penn. The characters were already so vivid in her mind; she'd even doodled a picture of the Loman's kitchen in her Algebra 2/Trig notebook.

"I think it sounds great, Penn. Oh! And I finished your book. You'll probably want it back." She rifled through her bag and handed it over to him.

"Wow, you finished it already?" Penn asked, astounded. Ava furrowed her brows at him. "I mean, I guess I figured you would need some more time. That's all!"

"You think I can't keep up with you?" Ava sassed, surprising herself with a sudden need to prove herself.

"I absolutely think you can. In fact, I wouldn't have given you my book had I not thought so," he said. Ava smiled and turned her head to the field. She didn't want him to catch her pink-tinged cheeks. As a distraction, she shot him a question she knew he couldn't resist answering.

"So, who is your favorite character?"

Penn immediately fell into concentration mode, screwing his face up in thought.

"I think I'm going to have to go with Happy," he said.

"Happy! But he's the worst!" Ava said, taken aback.

"Maybe I shouldn't have said he's my favorite, but I find him the most interesting."

"Seriously, Penn? He really is the worst. He might even be worse than Willy."

"What makes you say that?"

"Because he sees his dad living a complete lie and chooses to do the exact same! He buys into it all, without question, believes he doesn't have to work hard for anything, and while his father is having a complete breakdown, decides to, like, run off with a prostitute!"

"I'm going to guess your favorite character is Biff, then?"

Ava didn't want to admit it. "How did you know?"

"Well, I think because you clearly hate that Happy doesn't evolve or change throughout the entire story, while Biff has the most character development of all."

"Yeah. I guess that's why. I really loved the line that you underlined several times. The one where Biff says, 'I know who I am, kid.'"

"Why do you think you love that line so much?" he asked, eyes wide with intrigue. Ava glanced toward the field, finding it funny how he shifted questions back in her direction.

"I think because it's one of the most important things, you know, in life. Or um, in a story, I guess. To know who you are."

"Yes! That's so beautiful, Ava. And also why I love Happy so much!" Penn's hands were lifted, ready to illustrate his point. "He shows us the danger, along with Willy, of going through life denying and ignoring who you really are and blindly following what you're expected to be. And the name itself! Happy! Such an overrated ideation of the American dream, to become blissfully, ignorantly happy!"

Penn's hands had become so animated that if someone were looking into the class, they'd think he was trying to swat at a persistent fly.

"But life is so much more than finding happiness! It's about discovering who you are and failing, and persevering, and . . . and . . . and . . . growing in relationship with both yourself and others!"

Ava nodded fervently along with Penn. She felt nervous about speaking up and adding to what Penn was saying, but her sudden passion for the topic overrode her nerves.

"And like, what if Willy was honest with Biff about cheating on Linda?" Ava added. "What if he would have shown Biff it's okay to admit when you screw up? That it's actually brave, to tell the truth instead of lying all the time?"

She winced as her comment, spoken out loud, hit closer to home than expected. However, she wasn't ready to look at whatever it was just yet.

"Exactly, Ava! That's wonderful. Really, really brilliant."

Ava beamed, knowing Penn wouldn't say it unless he meant it.

"And you see, *that's* why I love the 'worst' character in a story," Penn continued. "They allow us to see ourselves in them. Happy didn't just become a douchebag of his own accord. He is a product of his father's lies and societal norms."

Penn's eyes sparkled as he spoke, distracting Ava as he continued.

"What has led to our flaws that we don't have much control over? When Happy faces an opportunity to change, he ignores it. What is calling out to us that we need to change in ourselves but are too afraid to answer? Are we strong enough to be like Biff, who remains incredibly flawed, but willing to accept it and move forward on a new path? Or do we, like Happy, ignore invitations to change and find ourselves content with complacency?

"Without Happy," Penn leaned in closer to Ava. "We can't fully celebrate Biff's decision to carve his own path. Without Biff, we can't see that change is possible, even if ridden with pain and the death of our heroes. In a well-written story, all characters are meaningful; even 'the worst' has something valuable to teach us about ourselves."

Ava found herself deeply connected with what Penn was saying. She was struck not only by how intelligent Penn was but how he didn't come off as annoying or intimidating. His way of including Ava, building around what she said instead of dismissing it, made her wonder if he knew how natural a teacher he was. She had yet to meet any teacher who could get her to care much about any subject, let alone stay up all night learning more about it. It was suddenly apparent why Mrs. Papayanni and most of the teaching staff loved Penn and why classmates frequently referred to him as a know-it-all.

They spent the rest of their class period exchanging thoughts and creating a detailed map of their project plans. When the bell rang, they stood up together, continuing their conversation up the stairs and down the hall until they had to part ways. Ava was already counting down the minutes until lunch, wondering what delicious food Penn had packed in his bag today.

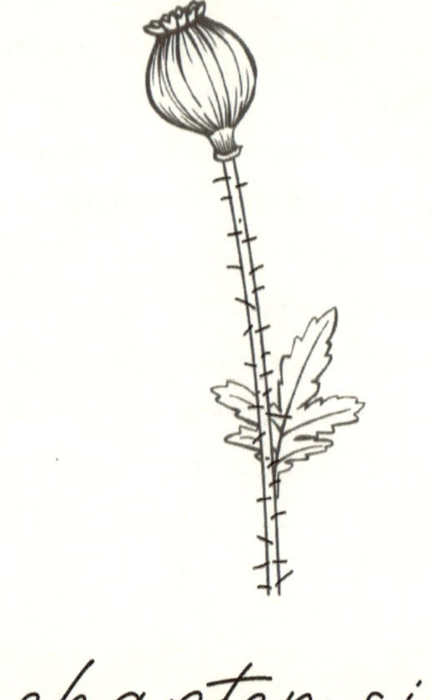

chapter six

Penn sat in the same booth with a different book propped up on his shoulder bag. His lunch was already open in the middle of the table. Ava smiled warmly at this gesture, feeling welcome at a table for the first time since Jacklyn left.

"You don't have to feed me every day, you know, I do have a lunch account," she said, scooting into the middle of the booth seat opposite of him.

"Paola would die if she thought my friend was eating whatever it is that they serve here. You'd think with the ridiculous amount of taxes our parents pay, we'd get some decent cafeteria food," Penn complained, making a puke face as a sad-looking plate of spaghetti passed.

"First of all, the food isn't that bad!" Ava said as an even more depressing plate of taco salad floated by them. "Second, do you call your mom by her first name? And third . . . did you talk with your mom about me?"

Ava studied a slice of his fresh mango with some sort of spice on it instead of looking at Penn as he responded.

"One: the food here is outrageously mal-nutritious," Penn answered, scooting the mango closer to her. "It's disturbing! Two: sometimes, I call her Paola for dramatic effect, but to me, she's Ma. And three: I may have mentioned I finally found someone who I might consider a friend. Why, did you not tell your mom about me?"

Ava shoved the fruit in her mouth, hoping he'd change the subject. His eyes didn't leave her face.

"I don't . . . we don't . . . talk about stuff like that," Ava answered with reluctance. Penn let the silence hang for a few moments before changing the topic.

"Okay, Ava, another serious question for you," Penn said as he looked outside the window closest to them, near the back parking lot. He leaned his body into the table to whisper to Ava. "Have you ever ditched school before?"

Penn looked nervous as if he was asking Ava if she'd committed a felony. Ava leaned back and tried to suppress a laugh.

"Of course, I have, Penn, but why are *you* asking? You couldn't possibly . . . ," Ava said, watching his fingers drum rapidly on the table. "Wait, are you asking me to ditch with you?"

Penn leaned back in his seat, eyes roaming around the lunchroom.

"I just, I kind of hate my study hall? It's mostly football players and then that girl Leona? The one that was terrible to you yesterday. I knew she looked familiar, but I didn't put together why. Anyway, something in me says she's not exactly thrilled about what I said to her."

"Yeah, no one talks to her like that. My sister, maybe, but wait, are you telling me you're scared of her? You sure seemed brave yesterday!"

"I'm not scared of her!" Penn shouted. Ava raised her eyebrows. "I'm not! It's the . . . the . . . the teacher is terrible too! She's always flirting with guys and sucking up to Leona."

Ava made the mistake of looking over to see Leona and Trish staring at her through the windows. Their heads were tilted to the same side as they studied Penn and Ava together. When Leona caught Ava looking back at them, she leaned in to whisper something in Trish's ear.

"So, you want me to ditch school with you? Today?" Ava said, still not believing it.

"I mean not if you have an important test or anything. And not if you think we'll get into serious trouble. Maybe you're right, it is a bad idea. I shouldn't be scared of Leona."

"No, I'm all about this! And, honestly, you probably *should* be afraid of Leona. When is your study hall?"

"In twenty minutes."

"Penn! Your next class? Are you serious!?"

"Completely serious. Ugh, you know what, forget it. You're right, it's crazy. I'll be fine. It's just an hour," Penn said as he packed up the remainder of his lunch. Ava eyed the parking lot to her right, weighing their chances of escaping undetected. Her heart began to dance in her chest.

"No, we're doing this," she said. Penn's eyes lit up.

"I can't believe it! This is crazy! Okay, what do we do?" Penn asked, shoveling all of his things into his shoulder bag.

"Okay; when the bell rings, we slip out these side doors as the moving crowd distracts the teachers on lunch duty. Follow my lead, don't hesitate, and, most importantly, duck down as we pass Ms. Somerson's classroom windows near the south parking lot. She's always catching escapees. Got it?"

Penn nodded, checking his watch. They both sat in nervous silence for what felt like an eternity until the bell rang. Ava quickly stood up and looked around before heading for the back parking lot, Penn close behind. She approached the doors with caution as the wave of students exited through the other side of the cafeteria. With a quick nod back at Penn, she inched the exit open enough for both of them to squeeze through.

They ran with abandon into the brilliance of a clear October afternoon. Bright rays of sunshine reflected off windows and onto the hoods of cars. The sun's heat complimented the chill of the wind; it was undoubtedly the perfect weather for an adventure. Ava motioned at Penn when it was time to duck, and they crawled beneath Ms. Somerson's classroom windows before running the final stretch to Ava's car.

Penn hesitated when he reached Ava's passenger side door.

"Everything okay, Penn?" Ava gasped, out of breath. "Honestly, if we turn back now, we'll definitely get caught."

"No, no. I'm good," Penn said, taking a deep breath and climbing inside. Ava slid in and shut the door behind her.

"I've never done anything like this before! Look at my hands," Penn said, holding them out as they shook. Ava felt nervous too but didn't want to worry Penn more by admitting it.

"I think I've got the perfect place we can go," Ava said, turning the car on and backing out of the space. Penn looked skeptical.

"Go somewhere? Ava, I don't know. We have less than an hour now to get back. I figured we could just sit in the car."

Ava shot him the dirtiest look she could muster.

"Penn! You don't waste a perfectly good skip period sitting in a parking lot!"

"Fine, fine! Can we just get ice cream or something at Poppy's and come back?"

"*Sure!* Then the whole town can see two high school students waltzing downtown in the middle of the school day. Good thinking!"

"Okay, OKAY! I'm not good at this! This is so stressful! I don't do stuff like this, okay? I just don't!"

Ava waited for him to settle down, watching as he sucked in air to try to calm himself.

"It's going to be alright," Ava said, hoping she sounded confident. "We'll get back in time for your next class, okay? I promise where I'm taking you will be worth it. Do you trust me?"

Penn's feet jiggled up and down on the floorboard. He nodded slightly, looking straight ahead. Ava pulled out of the school parking lot and headed north, away from the town. She turned the radio on to fill the silence as they crossed into Castlewood Reservation.

"Welp, this looks like a great place to bury bodies," Penn said, breaking the tension. "Tell my ma I love her after you murder me, okay?" He shifted uncomfortably in his seat. Ava rolled her eyes as they started up a winding path, trees growing denser around them.

"Have you been here before?" Ava asked, her eyes glued to the road as it twisted up a steep incline.

"No, actually. I didn't even know this was a thing."

They sat in quiet as Ava continued to weave up the mountain.

"Just a few more minutes, and we'll be there, I promise," she said, hoping Penn would start talking up a storm like he usually did.

"Good. I guess I should have told you I get car sick."

"Really!? Do you need me to stop?" Ava asked, feeling terrible as the road began to narrow.

"Nope, just need to be quiet and get to wherever we're going."

Ava nodded, slowing down for the steep curve before pulling into a small dirt patch, wide enough for two cars.

"There's a short trail to hike, and then we'll be there. Doing okay?" Ava asked, noticing Penn's cheeks were stripped of their natural rosy glow.

"Yep, but I need to get out of here!" he said, hopping out of the car and hesitating for a moment in the bushes. He steadied himself against a tree trunk before giving Ava a thumbs-up.

Ava grabbed her blanket from the back seat and motioned him over to the lightly beaten trail. Though it was a short path, she forgot it was full of uneven tree roots. They tripped and clawed their way to the top, gasping as they reached the top of the incline.

At the end of the trail Ava pulled aside a stooping branch and held it up for Penn. She led the way toward a quaint, grassy clearing ahead of them, stepping between two towering beech trees. She didn't speak, wanting to watch his face as it drank in the sights around them.

"*Wow*," he gasped, the landscape unveiling itself with each of their steps forward. Below, the town of Westwood sat nestled between rolling hills. Trees with leaves of every color lit up their periphery: shocking yellows, vivid reds, burning oranges, and every shade in between.

"It's . . . ," Penn whispered, but he couldn't find the words for once. Ava watched him scan the horizon, the warm colors reflected in his eyes. He rested his hands on his head in disbelief as he spotted Westwood High down below and his neighborhood to the far right, near the southern edge of town. He pointed to the center of downtown where Poppy's Ice Cream Shoppe sat, its bright pink storefront visible from where they stood.

Ava laid out the blanket behind him and sat down, stretching her arms up and back behind her. She closed her eyes and found solace in the breeze as it swept through the trees and under her hair. Penn continued to stand in front of her, his head surveying the horizon.

"My sister and I call it 'The Lookout.' Although I don't think it has an official name," Ava explained.

"I've never seen anything like it," he said a few minutes later, taking a seat beside Ava.

"Really? I mean it's great, I guess. I didn't expect you to be *this* impressed. But for Westwood, it's pretty great."

"That's *our town* down there," he said. Ava looked away from him to take in the expansive view for herself. She'd always felt like it was Jacklyn's, or even her father's, but her town? Penn looked over and caught her chewing her bottom lip.

"Did I say something weird?" he asked.

Ava shook her head.

"I did. You can tell me if I did, Ava. I hope you know that."

Ava sighed. "Do you really feel like it's your town? I mean, you've lived here less than a year. I've lived here my whole life and don't feel much of a connection to it."

Penn continued to study her. Ava squirmed as he did, feeling like he could see more of her than she ever cared for anyone to see.

"What would make you feel like you do belong here?" he asked after a while. She wondered if he knew how annoyingly intuitive he was.

"How am I supposed to answer that question, Penn? Seriously?"

Penn shrugged his shoulders. "Let's try this, what makes you feel like you don't belong?"

Ava thought for a moment, scratching an invisible itch on her chin in agitation.

"I mean, it's kind of obvious, isn't it? The friends I thought I had, hate me. My sister is on the opposite side of the country and hasn't spoken to me since June. And, oh! My parents barely acknowledge the fact that I exist. I can't even remember the last time I saw my dad now that he's going into the city for work. Need I go on?"

"So, belonging for you depends on other people," Penn said.

"What?!" Ava spat, unexpectedly offended.

"You depend on other people to determine if you belong or not."

Ava suspected Paola had packed him the wrong kind of mushrooms in his lunch today.

"I'm just speculating here, and you don't have to take anything I say to heart, but I think if you had people around you, people who really cared for you . . . and I mean you, not the person they think you should be, you might feel like you belong here. Or there's always another option."

"Which is?"

"Don't care what people think and decide you belong no matter what."

"*Easy for you to say,*" Ava scoffed.

"What is that supposed to mean?" he asked, sounding defensive for the first time.

"I've never met anyone who has more confidence than you," Ava said. "It's like you were born knowing exactly who you are."

Ava observed Penn's jaw muscle tighten. "Why won't your sister talk to you?"

"I . . . I'm not . . . I'm not totally sure," Ava said, evading the topic.

"Jacklyn, that's her name, right? I remember her."

Ava nodded, looking anywhere but at Penn, hoping he would stop asking about her sister. When the silence became too much to bear, she forced herself to answer.

"It's impossible not to know who she was. This whole town used to revolve around her. In some ways, it still does. Why, what do you remember?"

"She was the only person who said anything to me on my first day of school. We had Sociology with Mr. Jenneman together. She introduced herself to me after class and told me if I needed anything to let her know."

"Sounds like Jacklyn. I think . . . I've never cared that much that she's prettier, and more popular, and better at volleyball than me," Ava said as she looked in the direction of Westwood High. "But that she is *so damn nice* on top of it all makes me feel so . . . inadequate."

"Well, I think you are far from that, if it's any consolation. Bet you miss her a lot though, don't you?" Penn asked. Ava was seriously considering pushing him off the cliff's side as her eyes welled up with tears.

"I remember seeing you, too," he said. "The first week I moved here. I didn't know your name or anything, but I saw you walking around with Jacklyn."

"Yeah?" Ava asked, still upset with him for pointing out her dependency on others.

"I didn't think you were an asshole or anything, but just, kind of . . ."
Ava was afraid to ask him what that meant.

"You're just different than I thought you would be, that's all. You normally wear all the makeup and heels. I didn't recognize you the other day without all that stuff on your face," he said, sounding less confident than usual. Ava remained silent, afraid of what he thought about her now.

"Getting to know you, though, I've found there's a lot more to you, Ava, than there is to a lot of people. And I don't think that's something your sister has. Maybe your gifts don't sit so pretty on the surface, like Jacklyn's, but from little time I've known you, well. There's always more to know."

Ava felt her face burn with embarrassment. She tried to hide it by looking away, but Penn turned his body to face her full-on.

"I'm so glad you're here, in Westwood. And I think Westwood is lucky to have you, too."

Ava figured her cheeks now matched the most scarlet of leaves falling from the trees. Luckily, Penn looked down at his watch and jumped up, saving Ava from having to respond. She grabbed her phone out of her waistband to check the time.

"We gotta go!" they shouted in unison, running down the trail in record speed and nearly sliding their way back to the car. Their conversation hung behind them, suspended in the sacred space of The Lookout.

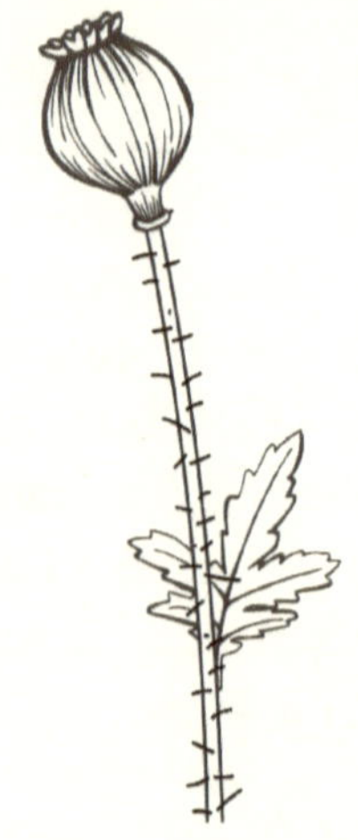

chapter seven

Penn and Ava pulled into the Westwood High parking lot with minutes to spare before their next class began. Thankfully, a freshman volleyball player recognized Ava standing outside the locked doors and let them in.

Adrenaline pumped through Ava's veins through Anatomy class, pitying Ms. Hubeny as she tried her damnedest to persuade them that the nervous system was something to wonder at. Ava wanted to focus, but her mind was drawn back to The Lookout. To Penn. She felt a complicated mixture of emotions, but anger kept boiling back to the surface.

"What does he know," she muttered under her breath, jogging up the upper gym stairs for volleyball practice after school. "He barely knows me. He skips on into my life, thinking he can tell me everything about myself when he just moved to this hellhole."

The locker room dynamic had changed over the past week, with Trish choosing to change in the back corner with the other two seniors. Ava stayed near the front with the rest of the team. She smiled at the freshman who let her and Penn inside earlier. Ava felt a tug of guilt for previously sniggering at her during practice with Trish; her tall white socks and purple sports goggles made her an easy target.

The girls split up for their usual scrimmage as soon as they were done changing. Coach Arruda stood on the sidelines, taking notes as they began to practice. Ava loved the way she coached. Instead of screaming at the players, as so many other coaches did, she studied the girls during practice and called them softly to the side to discuss how they could improve. When their time together ended, she'd hand out notes to each teammate and share some encouraging words.

Ava was distracted through practice, missing every serve that came in her direction. She couldn't switch off the part of her brain that combed through every word Penn had said earlier. Some of his words overwhelmed her, swam around her mind, and settled warmly in her chest. But telling her how to belong and not care what people think, who did he think he was? She wasn't about to take advice from someone only a year older than her, especially when she was pretty sure he didn't even have a driver's license.

Coach Arruda motioned Ava over as the ball flew right by her and out of bounds. The teammates on her side of the net looked like they wanted to spike the ball at her head.

"Hey, Ava," Coach said in her gentle, unassuming tone. "How are you doing today?"

Ava shrugged one shoulder and crossed her arms over her chest. "Doing okay, Coach," she lied as Coach Arruda studied her.

"I've noticed you're not hanging out with Trish much lately?" Ava nodded again and began to chew her bottom lip.

"Look, it's none of my business what goes on outside of practice. But you seem distracted lately."

Ava shifted her weight from side to side.

"I know it can't be easy with Jacklyn gone," Coach continued. "You two were glued at the hip. How is she doing in California; is she enjoying it?"

Ava answered with quick nods, anything to change the topic.

"Good, good. I think she made a good choice going there. That scholarship she got was well deserved, it's a great program they have going. But I bet you miss her?"

Ava looked up at the wall clock, hoping it would speed forward an hour. If one more person asked her about Jacklyn today, she would lose what sanity she had left.

"I completely understand if you don't want to talk about it. But I must be honest with you: I don't think your heart is on the court. I know you are aware you aren't our star player, but you've always shown up ready to play. I can't help but notice since this season started, it's almost as though you're just trying to get through it."

Ava inhaled sharply, worried Coach was going to kick her off the team right then and there. But Coach Arruda's facial expression remained as caring and kind as always.

"I want you to be on this team, Ava, I really do. You're a great team player, and you never make this game about yourself; that's important. You always show up, usually on time, and I know I can count on you. I really hesitate to say this, but maybe you need to ask yourself if you still want to be a part of this team."

Coach's disappointment poured over Ava. This was a place Ava had always felt safe, a place where she didn't have to act like someone she wasn't. But Coach was correct; something had shifted. She no longer looked forward to practices or cared how well the team performed. She couldn't put her finger on what exactly it was, but she knew it didn't feel quite like a place of her own.

"I don't want you to feel like you need to be on this team because your sister did this, or because you feel like you owe me something. I've been holding off on saying this, selfishly, because I wanted to make this season work. But I'm beginning to feel this lack of interest you have isn't a passing phase."

Ava looked down at her feet, studying the navy tennis shoes she'd worn to every practice for the past three seasons. "Can I think about it Coach? And let you know?"

Coach nodded. She raised the center of her forehead with understanding. Ava thought she looked a bit sad, like she already knew what Ava's decision would be.

"Of course, Ava. Can you do me a favor and let me know by the end of the week? I just ask you to show up to practice until you make your decision. Is that fair?"

Ava agreed, then took her spot back on the court for the remainder of the scrimmage.

She felt a strange sense of loss as Coach gathered them in a circle at the end of practice. It felt like she was on the outside looking in on this part of her life she'd never taken the time to fully appreciate. She locked eyes with Coach for a moment, gave a small, half-hearted smile, then left the court to change back into her school clothes.

Ava was overwhelmed with thoughts on her short drive home, so much so she nearly careened into her father's car now parked in the driveway. After finding space on the street, she tried to brace herself while walking up to the house. Mac sat on the bottom porch step, blocking the front door.

"Hey, Mac Attack, what's going on in there?" Ava asked, pointing at the front door.

"Come *on*, Ava. I'm thirteen years old. Can we stop with the 'Mac Attack'?"

Ava sighed and sat down next to him. "Sure, if you tell me why you're out here."

"Since when do you care about what's going on with me?" Mac asked, looking in the opposite direction. Ava fell silent. It was a fair question. She had never been close to Mac. He and Jacklyn had a bond Ava couldn't quite tap into.

"Mac, I—"

"You're not the only one who misses her, you know."

Ava stared at the concrete sidewalk in front of them.

"Have you heard from her?" Ava asked, though her gut twisted at the thought.

"Yeah, we try to talk once a week and text every couple of days. You?"

Ava was relieved Mac didn't know why Jacklyn wasn't talking to her either.

"Yeah, yeah. Us too," Ava fibbed.

They sat silently for a while, long enough for Ava to hear raised voices behind their front door. She looked over at Mac, still surprised to see so much of her father in his face.

"How long has he been home?" she asked.

"Only about an hour."

"And already?"

"Yeah," Mac whispered.

Ava shook her head in frustration; it was the same argument every time her dad came home after an extended stay in the city.

"Same fight as always?" she asked Mac.

"Actually, I think it might have to do with Jacklyn this time."

"Is she okay?" Ava asked, fear creeping up her spine.

"I thought you said you talk with her all the time?"

"Oh-oh yeah … I … I haven't checked my phone today."

Mac eyed her, sensing she wasn't telling the whole truth. "She's been struggling."

"Struggling … how?"

"I think you need to talk to Jacklyn about it."

"But I, can't you just tell me?"

"Honestly, you might be able to ask her in person soon."

"What does that mean? Is she sick or hurt or—"

"I won't be your go-between. If Jacklyn isn't speaking to you, she probably has a good reason. But you two might have to work it out sooner rather than later."

Ava was highly annoyed with Mac's sudden elevation in maturity level. But she knew he was right.

"When did you become such a grown-up?" Ava asked, nudging him with her elbow. Mac smirked, smoothing his front curls down.

"Well, when you've got parents like ours … ," Mac started. They exchanged a knowing look.

"Do you want to like, blow off dinner and come get Poppy's with me? I figure they have another hour of fighting left in them before they notice we aren't home. Plus, you know they'd only force us to eat fancy freezer food that tastes like dog crap."

Mac smiled widely in response, his eyes lighting up. She'd forgotten how closely they resembled Aunt Brene's. She always envied her siblings' eye colors: Mac's a deep oceanic blue, Jacklyn's lighter than his but electric, while Ava's light gray eyes most resembled their father's.

Mac wore a goofy smile on his face as they rode together downtown, even though Ava smelled like an old gym sock from volleyball practice. She rolled the windows down, but it didn't do much to help. She tried to remember if they'd ever gotten ice cream, just the two of them.

Inside Poppy's, Mac ordered birthday cake flavor, while Ava stuck with her traditional one scoop of dark chocolate, one scoop cookie dough. They took their cones out to the sidewalk, finding a metal table painted a bright magenta to sit at with the least number of leftover drips.

"Hey Mac, could we do this more?"

Mac licked his cone and nodded excitedly, looking more like the little brother she remembered.

"I'm sorry, you know," Ava said. "That I don't seem like I care. I just figured I didn't have much to offer you. She was more fun and caring and, you know. Jacklyn."

Mac stopped licking his cone to look up at Ava.

"I love Jacklyn and all, but you never make me feel like I'm your kid that you have to take care of, if that makes sense? You just feel like, like my sister. Instead of another mom."

Ava had to look away, her heart so full of love for Mac it hurt. "I think with Jacklyn around, it was easy to take a back seat because I knew she'd take care of everything. But now, now I have to figure everything out for myself. I hope I can figure out how to be a better sis, too."

Mac licked up the drips running down his cone. "I'm here with you too, you know, and I'll be in high school next year. We can figure some stuff out together."

If her family were the type to show affection, she would have stood up and hugged him close. But that just wasn't the Pierson way.

"That sounds nice, Mac. Really nice."

They shared a smile and continued to eat their cones. After a few minutes, Mac made a weird face.

"Some dude is waving at us from across the street. Should I be worried?"

Ava looked around and spotted Penn, a to-go bag in hand, waving his arm around and shouting at them.

"SEE!" Penn shouted as he crossed the street and pointed to their cones. "Poppy's would have been a great place to come today! You made me sound crazy when we . . . wait, who's this?" he asked, turning to Mac and sticking out his hand.

"This is my brother, Mac," Ava said. Penn looked at her in disbelief.

"You didn't tell me you had a brother!"

"Sorry?" she said, chuckling at the sight of Mac's eyebrows raised high. Mac cautiously shook Penn's hand. Penn gripped it professionally, as if Mac were an important political figure.

"Mac, it is SO good to meet you! Anyways, I better get this food back to Paola before it gets cold," he said, gesturing to his brown paper bag.

"Paola approves of carry-out?" Ava asked.

"Okay, no. Not at all," Penn said in a hushed tone. "But! Honestly, we really love Mei, who owns the place. She tries to make the food as healthy as she can for us. So, okay, yeah. We kind of love it. But Paola would hate if you knew that! The school cafeteria food is still garbage. Okay, okay, I'm talking too much again. Eat your ice cream! And Ava! This Sunday! My house! You get to meet Ma—I mean—Paola! Okay. Bye! Mac, nice to meet you! Okay, leaving now! Bye!"

Penn turned around and headed for his bike. Ava opened her mouth to ask if he wanted a ride, but he had already snapped on his helmet and headed in the opposite direction. The anger she felt earlier dissipated, replaced with a newfound appreciation for Penn's sincerity toward Mac.

"So . . . Penn, huh?" Mac smirked as Ava turned back in her seat.

"What is *that* supposed to mean?" Ava asked, biting into her cone now that she'd eaten most of the ice cream.

"I don't know if I've ever seen you like this," Mac said, an annoyingly smug look on his face.

"Like what?!"

"Your face is all . . . dreamy. You didn't tell me you have a *boyfriend*."

"I DON'T! We just met. We're not dating. Not even a little bit. It's not even *like* that."

"Like what?"

"You met my old boyfriends, they aren't like Penn. And what do you know about relationships anyway?"

As Ava grew more irritated, Mac continued to smirk. "Your ex-boyfriends, and all of Jacklyn's ex-boyfriends, now that I think of it, were total idiots. That guy is maybe the nicest human this town has ever seen. A little spastic, but, completely into you. I *like* him."

"Oh, shut up, Mac. He's not *in* to me. He's just nice. He's like that with everybody."

"*Puh-lease*, Ava. I may be in eighth grade, but I know that look on his face."

"What look?! That's just his face! It's always annoyingly happy!"

"No, Ava, *trust* me. It's because of you. He's stupidly into you."

"Nothing about Penn is stupid. Especially not his face, and not because of me! We're just friends. That's it."

"Mm-hmm. You might want to tell him that."

Ava picked up a stack of napkins in the middle of the table and flung them at Mac. Mac broke into a fit of laughter and chased them as they tumbled down the sidewalk. For the rest of their time together they sat peacefully, watching the sun sink behind buildings.

As the light faded to darkness, their phones buzzed simultaneously on the table. A knot tightened in Ava's abdomen. Mac's remaining smile disappeared, replaced with a look of dread. They walked reluctantly back to the car, not speaking a word on the drive home.

chapter eight

Ava backed out of the Pierson driveway and down her perfectly paved and shrub-lined street on Sunday afternoon. She'd heard of Baile Avenue, but it wasn't often she crossed over the invisible line to the "other" side of town. Though it was a ten-minute drive, her surroundings changed drastically from her house to Penn's. Houses sat closer and closer together, and in place of trimmed shrubbery, gardens grew wild. Her neighborhood's earth-toned siding was replaced by brightest blues, terracotta-oranges, and even a striking salmon-pink row home that occupied the corner where Ava turned toward Penn's house.

Distracted as she was by the buzz of people walking, laughing, and playing together on the sidewalk, Ava passed right by Penn's street. With so many cars lining the neighborhood, she barely managed to maneuver her car back down the way she came. A prickle of excitement rose on her forearms at the sight of Penn's street sign, hanging cockeyed on its post. She was relieved to find enough room to park in the driveway, considering her parallel parking skills were nonexistent.

Ava took the keys out of the ignition and paused to breathe before walking down Penn's driveway. She hadn't anticipated her nerves would skyrocket all because of a silly school project. She somehow convinced herself to get out of the car, pulling her sweater close as the wind picked up around her. Rambles of lavender, wild coneflowers, and cracked pots of varying bright mums blocked her path on the sidewalk. She sidestepped, hopped, and took a long leap to find herself standing on the top step of Penn's porch. Her excitement nosedived into anxiety as she stared at the door, worried what Paola might think of her.

"Ava!" Penn exclaimed, throwing the door wide open, Ava's fist still raised to knock. His sudden appearance caused Ava to bump into an unsuspecting pot, which shattered near her foot.

"Oh, god, I'm sorry!" Ava shrieked. She bent down to pick up the pieces, cursing herself for being such a klutz.

"No, no, no, leave it there!" Penn shouted, shaking his head as he looked out at the front yard. "Please, don't worry about it. I told Ma to clear this dang sidewalk for you; I knew I should have checked before you got here. Anyways, we're so glad you made it! It's cold out here, come in, come in!"

If Ava thought their garden was colorful, she wasn't prepared for what met her eyes when she shut the front door behind her. The small living room had no furniture but for a worn teal velvet sofa, which sagged in the middle. An ancient-looking television with an antenna sat in the corner, a black and white film playing on the tiny screen. Though this was interesting in its own right, it was the walls themselves that stole Ava's attention.

There was no white space from top to bottom, only swirling paint strokes of ruby red intermixed with sapphire blue, which faded into blood orange marked by hints of softest pink. It looked as though the paint was thrown from the can to the wall, but moving closer, each color expertly blended into the next. Ava's senses went into overdrive; all the neutral tones of her upbringing had bleached her palette. Her eyes were desperate to drink in every spectacular tint and hue displayed in Penn's living room.

And then, there was Paola. Ava hardly had time to catch her breath before one of the most striking women she'd ever seen appeared before her. Paola's outfit was as colorful and inviting as the walls around them. Her thick black hair fell in loose natural curls to her waist. Her eyes were as beautiful as Penn's, but a shade lighter, almost amber, framed by long, thick lashes. Though Paola was shorter than Ava by several inches, an electric energy emanated from her, filling the room with her presence.

"Ava! Welcome! Penn has told me so much about you!" Paola exclaimed, wrapping Ava up in a hug. Ava moved to end it, but Paola held on tight, rocking her back and forth.

"Ma! Give her some space! Sheesh! You are a little *too* excited," Penn insisted, walking forward to intervene. With reluctance, Paola let go and waved Penn off. She still held on to Ava's wrists, smiling into Ava's worried face. Ava felt self-conscious as she did this, wishing she had applied any amount of makeup to her face that day.

"You're so pretty!" Paola gushed, swatting the air in front of Penn. "You didn't tell me she was this pretty!"

Penn rolled his eyes and brought his hands to his forehead in disbelief. "Ma, Ava is here for a school project. She is not here to be assessed as a potential mate for me," he reminded her. Ava's eyes widened in shock.

"Oh, Penn, give your poor Ma a break. You know I want grandkids someday."

"Ma! What did I JUST tell you!"

"Fine, fine, fine. Ava! You have to taste what I'm cooking!" Paola demanded, taking Ava's hand and dragging her into the kitchen behind the living room. Ava passed by Penn, who mouthed, *"I'm sorry."*

The kitchen smelled of scents Ava had never experienced before; sweet and spicy notes wafted in and out of her nostrils.

"*Wow*. What are you cooking, Mrs. Abrams?" Ava asked as she investigated the large pot simmering on what looked like a 1950s-era stovetop.

"Oh, Ava, please just call me Paola." She said this as she glanced over at Penn, whose face suddenly clouded. "But oh, you know, just a bit of this and that!" Paola tossed in a leaf of what Ava guessed was an herb grown in the front garden.

"She doesn't believe in following recipes," Penn explained, his face returning to its usual exuberance as he leaned against the counter. Ava took notice that he dressed more casual in his home; a plain black tee replaced his usual button-up.

"What do you always say, Ma? What's the point of cooking if you're tasting the exact same thing you've had before?"

"Taste, taste!" Paola insisted, forcing Ava to blow on the steaming mystery concoction and take the spoon from her hand. Ava waited until it cooled and savored the dish's complexities as it hit her tongue full force. Like the garden out front, or the art on the walls, it shouldn't have worked; but as the flavors combined on her tongue, Ava knew it would be devastating to taste any of the ingredients again on their own.

Paola turned the volume up on what Ava thought looked like the same boombox from the movie *Say Anything*. Ava shrank against the counter as Paola began to move her hips back and forth, feet stepping in small but intricate movements. She reached out for Ava's hand.

"No, thanks!" Ava yelped.

"You don't dance! What?! *Why?* Because you're afraid or because you don't know how?" Paola asked, astonished. Penn snapped his head up from the stove where he was now stirring.

"Ma, *let her be*. If she doesn't want to dance, she doesn't have to dance."

"Fine, fine! But if she won't dance with me, you have to!"

"Seriously?" Penn groaned as Paola dragged him into the living room, leaving Ava to step into the role of stirring.

Ava watched Penn and Paola through the curved doorway as they spun and shimmied to the beat. Their laughter filled the small space, blending together with the racing melody and repetitive chorus blaring through the dusty stereo speakers. Penn's calculated movements became fluid, beautiful. Ava couldn't look away. Together, he and Paola made up two parts of one whole; they seemed interconnected, impenetrable. Envy wound itself around Ava, blurring the edges of her vision. She wished she had it, whatever it was they had. She felt sick with longing for it.

"How's it looking, Ava!?" Paola asked minutes later, twirling in from the living room. She wrapped an arm around Ava's waist.

"Honestly, I have no idea what it's supposed to look like," Ava answered.

"Me neither!" Paola said, laughing a full, deep belly laugh. She slurped juices from the spoon. "It needs more time. You two go get started on your project thingy, and I'll call you back in here when it's ready."

"You just want to finish up the piece you're working on without us around," Penn teased.

"Oh, so what!" answered Paola, heading to the kitchen table where what looked like thin metal shavings lay waiting. Penn kissed Paola on the cheek and headed down the small hallway, which split at the end. Ava followed Penn as he turned right. She noticed the start of a new mural beginning on either side of the hallway, twisting and whirling until she crossed the threshold into Penn's bedroom.

His room looked like a study she'd seen in movies about important college professors. The walls were a solid shade of deep cerulean blue. The wall to the far left was covered in a floor-to-ceiling bookcase. Books of every size and color were crammed on the shelves, some in piles on top of rows. Straight ahead, there was a desk made from oak under his window, which looked out onto a small patch of grass leading into a dense stretch of woods. On the wall to her immediate left was a cognac leather armchair, cracked and worn but timeless. A small twin bed sat innocently to her right, covers rumpled and unmade. Notebooks jutted out from underneath his bed. Ava felt the sudden urge to lie down on the floor, pick up a note-book, and spend the rest of the day inside his brain.

"I know it's not much, but . . . it's mine," Penn said, standing in the middle of the room, cracking his knuckles. Ava wondered if a girl, outside of Paola, had ever been in his room before. She perched on the edge of the leather chair, avoiding his bed.

"I think this room couldn't look more like you," Ava said, hoping to ease Penn's nerves as well as hers. Penn smiled, then awkwardly took a seat on his bed. "This is a nice chair," she remarked, scooting backward to rest fully into it.

"Thanks! It was my dad's, actually," Penn shared, looking down at his hands, now gripping his knees.

"Oh, I um, oh, is he not?" Ava asked, wishing she'd chosen the desk chair across the room.

"No," Penn said, clearing his throat. "He passed away last year. He had ALS. I don't know if you know what that is."

Ava shook her head, wishing she did so he didn't have to explain it to her.

"It's a nervous system disease that progressively paralyzes you over time. There's no cure or anything so eventually it leads to, well, you know."

"Shit, Penn. I'm so sorry, I'll move," Ava jumped up, her face hot. She realized the other chair might be his dad's too. She settled for sitting on the floor, her back against the bookcase.

"No, no! You can sit there! It's a chair! Please, Paola would kill me if she saw you sitting on the ground."

Ava refused to move, hating herself for not finding any words more comforting for Penn than "shit" and "sorry." They sat there, avoiding eye contact with one another.

"It's just that I don't think anyone but my best friend Kaysar has sat in that chair since my dad passed, and even he felt weird doing it," Penn recalled. Ava looked out the window above Penn's desk, praying any sort of soothing sentiment would come to her.

"We don't have to talk about it," Ava offered. "I didn't . . . I just . . . we can start our project if you don't want to talk about it, okay?" Ava suggested, memorizing the tree line outside. Penn sat back on his bed so that his back slumped against the wall.

"Unless, like, you want to talk about it?" Ava asked.

"It's so . . . *weird*. That no one knows him here," Penn whispered. "Everyone knew my dad back in our old neighborhood. In Baltimore. I don't know if I told you that's where I'm from. But he took care of everyone, and everyone took care of him. We were all like one big family, you know?"

Ava nodded like she understood, though she barely spoke to her own neighbors. She stayed quiet, realizing this was the first time he'd talked about himself without deflecting questions back at her.

"We watched him deteriorate for years until it happened. I think when he finally did pass, Ma and I needed to be anywhere else, if that makes sense? And this neighborhood is great, don't get me wrong. Ma loves it and knows everybody already. But the other day, when you said that thing on The Lookout about not feeling connected to Westwood? I feel it too. I didn't want to admit it because I want this place to work. But, I feel it too."

Ava wanted to sit next to him, to do anything useful, but she didn't know how to comfort people. No one had ever taught or showed her how. She tugged at her ponytail until her eyes fell on a framed photograph across the room. She stood up, picked it up, and held it in her hands.

"*Wow*," she gasped.

"I know, I know. I look just like him," Penn said.

"I mean, it's scary how *much* you look like him. Outside of your eyes and, well."

Penn looked up at her. "And well, what?"

"I mean, he's, well he's . . ." Ava set the photo down and rubbed her lips together. Penn searched her face.

"You can say it, Ava. Though it's totally insensitive, considering he is no longer alive and I'm trying to have a heartfelt conversation with you over here."

"I, oh, my god—I didn't say anything!"

"You think he's a babe," Penn teased, his face softening.

"I don't—I mean that's, no! I mean . . ."

Ava wished she'd burst into flame on the spot. She looked up to find Penn convulsing with laughter.

"Don't worry, I'm *messing* with you. I know I have attractive parents. I missed the gene, somehow, but I make up for it in intelligence, I think. Though both my parents are or have been college professors . . . ah well. I do the best I can with what I've got."

Ava set the picture down and looked at Penn, still slumped against the wall. She crossed the distance between them to sit on the corner of his bed.

"I, um, I am sorry, though, Penn. For your loss. And thank you for, well, telling me. I don't really know what the right thing is to say, but if it means anything, I'm glad you're here too. I meant to say that the other day when you said it to me. I'm glad you are here in Westwood too."

Though Ava spoke more to his bookcase than to him, it was the best she could do. When he didn't speak for a while, she turned around to find Penn's face buried in his hands.

"Penn, are you—" Ava asked, but she stopped as she saw his shoulders shaking. She joined him up against the wall and placed her hand somewhat awkwardly on his shoulder.

"For so long, Ava," he said, his voice muffled, "I've felt stuck. Like I'll never get over missing him. Like I'll never heal from this. Like it will never go away. And I'll never be half the man he was. No matter how hard I study, no matter what university I get into. I can't be him, or replace him, or bring him back. No matter how far I live away from Baltimore."

Penn shook harder. Ava put her arm around both of his shoulders. She opened her mouth to try to say something, but Penn wiped his face with the inside of his shirt. He reached over to grab his shoulder bag, putting an end to the moment.

"Anyways, sorry about that, Ava. I—"

"Hey, Penn," Ava interrupted, setting her hand on his wrist.

"Yeah?"

"You don't have to apologize for having feelings," she said, the only thing she could think of to say that might comfort him.

Penn reached down and squeezed her hand with his. Their eyes met for only a second before they jerked their heads away.

"Well! I hope you're ready to talk about death some more," Penn joked as he unpacked his bag and pulled out his copy of *Death of a Salesman*.

Ava grinned but couldn't fathom the depth of loss Penn and Paola must feel. The creeping envy she experienced in the kitchen earlier faded; instead, she tried to beat back the seed of hope growing within her. The one that took root sometime over the past week. The one that felt it might burst into bloom if she admitted the person sitting next to her was beginning to feel like home.

chapter nine

The next two weeks flew by as Penn and Ava continued working on their project during class, lunch, and on Sunday afternoons. On Ava's latest visit to Penn's house, Paola taught her how to sketch and use watercolors to bring her costume and set designs to life. While Ava continued to turn down Paola's invitations to dance, she studied her movements closely, storing each step and spin in her mind.

Ava wasn't sure if she was looking forward to her final volleyball game on Friday. Coach Arruda appeared relieved when Ava told her she wanted to finish out the season. Part of Ava wanted it all to be over with, but the other part felt something slipping away, something she wasn't sure she'd be able to get back.

When Wednesday morning rolled around, Ava found Penn standing in front of Mrs. Papayanni's desk as she walked into class. They were engrossed in conversation, Penn's hands flying as animated as ever. Mrs. Papayanni was uncharacteristically smiling, using her own sharp gestures to respond. Not wanting to bring attention to herself, Ava found her usual seat next to the windows and waited for them to finish. She took out her English folder, studying the project notes she needed to discuss with Penn.

"BIG NEWS," Penn shouted as he headed back from Mrs. Papayanni's desk, his hands jutting up and down in unison as he spoke.

"Yes, Penn?"

"We are going first next week when we present!" he exclaimed, waiting for Ava to respond with equal excitement.

"That's . . . a . . . a good thing?" she asked, searching his face for a sign. She took his massive smile as meaning it must be. "Great, how great!"

The class quieted as Mrs. Papayanni took the front of the room.

"This will be your last block period to work on your project. Mr. Abrams has asked to go first next Wednesday to present; do I have any volunteers to go second?" she asked, hopeful. The class went dead silent.

"All right then! I'll call at random on Wednesday, but please be prepared! I plan on getting to as many groups as possible. Don't count on getting the extra time to go on Friday," she said. A few students appeared crestfallen.

"On Friday, we will begin our unit on poetry. You have the option to choose one of your favorite poems, or I will assign you one. But be aware you will need to memorize, perform, and even write your own poem inspired by the original. I encourage you to bare your soul and speak your mind! That, after all, is what poetry is about. I've talked enough now! Let's get these projects finished up."

Mrs. Papayanni began her usual slow pace around the room. Penn's leg was shaking more than usual. Ava pulled her long sleeves down over her knuckles and scratched the back of her neck.

"Uh, Penn?" Ava asked.

"Yes, Ava?" Penn asked, throwing his chest over the sidebar of the desk to lean closer toward her.

"Did I miss something? Why is it so great we are going first?"

"Because going first is the best! We get to set the bar for the rest of the class, and I think we can set it fairly high! Plus, nerves are less likely to get the best of us. I mean, I'll speak for myself, but if I sit around too long listening to other people, I get restless. AND it means we can sit back and listen when others present after us! It's so great!"

Ava considered this, not wanting to admit to Penn that nothing would stop her nerves from getting the best of her. The thought of having to do any sort of public speaking made her want to vomit.

"Okay, Ava, I know most of our project is complete, but we need to nail down our presentation order and exactly what we're going to say. I think the more we rehearse, the better it will be. Do you think you could meet one more time after class? On Friday, maybe?"

"Oh, sorry Penn, I have my last volleyball game of the season on Friday, so that won't work for me. And we have, like, a whole week before next Wednesday. Don't you think that's enough time?"

Penn stopped jiggling his legs. "Your last game? Can I come?"

Ava wasn't sure how to respond. No one attended her games anymore. Her parents usually worked late on Fridays, Mac didn't have a ride, and Ava guessed Leona only came the past couple of years to support Jacklyn and Trish.

"I, well, are you sure you want to? We're pretty bad this year," Ava said, looking down at Penn's oxfords.

"Of course, I want to come! It's your last game of the season! And I've never gotten to see you play."

"Well, it might be my last game, period," Ava said, dragging her eyes upward to meet his. His energy calmed as he waited for her to continue. "Yeah, I just decided . . . well, I guess Coach Arruda helped me decide that maybe I wasn't really there because I wanted to be there. So, I won't be trying out for the team next year."

Penn's stare was so piercing she had to look away. She fixed her gaze on her unpainted fingernails, now tracing the J & S carved on her desk.

"I think it's a courageous move, Ava."

"Courageous? That's a big word considering I just quit a thing."

"Too many people stick with things they don't like because they think they should. It takes a lot of courage to walk away from something you don't love to find things that you do."

Ava didn't believe him completely, but she had to admit it sounded a hell of a lot better than the internal voices of guilt she'd been fighting over the past couple of weeks.

"And OH!" he shouted. "Can you pick me up next Wednesday morning and take me to school? That way we can put all our project stuff into your Jeep."

"Do you think you'll ever get your driver's license?" Ava asked, giving him the side eye.

"Probably not if I continue to have such a great chauffeur service," he shot back, grinning.

* * *

Ava entered the locker room for her last practice on Thursday afternoon feeling much lighter after her conversation with Penn. She looked around the room and thought back over the past seasons: how Jacklyn would turn the music up loud and the team would sing together at the top of their lungs. Or the time they stashed cheesy puffs in Trish's locker to slip in and eat during practice.

"Ava?" a soft voice whispered. Ava finished tugging on her gray Westwood High t-shirt to find Trish standing there, a glittery pink scrunchie tying up her curly mane of hair.

"Yeah? Does Coach need me or something?" Ava asked, surprised. Trish hadn't spoken much at all to Ava since Penn called Leona out. Trish pulled a curl out of her ponytail and stretched it out in front of her.

"No," she continued in a near whisper. Ava had to bend toward her to hear. "It's my eighteenth birthday the weekend after this, as you probably know and you haven't missed any of my parties as long as we've been friends. I mean, I was thinking, I don't know if you'd want to come. I know Leona is coming too, but, it would mean a lot to me if you could be there."

Ava's jaw fell open.

"I get it if you don't want to come. But, like, you totally could if you want. And you can bring that boy you're always with. Penn, I think he said his name was? The one who walks everywhere really fast? Bring whoever, really. I'd just, um, I'd really like it if you could make it."

Trish continued to stare at her, her light brown eyes hopeful. She was so delicate, so innocent in her pink sparkling glory that Ava couldn't muster the word no.

"I-I'll do my best to be there, okay? And I'll ask Penn."

"Thanks, Ava! Even if Leona doesn't want you there, I do," she said firmly, then gracefully spun around and left Ava alone in the locker room.

Ava couldn't believe she was considering Trish's invitation. The idea of being anywhere near Leona without adult supervision was terrifying. But then Ava thought of Penn, in his business casual slacks and ironed button-down, attending his first ever Westwood High party. It might not be so horrible, she thought, if he was there by her side.

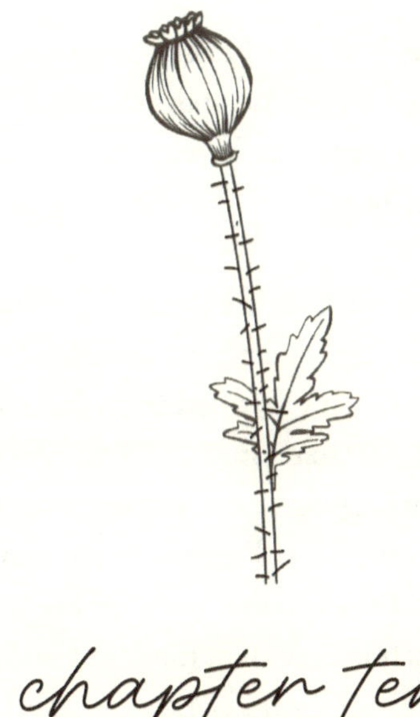

chapter ten

Thoughts of Trish's impending party were so distracting Ava hardly noticed the extra car parked in the Pierson driveway. She absentmindedly pulled into an open spot on the street, wondering if Trish was genuine or if Leona was orchestrating some elaborate scheme to get back at Penn. Distracted as she was, she didn't hear the shouting as she walked up the drive, or feel her phone buzzing in her bag. Utterly oblivious to anything going on outside of her own brain, she turned the golden doorknob attached to her front door, expecting to find nothing out of the ordinary.

Two screaming voices hit Ava full on in the doorway. Her eyes raced between the two figures: her father dressed in his best charcoal gray suit, jacket still buttoned, and a girl who stood in the middle of the open entrance hall. Ava struggled to identify her. Then she knew. What was once thick, luscious auburn hair now hung stringy and lank around the girl's face. Her cheekbones, which were once the envy of every girl at Westwood High, jutted out unnaturally over her sunken cheeks. Her curves had eroded; leggings sagged around her hips. A baggy sweatshirt nearly swallowed her whole.

"*Jacklyn?*" Ava whispered in astonishment.

"Close the damn door, Ava!" Mr. Pierson bellowed, spittle flying off his curled lips as Olivia trotted down the stairs to greet her. Jacklyn watched Ava scoop Olivia up in her arms, not looking Ava in the face.

"Get that thing out of here!" Mr. Pierson demanded. "You know how much I hate it!"

Ava shut the front door with her free arm. She spotted Mac on the sectional, staring down at the rug beneath his sock-covered feet. Ava jogged up the stairs two at a time, closing her bedroom door softly behind Olivia. She thought about hiding out there until the fight resided, but she couldn't leave Mac alone downstairs. Quietly, she walked back down the steps and sat close to Mac on the sofa. Mrs. Pierson had entered the scene in her absence. She leaned against the kitchen counter, keeping her distance.

"You will go back to school, Jacklyn; that's the end of it. I'll have a talk with your dean, threaten to sue him if I have too. But you're going back," Mr. Pierson said stonily, his handsome face contorted with rage. Though she'd seen her parents fight hundreds of times, this was different. Hatred flickered in her father's cold, gray eyes.

"I'm not going back there, *James*," Jacklyn said with defiance, her withering frame still emanating strength.

"Don't call your father by his first name, Jacklyn," Mrs. Pierson said, her words carrying across the foyer.

"Amazing how much respect you ask from us kids when you never were able to give much of it to each other," Jacklyn snapped back.

"What do you think you're worth without a college education?" Mr. Pierson asked, slamming his briefcase on the marble floor. "Nothing. The world will never take you seriously without a degree. You're going back. I'll book us both a flight so I can fix this fucking mess you've made. You will graduate."

"No," Jacklyn said with a smug smile.

"*What did you say to me?*" Mr. Pierson asked. He took two steps closer, standing inches away from Jacklyn. His tall body towered over hers, his chest puffed out, daring her to cross him. He'd never hit any of them before; his ways of causing pain were much more manipulative, inflicted beneath the surface consistently over the years. Ava felt the urge to run to her sister, to throw herself in front of her.

"I don't give a shit what Piersons are supposed to do, or look like, or become. You can take your sham of an American Dream and *shove it up your ass*," Jacklyn hissed.

Mac, Ava, and Mrs. Pierson audibly gasped. No one talked to Mr. Pierson this way. Not his wife, his clients, his partners, and especially not his daughter.

"Get out of my house," was all he said, his face draining of color.

"It's not just *your* house, it's Mom's—"

"I said, get out of *MY* house. NOW!"

Jacklyn sized him up one last time, then looked him square in the face, her expression dripping with disdain. When he didn't move, Jacklyn looked over at Mrs. Pierson, expecting her to stand up to him. But Mrs. Pierson stood there, silent as ever, staring at the spotless stainless steel refrigerator door.

Jacklyn let one small, resigned laugh echo around the entryway before picking up her things and heading toward the front door. She glanced back at Mac, whose look of despair broke Ava's heart in two.

"I'll be at Leona's if you need anything, okay, Mac Attack? Just text the word, and I'll come to get you," Jacklyn said. Mac's face fell as the small hope he held of Jacklyn taking him with her extinguished. Jacklyn hesitated for a moment, then looked a bit to Mac's right but not directly at Ava. Then she turned back to the door, opened it dramatically, and slammed it behind her.

Mr. Pierson muttered something incoherent under his breath as he undid his tie, then headed up the stairs. Mrs. Pierson continued to stand against the counter, fiddling with her tennis bracelet, pieces of her hair beginning to fall out of place. Mac lingered for a moment before making his way up the stairs. Ava pulled her legs under her, grabbed the remote, and turned on the TV without watching it. Eventually, Mrs. Pierson headed upstairs and left Ava with the first floor of the house to herself.

Though the sound of the TV helped to numb her pain, Ava couldn't take her mind off Jacklyn. Her phone stared up at her as she locked and unlocked it, wishing Jacklyn would explain to her why they weren't speaking. She just needed a single text message, or an emergency meeting on The Lookout, anything to break this painful silence. All she could picture now was Jacklyn arriving at Leona's, the two of them picking up right where they left off. She imagined Jacklyn replacing her completely with Leona, the two bonding over their hatred for her.

Ava turned the volume up louder to drown out her ruminating thoughts. Trish's party, her last volleyball game, and next week's presentation all seemed laughable now. Ava doubted she'd even be able to drag herself out of bed in the morning after this.

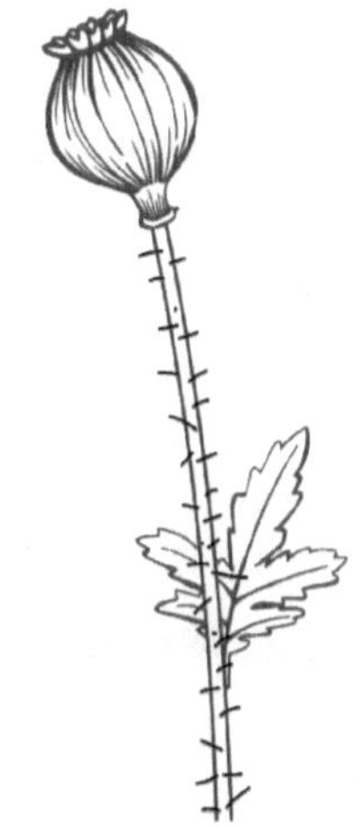

chapter eleven

A phone alarm blared rudely next to Ava's ear the following morning. She cracked her eyes open to stare up at the ceiling. Her eyes fluttered shut again as she recalled the events of last night. The front door opened downstairs, then slammed shut. A few minutes later, it opened and closed again, softer this time. The sound of Mac's heavy footsteps stopped right outside her door, but no knock came. Eventually, she heard him pound down the steps, the front door opening and closing once more. As she rolled onto her side, Ava doubted her mother would pick up the call from Westwood High to verify her absence.

She slipped into a dream of Leona stalking Westwood High's halls, waiting for an opportunity to jump down Ava's throat. It sprang forward to Trish, fairy-like in an extra sparkly outfit at her party, laughing at Ava for showing up. Ava thrashed beneath her covers; she had hoped sleep would take her away from her nightmares. She sprang awake as her phone vibrated in the jumble of twisted sheets. Shaking out her blankets, her phone fell to the floor. Penn's name flashed across the screen.

"Yeah?" she answered, her voice still gravelly from sleep.

"Hey! Ava! It's me, Penn! Sorry, I, uh, I know you're not big on phone calls, but I was looking for you this morning, and it looks like you aren't here. The bell is about to ring. Everything okay? Are you not feeling well?"

"I'm . . . ," Ava paused, about to tell Penn everything that happened yesterday. Instead, she listened to his heavy breathing. It sounded like he'd run around the whole school searching for her. She maneuvered herself to the edge of her bed, allowing her feet to dangle above the carpet. "I'm just running late this morning. I'll be there soon."

Penn hesitated; his annoying radar lie detector likely going haywire. "Great! I'll see you in class then?"

"Yeah, yeah. I'll see you then."

Ava hurried around her room, sniffing out the least smelly clothes to wear from her overflowing dirty laundry. She sensed Penn's probing glare through the line. "I'm serious, I'll be there! Bye!"

She hung up before he could ask any more questions.

Ava nursed a sick feeling in her gut as she arrived late to class. A strange dizziness hung around her head, causing her to feel like she was stuck in a relentless haze. It wasn't until Penn asked in English class about her game that Ava remembered it was Friday. The thought of it made her wrap her arms around her stomach, trying to hold its contents from spilling out.

When the bell rang to end the school day, Ava ran to her favorite bathroom, hidden near the library. Not many people bothered to go out of their way to use it. She rushed to the stall in the far back corner and threw her head over the toilet. When nothing came up, she slumped against the stall wall, her head in her hands. Her white converses stared up at her, waiting, but they didn't spark the same magic they did a few weeks prior.

Minutes passed before she heard the sound of heels clicking across the tile floor and a stall door shutting beside her. It was enough to motivate her to stand up, wash her hands, and put one foot in front of the other to arrive upstairs in the girls' locker room.

"I heard this might be your last game?" Ava was surprised to hear the freshman with purple glasses ask her as they changed next to each other. Ava turned to look at her, her low pigtails with poofs of bright blonde curls spilled out innocently.

"Oh, yeah. Yeah, I think it will be, actually." Ava smiled with what she hoped looked like politeness, unsure what to talk to her about.

"I-I-I've really enjoyed playing with you, Ava," she said. Ava stopped pulling on her own sock, relieved the girl's name finally came to her.

"You too, Leila, you're really good. This team would be total crap without you, and Trish, really."

"You're good too!" Leila exclaimed, a hint of nerves in her voice. "I hope you'll come to watch us next year, maybe? I know the seniors will be gone, and there's no one else from your year, but, it'd be nice to have a friendly face in the stands. Not many people come to see us, as you know."

Ava felt a small pang of regret. She wished she would have talked to Leila sooner, gotten to know her better.

"You know what? Maybe I will," Ava said, thinking she might just mean it. Leila's face split into a wide smile.

"Are you ready? Would you want to walk down to the main gym together?" Leila asked. Ava nodded, grateful to have someone to walk with who wasn't Trish.

Leila chatted happily beside her as they descended the stairwell. With each step, the haze from earlier thickened into an opaque fog. Her nausea magnified as they drew closer to the bottom. When they reached the main gym floor, Ava felt her knees buckle. She grabbed on to Leila's forearm for support.

"Oh, gosh! Ava?! You don't look so good," Leila said, though her voice sounded far away. Ava looked around to see where Leila had gone, but she felt like she was swimming underwater. Everything and everyone around her moved in slow motion, their faces distorted. She thought she spotted Penn, waving his arms in the stands across from her. But her eyes, struggling to focus through the obscurity, rested on Leona. She stood next to someone Ava couldn't quite make out.

"Are you going to be sick?" Leila asked, her voice even further away now. Ava thought she might fall into the black hole forming in front of her if she took a step forward. She squeezed her eyes shut. Ava tried to recall a breathing technique Ms. Delic had posted in her office: breathe in for four, hold for four, out for four. When she opened her eyes again, Mac and Penn stood in front of her, their expressions panicked.

"What's going on?! Ava, what do you need right now?" Penn shouted, his laid-back demeanor replaced with one of parental concern. Mac looked between Penn and Ava with fear.

"I don't know . . . I don't know if I can do this," Ava croaked, struggling to find her words. Mac, Penn, and Leila hesitated, looking at one another helplessly.

"What's going on over here? Ava? Ava, you don't look well," Coach said, breaking into the small circle. "Ava, can you tell me where you are right now?"

Ava's eyes followed Coach Arruda's silver whistle as it swung from side to side. She looked around to try to answer, but her focus fell on the swish of Trish's long, curly ponytail springing behind her as she too joined the circle surrounding Ava.

"Someone take her to the nurse, now. Get her away from all these people!" Coach demanded.

"Or maybe we can still catch Ms. Delic?" Penn suggested.

"I need . . . I need air," Ava squeaked. Penn reached out his hand, but she shook her head violently. "Alone. I need to go get some air alone."

Ava couldn't absorb the look of hurt in Penn's eyes. She ran with abandon toward the exit, pushing past anyone in her path, slamming her full body weight against the crash bar. The cold air welcomed her into its midst, a single heavy raindrop exploding across her forehead. She sucked in the fresh air as she raced around the building, finding the spot she was searching for.

She jogged down a small alleyway, formed by two mismatched school buildings. Her fingers traced over the brick on one side, the cinder blocks on the other. Dots of flashing light raced in and out of her vision. She stopped in the middle of the alley and sank down against the cinderblock wall.

"Breathe," she said out loud. "Breathe."

Ava sat counting breaths until she began to hum. She hummed louder and louder until all she heard was the calming sound of her own voice. It crested over the flashing images and grounded her to the pavement. When calmness stole over her, she lifted her head to face the multicolored bricks in front of her.

"Ava?" a voice called from the top of the alleyway. Ava kept staring ahead. If she stopped, everything might tremor and collapse. She sensed footsteps draw close and hesitate a few feet from her.

"Hey, can you tell me what's wrong?" the voice asked, hovering above her.

Ava wished she could grab hold of the figure next to her, for her body shook with longing for it. Instead, she hugged her knees in close, tugged them to her chest, burrowing down into the pavement.

"Ava, please talk to me," the voice pleaded as it sank down next to her.

These were the words Ava had been starved to hear for months. She thought they would fix everything, put her right again. But instead of relief, a burning, all-encompassing hatred erupted inside her. Ava couldn't bring herself to understand how someone she cared for so deeply could abandon her so suddenly.

With a blazing fury, Ava turned to meet the electric blue eyes she'd looked to for guidance as far back as she could remember. But instead of the glowing confidence they once held, Ava glimpsed something else. It made sense now: the sudden weight loss, the thinning hair, the sallow skin. Jacklyn hadn't come back to Westwood to spite their father or to mend her relationship with Ava: she'd come home to find herself.

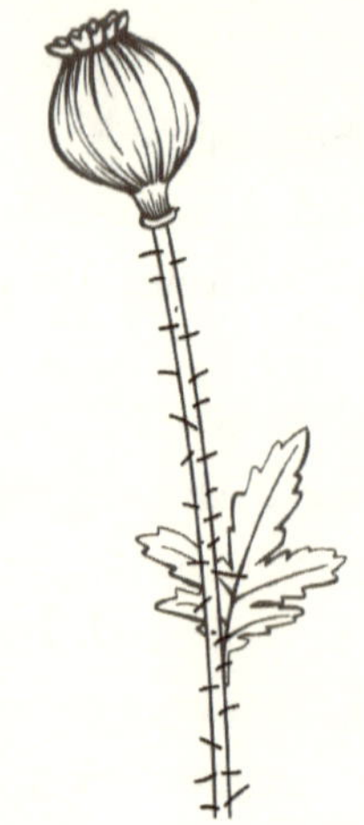

chapter twelve

"Leona will kill me for coming out here," Jacklyn said, glancing back toward the mouth of the alley. "But, you're still my sister. After everything. I don't like seeing you like this. It's pretty screwed up, you know, what you did. If I'm the reason you're out here, though, maybe we need to talk about it?"

Ava's anger and confusion dueled within her chest. Jacklyn waited for Ava to speak, accusations simmering beneath her calm and collected surface.

"Come on, Ava, you can't expect me to get over something like that! I don't even know how you think I'd ever talk to you again! But I'm trying. Okay?"

"What . . . what are you *even* talking about?" Ava whispered.

"You seriously won't even admit what you did! You thought I wouldn't find out?" Jacklyn half yelled, half laughed.

"Find out about what!?" Ava roared. Ravens rose from the top of the buildings, cawing madly as they flew in all directions.

"I *seriously* have to spell this out for you?" Jacklyn cried.

Fragmented images returned, blurring Ava's line of sight once more. Each memory began to separate and find its proper place in the timeline.

"Leona saw you with Bradley that night at Trish's," Jacklyn explained. "She saw you disappear upstairs with him. She said she'd suspected it for weeks but didn't want to tell me until she had proof. I *knew* you liked him, Ava. I just didn't think you'd go that far."

Ava tried to slow everything down as the pieces of that night snapped together with rapid precision.

"Leona didn't see what she thought she did," Ava sighed.

"Oh please, Ava, you've never been a good liar. Admit what you did!"

Ava's hands quivered, her forehead breaking out in a cold sweat. "Jacklyn. Can you believe me on this? It wasn't what she thought it was."

"What do you mean, 'it wasn't what she thought it was'? What does that *even mean*? I mean what else . . . could it have been?" Jacklyn sat down on the ground to face Ava, her back propped against the brick wall. Though every part of her body resisted, Ava closed her eyes and started from the beginning.

"Everyone passed out in the living room that night, remember? You were asleep on the couch with your head on Bradley's lap. You were snoring so damn loud, and I couldn't fall asleep. I got up to throw up those gross Jaeger bombs we took, and I tripped on someone sleeping on the floor when I came back. Bradley woke up and asked if I was doing okay. We got to talking for a bit after that."

Jacklyn still looked angry, but she sat quietly, watching Ava with suspicion.

"You're right, I did have a crush on Bradley. He can be so kind, unlike other guys. I mean, I'm sure you know, you dated him. I felt like he really did care about me. It felt nice to be . . . cared for, you know?"

Jacklyn gave a restricted nod in response.

"So, when he asked me if he could show me something upstairs that night while everyone was still asleep, I was so excited. I knew your birthday was coming up, and I was happy for you, Jacklyn. More than I liked him, I was happy for you! You finally found this person who treated you well, someone I thought might deserve you. When he led the way up to Mr.

and Mrs. Sterling's bedroom, I figured he didn't want to wake you and ruin your surprise gift. It was stupid. *I* was stupid."

Jacklyn's anger dissipated as concern crept around the edges of her mouth.

"When he locked the door behind us, I thought it was weird, but I trusted him," Ava laughed at herself, thinking of how naive she'd been. "I remember he patted the silky purple comforter, and like an idiot, I plopped down next to him. I even bounced up and down on the mattress, thinking he would pull out a necklace or something from his pocket to show me. I think I was hoping some boy would care this much for me one day. And then it . . . it . . . I don't know how it . . . it just . . ."

"Are you telling me that Bradley? That he—" Jacklyn's voice trembled.

"It happened so fast, Jacklyn. He took my clothes off so quickly, and then he was naked and . . . I didn't stop it. I didn't know how, or what to do. I just . . . I wish I could have stopped it."

Ava waited for tears that wouldn't come. She felt numb recalling it now, like she was sharing a story from someone else's life.

"I couldn't tell you. I couldn't tell anyone about it. I should have been strong enough to stop it."

Silence filled the space between the two sisters. They mirrored one another in the alleyway, one knee up, the other leg straight. They stared up at the narrow strip of sky above as dark clouds threatened to spill their contents.

Ava finished the rest of the story in her mind as they looked above. She'd never tell Jacklyn about the cry of pain Bradley mistook for pleasure as he thrust harder, faster. Or how she focused intensely on the white crown molding in the corner of the bedroom until he finished, not once looking Ava in the face. She would never tell anyone his breath reeked of buffalo chicken dip and malt whiskey. Or how his unshaven chin scraped at her forehead, rubbing it raw. How afterward, he ignored her tear-lined face and rolled off her, patting her twice on the upper left thigh.

Until then, she had forgotten she didn't move an inch until he put his clothes back on and left her alone in the bedroom. She laid there for what seemed like forever, until a sliver of strength swam its way to the surface, allowing her to roll over onto her side. Ava recalled now how she grabbed a Kleenex out of a box flecked with tiny pink hearts, wiped herself, and gathered her things which had been carelessly thrown across the room.

Memories from that evening flooded back; the long descent down Trish's stairs, her legs shaking. How she pulled herself into the backseat of her Jeep, reached for her red blanket, and wrapped it around her aching body. The feeling of the soft fleece against her face brought little comfort as it cradled her cheeks. She lay there, Bradley's spicy cologne still clinging to her skin, until the last shining star disappeared with morning light. The sun rose magnificently through her windshield, lighting up her mascara-stained face. In those early hours, Ava made a vow to herself to never speak of what happened that night to anyone. She believed if no one else knew it happened, she might convince herself it never did.

"I don't know what to say, Ava," Jacklyn whispered hoarsely. "I wish you would have told me ... I just ... I can't ... I ... you ... I ... why didn't you tell me? I could have done something. I could still do—"

"No!" Ava snapped.

Jacklyn leaned forward, placed her hand lightly on Ava's bare shin. "You're my sister, Ava. He can't get away with this. We have to do something!"

"It wasn't, I didn't ... I didn't try to stop it, Jacklyn, don't you get it? I let this happen. I let him do it."

"But, Ava—" Jacklyn pleaded.

"No!" Ava screamed, bolting to her feet.

"Okay, okay! Can you sit down? Can we talk more? Please?" Jacklyn reached up to hold Ava's hand, squeezing it hard. "I don't know how to ever apologize enough to you. I'm so sorry. I'm so sorry that he did that to you. If I would have ..."

Ava snatched her hand away and ran up the alley. Jacklyn followed close behind.

Ava turned back around at the opening. "I wanted you to know what really happened so we could go back to normal. I don't want to talk about it anymore, or ever again. Got it? Let's just go back to the way it was before this all happened."

Jacklyn attempted to reach out again, but Ava took a step back.

"Don't touch me right now, okay? I need to get back to the game."

"Are you sure you're okay to play? Coach Arruda would understand if you need to go home," Jacklyn insisted.

"No. It's my last game. But I guess you wouldn't know that. And Penn really wants to see me play, so, you're welcome to watch, but . . . Jacklyn. Don't tell anyone about this. This stays between us."

"Of course, it does, Ava. I would never—" Jacklyn began, but Ava was already sprinting back toward the gym.

Once inside, Ava pressed her back up against the far gym wall, re-orienting herself as her heart raced. When she felt steady, she spotted Penn staring at her in the stands. He sprinted down the steps toward her, his curly hair standing on end.

Ava focused on his worry-lined face as it drew near, his eyes the most vivid thing she'd seen all day. When he arrived in front of her with his arms open, he hesitated, but Ava threw herself forward. She buried her face into his faded button-down and breathed in his distinctly soapy scent, each inhale erasing all lingering thoughts of that night in June.

When Penn stepped back, Ava pulled him closer still, giving herself what she needed most: faith that good humans existed in the world, even one who cared enough to show up for her time and time again.

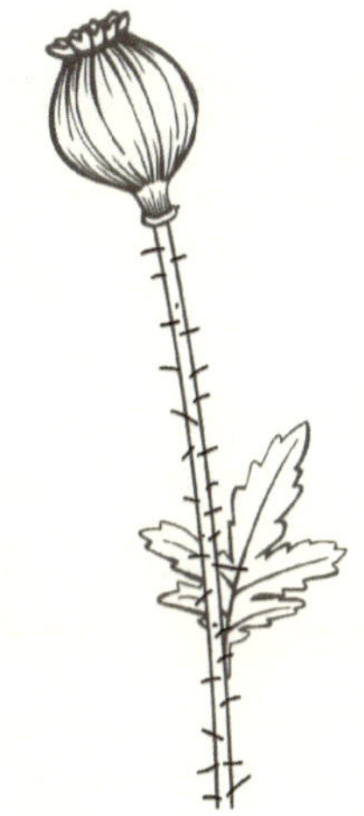

chapter thirteen

A buzzer rang throughout the gym. Ava jumped back, away from Penn. He opened his mouth to say something, but Mac rushed over to them from the stands, interrupting the moment. Jacklyn reappeared from outside and threw her arm around Mac's shoulders, guiding him back to their seats on the bleachers. She shot Ava a knowing glance, leaving her alone with Penn.

"There's one more game left, Ava. I don't know if...," Penn said.

Ava glanced over at her teammates huddled together, then up at the scoreboard on the opposite wall. They had won the first game, lost the second. The third was about to begin. Trish and Leila stood on opposite sides of the huddle, checking on Ava over their shoulders when they thought Coach wasn't paying attention. "Do you want to go somewhere to talk?"

"No, I, uh, I'm going to join the huddle. Let's talk after," Ava said, rushing away.

She jogged toward her teammates as they placed their hands together in the center of the circle, shouting "Westwood Warriors!" as they broke apart. The starters ran to their spots on the court as Ava took a seat on the bench.

"Are you sure you're okay to join us?" Coach asked, her deep brown eyes drilling into Ava's.

"Yeah, Coach, I'm fine! Just ate something weird at lunch," Ava lied. Coach squinted at her, then turned back to the game as the starting buzzer sounded.

Ava sat down and tapped her foot anxiously on the gym floor, hoping Coach would put her in at some point soon. She couldn't bring herself to look up at the stands. She could sense Mac, Jacklyn, Penn, and Leona's eyes drilling into the back of her head.

As usual, Leila's serves were flawless, the ball arcing beautifully over the net each time. But when the ball came back over the net, her team-mates struggled without Ava in her usual position. They managed to stay ahead of the other team by one point, but just barely, as the time ticked away. Coach looked pleadingly over at Ava, who gave one confident nod in response. She sent Ava in with minutes to spare.

The other team's serve wasn't anywhere as beautiful as Leila's; the ball went directly to Trish. Trish's small frame bent beneath the ball, sending it up with such force you wouldn't suspect she had it in her. Ava's heart pounded as a surge of electricity coursed through her veins. The ball was no longer just a ball. Instead, it stood for every place on her body Bradley had touched her without asking. It stood for the door he locked her behind, the clothes he'd stripped from her. It stood for more than winning a volleyball game. Above all else, it stood for her power, which had been so unceremoniously taken away by someone she thought she could trust.

Every muscle in her body lit with a burning anger as she jumped high into the air, palm colliding with the center of the ball. With a strength she'd never felt before, she smacked it over the head of the opposing team's tallest player and into a hole on their side of the net. It hit the waxed gym floor with a resounding 'WHOMP' just before the buzzer sounded to end the game.

Ava fell to her knees as her teammates closed in around her. They hugged her tight around the neck. She thought she'd hate them being so close to her, but instead, joy welled up inside her. Coach joined the tangle of girls and found her way to Ava. She put her hand out and helped her to her feet.

"Thank you for serving this team so well, Ava," she yelled over screaming teammates and clapping fans from their small crowd in the stands. Coach's eyes were glimmering and slightly red. "Not just today, but over your years with us. I know you're ready to be done, but please know how much you will be missed."

A fount of emotion sprang up inside Ava, the look on Coach's face sending her over the edge. Ava's chest heaved, but no tears came, not even when Coach put an arm around her shoulders.

Teammates surrounded once more to congratulate her on the winning point. She managed to fake a smile for the next few minutes before they headed into the stands to be with family. Ava was left with nothing else to do but walk toward the stands.

Penn, Mac, and Jacklyn stood waiting for her, faces slightly concerned but still smiling. Leona sat up a few stands, staring in the opposite direction with arms crossed.

"That was awesome, Ava!" Mac shouted as Ava drew close.

"I thought you said you weren't good, you liar," Penn teased, his hair a bit more tamed than when she had walked away from him earlier.

"Where was all that skill when we played together?" Jacklyn joked, though she stayed at a distance, unsure of where their relationship stood. "Do you want to do the ol' tradition of grabbing Poppy's after the game?"

A wave of exhaustion washed over Ava. She wished she had the energy to enjoy the evening with them, but beneath it all, she felt like the carved pumpkins now sitting all over town: her insides ripped out, scraped clean, and tossed aside.

"I, um, I think I might just go home," Ava said, looking down at her feet.

"I'm sure you're tired!" Jacklyn said, saving Ava from further questions. "Mac, why don't you come to get ice cream with Leona and me?"

Leona rolled her eyes from her seat above them. Ava was relieved. She knew she'd have the house to herself with Mac gone and her parents away.

"Thanks for coming, you guys," Ava said, looking more at Penn than her siblings. "It . . . it really does mean a lot."

Penn's face fell when she didn't say anything more. Ava made her way back down the stairs, passing Trish on the way.

"Great job today, Ava!" Trish shouted on her way to say hi to Leona. "Let me know about the party soon, okay? Jacklyn said she's coming now!"

Ava nodded politely, feeling more and more exhausted as she walked outside. The air was chillier, less muggy now that the rain had fallen during the game and passed. It smelled of damp asphalt and smoke coming from a neighboring fireplace. She took her time, dragging her tired feet to her car, parked in the furthest lot from the gym. When she arrived, she slung her duffle bag into the back seat, then rolled in behind it and closed the door.

She pulled her red blanket up from the floorboard and slung it around her body, lying down on the back seat. It was there she finally let hot tears release, her sobs filling the space. No one was ever supposed to find out what happened that night in June. Jacklyn, especially, was never supposed to know. But now there was no going back. There was no normal to return to. She felt it when she allowed Penn to close his arms around her. She felt it in her body as she released pain onto the court. It was time to stop ignoring the past. Even if the pain of it had to swallow her whole before she could rise.

* * *

On Sunday afternoon, a loud knock sounded on Ava's door. Ava pulled a pillow over her head. The knocking grew louder. Groaning as she stood up, she stumbled to unlock the door before rolling back on the bed.

"Shit! I can't see a thing," Mac said, stepping over piles of laundry and schoolbooks. "Okay, *dude*, your blackout curtains are *scary* good. I've got to turn on a damn light; cover your eyes."

Ava tugged her comforter up over her head, wishing he'd leave her alone.

"Here, I made you some mac and cheese," he said, plopping down on the foot of her bed and resting a warm bowl on her leg. "Mom and Dad have something tonight. I can't even keep track anymore. They forgot to leave cash, and this is all I know how to make. *Ava, wake up!*"

He pulled at the comforter. Ava's head felt like it was splitting in two. She pulled the covers down to just below her eyes, shooting him her most furious glare.

"Eat," he said, shoving the bowl in front of her face. Ava sat up on her elbows with her face scrunched. She speared a single noodle with her fork and ate it. Her belly ached for more. Soon she was scraping the bottom of the bowl.

"Welp, that's the last of our food supply, so we're screwed," Mac joked. Ava set the bowl beside her and tried to lie back down.

"No! You've been in here all weekend. We're worried about you!"

"Who is this 'we' you speak of?" Ava croaked, surprised her parents even noticed she had slept all weekend.

"Well, me . . . and Penn. And Jacklyn."

Ava stared up at the ceiling, then closed her eyes again. She wanted nothing more than to go back to sleep and never wake up again.

"Penn asked for my number after the game in case you—"

"In case I what?" she asked, fully alert now.

"I don't know, Ava, he seems to know you pretty well. I guess he knew you might . . ."

"What are you trying to say, Mac?"

"I don't know, take it up with Penn! He's the one who told me to come check on you and not leave until I made sure you were doing okay. Jacklyn said to give you space, but Penn is persistent."

Ava scoffed and leaned her torso up against the wall. She felt weak and heavy at the same time.

"What is going on with you, Ava?"

Ava studied Mac. She hated how his boyish features were sharpening. It didn't match his caring, if annoying, demeanor. She wondered if before her father became Mr. Pierson, he might have been something like Mac.

"Can I ask you something?" Ava questioned.

Mac hesitated. "Sure?"

"When you think of growing up, or like, becoming an adult, what do you think you'll be like?"

Mac stared back at her, confusing spreading across his face.

"I don't get it. What do you mean?"

"I mean, not like a firefighter, or whatever. But like, is there some adult you look at and think . . . that's the kind of person I would like to become?"

Mac gave her a funny look, wondering if this would somehow lead to Ava telling him what was going on with her.

"I don't know … well, I guess one of my friend's dads. My friend Will? I don't think you've met him. But every time I'm over there, his dad comes home with this big goofy smile on his face, like he's had the greatest day. Even though I think he works in maintenance or something. And he gives all the kids, all *five* of them, a huge kiss on the forehead. And then he gives Will's mom the biggest kiss of all. Will hates it, always gets so embarrassed. I laugh along with him but when his dad greets me, he claps his big hand on my shoulder. And it feels like I'm part of the family too. I don't know, it's not much, but …"

Mac's lovely answer washed over Ava. She had a warm feeling, whoever Mac would become, he wouldn't be Mr. Pierson, or Bradley, or any of the boys she'd dated over the past years.

Mac stood up and searched around the wreckage for her phone. When he found it, he plugged it in for her on the desk.

"I know I'm your little brother and everything, and we don't know how to talk about stuff. But I'm here. And as soon as this thing charges, give Penn a call, okay?"

Ava didn't answer, but smiled as Mac took dramatic steps over her mess toward the door.

"And uh, no offense, I say this out of nothing but love for you, but you smell like shit. A shower might be good too."

Ava launched a pillow at his head, but Mac escaped through the door, shutting it gently behind him. Her grave expression broke as a small laugh forced its way out of her. It warmed her features like a glowing campfire, softening all of her stiffness. Suddenly she was convulsing with laughter, gasping for air, sadness and joy colliding.

She stopped as she heard her phone buzz on her desk. Ava stared at it, urging herself to pick it up and hear the voice she most wanted to hear. Instead, she scooted to the edge of her bed and dragged herself into the shower. She stepped under the warm stream, allowing the water to wash her clean, hoping Penn would act as though nothing happened tomorrow.

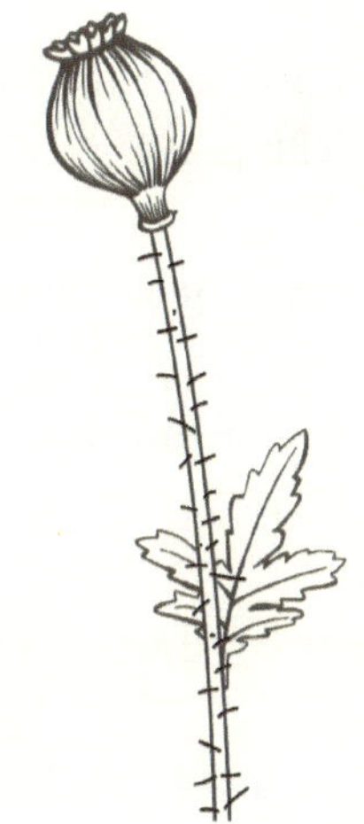

chapter fourteen

Monday morning brought with it constant questioning and worried looks from Penn. Thankfully, with their presentation days away, Ava distracted him with questions about the project. It wasn't until Tuesday that Ava's stomach began to flutter with nervousness. She'd been so preoccupied over the past week that her stage fright hadn't yet begun to take root.

"Are you still okay with picking me up tomorrow morning?" Penn asked as they walked out of the lunchroom. "I could try to see if Paola will wake up early to take me, but you know how much of a gamble that is."

"Oof, not worth the risk. I'll be at your house bright and early, okay?"

"You're sure it's not a problem?" Penn asked. He kept looking at her like she was about to crumble to pieces.

"Penn. I said I'll be there, so I'll be there."

He nodded but didn't look so sure. Ava knew how concerned he was about her. But Jacklyn was the only person who could know the truth about what happened with Bradley. If Penn knew how many people she'd slept with she couldn't imagine what he'd think of her.

Ava pulled up to Penn's house on Wednesday morning to find Paola standing on the sidewalk in a bright pink, bell-sleeved floral nightgown.

Without seeing Ava, she bent over and attempted to move a giant pot of mums. Ava parked her car quickly and jogged over to help.

"Oh, Ava! Good morning! Penn threatened to break all of my pots if I didn't move them. I totally forgot until I heard him banging around this morning!"

Ava grabbed the other side of the heavy terracotta pot and helped Paola slide it further into the grass. Paola struggled with her side, tripping over her small feet.

"I can get this one alone if you'd like," Ava said, hating to see Paola nearly twist an ankle several times.

"No, no, I'm stronger than I look! I promise! I have to move all kinds of crazy stuff for projects I'm working on. This . . . is . . . *nothing*," she heaved. Paola remained stooped over the pot after they set it down, her backside high in the air.

"Thank you so much for helping us with our project. It turned out way better than I ever expected," Ava gushed, savoring her time alone with Paola.

"Oh, please, like you put me out! I loved it! Penn hardly ever lets me help him with anything. And you're such a natural artist! You took right to sketching and watercolor. You're welcome over here anytime you like after this project is over."

They shared a smile as Penn walked through the open front door, balancing their not so miniature-sized stage in his arms.

"Ma, this sidewalk better be clear!" he shouted, his face hidden behind the backdrop. "If I trip you'll have to explain to Mrs. Papayanni why Ava and I have nothing to present!"

Ava ran to grab a small pot coming up on Penn's left.

"Oh, hi, Ava!" Penn exclaimed as she came into his limited vision. "You can go right inside and grab what you can!"

Ava walked inside, sniffing at some delightful scent that must have been Penn's breakfast. She dragged her fingers along Paola's mural that had expanded in the hallway. Inside Penn's room she grabbed her folder of drawings off of his desk. Something caught her eye underneath. She reached down, fanned out the stack of papers, and felt her heart drop to the floor.

"Got it all?" Penn asked. Ava jumped, sending her folder with the illustrations flying all over the room.

"Shit," she gasped, frantically gathering her favorite watercolor back into the folder. "Shit shit shit shit shit."

Penn knelt beside her, placed a hand on her wrist.

"Ava, seriously. Can we talk? You're clearly—"

"I'm fine! I'm fine."

"You're not fine, Ava. You haven't been fine since—"

"Were you going to tell me where you're applying for college?" Ava blurted out.

Penn hesitated, dropping his eyes to the mess around them. "It's still really early, and I don't know who will accept me. Don't worry about it. I'd rather talk about what's going on with you. Don't think I haven't noticed you're constantly changing the subject when I ask about it. Something big happened on Friday. Why can't you tell me?"

Penn handed Ava the last sheet of paper that had fallen. He searched her face as she took it. She held his gaze, her eyes burning equally into his.

"What's the point of telling you if you aren't going to be around much longer?" she asked, the words snapping out of her mouth like a whip.

Penn's face went blank as he stood up.

"That's not fair, Ava."

"Yeah, well. I'm not the only one keeping secrets here."

Ava had never seen Penn angry before. He balled his hands into fists, then turned on his heel and walked into the hallway. Ava followed him out the door, the air between them fraught with tension.

"Oh, Ava!" Paola shouted, breaking away from a neighbor as they stepped outside. "Did Penn invite you to his track meet on Friday? Kaysar is coming in to watch and stay for the weekend! You should come!"

Ava looked over at Penn, whose jaw was clenched shut.

"Oh, I'll be there!" Ava exclaimed, more to spite Penn than anything else. Penn gave Paola one quick peck on the cheek before heading to Ava's Jeep. Ava slammed her door behind her as they got in. They sat in silence as they buckled in and Ava started the car.

"I don't . . . ," Penn said as Ava said, "We should . . ."

"You go," Ava pleaded.

"I don't like this, whatever this is," Penn said. "Usually, we can talk about stuff. You really can't tell me what was going on at your game?"

"No, Penn. I just . . . I can't. Okay? I just can't."

"Do you not trust me or something? I would never—"

"It's not about trusting you! I just can't tell you this."

"Okay. I can respect that," he said, his hands releasing onto his knees. "And I'm sorry I didn't tell you about college. I really don't know what's going to happen, and it's kind of scary. I don't know how I'm going to leave my mom, but I also don't think I want to stay here. But when I know, I'll tell you, okay? And if you're ever ready to tell me what happened the other day, please know I'm not going to judge you. Whatever it is, I wouldn't do that."

Ava nodded down at her jean-covered thighs. She hated how he somehow knew exactly what she was afraid of.

"And your track meet?" Ava asked. "If you don't want me to come, that's fine. I just agreed back there to piss you off."

Penn nudged her forearm on the center console.

"No, I just thought you had a lot going on, and I didn't think you wanted to come sit through my boring meet. But of course, you can come, if you want."

"I'd love to," Ava said, glancing over at Paola, who was now standing on the curb, talking with a different set of neighbors. "I'm not like falling apart, Penn. I promise. It was just . . . it was a lot that Jacklyn came home."

At the thought of seeing Jacklyn again, Ava smacked her hand on the steering wheel.

"I forgot to invite you to Trish's party!"

"A Trish party? Trish that hangs out with Leona, that Trish?"

"Yeah, from my volleyball team?"

"Mmm, with all the pink and the glitter. And why do we want to go to her party?"

"She really wants me to be there, and she asked me to invite you, too."

"I'm not really a *party* kind of person, if you haven't noticed. Will Leona be there? This doesn't seem like the best idea."

"Yeah . . . ," Ava said, beginning to reverse out of the drive. "I just thought it might be fun to have you there. But you're right, I thought it seemed a little off that she invited me. Forget about it."

Penn watched as Ava's face fell.

"Well, actually, now that you mention it, Kaysar thinks that I'm living my best life out here, so maybe we could stop by? If it's okay that Kaysar comes?"

"I don't see why he couldn't. So, you're agreeing to this? Going to a party?"

"Yes, I think so. But they can't force me to drink or do drugs!"

Ava choked back a laugh. "If it helps, I won't be partaking in drugs, either, okay? I just plan on going for a little bit. Then you can watch your lame old scary movie as per tradition. What's the name of it again?"

"*Psycho* is not lame, Ava, it's an American classic."

"Classically lame."

Penn buried his head in his hands.

When they got to school, they dropped their project off in Mrs. Papayanni's classroom. She oohed at the sight of it, clapping her hands together in excitement. Penn was walking so quickly next to Ava as they made their way to his locker that she had to ask him to slow down.

"Ah! Sorry!" Penn said. "I get so pumped for presentations! And your drawings look so good, and the set and everything, I'm just so excited! This is going to be great!"

Ava tried to smile but felt bile rise on the back of her tongue, not nearly as elated for the presentation as Penn was. She spent her next class period with sweaty palms, attempting to ignore the huge surge of nerves she felt.

When Ava got to English class, Penn was already at the top of the room. Desks had been pulled to the front of the room to support the weight of their "miniature" set. He was ready to start presenting as soon as the bell rang.

Mrs. Papayanni took a moment to check attendance before giving them the floor. Penn looked over at Ava and gave her an encouraging smile before starting the presentation. Ava watched with dread as twenty of her classmates settled into their seats. Her throat dried up as her feet sweated, soaking the inside of her boots. When it was Ava's turn to present her illustrations, she panicked. She dropped her rendering of Linda Loman's costume on the floor. Penn kneeled down next to her.

"You can do this, Ava, I know you can. We've practiced! If it helps, just turn and present to me, okay? Pretend Mrs. Papayanni is Paola and we're back at my house," he whispered. "*You've got this.*"

Ava stood back up, still terrified. But she angled her body more toward Penn. She closed her eyes for a second, recalling the smell of open books, acrylic paint, and garden herbs. When she opened her eyes, all she saw was Penn, his curls spiraling as out of control as ever.

She didn't know what she said or how she got through it, but before she knew it, Penn was wrapping up the presentation. Justin Reuben whooped obnoxiously as the class applauded.

"That was really well done, both of you!" Mrs. Papayanni gloated. "Thank you for sharing your excellent work with us!"

Penn gave Ava a high five before breaking down their project.

"See," Penn whispered. "That's why you go first! Imagine the rest of these guys probably *freaking* out because their project isn't as good as ours. Meanwhile, we get to sit back and enjoy the rest of class!"

He wasn't wrong. Penn and Ava had gone above and beyond the rest of their classmates. Though the class clapped politely at the end of each presentation, Penn and Ava knew they had earned their applause.

"Great job, everyone," said Mrs. Papayanni after the final group presented. "Remember to come prepared on Friday with a poem, or else I'll choose one at random for you!"

Penn and Ava rehashed their presentation as they walked together to their next class.

"Oooh," marveled Penn. "Do you know what poem you're going to choose for Friday?"

"Uh, whatever Mrs. Papayanni assigns to me?" Ava answered.

"Ava! You've got to have a favorite poem!"

"Does something by Shel Silverstein count?"

"Actually, I do love me some Shel Silverstein, but I also can't believe you right now."

"I find poetry to be somewhat . . . pretentious."

"Pretentious!?" Penn stopped dead in his tracks, clutching his chest. "You're not reading the right poems!"

"Tell me a poem that's not pretentious."

"Okay, let me think," he said, walking back alongside Ava.

"Yep, see! There isn't one."

"No! The, uh, 'The Orange' by Wendy Cope! In fact, all of Wendy Cope's poetry is wonderfully accessible but still has depth."

"Fine, I'll do this Orange one you speak of," Ava sighed.

"You've got to read it first to see if you connect with it!"

"Meh, I trust you."

Penn tugged at his hair in his frustration.

"Why, what poem will you do?" Ava asked, hovering outside her classroom door.

"There's so many good ones! But there's this one by Rudyard Kipling that I love—"

"Oh, now he sounds pretty pretentious."

"Ava! He is NOT!" Penn stressed as Ava burst into laughter and turned sharply into her classroom.

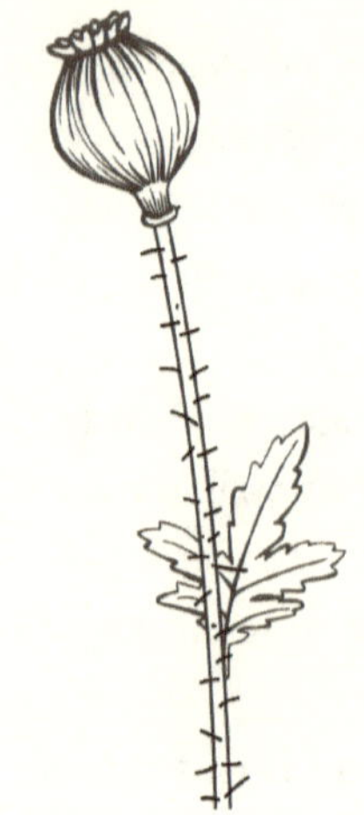

chapter fifteen

Ava was greeted Friday morning by a light layer of frost that covered the manicured Pierson lawn. She shuddered from the blast of cold that met her, turning back around to grab her black winter parka from the closet inside the entryway. On her drive to school, Ava remembered Penn's track meet was later that same afternoon. As much as she liked Penn, she wasn't looking forward to standing outside in the cold.

Trish stopped by her desk in first hour, her usual ponytail pulled into a graceful knot on the top of her head.

"Will you be able to make it tomorrow night?" she asked, sounding a bit anxious.

"I think I might stop by. Is it still okay if I bring Penn? And if a friend of his comes along?"

Trish's face lit up. "Yes! The more the merrier! But, Leona will definitely be there with your sister. I don't know if that's weird for you. I don't want you to be uncomfortable."

Ava's eyes wandered around Trish's face, still not sure if she was sincere. "It should be okay, thanks for asking. I think my sister had a talk with Leona so she should be . . . subdued."

Trish giggled knowingly before heading to her usual seat in the far back corner.

Ava arrived in English class earlier than Penn for once. Mrs. Papayanni paused her writing on the board as Ava walked in. "What poem did you choose, Ms. Pierson?"

"I um," Ava answered, cursing herself silently for not remembering the poem Penn suggested. She was wracking her mind for it when Penn strolled in, whistling.

"*Thank God*," Ava whispered as he sat down beside her, Mrs. Papayanni still waiting for an answer. "What's the poem I decided on the other day when we were talking about how much we love poetry?"

"That *you* decided on? You mean 'The Orange,' which I lightly suggested?" he whispered in response.

"Yes! 'The Orange'!" Ava shouted to Mrs. Papayanni.

"A Wendy Cope fan? Lovely! What about you Penn?"

"It was so hard to choose, Mrs. P. But I think I landed on 'If—' by Rudyard Kipling."

"Ohhh, yes. A wonderful choice. Any particular reason?"

Penn shifted uncomfortably in his seat.

"It's one my dad would read to me when I was little."

Mrs. Papayanni nodded, somehow knowing not to ask more questions as she turned to finish what she was writing on the board.

"Penn, if I would have known *that*, I wouldn't have called it pretentious," Ava said, feeling guilty for laughing at him yesterday.

"Oh, you didn't know. It's not a big deal."

But Ava could tell by the look on his face that it was somewhat of a big deal. She wanted to ask more about it, but the bell rang.

Mrs. Papayanni had an extra difficult time getting Justin Reuben to stop flirting with two pretty seniors near the back of the classroom. She stood in annoyance at the front of the room. "He-hem! Today we start our unit on poetry. I hope you've come prepared with your poem . . . or prepared to let fate decide," said Mrs. Papayanni as she held up an old dusty top hat. "You'll be pairing up again for this unit, so I encourage you to find another partner if your last didn't suit you."

The class murmured around her, some students looking around anxiously for another craning neck to pair up with. Ava tried to catch Penn's eye to make a joke, but he was staring off in the distance.

"In just a moment, I'll let you move around to pick your partner, but let me explain what we'll be doing," Mrs. Papayanni continued. "While you will have a partner, you'll also be required to complete work on your own. At the end of the project, you'll each perform your poem for the class from memory."

"If I would have known that I would have picked another poem!" someone whispered angrily behind her. Ava hoped the poem Penn had picked for her was mercifully short. She looked over at him to ask more about it, but he was staring down at his closed planner.

"During class you will be analyzing each of your poems through different literary elements. Each class, you will spend time discussing a different element through both of your poems. You'll want to take notes because you'll then need to write a paper summing up what you've learned, due before Thanksgiving break. Your performance and paper will count as your midterm, which makes up thirty percent of your grade this semester."

Some of Ava's classmates dropped their heads down to their forearms in response. She expected to see Penn bobbing out of his seat with excitement, but it seemed he had disappeared to somewhere else entirely, while leaving his body behind.

"Alright, let's get started! Ms. Negash will pass the top hat around if you haven't chosen a poem. I'm handing Ms. Pierson a sheet of paper to write down the poem if you've already chosen one. For those of you who haven't partnered up, please take the time to do so now. For today, read your selected or assigned poem out loud to your partner and have some light conversation on why you chose your poem and what you enjoy about it."

Ava looked over at Penn, who fiddled with his pencil but would not look up from his planner.

"Penn, I can go partner with Justin if you don't want me as your partner."

Penn finally looked over at her, a terrified look on his face.

"I'm joking! I'm not ditching you for that creep. But, honestly, I need to read this poem if you do need time to find a new partner."

"Ava! You didn't even read it?!" Penn gasped.

"No, I fully trust that you picked out a great poem for me."

"You have to write a paper *and* perform it, you really ought to love it before you . . ."

But Ava was already scribbling the title down on the sheet Mrs. Papayanni had handed her. Penn shook his head as she passed the paper over to him.

Ava took out her phone to read the poem. It was thankfully quite short and easy to read. She looked over to find Penn with a book open, running his finger slowly across each line of poetry.

"So, uh, do you want to read yours, or should I read mine first?" Ava asked.

Penn looked up from the book, befuddled. "W-what?"

"We're supposed to read our poems out loud to each other. *Sheesh*, I'm already the one pulling the weight in this partnership. Per usual."

Penn tried to smile at her, but it came off as more of a grimace. While Ava wanted to comfort Penn, the classroom didn't offer the same safety to speak in earnest as Penn's bedroom did. Ava tried to compensate by whipping her desk toward his and looking serious about her poetry reading.

"Okay, *I* will go first. 'The Orange' by Wendy Cope," Ava began and breezily rushed through the poem. She didn't bother adding much thought or emotion since it was so simple. But as she stumbled onto the last line, she stopped abruptly, her cheeks warming with embarrassment. She rushed all of the words together before looking back up at Penn, who seemed to have finally landed back in the classroom with her.

"Slow down a bit, maybe? When you recite it to the class?" Penn suggested. "And be sure to make eye contact with the audience." Ava's heart was beating so fast she struggled to nod. "And that last line, say it like you mean it."

"Mmm, your turn!" Ava shouted. Penn looked at her quizzically, then smoothed out the page in his book of poetry.

"'If—' by Rudyard Kipling," he started, but didn't actually need to reference the book at all.

Penn kept his eyes on Ava, reciting each line of the poem by heart. His voice took on a whole new character as he read, his tone deep and profound. He paused after each line, leaving room for Ava to soak them in. With each stanza, his voice crescendoed. He spoke each word as if they had been written just for her.

At the phrase "hold on" his volume reached its loudest peak, enough that other students quieted to listen. Mrs. Papayanni stopped circulating to hear the final stanza, but Penn's eyes never once left Ava's face. After Penn delivered the final line, Ava sat waiting, wishing he'd continue on. The class remained utterly silent, left in a stupefied trance.

"*Shit*," said Justin from the other side of the classroom.

While Mrs. Papayanni scolded Justin for saying it, Ava couldn't help but feel the same way. She shot her hand high into the air.

"Can I go first when we recite our poems?"

Ava's question broke the enchantment, and the class went back to reading with their own partners. Mrs. Papayanni nodded at Ava, a smile playing on her lips. Penn was still looking at her, but his eyes had glazed over.

Wherever his mind kept wandering to, Ava knew he needed to spend a little more time there. She unlocked her phone to read "The Orange" again and tried to picture herself performing it with even an ounce of Penn's talent.

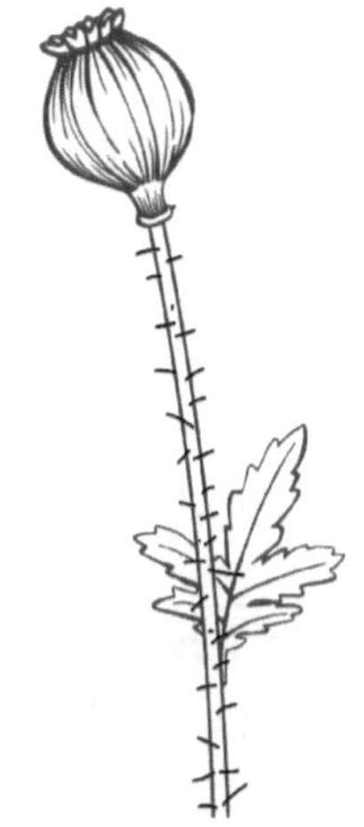

chapter sixteen

Ava dawdled around Westwood High's hallways after the final dismissal bell rang. She was trying to waste time before Penn's track meet which was located down the road at Blackbranch Park. It was surreal in a sense, walking the halls with hardly any students in them. It dawned on her she'd be graduating in a little over a year and a half. She passed by Penn's locker, and the college applications she had been trying so hard to block out swam to mind. A surging sadness enveloped her, thinking of her senior year without him around.

"Ava!" a cheery voice rang out from behind her. "I feel like I haven't seen you at all since our meeting last spring!"

"Oh, hi, Ms. Delic. It's been, uh, a-awhile," Ava stammered. She'd been meaning to meet again with her but kept putting it off.

"How is that AP English class going with Mrs. Papayanni? Did you end up making some new friends?"

Ms. Delic leaned on the locker next to Penn's in the bright white hallway, the sun from the skylights above streaming down on her chocolate brown curls. She looked as stylish as ever in a mauve silk cowl neck top, navy blazer, and matching dress pants cropped at the ankle.

"Yeah, I did make a friend, actually."

Ms. Delic beamed at her, her coral lip gloss sparkling in the daylight. "Do you mind if I ask who?"

Ava glanced down at the top of her converse laces. "Penn Abrams? Do you know—"

"Yes! Penn! He's one of my fav—, I mean, he's a very good friend to have. Everything else going okay outside of classes?"

Ms. Delic's open, friendly face tempted Ava for a moment.

"Well, I, um," Ava started, then heard voices coming from the end of the hall. "I mean, yeah. Everything is going well. Fine."

Ms. Delic's smile faltered the slightest bit. She waited until the students passed by, but the moment had passed.

"My office is always open to you, Ava. We don't just have to talk about class schedules, you know. If there's anything you want to talk about, anything at all, that's what I'm here for. I'm here to advocate for you, not just as a student but as a person. Okay?"

Ava's heart began to pound, wondering if Ms. Delic had heard a rumor or something about her. "Look I, um, I gotta go. I've got a . . . I've got a thing."

Ms. Delic seemed disappointed, her warm smile melting away.

"Sure thing, Ava. There's a sign-up sheet on the outside of my door if you'd like to set up a time with me."

"Yeah, thanks, Ms. Delic," Ava said, dismissing her.

Ms. Delic shot Ava a look of concern then walked down the remainder of the hallway, the click of her heels echoing behind her. Ava took a minute to stare up at the skylights on the ceiling, squinting into the glaring sun. If her parka wasn't slung across her arm, she'd believe it was a warm summer day—a warm summer day where she could be anywhere and anyone but herself.

She took a deep breath and headed out to the parking lot, pulling on her parka as she jogged. The sun could only do so much to nip the chill in the air. On the drive to Blackbranch Park, she noticed how alone she felt, never having gone to a sporting event by herself. The thought of texting Jacklyn crossed her mind, but she wasn't ready to hang out with her again. Not just yet. And picking up Mac would make her late for the meet.

Pulling into the gravel lot of the park, she surveyed the wide-open area behind her windshield before stepping back out into the cold. It took another minute before she spotted Paola's long mane of hair blowing wildly in the wind next to a tall, muscular figure standing close by. Ava closed her eyes and squeezed the steering wheel; she'd forgotten all about meeting Kaysar. Anxiety pulsed through her forearms, while her legs became heavy, like they were filled with lead. She couldn't figure out why meeting Penn's best friend meant so much to her.

Paola's engulfing laughter drew Ava forward, while Kaysar's towering frame became more intimidating as she drew closer.

"H-hey!" Ava managed to say.

"AVA!" Paola shrieked and pulled her into a tight hug. "You wouldn't happen to have some kind of hair tie, would you?" She looked pleadingly at Ava as hair blew into her eyes and stuck to her lipstick. Ava pulled a black scrunchie off her wrist and handed it over. "You're a lifesaver!"

Paola secured her hair while Ava tried to smile up at Kaysar. His dark aviators blocked his eyes, and his face remained blank even though Ava knew he heard her. She couldn't help but think he was far too cool for Westwood with his all-black wardrobe complete with a wool cap, vintage leather jacket, and lace-up boots.

"Oh my god!" Paola exclaimed as soon as her hair was out of her face. "Ava! This is Kaysar! Kaysar, this is Ava!" Ava stuck out her hand, but Kaysar responded by turning his body forward to where Penn was warming up with his team ahead of them. Ava pulled her hand back into herself, embarrassed.

Penn was stretching several feet away from the rest of his teammates. He caught sight of Ava and waved dramatically, causing Ava to laugh and return a sheepish wave back. Kaysar let out a strange, muffled sound.

"So, uh, Kaysar," Ava attempted. "Have you been to one of Penn's meets before?"

"Yeah. I never missed one before he moved . . . here," he growled, not bothering to face her when he spoke.

"Nice! Do you, um, do you run cross country too?"

"Hell no," Kaysar scoffed, shoving his hands into his pockets. Paola was too busy taking photos of Penn on her phone to notice anything amiss.

Ava scraped her bottom teeth across her top lip; Penn hadn't warned her that Kaysar wasn't a big talker.

"You're going to do great, Penn! You've got this!" Paola yelled, stepping a few feet forward to shout to Penn. Penn's teammates looked at her as if she were certifiably insane.

"So, Penn tells me you guys have been friends since you were little? That's pretty cool," Ava said in between Paola's loud cheers. Ava was dying inside, hoping Paola would do anything to break into this awkwardness. Kaysar didn't even bother to respond this time.

"Oh, Kaysar!" Paola said, finally stepping back to join the lack of conversation. "Have you told Ava about our neighborhood? I bet she'd love to hear about all of the characters on the block. Remember Old Man Ivanov?"

Ava was surprised to hear Kaysar respond with a low, warm laugh.

"That dude was insane! He'd walk outside in a blizzard wearing nothing but his undershorts and tattered old boots, singing at the top of his lungs! Ah man, but he did shovel the sidewalks for everyone. After he, you know, passed, Penn and I—"

"I forgot about your sidewalk clearing business! It only lasted what . . ."

"About a month!"

Paola and Kaysar held on to each other's arms as they doubled over in laughter. Ava felt like an outsider. She looked around the park, pretending she saw something interesting in the woods. Thankfully, the woman with the starting pistol headed to the starting line, and the runners followed suit. After a few minutes, a loud shot rang in the park, and Penn took off, settling himself into the middle of the pack.

"Oh, you know, he just stays in the middle there for the first few laps," Paola explained as Penn disappeared out of sight through the trees. Ava realized she wouldn't get to see much of Penn running at all; she was stuck speaking, or not speaking, with Kaysar.

"So, Ava, Penn tells me you guys are going to a party tomorrow night?" Paola asked, eyebrows raised.

"Oh, he told you about it?" Ava asked.

"Of course! Penn can't keep a secret from me. I'm so excited for him to have friends to go do teenager things with!"

"I told him I won't force him to do any hardcore drugs or drinking, in case you were worried," Ava joked.

Paola burst out laughing. "I'd be very impressed if you managed to get him to have any fun at that thing at all, honestly, Ava."

"He'll have fun if I'm there," Kaysar said, adjusting his sunglasses further up the bridge of his nose.

Ava tried to not read too much into it but was very aware Kaysar was not her biggest fan. Paola still seemed not to notice; her eyes glued on Penn as he came around a bend. He'd already managed to move further up in the pack. Kaysar joined Paola in the cheering this time around, while Ava clapped her hands pathetically. She'd never been much of a cheerleader. She liked to think Penn would appreciate that.

Kaysar began to speak more as Penn started another lap but only on topics Paola could relate to. Paola tried her best to bring Ava back into the conversation, but Kaysar was a pro at edging her back out. Eventually, Ava resigned by taking a few steps away from the two of them, acting as though she had a critical text message to respond to. She didn't look up until the shouting grew louder from all over the park, which she assumed meant the race was ending soon.

Penn was now at the very front, only two other boys ahead of him. She attempted to clap harder, but it was drowned out by Kaysar and Paola's shouting. When Penn crossed the finish line in second place, she couldn't help but let out a loud "whoop" but stayed behind as Paola and Kaysar ran to hug him.

Ava watched from a distance as they embraced him, crossing her arms over her chest. She felt it all afternoon, but seeing them together like this, it was clear: Kaysar was part of the family. The inseparable duo of Penn and Paola opened wide to welcome Kaysar, but Ava felt she'd always be watching them from a distance. Even as Penn craned his neck around Kaysar to wave at Ava with both hands, she felt numb. She was silly for thinking her friendship with Penn was somehow special. She couldn't compete with the seventeen years Kaysar and Penn had together.

"Can you believe this?!" Paola asked with giddiness as they made their way back over to Ava. "He's never come in second before. He's been in the top five but never second! Maybe it was having you here, Ava!"

Paola threw an arm around her and hugged her close. Kaysar took off his glasses, and the scathing look he threw at Ava couldn't be mistaken this time around. However good-looking he might have been, Ava mentally declared he was downright terrifying.

After Penn's team huddle broke apart, he bounded over to them like he hadn't just run over three miles. Kaysar opened his arms to give Penn another hug, but Penn didn't see it. Instead, he came to stand right in front of Ava.

"I'm so glad you came! I know these things can be pretty boring, but, I'm really glad you stuck it out. It's so cold and everything! Thank you for coming," Penn said to her, his eyes going soft as he said it. He did a weird dance with his arms, but Ava kept her arms crossed as Kaysar looked on. Penn settled on patting her oddly on the shoulder.

"It's getting chilly, Kaysar, let's go to the car," Paola suggested.

"It's not that cold," Kaysar began.

"It most definitely is! I'm freezing!" Paola said, fake chattering her teeth. "Penn, see you there in a minute, okay?"

"But—" Kaysar argued as Paola grabbed his arm and pulled him toward the parking lot. Penn watched them go, a confused expression etched on his face.

"Did I miss something?" Penn asked.

"Nothing at all! Oh, just like, your best friend *despises* me, that's all."

"Kaysar?"

"Oh yeah. He big-time hates me."

"Well, that's weird. Are you sure? That doesn't sound like him. He's one of the nicest people I know."

Ava searched Penn's face to see if he was being sarcastic, but he continued to look flustered.

"I'll talk with him," Penn said. "Maybe he didn't put together that you're the friend I talk about all the time. But, hey! We started a new tradition of going to Mei's after my meets. Do you want to come?"

The amount of hope in Penn's eyes was enough to make Ava feel guilty, but she wanted nothing more than to avoid Kaysar for the rest of the day. Or the rest of her life, if that was an option.

"I don't want to intrude. You should enjoy time with your best friend."

Penn scrunched up his eyebrows, as if Ava had said something hurtful. "You aren't intruding. I want you to come."

Ava swore silently, hating that it was impossible to tell him no when he was this direct. "Okay, but only because I'm making you go to Trish's party tomorrow night."

"Crap! I thought you would forget about that," Penn joked, tugging on his hoodie. "I'm starving. You can ride with us to the restaurant—"

"No!" she shouted. Penn shot her another probing look beneath his hood. "I mean, I'm good! I'll drive myself."

Penn walked with her back to her Jeep. Kaysar pulled up next to them, with Paola in the passenger seat. Penn waved goodbye to Ava as he ducked into the back seat. Ava didn't miss Kaysar's utter disdain for her as he rolled his eyes in her direction. He then backed up and accelerated quickly out of the lot, sending a spray of gravel behind him. Ava shook her head while trilling her lips, admitting to herself it was going to be a very *long* dinner.

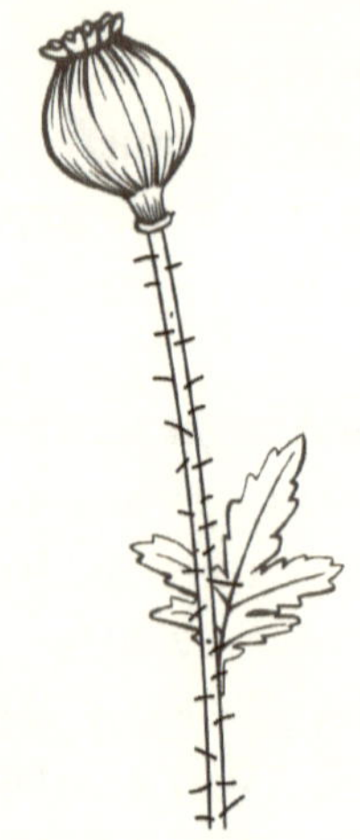

chapter seventeen

While her heels dug into the sidewalk, the wind picked up around Ava, pushing her toward the entrance of Mei's. Through the glass door she spotted Penn, Paola, and Kaysar at a table in the far left of the small dining room, roaring with laughter. She contemplated turning right back around, noting how they, or at least Kaysar, seemed much happier without her there. As she released her hand from the door handle, Penn spotted her and jumped out of his seat. He ran toward the door as Ava looked back at her car on the other side of the street, thinking how easy it would be to make a run for it.

Warm air embraced Ava as Penn flung the door open. The tantalizing scents of fresh ginger and simmering garlic greeted her nose as she followed behind him, not paying attention to what he was saying. She was far too busy studying a mural that took up the entire left side of the restaurant. The scales of an enormous dragon were painted in honey gold, burnt orange and fire engine red. The dragon looked as if it were about to take flight off of the wall, its broad webbed wings spread wide and waiting.

"Paola, did you paint this?" Ava asked in awe as she reached the table.

"Oh, Ava! Hi! Sit, sit!" Paola exclaimed, gesturing to the spot on her right and across from Penn. "Yes! I don't usually do fantastical paintings, but this has become one of my favorites."

"And she should be well paid for her incredible work," sternly suggested the woman who arrived at their table with a tray of water glasses.

"I told you, Mei, I don't want to be paid for it!" Paola insisted. "It's my gift to you for opening up your own restaurant!"

Mei pouted her bright red lips and rolled her eyes. She was petite, but Ava thought she still might be taller than Paola by a few inches. Mei's hair was cropped smartly to frame her sharp, high cheekbones. Ava envied how posh she looked in an aquamarine-colored wrap dress.

"And don't even *think* about trying to give any of this food away for free," threatened Paola. "You sent Penn home with enough extras to feed us for a week the other day! I will be making up for it in your tip tonight."

Mei refused by violently shaking her head before turning to Ava.

"And you must be Ava?" Mei asked, her lips turning upward into a magnificent smile that lit her face up from within.

"Y-Yes! Penn has said nothing but great things about this place. I'm sorry I haven't been in here yet. How long have you been open now?"

"Oh, it'll be about three months now. Business is slower than I'd like; I still haven't really gotten the hang of Westwood. We've only lived here about a year."

"Mei lives just a few blocks from us," interjected Penn, leaning across the table. "She walks with her five boys through our neighborhood every morning. She was the first person to welcome us to our neighborhood."

"Well it's really love to meet you Mei," Ava said as Kaysar cleared his throat in the seat next to Penn. She'd been too distracted meeting Mei to notice him sitting there, but his narrowed eyes in her direction were a not-so-gentle reminder.

"So, Ava," Paola asked as Mei walked back into the kitchen. "How did you like going to your first track meet?"

"She didn't look like she liked it at all," Kaysar answered before Ava could speak for herself.

"I mean, I . . . ," Ava tried to say.

"Oh!" Penn piped up. "Kaysar, Ava is the friend I've been telling you so much about. I thought I told you she'd be at my meet."

"You did," Kayser said, completely deadpan.

"Okay, is something wrong?" Penn asked, confused.

"Nope. All good here," Kaysar answered, slurping his water obnoxiously through his straw.

Penn looked over at Ava and shrugged helplessly. Mei graciously arrived back at the table, setting down dumplings before taking their order. Her presence eased the small amount of tension that had mounted. She memorized everyone's order without having to write it down, even with Paola's many substitutions. As soon as Mei left, an awkward silence descended over them.

"So, Kaysar, did I tell you about the project Ava and I worked on together?" Penn asked, attempting to open the conversation. "You would have *hated* it."

"I thought I would hate it too!" Ava said, joining in. "But it didn't end up being so bad. I think we did a pretty good job."

"Good job?!" Paola exclaimed. "Their teacher was super impressed! Ava is a natural artist, just like you, Kaysar."

"She's nothing like me," Kaysar shot back in disgust. "Don't compare her to me."

Paola and Penn looked at each other, a conversation playing out in silence between them. Ava felt blood rush to her face.

"Kaysar, do you want to go outside and talk?" Penn asked, standing up from the table.

"No, I don't, actually," Kaysar said, ripping the black beanie off his head and throwing it down on the table. "All you've talked about for weeks now is Ava. Ava this, Ava that, Ava and I went here, I went to Ava's volleyball bullshit, now she's coming to my meet."

Kaysar began to raise his voice, causing the couple a few tables away to pause their eating to watch.

"I don't see what's so great about her," Kaysar continued. "Have you seen her parka? I bet it costs more than I make delivering pizza in a month. And her brand-new Jeep? Are you *kidding* me? You'd never be friends with someone like that in Baltimore. She's not even pre—"

"Please don't talk about Ava like that," Penn said, a hint of warning in his voice, though he stayed calm. "I would never let anyone talk this way about you."

"There's nothing bad to say about me! I'm, well, at least interesting. She barely even talks! The way you described her I thought she was this amazingly talented, intelligent, beautiful person. She's just—"

"Kaysar, stop talking," Penn demanded. "Outside. Now."

"But—"

"Now!" Penn yelled. It was the first time Ava had seen Penn lose his temper. He'd been upset with her before their presentation, but it was nowhere near this.

"*Unbelievable*," Kaysar spat, his chair scraping loudly on the stone floor as he pushed it backward. Penn followed behind him as he stalked out the door.

"Oh, Ava," Paola whispered, placing her hand on Ava's shoulder. "I'm so sorry about this. He's been nothing but a good friend to Penn. Like another son to me. I just don't know what this is about."

Ava watched through the storefront windows as they argued on the sidewalk. She couldn't make out what they were shouting, but it didn't look promising. Ava wished she would have run back to her car when she had the chance. She knew she shouldn't have come.

Mei arrived back with a tray full of food, balancing it effortlessly on her shoulder before placing it on a stand. She began handing out plates before noticing half the party was missing.

"Everything okay?" she asked, looking toward the front where Penn and Kaysar now stood silent, arms crossed.

"We'll be just fine, Mei," Paola answered for the both of them. "Thank you so much! This looks wonderful, but I do want to remind you that you own this place. You don't have to serve us."

"Nonsense! I want to serve my customers with my own two hands. Let me know if you need anything," Mei said, patting the table before walking away.

Penn and Kaysar walked through the doors a few minutes later, their cheeks tinged with pink. Both dropped heavily into their seats, digging into their food without saying a word. Not even the tantalizing fumes rising from Ava's plate could stir up any hunger in her. She pushed it around without eating it.

"I, um, I think I'm going to go," Ava whispered to Paola. "I'll just take this to go when Mei comes out next."

Penn looked up, the same pained expression on his face that she'd seen at her last game. "Ava. I want you here. I want you to stay."

Though Kaysar shoveled an extra-large bite into his mouth, Ava still heard him grunt.

"Really, please stay," Paola pleaded. "Finish your food at least?"

Ava nodded, though staying went against her better judgment. She continued to move her food around without taking a bite as Penn and Paola made light conversation about the weather. They somehow managed to make it through the rest of the meal without another eruption from Kaysar. It wasn't until Mei came and dropped off the check that Ava felt Kaysar's eyes on her again. Paola reached forward to grab it.

"I'll get it," Kaysar said, snatching it from Paola's reach.

"Kaysar, come on. You don't have the money for this," Penn said, pulling out his own wallet.

"Like *you* do?" Kaysar scoffed, eyeing the bill and trying to calculate the total with tip. Ava could feel her heart beating in her throat. Kaysar put the bill down with his card, staring at Ava as he did it.

"Thanks for dinner, Kaysar," Ava murmured. Penn and Paola's eyes were wide, unsure what to do next. Kaysar's expression turned from glum to smug as Mei came back to the table to pick up the check.

"Mei, I'll, um, here's . . . ," Ava fumbled, pulling out her parent's credit card and tossing it on top of Kaysar's card.

"You've got to be *shitting* me," Kaysar complained as Mei took both cards and left the table before they could argue about it. "I said that I'll get it. We don't need your daddy to pay for dinner."

Penn opened his mouth, but Ava got there first.

"I-I-I don't know what I did to you, Kaysar, to make you dislike me so much," Ava said, clearing her throat. She felt her entire body shaking as she did it. "I-I wanted to help pay because Penn and Paola have fed me every Sunday for over a month. And I agree with you; I don't know why Penn said all that great stuff about me. I know I'm pretty ordinary. But

I also don't know why he said great stuff about you either. You've been, frankly, *sort of a dick*."

Ava didn't know where any of this was coming from, all she knew was that she was tired. Tired of being stepped on, overlooked, underestimated. Tired of everyone else speaking for her.

"I've let people take their shit out on me enough," Ava said, her voice strange and loud in her own ears. She glanced over at Penn whose eyes were gleaming. "But, honestly, I've got my own stuff to deal with. I-I get it; my parents have money and I know I'm very, very privileged. But that doesn't mean I wasn't handed my own bag of crap."

Kaysar opened his mouth then closed it again. Mei came back to the table, setting Kaysar and Ava's credit cards in front of them cautiously. Ava signed the check sloppily and thanked Mei before nodding curtly at Paola and Penn. She rushed quickly out of the restaurant and into the thrashing wind. Her heart was still racing as she reached her car and fumbled around in her bag for her keys. She was so distracted by the sound of her own blood pounding in her ears that she didn't notice Penn jog up behind her.

"Ava, I'm *so* sorry," Penn said. "You didn't deserve that. He won't tell me what is going on with him!"

"I think I might have an idea," Ava said, jiggling her keys in her hand.

"What do you mean?"

"I think he might believe I'm . . . replacing him."

Penn stared at her blankly. "What do you mean *replacing* him?"

"I, um . . . as someone who was just ditched by her own friends . . . I think he feels like he's losing you."

"Kaysar? No way! He's been my best friend since, well, ever."

"I don't know, Penn. It's just a thought. Like you said, you don't have to take anything I say to heart. But I think you should spend tomorrow with him instead of going to the party with me."

"No! Ava! I'm coming. With or without Kaysar, I said I'd be there."

"You were probably right, though, the party is a bad idea. It's better if we stay home."

"Ava, look at me," Penn said. Ava reluctantly dragged her eyes, which had been darting everywhere but his face, to meet his. He held her gaze for a few seconds before speaking.

"I want to come tomorrow. I want to be there for you. Will you let me?" he asked, his eyes sparkling, breath warm. Ava dropped her gaze to rest on his lips, then his Adam's apple. She felt suddenly uncomfortable, aware she was only inches away from him. She thought back to their hug last week, to the safety his body provided for her. It took everything not to bury her head into his chest and inhale deeply, allowing her, for the shortest of moments, to forget the day, the week, maybe even forget Bradley ever existed.

"Okay," she said, taking a step back instead. Ava hoped the physical distance would quiet her senses and cure the ache of wanting him close.

"Pick me up tomorrow night then?" he asked, breaking eye contact to look across the street. "I'll talk to Kaysar. I hope he decides to come. I really do think the two of you could be friends someday."

Ava didn't have the heart to ask him, "*In what world?*" Instead she raised her hand to say goodbye. Penn responded with a weird dance where he stepped forward, then back, his arms flailing out and back into his body. Somewhat embarrassed, he gave her a spastic wave before jogging back toward the restaurant.

As soon as Ava closed the Jeep door behind her, she banged her head lightly on the steering wheel, realizing too late that Penn had tried to hug her goodbye. As she drove past the restaurant, she tried to catch his eye, but he was engrossed in conversation with Paola. It was Kaysar who locked eyes with her, arms crossed. Though the light was fading, Ava could just make out the traces of contempt etched on his face. It was official, no matter what Penn said: there was no way in hell the two of them were going to be friends.

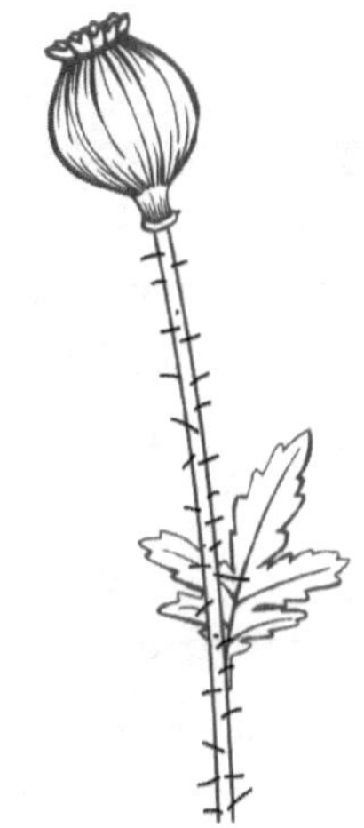

chapter eighteen

Penn sprinted in and out of Ava's dreams all night. She never saw his face; only the back of him as he raced onward, never turning or slowing even as she called out after him. After a fitful sleep, she awoke drenched in a cold sweat. She rolled over on her phone and picked it up to find it was 6:04 a.m., far earlier than she ever cared to wake on a Saturday.

Low voices drifted up from below as she opened her bedroom door to let Olivia out. Stepping further into the hallway, she peered over the second-floor balcony. The front door stood open, her father arguing with her mother before slamming it abruptly in her face.

Ava sighed and walked back to her bedroom with little hope of falling back asleep. She began to tidy up her room, sorting her dirty laundry by color and trying not to think of the party later that night. Though she wanted to trust her sister and Trish, she knew Leona was bound to have something up her sleeve.

Gathering a hefty pile of dirty clothes in her arms, Ava walked down to the washer and dryer on the first floor and dumped her clothes in the wash. With her mother nowhere to be found, she curled up on the couch and slung a faux fur throw over her legs in hopes of drifting off to sleep.

"Wake up!" Mac shouted over her. Ava groaned as a pillow hit her in the face. "I need to do laundry at some point today."

"Since when do you do your own laundry?" Ava groaned, trying to throw the pillow back in his direction, but it flopped sadly onto the ground.

"Since Mom stopped doing it for me," Mac complained, plopping dramatically down on the couch, looking agitated in his red and black flannel pajamas.

"When did she stop helping you with laundry?" Ava asked, looking around to find their house was nowhere near as tidy as it usually was.

"Like a month ago. I get that Jacklyn and you decided to be all independent by doing your own laundry starting in high school, but I don't know what in the hell I'm doing. I swear Mom and Dad take all their clothes to the cleaners, and I'm just left to figure everything out by myself."

Mac jerked the remote up from next to Ava and flipped aimlessly through Netflix.

"I'll throw your stuff in with mine," Ava offered, standing up and stretching. "Will that help you to be less cranky this morning?"

"Oh, shut up; you slept through Mom and Dad fighting all night last night. I'm so sick—"

They heard a door slam upstairs.

"*Great*, now I've pissed her off too," Mac sighed. Ava threw her blanket over to him and padded back upstairs to grab another load of laundry.

As the evening drew closer, Ava felt so anxious she picked up her phone several times to text Penn, making up excuses on why she couldn't make it, each time deleting it and starting over. Just as she was about to hit send on the perfect scenario involving Mac, a fever, and a fight with her mom, her phone buzzed in her hand. It was Penn asking if he needed to bring nonalcoholic beverages or side dishes to the party. Ava snorted, assuring Penn none of that was necessary.

Ava took her time in choosing an outfit, sorting through her freshly laundered options. It was the first time in weeks she'd needed to dress up for anything. The party she had walked out on seemed months, almost years, ago now. It was odd just how much had changed since then.

She tried on a muted-pink, chunky sweater Jacklyn had gotten for her last Christmas along with her favorite pair of high-rise jeans. At the time,

Ava figured her sister had bought the sweater for herself then regifted it to Ava as an afterthought. But looking at herself in the mirror, she thought maybe Jacklyn knew it would set off her gray-blue eyes and skim the perfect place on her hips.

In an attempt to pass the time, which seemed to be crawling forward, Ava started to curl her hair. With an insane amount of adrenaline pumping through her veins, she wound up burning several fingers along the way. Switching to makeup, a much safer option, Ava dropped her favorite blush, which shattered to pieces on the ground. After getting it cleaned up, she switched to eye makeup, where things got out of control due to shaky hands and liquid eyeliner.

"Screw it," Ava said, wiping off her eyeliner for a final time and settling for a more natural eye look. "There's a reason I started going for this 'no make-up look.' Leona can *suck it*."

With her and Mac's laundry folded, and her stomach fully covered, Ava picked up her bag and made her way downstairs.

"I'm heading out," Ava shouted up the stairs, without realizing Mrs. Pierson was already sitting in the kitchen next to an empty bottle of wine. She still wore her bathrobe, her hair uncharacteristically greasy and disheveled.

"Did you hear me?" Ava asked, pausing in the foyer.

"Yeah, yeah. Don't be too late, Jacklyn," Mrs. Pierson answered, her head swaying. Ava looked over at Mac who was playing video games on the couch.

"I'll keep an eye on her; you go have fun," Mac replied, unconcerned. "And tell Jacklyn she still owes me ice cream. Dumb Leona wanted coffee instead after your game last week."

Ava smiled at her little brother, though she felt guilty for leaving him alone with their mom like this. If she hadn't done his laundry all day, she would have felt worse.

"Thanks, Bro, call me if you need anything," Ava said, slipping out the door and heading to her Jeep. She hoped her mom would be back on her feet tomorrow.

As Ava pulled up in front of Penn's house, she noticed the pots of now dying mums had returned to their precarious positions on the sidewalk.

She laughed as Penn headed down the walkway and out to her car. For a wonderful half of a second, Ava thought Kaysar had decided not to come, but all hope was squashed as he walked out a minute later, his hands buried deep in his black jean pockets.

The Jeep's dome light sprung to life as Penn opened the passenger side door. Right away Ava noticed his curls were glossy and much more tamed than usual. Though she thought he looked nice, she found she preferred them in their natural state of chaos. Something about the way they spiraled wildly was comforting to her. He also wore a pair of glasses with a deep blue frame flecked with gold, his eyes shining bright behind them as he took in Ava.

"You look . . . ," they both said at the exact same time, but neither finished their sentence due to Kaysar slamming the passenger door behind him.

The dread she felt earlier had dissipated at the sight of Penn, but glancing back at Kaysar's brooding face, it returned in full. Ava backed quickly out of the driveway, hoping to make the awkward drive as fast as possible. Penn got the hint and turned the volume up on Ava's stereo as they crossed back over into the east side of town. No one spoke as the homes grew exponentially larger on their way to Trish's.

Ava pulled up to the curb, parking in her usual spot. They shivered all the way up the street and down the long winding path to Trish's front door. Music pounded from inside the house as they reached the end of the walk. Halloween decorations still hung on the front stoop, fake cobwebs framing the entryway. Kaysar let out a low whistle, watching Ava closely as she stepped up to the intimidating round-top mahogany door. She hesitated, with her hand stretched toward the doorknob, her body unwilling to go any further. Kaysar sighed loudly behind her and stepped forward. He shot her a look of annoyance before throwing the door wide open and stepping inside. Ava looked over at Penn, who used both arms to gesture her forward.

"Ladies first," was all he said, his voice shaky and unsure.

Once inside, the scene was all too familiar. Even Lukas and Liam were in the same places in the living room as last time. Penn followed closely behind Kaysar, who pushed rudely through the crowd on his way back to the kitchen. Penn apologized in Kaysar's wake, not noticing that Ava had fallen behind. She allowed herself to get stuck behind classmates, hoping to avoid the kitchen for as long as possible.

Within a few minutes, Penn returned to her with a Coke and waved her forward.

"It's quieter in the kitchen!" he urged, motioning her to follow him. Ava tried to tell him she needed a minute, but her voice was swallowed up by the music and crowd.

Once inside the kitchen, Ava spotted Jacklyn right away. A small circle, including Trish and Leona, had gathered around her at the top of the island. Jacklyn wore a long-sleeved, flowy white dress with small, embroidered flowers around the collar. Her makeup was applied so that her face appeared fuller, her cheeks rosy and healthy. If Ava didn't know any better, she'd think no time had passed at all since last June.

"Ava, you came!" Trish shrieked, cutting off Jacklyn's story. Leona looked both furious and stunned as Trish broke from the circle, rushing forward to give Ava a hug. Trish's glittery gold mini-dress complimented her beautifully; usually, she looked far younger than she was, but tonight she seemed much older than eighteen.

"Ha-Happy birthday," Ava stammered into Trish's hair, which tumbled freely down her back.

"Thanks! And Penn, hello!" Trish said, turning to Penn and waving. "And this is?"

Kaysar finished chugging the beer he was holding to look several feet downward at Trish. Ava was surprised to see a small smile appear on his face; he didn't seem to mind one bit that Trish's parents had money.

"I'm Kaysar," he answered, sticking out his hand. "You're the birthday girl, I presume?"

Trish giggled before handing Kaysar another beer from the refrigerator. Ava tried not to look too shocked at her discovery that Kaysar could be charming when he wanted to be. She almost forgot he detested her for a moment.

"Hey, Sis, glad you came," Jacklyn said, sneaking up to slide an arm around her waist. "I like your hair curled like this. Also, nice sweater. I *knew* it would look good on you."

Jacklyn turned toward Penn to compliment his glasses before Ava could respond. She wiggled out of Jacklyn's grasp and around the counter, pretending to pour herself a shot to get away from everyone.

"Didn't think you'd be brave enough to come," said Leona, her voice silky. "Why don't you pour me one of those? We can take it together."

Ava dared to look over at her; tonight, she was dressed all in black. Her leather mini-skirt and thigh-high boots were a very Leona choice, one that made Ava feel woefully underdressed. Leona stared back at her, a daring look in her expertly ink-black lined eyes. Ava searched over her shoulder for Penn, who was now engrossed in conversation with Jacklyn. Her insides twinged with jealousy. Leona stole the bottle of vodka out of Ava's hand and poured out the two shots, sliding one in Ava's direction.

"To burying the hatchet," Leona said, eyes twinkling as she lifted her shot glass in the air. Though every cell in Ava's body begged her not to do it, she clinked her glass against Leona's and threw her head back. The shot burned down the back of her throat, causing Ava to cough several times before catching her breath.

"Did you forget how to drink?" Leona purred, a playful smile on her lips. She poured another shot for herself and drank it down again without a chaser.

"No, I—" Ava said as Leona's phone buzzed on the counter.

"Gotta take this," Leona mouthed, stepping away abruptly.

The slight feeling of dizziness Ava felt before her last volleyball game appeared again, but she shrugged it off, chalking it up to the shot she just took. She walked back over to Penn and Jacklyn, both fully animated in their discussion. Neither noticed her return. She stood there awkwardly until Trish excused herself from Kaysar.

"Here," Kaysar said, handing Ava a beer. Ava took it with caution, examining it for any signs of tampering.

"Cheers," he said, raising his can to hers. Ava bumped her can with his but set it back down on the counter. She was not about to let Penn drive her car illegally tonight, and she'd be lucky if Kaysar would be able to walk back to the car later.

Leona sashayed back into the kitchen, tossing her hair behind her. A familiar spicy scent wafted in after her, dominating every other smell in the room. Ava placed both of her hands flat on the countertop, physically bracing herself, though not sure why. She felt Kaysar step in close beside her. He asked her something, but Ava couldn't hear anything outside of her sister yelling a few feet away from her.

"What is he doing here?" Jacklyn yelled at Leona, breaking away from Penn to confront her. Leona stood casually in front of the sink, examining her fingernails.

"Who?" Leona asked Jacklyn, amusement in her tone. She appeared to be reveling in the attention. "Oh, *Bradley*? He's home from college. I thought, maybe, the Pierson sisters might like to see him again."

Ava tried to look anywhere else, but her eyes were drawn like a magnet to the sharp angles of Bradley's shoulders as he high-fived Liam in the living room. The reddish hue of his hair still made her skin crawl, sending goosebumps down her arms. Ava picked up her beer and attempted to chug it, but she choked on it instead. Kaysar grabbed a water bottle and handed it to her. She looked up, half expecting Kaysar to try to humiliate her for it. But his gaze, like everyone else's in the room, was on Leona and Jacklyn.

"Jacklyn!" Bradley exclaimed, sauntering into the kitchen. "Leona didn't tell me you'd be here! I thought you'd still be in Cali! Why is everyone . . . ," he paused as he surveyed all sets of eyes on him in the kitchen. "What's going on?"

No one said a word as Bradley looked blankly around the room, his face lighting up at the sight of Ava.

"Ava! Haven't seen you since—"

"Don't you *dare* speak to my sister," Jacklyn spat. "Leona, what were you thinking?"

Leona ran her tongue over her upper lip before grinning mischievously. "I thought Ava might like to see an old friend."

"You have no idea what happened that night, as much as you think you do!" Jacklyn shouted, her face purple with rage, a vein popping out of her forehead. "I-I told you, you PROMISED me you wouldn't talk to him again . . . let alone invite him here when you knew Ava was coming!"

Penn's head was rapidly turning from Jacklyn back to Ava, then to Leona, and finally resting on Bradley. Kaysar was standing as close to Ava as possible now; she hadn't realized she'd begun to lean on him.

Trish fought her way back into the room, shoving through a dense crowd who had now gathered around the kitchen after Jacklyn's shouting. "Are we playing flip cup?! *Move!* Sorry, I just had to pop outside for a . . . ," Trish paused as she reached the kitchen. "Why is it so quiet? Is everything alright?"

"Hey, Trish!" Bradley piped up when no one else responded, tipping his cup toward her. "Happy birthday!"

"*Bradley?* You can't, you're not supposed to be here," Trish said, her voice soft but firm.

"What is *with* you people tonight?" Bradley asked, sipping on his drink. "Leona told me this was supposed to be a fun time."

"Bradley, this is my house, and I'm going to, uh, I'm going to ask you—you need to leave!" Trish sputtered.

"I just got he—"

"She asked you to leave, *bro*," threatened Kaysar. He left Ava's side to step toward Bradley.

"Are you supposed to scare me or something?" Bradley asked, laughing and pointing at Kaysar. "Who the hell is this guy anyway? I can stay if I want to stay."

"You heard them! Get out!" Jacklyn yelled, pivoting away from Leona to face Bradley full on. Her fists were clenched at her sides. Ava wished she could say something, anything at all, but the strength she had to stand up to Kaysar last night was nowhere to be found.

"Damn! You were never this crazy when we were dating," Bradley joked. "What did California do to you?"

Jacklyn lunged at him, but Kaysar ran between them. He let Jacklyn pummel his chest instead of Bradley's, who stood wide-eyed behind him, clueless.

"Let me—I'll show him!" screamed Jacklyn, her dress falling off her right shoulder. "That-was-my-baby-sister-you-piece-of-human-garbage! Let-me-at-him!" Jacklyn tried to push against Kaysar, but his tall muscular frame stood still, blocking her.

"He's not worth it," was all Kaysar said, letting Jacklyn continue to hit him until tears fell down her face. Kaysar pulled her into him, allowing her to scream into his chest. Penn stood eerily still, keeping a few feet between himself and Ava. His face looked paler than it had on the winding drive up to The Lookout.

"Thanks for protecting me, man," Bradley said as he cowered behind Kaysar. Kaysar's bicep bristled beneath his shirt as he released Jacklyn.

"Let me get this straight, this is all about Ava? *Come on*, Jacklyn. You and I weren't even that serious, and Ava clearly had a crush on me. I was just, you know, giving her what she wanted. Right, Ava?"

Ava watched Penn's eyes flash with fury. He stepped further away from her. Ava wished she'd blend into the wall behind her. Everything she'd been trying to hold inside, to hide from everyone, was spilling out all over the room. The worst part was Penn was there to watch, to see her for what she really was. Kaysar was right. She wasn't smart, or beautiful, or interesting. She was stupid. A stupid girl who followed a boy up to a bedroom expecting to be cared for. He had every right to step away. Ava was surprised he wasn't already sprinting toward the door.

"You need to leave. *Now.*"

Ava lifted her head up to find it was Penn who spoke. He hadn't left at all, instead he was moving in toward Bradley. He stood in such a way that Kaysar, Jacklyn, and Penn's bodies created a blockade where Ava could no longer see Bradley.

"In fact," Penn declared, his voice stern and clear, "Everyone watching this little show needs to get out of here too. Trish, I know it's your party but—"

"Y-yes!" exclaimed Trish, coming out of her own state of shock to shoo people away from the kitchen and toward the front door. "This party is so over people, out. OUT!"

"I still don't see what the big deal is!" Bradley said, refusing to leave the room.

"*I will call the police if you don't leave*," Jacklyn hissed, stepping around Kaysar.

"Like hell you will!" laughed Bradley. "This all has to be some kind of joke. When did you get so sensitive?"

"I don't know, Bradley," Jacklyn sneered. "Maybe when you decided to—"

"No!" yelled Ava, though she wasn't sure her voice was coming from her. "No one can know Jacklyn!"

"Ava, it's pretty much already been said," Jacklyn argued.

"Wait," Bradley paused. "Are you saying that I . . . that I . . . Is this about the bullshit complaint filed against me this summer? My uncle cleared my name immediately of that nonsense. Are you telling me it was *Ava* who reported me?"

Bradley pushed between Kaysar and Penn, his face screwed up in disgust. "You *followed me*, Ava. You—"

"Leave her alone! It was me," Trish squeaked, stepping back inside the kitchen. "I reported you!"

"*What?*" Bradley gasped, spinning on his heel to face her.

"I. Reported. You," Trish declared, drawing out each word for him. "I didn't know, at the time, that your uncle was on the force, or I would have . . . well . . . anyway . . . it was *me*."

No one spoke, the reality of the situation dawning on those still left standing in the kitchen.

"You must be drunk or something, Trish," laughed Bradley, breaking the silence. He threw his cup into the sink, its contents splattering across the white backsplash. "What could you possibly have had to report?"

"I haven't had a drink yet tonight," Trish responded evenly. "I was too busy trying to host my eighteenth birthday party until you showed up here and ruined it. I reported you after you assaulted me in my parents' bedroom this past summer."

"A-A-Assaulted? Wh-what a joke," stammered Bradley, pleading to Penn and Kaysar. "She *wanted* me. Just like Ava did. You would've done the same, guys. Jacklyn was a great girl, and all, but I'm the kind of man who needs options."

"Wait, are you saying," Leona asked, half laughing as she cut off Bradley. "What do you mean, Trish? You can't possibly have been . . . you would have . . . you would have told me if something like that happened to you, right?"

Trish looked around the room, opening her mouth then shutting it again.

"You would have told me, *right!?*" Leona asked again, shifting away from the sink.

"Well, I, um," Trish shrank as Leona drew up to full height. "Maybe we should go somewhere to talk? I didn't mean for it to all come out, not like this. But I had a feeling when you told me about Ava this past summer that it might have happened to her too. That's why I invited her here, so that I could tell her. I didn't think you'd invite *him* here. Not after . . . not after Jacklyn and I asked you not to."

"I . . . ," Leona looked around the room, at Jacklyn's furious face, at Trish, and lastly at Ava. "I-I've got to . . ." Leona ran from the room, brushing past Trish on her way out. Everyone watched as she left, not bothering to chase after her.

Bradley stood alone, seemingly dumbfounded. "You two get it, right?" He looked from Kaysar to Penn. "You guys know what it's like when a girl is into you, right?"

Penn and Kaysar stood together, arms crossed, jaws set. Bradley stepped out from around them and toward Trish. Jacklyn narrowed her eyes as he passed her, her body still heaving.

"I didn't do anything wrong, right Trish? You know that I . . ."

"I asked you to leave," Trish responded, her head held high. Ava wished she could muster that kind of strength, but her legs felt like rubber. She clung to the edge of the counter as Bradley turned toward her.

"Ava, you followed me up the stairs that night. You wanted it to happen. You *agreed* to it."

Ava averted her eyes, though Bradley was unavoidable as he stood in front of her. The smell of him was sickening.

White crown molding flashed in front of her. She closed her eyes, sinking into that night in June, letting the wave of it crash over and around her. She didn't try to fight it. Down, down, she went, letting the memory of it fill her lungs. She was gasping for air when a simple word rose to the surface and burst out of her in a hoarse whisper.

"No," she said.

"What did you say?" Bradley asked, moving in closer. Ava opened her eyes and rotated toward him, still holding on to the counter. She found Penn's eyes behind Bradley's shoulder and held them before staring Bradley directly in the face.

"N-no. I never agreed to anything that night. You just, you took what you wanted. I never wanted, I never meant to hurt my sister. A-A-And I want you to leave. Now."

"Come on!" Bradley protested, reaching out toward Ava, but Trish, Jacklyn, Penn, and Kaysar ran forward, blocking him once more. None of them spoke for her, letting Ava's words stand as the last Bradley would hear from anyone that night.

"Alright, *alright.* I'll go," Bradley said, stepping away with his hands up as he moved toward the hall. "But all of this is absolute bullshit. I didn't do anything wrong, and my uncle believes me so, that's all that matters. Not whatever lies you all choose to believe."

No one answered, staring at him, waiting for him to leave.

"I DIDN'T DO ANYTHING WRONG!" he screamed as he turned and stomped away. He slammed the front door shut behind him, the echo ringing through the near-empty space of Trish's first floor.

* * *

"Ava, I-I'm," Trish spoke first, ending the prolonged silence. "This shouldn't have happened like this ..."

"I'm ... I need to go outside," Ava said to no one in particular. In a trance, she edged her way out of the kitchen.

She found herself drawn to the patio door and slid it open. The moon was nowhere to be seen tonight, hidden behind dark rolling clouds. The fresh fallen leaves from her last visit had dried up and blown away, leaving only the smell of winter on the wind. She inhaled deeply, finding that the cold air brought life back into her lungs.

Ava heard the door slide open behind her but didn't have the strength to ask them to go away. She wasn't even sure if she wanted to be alone. Someone's warm hands draped a jacket around her shoulders and took a seat next to her.

"I, I didn't want anyone . . . ," Ava began, staring down at a speck of dried mud clinging to her shoe.

"Ava, it's okay," Penn's consoling voice met her ears.

"No, but I, um, I don't mean just anyone. I really didn't want *you* to know. I didn't want you to think less of me."

"Can you look at me, for just a second?" Penn asked. Ava tipped her face up toward his, his eyes now burning like embers after the fire had ignited in them earlier.

"Whoever you've slept with, consensually, in the past, those were *your* choices to make. Not my choices to judge. But what that person did to you was take away your choice. It wasn't your fault. Nothing that happened that night was your fault. Please, *please* know, that I will never think less of you. Not for any mistake you think you've made, and especially not for any pain carelessly . . . and horrifically . . . inflicted upon you by someone else."

Ava had to look away. Overwhelming emotions were welling up inside her and on the brink of overflowing.

"I am . . . ," Penn continued. "I become more and more *impressed* by you as I get to know you. At the person you're becoming. I think more and more of you, Ava. All of the time."

Ava clutched the edges of Penn's jacket, as every feeling she'd had since last June broke forth. She let out a strangled sob without trying to repress it. She knew Penn would want her to feel it all, every bit of it. To not apologize for a single tear.

"Do you want me close to you?" he asked. Ava began to shake her head no, but she let out a loud, screaming cry as she did. Hot tears burst out of their hiding places, and all she could do was shake her head yes until he was near. He closed the gap and cautiously put one arm across her shoulders. Ava threw herself into him, swinging her head into his chest. He held her close as she heaved, releasing all the pain she hadn't yet allowed herself to feel. She held on to him for what could have been hours, neither of them caring to move.

"Hey, can I speak with Ava, for just a moment?" asked a deep voice from behind them. Ava shot straight up, afraid for a second that Bradley had come back. She looked back to find it was Kaysar standing in the doorway.

"Why don't you ask Ava yourself?" Penn asked him.

Kaysar rubbed the back of his neck. "Sure, yeah, of course. Ava, can I please speak with you?"

Ava wiped her face with the inside of her sweater. She gave one slight nod, though she wasn't sure what Kaysar could possibly have to say to her. Penn stood up and whispered, "*Be nice,*" to Kaysar before sliding the door shut behind him.

"Damn, it's cold out here," Kaysar commented as he remained standing on the stoop. He sounded somewhat lame now that he didn't have anyone around to impress. "Look, I'm, uh . . . I'm not good at apologies but I am, uh, I am sorry."

"It's fine, Kay—"

"No, it's not. I know Penn cares about you, I just didn't know how much. When I saw it in real life, I just, kind of . . ."

"Turned into an asshat?"

"Yeah, well," Kaysar smiled sheepishly.

"I really do appreciate you coming out here and everything, but I'm just . . . I'm really exhausted after everything," Ava said.

"Totally, I get it. I'm not a big talker, but I need to speak to you about something."

Ava nodded, glancing back behind them. Penn stared at them from the hall, pretending to clean up a bookshelf. When he saw that Ava spotted him, he went back to collecting cans from the counter. Ava repressed a laugh.

"I've known Penn since for, well, forever," Kaysar began. "I knew Penn when Mr. Abrams was alive and healthy. I don't know how much Penn told you, but he was the man every kid looked up to on our block. When my mom lost her job, he made sure we had groceries. When I face planted on the sidewalk, his dad scooped me up and cleaned up my bloody nose."

Kaysar paused to sit down. He tugged his black beanie down on his head before continuing.

"You don't know how it was, when his dad got really sick. It was . . . fucking devastating. Penn holed up in the house, taking care of Paola on top of Mr. Abrams; she had stopped taking care of herself. He stopped going to school for a while, and I was the person who took care of Penn. I brought him homework, made sure he ate, slept on the floor next to him as he cried in his sleep. It *gutted* me to see them like that," Kaysar continued, his elbows on his knees, hands together as if in prayer.

"When they decided to move here after Mr. Abrams passed, we were all tore up, everyone on our block, but especially me. Because as much as I love my own family..."

Ava nodded as Kaysar stopped to collect himself, understanding how Paola and Penn felt like a home in and of themselves.

"I get why they had to get out. To start over. But I felt...abandoned. So, when Penn didn't love it in Westwood at first, I was, I hate to say it, happy. It meant they might come back. It meant I might get part of my family back. But when he started talking about you...

God, I just really started to hate you. Penn began mentioning you without even realizing it, and I knew it then. I knew I was losing my friend, and I would never get him back in the same way."

"But you have a bond with him that I will never have," Ava interjected.

"Yeah, but you get to be here with Penn now. It's like I get past-Penn and you get present-Penn. It's not fair."

"But you're here right now," Ava suggested.

"I am but I'm not. You get to make new memories with him, and I'm stuck rehashing the old ones."

Ava thought back to Jacklyn screaming earlier in the kitchen at the person who'd ripped them apart. They, too, would never be quite the same.

"I'm willing to share Penn if you are," she offered. Kaysar smiled, the first he'd given to Ava since they met. It was warm and welcoming, just as Penn had described him in the first place.

"And one other thing," he said, adjusting his beanie and shivering. "I had a...well, someone abused me when I was younger. That's why I caught on so quickly back there when Jacklyn flew at that asshole. From the way you froze up when he walked in. I recognized it in myself."

"I am so sorr—" Ava said.

"No! Don't be sorry for me. That's the last thing I want. I'm telling you because I've gone to therapy for years now, and I was just able to tell my Mom about it."

"Wow, I...," she whispered, but he held up his hand to stop her.

"I really came out here to tell you this; this is your story to tell, okay? Yours and yours alone. It's messed up that it came out back there in front of people. But it's not up to anyone else how you decide to live with this. You get to tell people, or not tell people, on your own terms, from here on out. *You* get to decide, for yourself, how you heal."

They sat together in silence, an appreciation for one another growing between them as an almost full moon poked through a hole in the clouds.

"It's getting late; ready to head out?" Penn asked, cracking the door open behind them.

Kaysar and Ava nodded in unison, standing up together to join Penn in the warmth of Trish's hallway. Penn handed Ava her purse and helped her to shrug on her parka. Trish and Jacklyn stood in the middle of the living room, bags of trash around them. They had somehow managed to clean up most of the house while Ava was outside.

"I—" Jacklyn said, moving toward her, but Ava held up her hands.

"I can't talk about it anymore tonight. I will call you when I'm ready, okay?"

Jacklyn opened her mouth to say more, but Trish spoke up first.

"When you're ready, I'm here too," she urged. "And Ms. Delic helped me process a lot of this if you ever want to speak with her about it, but no pressure, or anything."

Ava nodded in appreciation before turning toward the hallway where Penn and Kaysar stood waiting for her. On her way out of the living room, she passed by speakers on the fireplace mantle and halted to a stop. A song was playing, so quiet you could barely hear. It was the same one that had played in Penn and Paola's living room countless times over the past Sundays she'd spent with them. She turned the volume up, four sets of eyes monitoring her, afraid she might shatter. Then Ava began to sway.

She moved her feet slowly at first, attempting to match the beat. The tempo began to pick up, and she struggled to replicate the movements she'd tried so hard to memorize at Penn and Paola's. Then suddenly Penn was there, spinning her into him, guiding her feet in the right direction. The more she moved, the freer she felt, whirling across the space where her power had once been stripped away.

Jacklyn joined in next, wiggling her hips back and forth toward Ava, her white dress flowing around her ankles. Kaysar extended his hand to Trish, who curtsied and twirled to the center of the open room. Together they formed a circle, smiling and laughing into each other's faces, limbs flailing about as one song changed to another.

It was there that Ava felt herself float high above the scene as she let go of judging herself and judging the moment. She imprinted as many details as possible on to her memory, never wanting to forget the night she chose to dance her first steps toward healing.

part two

Dance with me
until the last note
rings out
in the kitchen

Don't remind me
in the morning
all we've lost
in an evening

Tonight,
let's pretend
this song was written
with us in mind

And our simple
two-step
will hold us together
across time

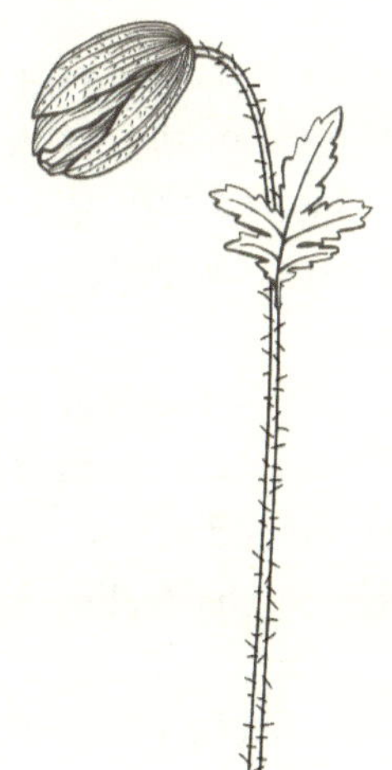

chapter nineteen

The sign-up sheet on the back of Ms. Delic's door stared blankly at Ava. The hallway surrounding her was quiet, aside from a giggling pair of freshman boys who were clearly supposed to be somewhere else. They reminded her of Mac, how soon he'd be in these same halls with her.

Ava jumped as the door in front of her swung open.

"Ava!" Ms. Delic said. "So good to see you! You look different. Did you want to speak with me?"

"I, um," Ava hesitated. There was so much to say, but she didn't know where to start. She glanced up a couple of inches to meet Ms. Delic's expectant smile. "I can just, like, set up an appointment or whatever if you're on your way out."

"No! No! Come in, come in!" Ms. Delic said, motioning Ava inside. Ava bounced nervously on her heels in the middle of the room, wishing she could word-vomit everything on her mind and be done with it.

"You're welcome to sit on the loveseat over there. Let me grab a few things from my desk," Ms. Delic told her, her tone warm and unassuming.

Ava sank back into cozy gray cushions and silently begged her heart to stop racing. She took in her surroundings as she waited. Ms. Delic's office hadn't changed much since the last time Ava had been there. Drawings created by students covered most of the walls, with an occasional poster pinned between them. Ava located the sign with breathing techniques she had recalled before her last volleyball game, hanging right above Ms. Delic's burnt-orange armchair.

"Did you get a new haircut?" Ms. Delic asked as she walked around her desk. Her high heeled boots were muffled by a fluffy teal rug, which covered most of the ugly brown and yellow tiled flooring beneath it. Ava hid her hands underneath her thighs, feeling a rush of vulnerability come over her.

"Hmmm . . . new top?" Ms. Delic guessed, sitting back into her armchair. She elegantly crossed one leg over the other. Ava shook her head, turning her gaze toward the desk to rest on a strange squishy object in the center. "Well, whatever it is, Ava, you look great! What would you like to talk about today?"

Ava tried to speak, but her clenched jaw refused to move. Ms. Delic followed her gaze, then stood up and grabbed the lime green squishy ball from her desk. She tossed it over to Ava.

"We can just sit here until you are ready to talk, okay?" Ms. Delic suggested.

Ava squeezed the ball for several minutes, calming as it ballooned out and gave the effect of oozing between her fingers. She wasn't sure how much time passed before she spoke, but when she peeked up, Ms. Delic was still smiling.

"I . . . can we talk about my schedule for next semester first?"

"Of course, we can! Let me take a look here," Ms. Delic set down her pen and notepad to check her computer for Ava's schedule. "It looks like we'll keep most of your classes the same, but we could switch out a couple of your electives. Have you decided on what you'd like to study in college? I can find some options that relate to your major that may sound interesting to you."

Ava shrugged her shoulders, not having considered it all that much. "I don't know, my dad wants us all to go into business or law so, I guess one of those."

"Interesting. What is it that you like about business and law?"

Squeezing the stress ball with all her might, Ava thought of her dad fighting with Jacklyn. "That I could make money, I guess?"

"Hmmmm," Ms. Delic responded, clicking her pen several times. "Okay, let me ask you this! What is something you really, really enjoy? Something that causes you to lose track of time while you are doing it? You don't even have to be good at it! Just something that feels like the most natural, challenging, yet interesting thing in the world to you."

Ava racked her brain for something, anything that fit this description. She thought about her classes, how each one seemed to bore her more than the next. Her grades were good, but she didn't excel at a particular subject. She bit her lower lip, feeling stupid that she couldn't think of a single thing.

Then her eye lingered on a piece of artwork on the wall. A sunny living room popped into her mind: Paola at her easel, showing Ava how to add shading to her sketch of the Loman's kitchen. Time disappeared every time she began working on a piece of art.

"I guess like painting and sketching stuff. So, art? Does art count as a thing?"

"Of course, art counts!" exclaimed Ms. Delic. She began to tap rapidly on her keyboard. "Let's add an art class to your schedule and get rid of your study hall. We can meet back together next semester and see if it's something you'd like to consider as a major in college! We can start talking about college options then too."

"But, wait!" Ava shouted, struggling to keep up. "Am I even allowed to study something like that?"

"What do you mean by that, Ava?"

"No one takes art seriously. I can't be expected to earn a living doing it."

"Oh, I don't know about that," Ms. Delic stepped from around her desk and leaned against the front of it. "I think if you love something enough, and have the courage to stick with it, you'll find a way to make a living out of it. You don't have to be a starving artist, you know. You can have a career as an art teacher, a graphic designer, or an illustrator. I even have a good friend who started as an art therapist and now runs her own nonprofit that provides affordable studio space to local artists."

"What's an art therapist?" Ava asked, her interest piqued. She set down the squishy ball and leaned forward.

"An art therapist is someone who encourages others to express their feelings and emotions through art. It helps people in all sorts of different areas including those who are healing from trauma, suffering from mood disorders, and can even help to improve social skills."

"That's a real thing? People actually make money doing it?" Ava asked in awe.

"Of course, it is! You may not become rich doing it, but you can earn a healthy salary. I've learned in my own experience working several jobs before this one that it's important to know what you value before a job decides it for you. If money is a priority for you, then maybe art is not the best choice as a major. Actually, I have something that will help!"

Ms. Delic held up a finger as she approached her tallest filing cabinet. She opened the third drawer down, ran her finger across the files, and pulled out a worksheet. "Got it! You'll put a number by each attribute from one to thirty, one being what you want most from your job and thirty being the least."

Her pale pink shirt billowed behind her as she rushed to hand the paper to Ava.

"You'll see there are so many options! Maybe you want to work with numbers, or have flexible hours, or you would like to be able to travel around the world. Maybe you want all three! Take your time while I'm searching for other elective options for you."

This time around, Ava didn't have to think quite as hard. She was inspired by Ms. Delic and Paola, who thoroughly enjoyed their work teaching and helping others.

"I'm ready!" Ava piped up after several minutes.

"That was fast! Hold on a minute here," Ms. Delic said as she hit the enter key on her keyboard several times. "What did you come up with?"

"I chose creativity as my first priority, helping others second, and flexibility as my third."

"Those are lovely choices! And I'm just curious, where did money fall on your list?"

"It's pretty far down. . . . I labeled it as my twentieth."

"See! It's important to know what matters most to you above all else, not to anybody else, when seeking out a career. With those choices, I have an idea for a class you can take but let me know what you think."

Ava nodded excitedly.

"Have you taken a psychology course yet?"

"No, not yet. What is it?"

"You'll get to study the human mind and learn why people behave and feel the way they do. Plus, Mr. Jenneman is one of the best teachers at Westwood High. Oops. *I shouldn't have said that.* But it's true! If you do love it, we can start talking seriously about art therapy or anything else you are interested in exploring, and we'll see what colleges have good programs. How does that sound?"

"I think it sounds really . . . exciting," Ava said, unsure if she was allowed to feel that way about something as overwhelming as her future.

"It is exciting! Especially when you start to discover careers that feel right for you, even if they aren't as mainstream as others! I want to say it's also okay if you get to college and decide to major in a completely different subject area than psychology or art. Some of us need to try all sorts of things before finding the right fit, but it's great that you have a starting point!"

"Thanks, Ms. Delic," Ava said, wishing she could convey just how grateful she was.

"You know what it is," Ms. Delic said, tilting her head so that her curls spilled over her right shoulder. "I thought it was something physical about you but it's almost like, like some weight has been lifted from your shoulders since I saw you last. Am I imagining it?"

Ava grabbed the couch pillow next to her and hugged it to her chest. It was the perfect opportunity to say what she needed to say, what she *wanted* to say, but she couldn't bring herself to do it.

"Hmmmm," Ms. Delic said again, shooting Ava a warm smile. "How is English class going; are you still hanging out with Penn?"

"Y-yeah," Ava stuttered, wondering if Ms. Delic would bring the topic up on her own.

"What about Trish and Leona, those were your close friends outside of Jacklyn, right?"

"S-s-sort of. Trish, a little. Leona, not so much."

"Do you want to talk about that a little bit maybe? You can start wherever you'd like, we've got time."

Ava lifted her gaze to the wall clock on the wall next to her. She watched the second-hand tick, following it as it completed one revolution.

"Leona is . . . Leona was . . . Leona always liked Jacklyn more than me. Without Jacklyn around at school to call her out on stuff she's just . . ."

"You can say it, Ava. The door is closed, and I won't tell a soul. In fact, I won't tell anyone anything you say here unless I believe you are a harm to yourself, a harm to others, or if you yourself are in harm's way. I also will need to report if you disclose any child or elder abuse. Does that make sense to you?"

Ava thought for a minute, then nodded, setting the couch pillow beside her.

"Good! Go ahead, she's just what?"

"She's, well . . . *mean*."

"And before, when Jacklyn was around? When she wasn't as mean, what did you like about her as a friend?"

"I guess she always told me what I should wear and how to do my makeup. And I don't know, she'd come to our volleyball games. She'd always pay for stuff, like if we all went to lunch or whatever. But she would get mad if anyone else tried to pay. Before Jacklyn left, she was harsh, but it was bearable. Afterward she turned malicious."

"I see. Well, is Leona someone you think you want to stay friends with?"

"I don't. After last weekend I don't think . . ."

"What happened last weekend?"

Ava hesitated, chewing at her lip. The story was there, waiting at the tip of her tongue, begging to be heard.

"Whatever it is, Ava, I won't judge you. Or we can always come back to it another time. Up to you."

"Well, I guess it . . . it started with . . ."

Ms. Delic gave her a supportive nod, urging her to say what she needed to say.

It was enough to pull the plug on all Ava had been holding in. She let everything out, starting with Trish's birthday party, then laying out every detail about Bradley and what he had done to her. Every word rushed across her lips, pleading to be out in the open, begging for understanding. Ms. Delic furiously took notes on her notepad, flipping the pages up as she filled one and then the next.

"Ava," Ms. Delic asked as Ava ran out of breath. "I do have to ask you, do you feel that you are in danger of being assaulted by Bradley again?"

"No," Ava said without hesitation, thinking of the circle of protection who had surrounded her at Trish's party.

"Are you sure? You don't feel threatened at all by him?"

"No, I feel safe now."

"Okay. First of all, *thank you so much* for sharing this with me. I can't imagine how difficult it has been to carry this terrible thing that happened to you around, not able to tell anyone. I can't tell you how glad I am to hear that you have safe people in your life to talk with. I am so sorry this happened to you in the first place. It sounds like you have friends and two siblings that really, really care about you. That must feel wonderful after feeling completely isolated after it happened."

Ava stared down at her kneecaps, her vision blurry as a thick wall of tears formed.

"I've written down every detail you told me," Ms. Delic explained, pointing to her notebook. "And I would like to encourage you to report this—"

"But," Ava cut her off, "Trish did and the police ignored it! They didn't even . . . I just don't see the point."

"It is *entirely* up to you whether or not you report, and given the circumstances with the Westwood Police Department, I understand if you decide not to. There are other options should you choose to go forward with allegations. If you want to talk about those, we, by all means, can."

Ava's eyes remained on her knees, far too tired to think about taking it further today.

"I want you to know I completely believe, on every level, that you were assaulted by Bradley against your will. And I'd like to stress that *none of this was your fault.* Just as your friend Kaysar said, it is your choice from here what you want to do, and I will support you in whatever decision you make."

"I don't think I'm . . . I don't think . . . I just need more time to think," whispered Ava.

"*Of course.* Let's leave it there for today, and you come back in when you are ready to talk about it more, okay? Let me print out your schedule for next semester and write you a hall pass.

"And oh! Some questions you might want to ask yourself when it comes to your friendships: Does this person show up for you when you need them? Do you feel supported by them? Do they encourage you to be the best version of yourself? If the answer is no on all counts, you may not have had much of a friend in the first place. Which means it's *totally okay* to walk away from a friendship and invest that time into relationships you feel are genuine."

Ms. Delic placed the papers she needed into her hands. Ava's mind was whirling in a flurry of different directions.

"Come back and see me, when you're ready. And don't feel like you're ever a burden to me. I'm here to support you, okay?"

"Y-yes, Ms. Delic, thank you," Ava answered, straightening up, feeling disoriented as she walked out the door and into the empty hallway. So much had happened in the last hour she couldn't tell if she felt relieved, overwhelmed, or some combination of the two.

Her phone buzzed in her bag as she walked to her class, grounding her back into the reality of the school day. She found her feet carrying her toward her favorite bathroom by the library. As soon as she closed the stall door, she took out her phone to find Kaysar had sent her an old photo of Penn and him from middle school. Penn sported lime green braces and a broad smile, his curls long and frizzy. Kaysar was scrawny, with spiky haired dyed a vibrant orange at the tips, not nearly as attractive as he was now.

A laugh tickled the base of Ava's throat, then erupted fully into the empty bathroom. With it, she released the tension she'd built up from speaking with Ms. Delic about Bradley. Joy spread through her fingertips as she texted Kaysar back, savoring the fact that she had not one but two friendships she could consider genuine in every sense of the word.

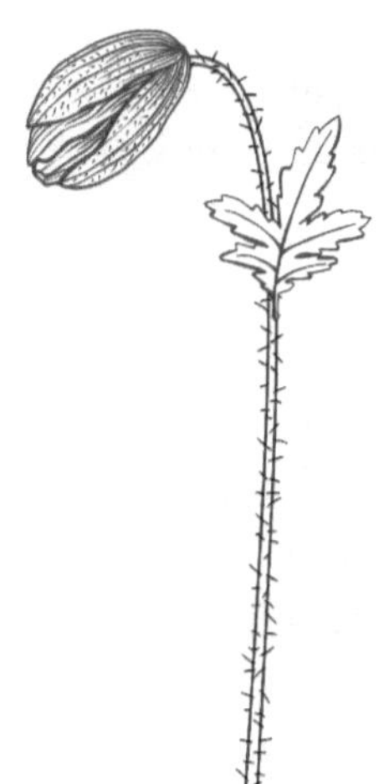

chapter twenty

It was a particularly gloomy Saturday afternoon in which Mrs. Pierson cleaned herself up and went into the office, leaving Mac and Ava alone with their boredom. Mr. Pierson's car had gone missing from the driveway, yet again, and the number of wine bottles lining the kitchen counter was multiplying by the day. Instead of discussing this, Ava argued with Mac over the remote, refusing to watch him play video games. Their bickering stopped abruptly as their phones buzzed simultaneously on the coffee table in front of them.

"Did you . . . ?" Mac asked Ava, reading his text message.

"Yeah, got it too," answered Ava.

"I mean, it's not like we have anything better to do right now. Unless you changed your mind and want to watch me *destroy* these zombies."

"It might be a better alternative to this," Ava said, glancing back down at her phone, wishing the text from Jacklyn would disappear.

"Come on," Mac pleaded. He turned the TV off. "It's just lunch. How bad can it be?"

"Things feel weird now," Ava groaned. "After everything."

"I won't ask what 'everything is' for the thousandth time. But she did pop out of the same womb as us. I think you can handle sitting in the same room with her for an hour."

"It's just . . ."

"Just what?"

"It feels like everything has changed."

"But she told me you guys, like, danced together at Trish's thing! It sounds to me like you've made up."

"Yeah, but we haven't actually sat down and talked since she's been back."

Mac rolled his eyes, then stood up and grabbed Ava by the wrists, pulling her up from the couch.

"Fine. . . . *I'll come.* But only under one condition," Ava said, dragging her feet toward the front door.

"You have conditions now?"

"Yes, I do. I want to go to Mei's to eat. So at least if it's awkward I can shove delicious food in my face."

Mac shrugged as he texted Jacklyn, then gave Ava a thumbs-up at the response. He picked up Ava's keys from the side table and tossed them at her.

"Time to get this so-called awkward meal out of the way," he said, throwing open the front door.

* * *

Jacklyn was waiting outside the front door of Mei's as Mac and Ava pulled up, hopping from foot to foot to stay warm. Though a coat engulfed her tiny frame, she shivered noticeably on the sidewalk. Mac bounded over to her, colliding into her with a hug that nearly bowled Jacklyn over. Ava lingered behind; her hands hidden in her coat pockets. Mac and Jacklyn had always been more affectionate with one another than their father liked.

"Hey, Mac Attack!" Jacklyn shouted, returning his hug with equal excitement. "Hey, Sis!" she said to Ava, withdrawing from Mac.

"He doesn't like being called Mac Attack anymore," Ava blurted.

"Oh, I'm sorry," Jacklyn stuttered.

"No, it's fine!" Mac argued, glaring at Ava.

"No, it's not." Jacklyn said. "You're almost in high school now; I get it."

They paused for a moment, staring around at one another. Ava shot Mac an "I told you this would be weird" look, to which he responded with a very annoyed shake of his head.

"Should we, um, go in?" Ava asked, pointing at the door. Mac was quick to pull it open, waving Jacklyn and Ava through.

Inside, Mei was bustling around the busy dining room. She shouted a quick "sit wherever you'd like!" without slowing down. Ava chose the same table she'd sat at last time, half wishing it were Kaysar instead of Jacklyn sitting across from her. It was funny how Kaysar was the person she texted with most now, even more than Penn.

"This place is . . . ," Jacklyn trailed off, staring around in amazement. Her eyes rotated toward the white tin ceiling tiles and drifted across the hanging clusters of red and gold lanterns. She paused for a long time on Paola's mural, taking in each brilliant scale before her gaze landed back at their table.

"Way too cool for Westwood?" Ava guessed, opening up her menu.

"Is that you, Ava?!" Mei shouted, passing their table on her way from the kitchen. She rushed up to the table, her cheeks flushed. "I didn't see you come in! Who is this with you?"

"My brother Mac," Ava said, pointing to her left. She then gestured across from her. "And my older sister, Jacklyn."

"Well, how lovely to meet you both! Can I get you all started with anything special?"

Jacklyn took charge before Ava had a chance to respond.

"We'll take the Peking duck wontons, oh, and the walnut sesame prawns—"

"And the pork dumplings," interrupted Ava. Jacklyn's face fell, but Ava was too frustrated to care. "They were amazing last time. Thanks, Mei!"

Mei gave a quick thumbs-up before jogging away.

"So, how did you become friends with Mei?" Jacklyn asked, shrugging off her coat and hanging it on the back of her chair.

"Penn and his mom, Paola, are friends and neighbors with her," Ava answered, sitting back in her seat as Jacklyn leaned in toward the table.

"Ohhhh," Jacklyn purred. "Did you and Penn, like, go on a date here?"

"No!" yelped Ava, as Mei returned with their waters. Mei raised one perfectly shaped eyebrow at Ava before leaving the table again. "I mean, no. We're just friends."

"Oh please, Ava," Jacklyn said, rolling her eyes.

"*Right?!*" Mac chimed in, raising his hands in the air.

"Why is it so difficult to believe two people of the opposite sex can be just friends?" Ava asked, crossing her arms over her chest.

"Well, I think it's totally possible," Jacklyn said, though rather snidely. "But not when one half of the friendship has a blatant crush on the other half."

"Exactly!" exclaimed Mac.

Ava shifted in her seat. She hated how Jacklyn and Mac fell right back into their same patterns. Every word Jacklyn spoke caused Ava to bristle with irritation. "He's not into me. I'm not into him. Besides, we didn't come here to talk about Penn, or about me. Why are you back from California?"

Jacklyn's expression clouded. She tucked a thin strand of hair behind her ear and rubbed her lips together. Ava thought Jacklyn's face looked the slightest bit fuller, though it may have been wishful thinking.

"We don't have to talk about that yet; we don't even have our apps!" Mac joked, though Ava nor Jacklyn cracked a smile.

"I think that I have more than shared what I've been going through," stated Ava. "And it feels like you told everyone *but me* what happened out there."

"I've been trying to get ahold of you, Ava," Jacklyn said, fiddling with her straw. "It's not like I didn't want to tell you. But it just seems kind of stupid now in comparison to what you went through."

"Are you both still not going to tell me?" Mac asked.

"No!" Jacklyn and Ava shouted together. They shared a brief smile before returning back to the conversation.

"I highly doubt I'll think it's stupid," Ava urged.

Mei returned with their appetizers, and they paused the conversation to order their entrees. Ava watched as Jacklyn loaded up her small plate, relieved her sister was eating a healthy amount.

"Looks like you liked it?" Mei asked ten minutes later on another run back toward the kitchen, her arms balancing stacks of plates.

"It was amazing!" Jacklyn shouted. Mac and Ava nodded fervently, stacking their plates at the end of the table.

"So ...," Ava said when Mei left again.

"Okay, here goes," Jacklyn sighed. She straightened up and pulled her hair back into a low ponytail. "Basically, I hated California, and I hated college. And I hated myself for hating it. Everyone around me was living, like, their very best lives. But I hated that every day felt the exact same as the next. It *never* rains, or gets cold, or is less than perfect there.

"I hated the stupid palm trees and the 'golden' hills and the fact that everyone walked around like it's the best place on earth. I hated my large lecture halls and the teachers who I tried to get to know but didn't give a shit about me. I hated the dorms. I hated Greek life. I tried so hard, every single day, to make myself love it. I ended up drunk and high every night just to fail my classes and wind up on probation for something I did that I don't even remember. I quit eating. I quit going to class. And every day I just freaking wished the rain would fall so I could feel..."

"Like it was okay to feel everything you were feeling?" Ava asked. Jacklyn nodded; her eyes misty.

"And the truth of it is, I missed Westwood. I missed high school. As lame as it sounds, I missed home. And I missed you, Ava, *so damn much*. Even though I was so mad at you, I just wanted to be near you. Even if I could barely look at you, I needed to know that you were okay."

"I'm ... I'm so sorry I couldn't ... I didn't know," Ava said, fumbling over her words.

"I'm sorry too, Ava. I hope you know that."

Jacklyn reached over and grabbed Ava's hand. Mac put his hand on top of theirs and squeezed.

"If it weren't for you, Mac," Jacklyn continued, "and I know you'll hate this, Ava, but for Leona too, I don't know what I would have done out there. They both told me to come home even if Mom and Dad would freak. They knew I was losing myself."

When silence fell, the three of them welcomed it, leaving space for their collective emotions. They let go of each other's hands as Mei arrived back with their meals. Ava couldn't help but notice Mei looked exhausted and the lunch hour had only just begun.

"Enjoy!" Mei chirped, then headed over to greet two new parties standing by the door.

"I guess I thought you'd love it out there," murmured Ava as she dug into her food.

"Everyone else did. I thought I would too," Jacklyn said, shoveling food into her mouth. "I know I'm a failure," she continued between bites. "And an embarrassment to the Pierson name. I ruined my scholarship, probably my whole future, too. But if that was what my future would look like, what my life would look like, I knew I would struggle every day to live it."

"Failure is a pretty harsh word for yourself," said Mac, sucking down a noodle. "Especially when you were probably one of the most accomplished graduates of Westwood High."

"Yeah," Ava chimed in. "I think you are . . . ," she searched her brain for the words Penn had said to her, "brave for quitting something you didn't love to find something you do. Or somewhere you didn't love to find a place you do."

Jacklyn prodded a piece of chicken for a minute before looking back up. "When did the two of you grow up on me?"

Ava and Mac caught each other's eye and shared a slow smile.

"So, uh," Jacklyn said, changing the topic. "Mac told me Mom's been hitting the bottle again? I know this might sound a little crazy. But I have the weirdest feeling Dad isn't just going into the city for work."

"Yeah," Mac said. "I think you might be right. And I think Mom knows it too, hence the wine."

"I don't think this is the first time, either," Jacklyn continued. "I'm pretty sure when I was in middle school, Aunt Brene caught him out with some lady in Pittsburgh."

"Wait," Ava said as it dawned on her. "Is that why we haven't seen Aunt Brene in, like, four years? *Why do I take so long to catch on to this stuff?*"

"Well, Ava, you've always been a bit . . . in your own world," Mac said. Jacklyn giggled but stopped abruptly at the sight of Ava's highly offended expression.

"Room for dessert?" Mei asked several minutes later when placing a plate in the middle of the table.

"Whoa!" Mac exclaimed.

Together the Pierson siblings marveled at the glistening arrangement of sugar-glazed cherries, apricots, and raisins atop sticky rice in front of them. They dug in, finishing the beautiful dessert within minutes.

"Guess you all enjoyed it?" Mei asked a few minutes later. She picked up the empty plate and set down the bill. Ava grabbed it before Jacklyn could.

"Mei, you didn't charge us for one of the apps or the dessert!"

"My treat!" she shouted, bustling away to another table.

When Mei returned to pick up the check, Jacklyn caught her before she rushed away. "I was wondering . . . I see you rushing around this place and, well, if you need help, I'm in need of a job."

Ava raised her eyebrows. Mr. Pierson had never allowed any of them to get a job, purely because he didn't want anyone in Westwood thinking he couldn't pay for everything they needed.

"I can help with bussing or serving or getting the word out around town. I know a lot of people who would love this place!"

"I can't pay much, but tips are decent," Mei said, looking hopeful but hesitant.

"Can you feed me?" Jacklyn asked.

"That I *can* do!" Mei answered with a laugh. "Come in for a formal interview tomorrow at three?"

"Absolutely, I'll see you then!"

Ava waited until Mei was out of earshot. "Did Dad cut you off?"

"Pretty much. He said he'll pay for things again when I go back to school in California. But I've decided if I want a life and job that I love, I'm going to have to do it my own way."

"Even if you're broke?" Mac asked.

"I'm not broke! I'm about to have a job!" Jacklyn exclaimed as she stood up. Ava smiled to herself as they exited Mei's, mesmerized by Jacklyn's ability to ask for exactly what she needed.

"Oh, and Ava," Jacklyn said, turning to Ava before they parted their separate ways, "now that we've talked and everything, do you want to come over to Trish's tomorrow? Leona will be there and she'd like to apologize to you."

"I can't!" Ava shouted, louder than she intended. "I go to Penn's house every Sunday afternoon."

"Okay what about Monday, after school?"

"I-I don't know," Ava hesitated, scuffing the toe of her shoe on the sidewalk. "I don't get why you still hang out with her. Especially after what she did."

"We talked about it after Trish's party. She really didn't know the whole story. She was looking out for me, and I believe her. I admit, I don't think it was her best idea but we all used to be such good friends, you know? Maybe just come and hear her out."

"I'll think about it," Ava whispered, though every cell in her body screamed at her not to go.

"Let me know on Monday?" Jacklyn asked, hopeful. "I really do think it will be a good thing for all of us."

Mac stepped forward and hugged Jacklyn goodbye. When Jacklyn opened her arms to embrace Ava, Ava found she could raise only one arm half-heartedly in response.

"See!? Not so bad," Mac said as they climbed back into the Jeep. They watched as Jacklyn pulled out onto the road ahead of them.

"Yeah, not so bad," Ava replied. It was pure relief to have Jacklyn back in Westwood, and frankly, back on her side. But she couldn't ignore the chill scurrying down the length of her spine as the reminder of Leona's words *'to burying the hatchet'* flashed scarlet red across her mind's eye.

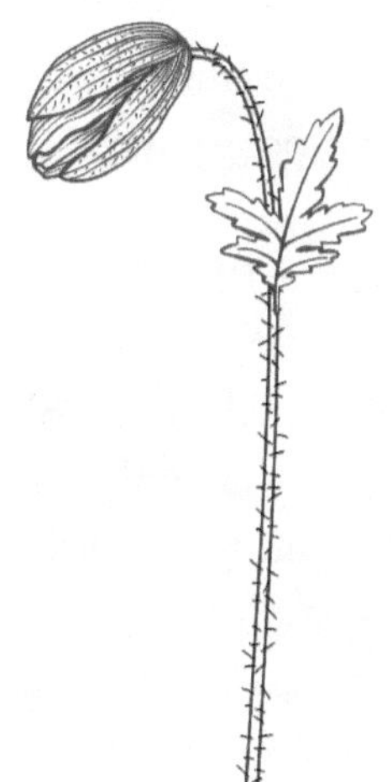

chapter twenty-one

The sound of Penn's pencil scratching across paper was driving Ava nuts. She'd been lying on the floor, staring out his window at the tops of bare tree branches, waiting for anything resembling a poem to come to her. Yet here was Penn, hand flying across the page, writing what could be a whole book of poetry before a single word formed on her page.

Ava glowered over at him as he sprawled out on his stomach, one foot dangling over the edge of the bed. His hair on the left side of his head stood up higher than on the right. Ava sighed heavily, hoping he would notice her, but he continued writing. Throwing her notebook to the side, Ava stood up and stretched. Penn paid her no attention as she walked out of his bedroom and into the living room. She found Paola set up in the living room, a large canvas on her easel.

"What are you working on?" Ava asked over her shoulder.

Paola jumped up, splattering paint across what looked like the beginning of her underpainting.

"Shit! I'm . . . ," Ava gasped, but Paola waved it off.

"Don't worry about it! I was trying to make it into something it doesn't want to be. Anyway, how's the poetry writing going?" Paola asked, setting down her paintbrush.

"You know, not so great. For Penn, it is going spectacular. So, that's a thing."

Ava plopped down on the small couch. She put her elbow on the arm and rested her chin on her fist. "How do you get started on a painting? Aren't you afraid you'll, like, mess it all up if your first stroke isn't just right?"

Paola untied her paint-covered apron, placing it lightly on the chair she'd jumped up from. She sat down next to Ava on the sofa.

"You know what's crazy?" Paola answered. "Maybe it's just me, but I find my favorite paintings are the ones I thought I messed up the most. There's something so *satisfying* to me about imperfections. If you learn to work with them, instead of against them, they wind up turning an average painting into something . . . extraordinary."

Ava studied the painting at length across the room. An ugly streak of black marred what was a beautiful blending of bold colors. She didn't have the heart to tell Paola there was no way something extraordinary could be made from that.

"What's got you held up on writing your poem?" Paola asked, picking at a glob of cobalt blue paint on her finger.

"I suck at writing poetry. I don't know what I'm even doing!" Ava shouted, frustration seeping through her usual stoic demeanor.

"I'm sure you don't suck."

"No, Paola, I *actually* suck. It's not like sketching or painting where I'm half-way decent at it."

"You're really good at both! Don't sell yourself short."

"Okay, thank you, but with poetry . . . the way Penn recites . . . it's embarrassing when I try."

"He did tell you why he picked the poem he's reciting for class, right?"

"Kind of. He told Mrs. Papayanni that his dad, or um, Mr. Abrams would read it to him."

"Exactly! Martin loved poetry, and by that, I mean he was *in love* with it. He read a poem every single morning in his study before starting his day, and another to Penn in the evening in place of a bedtime story. He passed his love for poetry down to Penn. You weren't given the same opportunities to love it."

"I don't understand how anyone can love it; it seems so snobby! The people who love it act like they are so entitled. Not Penn, but, everyone else I've met who likes poetry."

"Art can be snobby, as you say, too."

"You don't make art snobby!"

"But that's it, Ava, don't you see? Art and poetry aren't in and of themselves pretentious. I'm thinking of poets such as Rumi and Izumi Shikibu."

"And Wendy Cope?"

"Yes! Sometimes the simplest poems are the ones that move you the most. With anything creative, there are gatekeepers who try to make it available, and understandable, only to the elite. But the reason I create art, and I believe why many poets create poems, is because it's the place where we can best make sense of our own experience and hope to help others make sense of theirs. To me, there's nothing snobby about that."

"I think I get it. Though I'd never begin to think I understand your art or experience fully."

"But the fact you take time to try to understand it, that's all I could ask for! What about the poem you chose to recite in class? Penn told me you picked 'The Orange.' Can you recite it for me now?"

Ava screwed up her face and buried it into the armrest.

"Please!" Paola urged her, rubbing Ava's shoulder.

"Okay," Ava sighed. "Here goes. I just memorized it, so don't judge me if I mess it up."

"Never!" Paola said, sitting up straight.

Ava fumbled her way through the poem, having to look down at her phone several times to make sure she was on the right line.

"Brava!" Paola exclaimed when she finished. "What does that poem make you think about in your own life?"

"Uh . . . ," Ava stopped, never having thought about it in depth before.

"Don't you have to write a paper on this?" Paola teased.

"*Don't remind me!*" Ava groaned. "I guess it makes me think of sharing food with Penn at lunch. Of eating ice cream with Mac downtown. Going to Blackbranch Park. Having friends that are actually real friends. I think of trips up to The Lookout. It makes me think of the days, the ones that seem absolutely perfect, not because anything all that great happens, but because I feel content, or um, at peace with what I have, like the poem says. Like I have everything I'll ever need in good friends and good food."

"I don't know, Ava," Paola said, beaming. "It sounds to me like you know more about poetry than you think. And oh! I've been meaning to ask you. I've been thinking about putting together a free art class for the neighborhood; there are so many creative kids on this block! Would you be willing to help? Kaysar already said he's in!"

"I . . . ," Ava hesitated. "Are you sure you want me helping? I'm not that, you know, experienced."

"You'll be awesome! The kids will love you! I'll do most of the teaching, I'll just need you and Kaysar to help the kiddos open paint and answer questions. It will be fun!"

"I-I guess I can. When is it?" Ava asked, apprehensive about the whole situation.

"Not sure just yet, but I'll let you know! Thanks, Ava! Seriously, it's going to be wonderful, you just wait." Paola patted her knee then walked back over to her easel. She tied her apron around her waist and sat down in front of the ruined canvas.

Ava watched in awe as Paola dipped her brush into paint and created upward strokes in and around the splatter. Feeling inspired for the first time that day, Ava rushed back to Penn's bedroom.

"Where did you go off to?" Penn asked, sitting upright on his bed, his moleskin shut.

"Oh, you know, just learning about poetry from Paola."

"*Really?* I didn't think she liked poetry all that much. It was always my dad's thing."

"Maybe not, but she . . . I mean, you know this already, but she really loved your dad."

Ava sat back down in front of Penn's bookshelf. She crisscrossed her legs and opened her notebook without any further explanation. Penn watched curiously as she set her pencil down on the page, words flowing from her hand, each line as imperfect as the next.

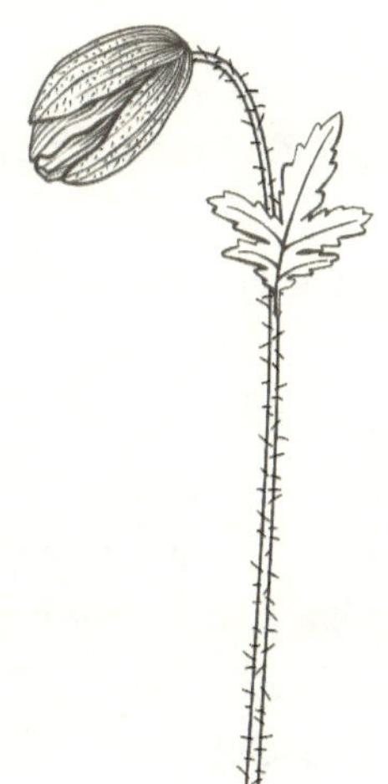

chapter twenty-two

Trish's front door was framed beautifully by a garland interlaced with gold ribbon. Ava sighed into the cold air as she admired it, releasing a misty cloud from her lips. She breathed in the comforting scent of pine as she knocked gently inside the large wreath hanging on the door. She still held a small hope no one would hear her, that there was still some way to get out of this arrangement.

"Ava! You came!" Trish shouted as she opened the door. She wrapped her arms around Ava's neck. Trish lowered her voice as she invited Ava in. "I didn't expect you to agree to speak with Leona, after what happened. I'm still not sure how I feel about it—"

"Hey, Sis!" Jacklyn interrupted, yelling down from the landing above. "We're in Trish's room, come join us!"

Ava hesitated in the entryway, wishing she could have just a few more minutes alone with Trish. They hadn't had a chance to speak in person since her party.

"You don't have to stay long," Trish assured her, voice still low. "I don't know how well this will go, honestly."

"Come up!" Jacklyn exclaimed, smiling as she leaned further over the banister. Ava shook her head in supreme annoyance, but Jacklyn didn't seem to notice. Ava reluctantly followed Trish up the stairs and toward her bedroom, which was on the opposite end of the hallway from Trish's parents' bedroom.

Jacklyn sashayed over to Trish's bed and flopped next to Leona on the glittery purple comforter. Leona sat poised on the edge, filing her fingernails. She didn't bother to look up as Ava entered. Ava sat down awkwardly on a furry pink poof near the bay window, as Trish chose a spot on the floor near the door they'd come through.

"Have you gone to see Ms. Delic yet?" Trish asked after a prolonged silence.

"Yeah, I, um, I did, actually. She was really helpful," answered Ava while twiddling her thumbs.

"Isn't she great?! She never made me feel pressured to go to the police or anything."

Ava didn't answer, allowing another pause to settle between them, broken only by the scraping of Leona's nail file.

"So, do you think you'll try to report him?" Trish asked. She tucked her feet under her, her hopeful light brown eyes staring up at Ava.

"I mean, does that even seem like a good idea?" Ava answered, half shrugging. "It sounds like it didn't go all that well when . . . when . . . you know, you did."

"You do remember your parents are lawyers, *right*?" Leona sneered, deciding to enter the conversation.

"Right," Ava answered. She tugged at the faux fur of the poof to restrain herself from ripping the nail file out of Leona's hands and shoving it somewhere else. "My dad who couldn't even support Jacklyn when she dropped out of school. And my mom who hasn't been sober in weeks. They would really make a lasting impression in court."

"But it is possible Mom will sober up soon," Jacklyn jumped in. "When they stop this round of fighting, maybe she could help you two put a case together against Bradley. She is somewhat experienced in these sorts of cases, even if it's not her emphasis. But she is a great lawyer when she wants to be."

Ava longed for Penn and Kaysar's presence, not expecting an onslaught of pressure about Bradley. She grabbed a throw pillow from the floor and placed it in her lap, trying to picture herself sitting back in Ms. Delic's office.

"I don't know if, I don't know if I'm ready," Ava said, looking out the window beside her. The sky was growing darker, and the bare branches level with Trish's bedroom were thrashing from side to side.

"Well, Trish," Ava said, ignoring her sister and Leona. "Do you . . . do you think it's worth it? To go through all this? Just for . . . I mean, what's the point of it all?"

Trish twirled a long curl around her finger. "It's worth it to me if it means it won't happen to someone else. I still don't know if I'll forgive myself for letting this happen to you. If I would've spoken up sooner, told you when it happened, maybe Jacklyn would've broken up with him and you never would have gone up to my parent's—"

"Trish," Jacklyn stopped her. "You know it's not your fault, right? This is purely Bradley's fault."

"Exactly!" shouted Ava, scooting to the edge of the poof. "It's his fault! Why should Trish and I have to go through all of this for someone who won't be held accountable for what they did!? Why is it on us? Why can't I just live my damn life without this expectation on me to report. The probability of the case being tried and of Bradley being convicted is . . . *I don't know, I'm not a freaking stats genius*, but I know it's not good!"

"Maybe you're right," Trish said, bringing her knees to her chest. "It makes me sick thinking of Bradley's uncle. They treated me like I was five years old at the police station. Maybe you're right, Ava."

"*Wow*," laughed Leona. Ava's fists clenched in her lap at the sound of her high-pitched cackle.

"What?" Ava spat.

"It's just, out of all of us, I never thought *you'd* be the one to break Trish's spirit."

"I-I'm not breaking anything!" Ava gasped. "I'm being honest about how shitty this situation is and how we're not likely to get anywhere with it."

"You know," Leona said, giving her hair a dramatic toss over her shoulder. "I really thought about apologizing to you today, like Jacklyn asked me to. But, it's kind of pitiful, really, seeing you like this, so I don't think I'll be able to."

"Yeah, yeah, Leona," Ava shot back, her body shaking with fury. "I'm *pathetic*, boys don't like me, my skin sucks, and I'm boring as hell compared to my perfect sister. *I GET IT!* Honestly, I think it's kind of pathetic that you are obsessed with treating me like shit! Don't you have, like, anything better to do with your life?!"

Leona smiled, a wide cat-like grin spreading across her face. "*Finally.*"

"Finally, what?!" Ava yelled, jumping to her feet.

"Finally, you care enough about something to get angry about it. As long as I've known you, you've let everything slide off of you. It's been like hanging out with a cardboard cutout."

"That doesn't mean it's okay to talk to her like this," Jacklyn interjected.

"Well, I didn't, when you were still around. But with you gone, she needed someone to light a fire under her ass."

"It really isn't okay, though, Leona," Trish said, coming to stand up alongside Ava. "You speak like this to me too."

"I said I was sorry!" Leona retorted, crossing her arms. "I won't grovel, if that's what you all are expecting. I shouldn't have invited Bradley to the party, Ava. I'm sorry."

"*That's it?*" Ava asked.

"Again, I don't understand what you are expecting out of me. You know who I am, and I won't apologize for it."

A bubbling in Ava's stomach crept up to her throat and exploded into a loud, manic bout of laughter. The girls stared at Ava, unsure how to react.

"After all of your insults, and the slut shaming, and the silent treatment," Ava gasped as her laughter settled, "that's all you have to say? Nothing about what Bradley did to me, nothing about what you said about me in front of Penn, nothing else?"

Leona raised her hand, and Ava thought, for a split-second, it was to reach out. Instead, she used it to flick the remaining hair off her shoulder. Leona blinked twice at Ava and crossed one leg over the other, staring at her in defiance.

"I'm done," Ava declared after a pregnant pause. "I'm done, Leona. I'm done with whatever this was because now I know it never was a friendship."

"Ava," Jacklyn reached up to grab Ava's wrist. "She's trying . . ."

"Why? Why do you ALWAYS stick up for her? Aren't you tired of managing her poor behavior toward everyone but you? Just stop! Stop trying to force us all to be friends with each other! I can choose my own friends! And you and I can go back to being sisters, which is the only thing we've been all long."

"But," Jacklyn pleaded, "we are friends too! All of us are friends! We can . . . we can work this out!" She looked desperately at each of them. Trish lowered her eyes to the rug, and Ava shook her head sadly. Leona pulled her phone out of her bag to distract herself.

"Jacklyn," Ava extricated her wrist from Jacklyn's grip. "I'm so glad you're home, but things changed while you were away. Let's decide for ourselves who we want to be friends with, okay?"

Jacklyn sunk back onto the bed as Ava turned toward the door.

"Ava," Leona said softly. Ava spun around, hopeful for a genuine apology.

"You forgot your bag."

Trish and Jacklyn stared in disbelief at Leona, her doe-eyes not showing a single sign of remorse. Ava jerked her bag up from the ground and gave a slight wave to Trish and Jacklyn as she strode, head high, out of the room.

Ava paused when she got to the landing, recalling the trio of freshmen who stood there in October. She ran her hand over the banister, remembering the lost expression of the girl who clung to her arm near the front door. She realized, until recently, that she, too, had attached herself to anyone who would be friends with her, no matter how they treated her.

As Ava descended the staircase, she felt a small flicker of pride with each step. Proud of herself that she no longer needed to hide from Leona or behind Penn. She was beginning to make her own decisions; however hard they might be. She reached for the doorknob and, without looking back, flung the door wide open.

Her steps were light as she walked down Trish's long stone driveway and back to her Jeep. She settled into her driver's seat, the wind pushing the door shut beside her. Ava reached backward for her blanket but stopped herself, finding she didn't need the extra layer of comfort. Instead, she turned the volume up on her stereo, singing at the top of her lungs as she drove away, leaving all thoughts of Leona behind in the rearview mirror.

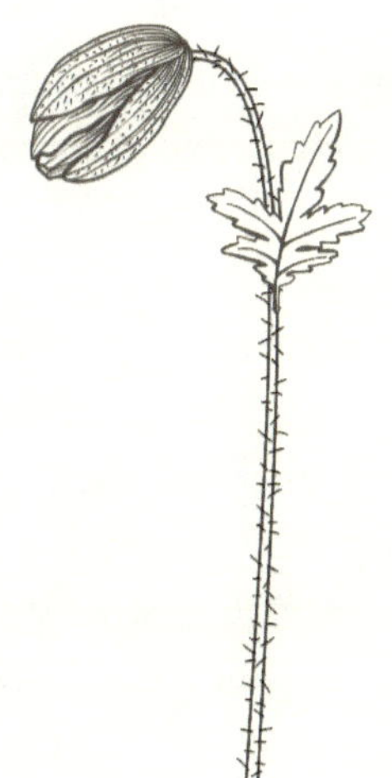

chapter twenty-three

Mac's heavy footsteps thudded in the hallway. Ava listened closer to find he was humming to himself. She squinted her eyes open, remembering what day it was. Dread spread through her limbs. She threw off her covers and heard something crinkle beneath her feet as she stood. The printed pages of her poetry essay lay scattered across her bedroom floor.

Ava picked up the pages and carefully placed them together in her English folder. She scanned the first lines of "The Orange," her pulse racing. Wendy Cope's words cycled over and over in her mind as she dragged herself into the hallway, ruminating on all the ways her presentation was bound to go wrong.

"What could you *possibly* be humming about this early in the morning?" Ava complained, passing Mac in the hallway.

"It's a beautiful day to be alive, Sis! Can't you feel it?" he asked, smiling broadly beneath his ever-growing mop of hair.

"It's cold and gray and depressing," Ava answered, scrunching her face up at her reflection in the bathroom mirror. "Just like it has been every other day this month."

"*Oh, come on!* It's the last day of school before winter break! Which means my teachers will show 'educational' films all day and then it's FREE-DOM FOR TWO WHOLE WEEKS!" he yelled, bending at his knees and pumping his fists in the air.

"Shhh!" Ava urged, pointing to their parents' bedroom. "You know better than to scream this early with Mom, uh, 'sleeping in' so much lately."

Mac shrugged while slinging his backpack over his left shoulder. "Could you pick me up today, after school?"

"Why? I thought you were riding home with Will now?"

"I'd rather be picked up by you today," Mac said, his cheeks turning pink.

His words stopped the internal war Ava had been waging against her nerves. She looked over at him to find he was fidgeting with his gray hoodie strings.

"I, um, I guess I can do that," Ava said, hiding her smile as she started to wash her face over the sink.

"Thanks!" Ava thought she heard him say before he ran down the steps.

Ava heard her mom's alarm go off and rushed to her bedroom to avoid a morning encounter. She grabbed out an old, burnt-orange cardigan from her drawers and paired it with black jeans. Then she braided her hair and swapped out her now broken-in Converse for a pair of heels, hoping to look somewhat confident for her presentation.

After reciting "The Orange" several times in the mirror, Ava scrambled downstairs. She stopped in her tracks at the sight of her mother standing near the door, staring out the window. Her bathrobe was stained and disheveled. She had a mug in her hand, but whatever the contents were, Ava guessed it wasn't coffee.

"Uh, good morning, Mom?" Ava greeted her, trying to hide the concern in her voice.

"Has your father called you?" Mrs. Pierson asked, eyes not moving from the window.

"No, should he have?"

"I suppose not . . . but . . . did you know?"

Ava dropped her bag to the floor and approached her mother at the window. "Know what, Mom?"

"About your father?"

"I'm not sure, w-what do you mean?" Ava stammered.

Mrs. Pierson took a sip out of her mug, then gulped more down. "Would you want to know? If you were me, would you want to know who your husband really is?"

"I think you need to go back to bed," Ava offered, reaching out to grab her coffee cup. Mrs. Pierson jerked it away, splashing it onto herself. Another dark purple stain blossomed on her once stark-white robe. She looked down, unphased, then turned her attention back toward the window.

"I thought if I just stuck around long enough he would . . . ," Mrs. Pierson said, slurring some of her words, "James would become all the things he promised he'd be to me when we were eighteen. But I always knew, Ava. I always knew he would take *everything* out of me until I had nothing left. Then he would find someone else to leech off of."

"Mom?" Ava said, stepping closer. As she did so, her mom's shoulders began to shake. Her now-empty mug fell to the floor, shattering across the marble tile. Ava led her around the wreckage to the living room couch. Her mom grabbed on to her arm, pulling her downward. She began to sob loudly into the air, screaming words that made no sense to Ava. Eventually, she ran out of tears and fell asleep, her head resting on Ava's shoulder.

By the time Ava propped her mom up on a pillow, cleaned up the entryway, and drove to school, her first hour had already passed. She ran through the halls in a panic, arriving to class as Mrs. Papayanni finished taking attendance.

"Ava! How nice of you . . . ," Mrs. Papayanni began but stopped herself short, her stern gaze softening as she caught sight of Ava's troubled face. "Please take a seat, Ms. Pierson. Are you still prepared to go first today?"

"Y-yeah! P-Please. If that's okay," Ava gasped, trying to catch her breath. She felt Penn's eyes burning a hole in the side of her head, but she couldn't bring herself to look at him as she sat down.

"More than okay!" answered Mrs. Papayanni. "Now, when each of you come up to present, please stand in this same spot I'm standing. Present with your hands free, and I'll collect your papers and self-authored poems at the end of class. If we have time, and if anyone would like to read their original poem to the class, I'd love to hear them. But I understand poetry is deeply personal, which is why I am leaving it optional. Any questions?"

The class craned their necks around, their eyes collectively landing on Penn. It was rare he didn't have something to add. But when Ava dared to glance over, he was staring down at his fingers, interlaced on his desk. After a short pause, Mrs. Papayanni clapped her hands together.

"Wonderful! Let's get started. Ms. Pierson?"

Ava felt her legs tremble as she headed to the front of the room. Looking around the class, it seemed as if the number of students had quadrupled. She watched as several classmates shifted uncomfortably in their seats, waiting for her to begin. When she opened her mouth, nothing came out. She'd forgotten the first line of the poem. A snigger met her ears from the back of the room.

"Mr. Reuben!" Mrs. Papayanni hissed. "Do I need to move you to a seat next to me?"

"No way, Mrs. P, I like my seat just fine," he said.

"Ava, please begin," she instructed between gritted teeth.

Ava opened her mouth again, but the words jammed up together in the back of her throat, spilling out in one line. "I'm-reciting-'The-Orange'-by-Wendy-Cope."

Everyone in the front row stared blankly at her, the silence growing unbearable. Her eyes shot toward the hallway, thinking how easy it would be to run and hide in her favorite bathroom stall.

A ray of sunshine cleaved its way through the gray sky above the soccer field, drawing Ava's gaze to the opposite side of the room. She followed it through the window and over to where it landed, across Penn's face. He squinted in the brightness, adjusting to the sudden exposure of light. When he finally found Ava's face again, his eyes shone bold and bronze, just as they did the first day they met.

"*Slow down. Breathe*," he mouthed, using his right hand to shield the sun, his left to illustrate a plane landing. Ava nodded, collecting herself. She took a deep breath, holding Penn's gaze as she began.

"'The Orange,' b-by Wendy Cope," she began, much slower this time. She stood up straight as Penn demonstrated for her in his chair. "*At lunchtime . . .*"

Ava spoke the first line to Penn but discovered it less scary to leave his face and address the rest of the class as time went on. She was surprised to find Mrs. Papayanni smiling at her and Justin Reuben actually paying attention.

As she progressed to the next stanza, Ava remembered what Paola had said back on Baile Avenue. She loosened up as her favorite memories came to mind, feeling the warmth of the sun as it broke its way entirely through the clouds.

When she reached the last line of the poem, Ava paused, angling her body toward Penn. With as much clarity as she could muster, she spoke the last seven words directly to him.

Penn beamed when she finished, applauding obnoxiously. Mrs. Papayanni joined in with him while the class gave an obligatory clap or two.

"You did awesome, Ava! You were so good!" Penn gushed as Ava sat down beside him. "That poem has never been one I read often, I always felt it was a little simplistic. But you really brought it to life and now it might be a new favorite! Poetry is great that way, isn't it?!"

Ava rolled her eyes, trying to wipe off the huge smile plastered to her face. "I'm sure you will do much better than I did."

"Doubt it!" Penn said, "I'm going last because I wasn't feeling so great that day we signed up. You know how I *hate* waiting for everyone else to go but, ah well."

Ava rode a brilliant wave of relief through the rest of class now that she'd already gone. She listened intently as her classmates recited poems by Maya Angelou, Mary Oliver, Pablo Neruda, Wendell Berry, Naomi Shihab Nye, Ted Kooser, and several others. She was struck by how each poem took on the student's character, transforming them into anything but pretentious.

"Mr. Abrams? It looks like you're up," Mrs. Papayanni said after quieting the uproar of laughter that erupted after Justin recited "Look at These" by Helen Farish.

"Wish me luck," whispered Penn as he stood up, tugging at his curls.

Like he'll need it, Ava thought.

Penn stepped in front of the classroom and rolled his shoulders back. He bent his arms at the elbow and raised his hands. The class quieted, holding their breath to not disrupt what was about to ensue.

"'If—' by Rudyard Kipling," he began, his voice transforming on the spot. "*If you can keep your head when all about you . . .*"

With that, Penn swept them away, drawing them in with each gesture, every word holding them captive. She imagined paint instead of words pouring out of Penn's mouth and splashing onto each student, each of them a canvas hungry for composition. The picture of Mr. Abrams on Penn's desk swam to Ava's mind; she felt he was present today, watching Penn with pride.

"*If you can dream—and not make dreams your master . . .*"

Ava's mind wandered back to her house, to her mother passed out on the couch. What was it her mom had said? That her own father had "*taken everything out of her until she had nothing left*"? That soon he would "*leech*" off of someone else? Ava didn't know what to make of any of it. The more the poem sank into the folds of her brain, the more she began to process her own relationship with her dad. She'd always thought her father was the strongest person she knew, never showing weakness, never entertaining emotions. But what kind of man was unfaithful to his wife? What sort of dad refused to take time to get to know his children? What type of person cared more about his work than his family?

And here was Penn, in front of her. Penn wasn't muscular or rich or particularly handsome. But as she stared hard at him, the reality of her father's weaknesses was illuminated. Penn, like his father before him, was this poem, come to life.

"*Yours is the Earth and everything that's in it,*" Penn recited, reaching the end of the poem. "*And—which is more—you'll be a Man, my son!*"

Applause broke out unanimously from around the classroom, and even Mrs. Papayanni smiled as Justin let out a wolf-whistle.

"You okay, Ava?" Penn asked, sitting back down in his seat. She realized she hadn't lifted her own hands to clap for him.

"Yeah, I'm . . . that was . . . you were . . . that was . . . thank you," Ava struggled to say.

"Thank you for what?"

"Oh, I just mean you were incredible, up there," Ava said, blushing bright red as Mrs. Papayanni walked between them to collect their papers.

"Well, class," Mrs. Papayanni said as she reached the front of the classroom. "We have a few more minutes, any takers on reading your original poems?"

"*You should read yours,*" Penn urged her.

"No! Don't try to trick me into letting you read the poem I wrote!"

"Please!" Penn begged. "I bet it's great!"

"No way, Penn. *No way.* You read yours!"

"Nah . . ."

Mrs. Papayanni scanned the classroom, stopping at Penn, who shook his head. "Alright then, how about you all take the last few minutes to chat amongst yourselves. It is, after all, nearly the start of your winter break."

The class hooted and hollered, turning toward each other to discuss upcoming holiday plans.

"Penn," Mrs. Papayanni called, sitting behind her desk, "Come see me, after class? There's a poetry competition I think you'd be interested in signing up for."

"Sure thing, Mrs. P! Sounds great!" Penn answered. He turned toward Ava, excitement manifesting in his legs as they bounced up and down beneath his desk.

"Cool . . . a poetry competition," Ava joked.

"Yeah, well, it will look good on my resume, you know, to have awards and stuff," he said rather sheepishly.

His words settled strangely onto Ava as she realized the first semester of Penn's senior year was ending. The bell rang, disrupting her thoughts, sending her alone into the hallway as Penn stayed behind to speak with Mrs. Papayanni.

* * *

Mac flew down Westwood Middle's steps, waving to classmates as he burst into Ava's Jeep. Kids were pouring out onto the front sidewalk with huge smiles on their faces, ignoring their parents' honking horns to speak just a bit longer with their friends. Ava felt a pang of nostalgia watching them.

It felt like it had been much longer than three years since she'd left the middle school halls.

"Pedal to the metal, Sis, let's get the hell outta here!" Mac shouted as he buckled himself in.

"Well, hello to you, too," Ava muttered.

Mac's cheeriness was contagious on their drive home. He rolled down his window and shouted, "*Freedom!*" at the top of his lungs at each passing pedestrian. For a glorious ten minutes, Ava felt like everything was going to be alright. Maybe even more than alright. They were still giggling as they tripped over each other and up the driveway to the front door.

Mr. Pierson stood on the front step, his cell phone pressed against his ear. He held a finger up to his lips as Mac and Ava approached. They both attempted to pass him, but he held an arm out to block the way. Confused, they waited impatiently for him to finish up what sounded like an important business call.

"Your mother is a mess," Mr. Pierson said blankly, hanging up rather abruptly to whoever was on the other end of the call. "Who left her like that?"

"Like what?" Mac demanded, stepping out in front of Ava.

Mr. Pierson loosened his tie, his jaw clenched. "You two should have called me, I didn't know she had gotten so . . ."

"So what?!" Mac asked, his voice cracking.

"I-I-I figured she'd clean herself up," Ava stammered.

"I knew she'd pull this *shit* as soon I told her I was—"

"*That you were what?*" asked Mac. Mac dropped his bag on the concrete and stepped in closer to Mr. Pierson. Ava couldn't believe they were nearly the same height now. Mac's hair brought him level with the top of their father's closely shaved head.

"Take a step back, son. She told me she already spoke with you all," Mr. Pierson said simply, angling his head toward his car. Ava followed his gaze to the silver Land Rover, doors open, seats filled with luggage and boxes.

"Wait you're-you're . . . leaving?" Ava asked, face scrunched in confusion. Mac's hands rounded into fists.

"Moving out, more like," Mr. Pierson said. "It's been a long time coming, frankly, the way your mother behaves. And especially now, she's revolting."

"You can't be serious?" Mac asked, bewildered.

"When your mother . . . *sobers up* . . . she will explain it all. I've got to get on the road if I'm going to make it back into the city in time."

"In time for what, exactly?" Ava asked. She did her best not to show him how angry she was, knowing he'd only use her emotions against her.

Mr. Pierson's jaw twitched. "You two call me if your mother pulls another stunt like she did today, got it?"

"Do you plan on coming back?" Mac asked.

"I'll try to visit sometime after the holidays. I've got a lot going right now."

"But what about Jacklyn? Don't you want to tell her?"

"*What about her?*" he spat. "If she thinks she's got life figured out, then she can figure this out for herself too," he said firmly. He looked down at his watch, and with a short nod, strode over to his car and slammed the doors shut.

They watched in awe as their father raced down the street. He rolled right through the stop sign at the end of their neighborhood and sped dangerously out of their lives.

Mac cursed beneath his breath and snatched his bag up in a fury. Ava took a deep breath as she followed behind him inside the house. They found their mom stooped over on the bottom of the staircase, still in her stained bathrobe. Mac and Ava sank down on either side of her, unsure of what to say. When she lifted her head from her knees, she was surprised to find them both sitting there.

"Is he . . . is he . . . is he really gone?" Mrs. Pierson asked.

"Y-yeah, Mom. He just left," Ava answered, unprepared for the next wave of sobs that exploded from their mother.

"Maybe let's get you up into the shower," Ava said, trying to calm her. "Mac, can you try to get a hold of Jacklyn?"

Mac nodded his head, trying to make sense of it all. He fumbled around in his pocket, searching for his phone.

It was a challenge to guide Mrs. Pierson up the stairs since she put most of her weight on Ava as they climbed. Ava felt weird entering her parents' bathroom. Her dad never allowed them in there. She propped her mom up on the toilet, helping her to undress. She turned the water on, holding her mom's hand as she stepped into the shower. Ava waited against the sink until her mom finished. When she was safely dressed, and back in bed, Ava left to find Mac. He was in his bedroom, finishing up a phone call.

"Was that Jacklyn?" Ava asked as he hung up.

"No," he answered, his voice far off. "I think she might be busy working at Mei's right now."

"So, who was that then?"

"Jacklyn told me to call her if . . . if Mom ever wasn't . . . well."

"Call who? Who are we talking about here?"

"Oh, I thought I said already. A-Aunt Brene. She'll be here in a couple of hours."

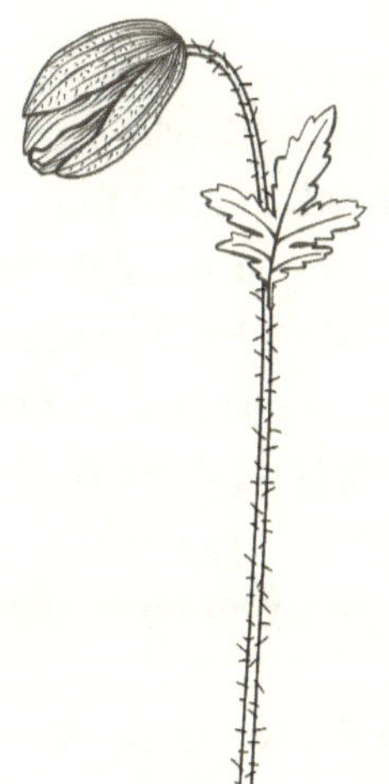

chapter twenty-four

"**H**ey, kiddos!" a voice as warm as a July afternoon called out to Mac and Ava as they shivered on the same step their father had casually strolled away from a few hours before. Aunt Brene pulled them both tight into a hug, squashing their faces against her ample chest. Notes of cinnamon and honey filled their senses, raising up memories Ava had long forgotten about.

"I've missed you both more than words can say!" Aunt Brene exclaimed, giving Ava a tight squeeze before letting go. "Now, I've packed a few bags; could the two of you help me unload?"

Ava and Mac nodded in unison, following Aunt Brene down the sidewalk. She was just as Ava remembered her: short and curvy with cropped auburn hair, though it was beginning to turn gray now. She wore a deepgold cardigan over a burgundy sweater with dark jeans. Ava was comforted by how little she had changed over the years.

The back of Aunt Brene's beat-up RAV4 was jam-packed full of luggage, groceries, and stuffed brown bags. Ava and Mac glanced over one another, working out that Aunt Brene clearly planned on staying for more than a few days.

As they began to unload, Jacklyn pulled up to the curb, rushing toward them in her apron embellished with Mei's logo.

"Is everything okay?!" Jacklyn yelled from the bottom of the driveway. She looked around in confusion at the sight of the RAV4 of which Aunt Brene had disappeared behind. "I left Mei's as soon as I—"

"It's alright, my darling," Brene said, coming out from around her car. She pulled Jacklyn into a hug and rubbed her back until she calmed down. "I'm coming to stay for a while so you kids can ... well ... *be kids.* This isn't the first time James, excuse me, your father, has caused Amelia to have an episode like this."

Ava was surprised to find how closely Aunt Brene and Jacklyn resembled each other as they stood side by side.

"Let's finish this unloading so I can make you all something to eat!" Aunt Brene urged, motioning them back to the car. "I imagine you all's fridge is a sad affair if Amelia was left to do the shopping."

The four of them entered the house, arms heavy with Aunt Brene's things. They found Mrs. Pierson sitting on the sofa, her eyes glued to the TV, unmoving as they made their way back to the kitchen.

"How are you doin', Amelia?" Aunt Brene asked on her way through the hall. Mrs. Pierson responded by turning the volume up on the television.

"So, Aunt Brene, how long are you here for?" Jacklyn asked, trying to make up for their mother's rudeness.

"Had some built-up vacation! I haven't taken time off for years now, so I'll stay as long as it takes to get Amelia back on her feet. Glad Mac here gave me that call; it's been hell not getting to see you all even though I live just a couple hours away. *I swear your father* ... well. I won't start bad mouthing him as much as he deserves it."

"Are you still working at the nursing home?" Mac asked, examining something in one of Aunt Brene's bags.

"Sure am! Still in charge of group activities and still loving it! It brings me so much joy to care for people, even though it's heart wrenching when they pass away. But out of all the many, many jobs I've had, this one is by far my favorite."

"Aunt Brene . . . what is . . . *this*?" Mac asked, his face scrunched in disgust.

"An eggplant?! Are you tellin' me you've never seen an eggplant before?"

"What do you do with it?" he asked, daintily handling it by the stem before setting it on the counter.

"Oh, all sorts of things! You can make eggplant parmesan, use it as a flatbread topping, grill it and pair with tomatoes as a salad. All kinds of things!"

"*If you say so,*" Mac muttered, moving to unpack another bag.

By the time they finished unloading, the Pierson kitchen counters were filled with fresh produce, enough that Ava thought even Paola might be envious. Their black glazed fruit bowl, which had been empty for weeks, was now kept company by ripening bananas, Pink Lady apples, and ripening avocados. Numerous shallots, bulbs of garlic, and bright yellow lemons filled a three-tier stand on the counter. Their refrigerator, which usually held only takeout boxes, was stocked full of all sorts of food Ava had no idea how to prepare.

As the Pierson siblings finished tidying the kitchen, Aunt Brene set about placing three-wick candles around the first floor. When she was finished, she went out to her car, returning with two thick, furry blankets. She draped one over Amelia, who still wouldn't speak to her.

"I always thought this place was a bit too . . . harsh," Aunt Brene whispered to Ava on her way back into the kitchen. She handed Ava a lighter and pointed to the candles around the room while she started prepping dinner.

The sun had already set by the time Aunt Brene had fully settled in. Ava dropped down in a seat on the living room sofa next to Mac and Jacklyn after a delicious dinner, downright exhausted. Mrs. Pierson had fallen asleep again without joining them for the meal, her head dipping over toward Aunt Brene. Aunt Brene scooted over. She tucked a strand of hair that had fallen across Mrs. Pierson's forehead behind her ear.

"Well, better be going," said Jacklyn, yawning as she stood up. "Leona's parents want me in by a certain time."

"You're not staying here?" asked Aunt Brene.

"They didn't tell you?" Jacklyn asked, looking from Ava to Mac. "Dad kicked me out."

"*Oh honey*, you should move on back here. James, I mean, your father, doesn't control who lives here anymore. He lost that privilege when he left today. I bet Amelia will agree once she . . . once she's better."

Jacklyn looked over at her mom, hesitating. "I think . . . I think I'll stay with Leona, for now at least."

"*Jackie*," Brene insisted.

"No one calls me that anymore!" Jacklyn cried, crossing her arms over her chest. Ava tried not to laugh at her sister's childlike reaction, but it escaped her lips. Mac elbowed her hard in the ribs. "I'll think about it though. We don't even know if he's really gone this time. He came back eventually, the last time this happened."

"Well, it's your call," Aunt Brene answered. "As long as I'm staying here, you're always welcome."

"Thanks, really. I'll think about it," Jacklyn said, ruffling Mac's hair on her way out the front door.

Ava felt her eyes drooping, the full weight of the day sinking in.

"Oh, you kids go up to bed! I'll take care of Amelia," Aunt Brene said, taking the mug out of Mrs. Pierson's slack hand.

Ava wanted to help, or act like she wanted to help, but she didn't have anything left in her. She followed Mac upstairs, collapsing in her bed with her school clothes still on. As tired as she was, she felt flooded with relief that her father might not be stopping in and out of their lives when he felt like it anymore. There was a sweet finality to seeing his bags packed, his car removed from the drive.

She stared at the ceiling, feeling a weight lift, now that she wasn't responsible for caring for her own mother. That, finally, Aunt Brene was there to be the adult her parents were incapable of being. A wave of guilt rode over her as her eyes fluttered shut, thinking what kind of daughter didn't miss her own father. She rolled to her side and hugged her knees into her chest.

She listened as her mother stumbled up the stairs, Aunt Brene whispering to her to be quiet as she supported her. Maybe, Ava thought as she drifted off to sleep, she was the kind of daughter who was sick of playing pretend in a family built upon lies.

* * *

In the days leading up to Christmas, Aunt Brene kept Mac and Ava so distracted they didn't have much time to think about their father's absence. Ava's arms were still sore from the boxes of decorations she and Mac hauled up from the basement, many of which were covered by a thick layer of dust.

There was something infectious about Aunt Brene's love for the holidays. Not once did Mac or Ava complain as they hung garlands around the tall archways of their house, though it took them a whole day to do it. They giggled as Aunt Brene sang carols during their poor attempt to staple lights to the roof; the house looked more like Clark Griswold's than James Pierson's by the time they were finished.

Jacklyn popped in and out between her shifts at Mei's to help decorate. Aunt Brene sent her large containers of leftovers each time, always urging her to move back home. Though Jacklyn refused, each visit she stayed a bit longer.

Mrs. Pierson still refused to speak to anyone, walking ghostlike throughout the house. But Aunt Brene didn't give up hope, still talking to her amidst the silent treatment. Ava thought she even caught the hint of a smile on her mother's face one evening as Aunt Brene recounted a story of Mac running naked through her kitchen on a particularly rough night of babysitting.

"Get up, get up!" Mac yelled, bouncing on Ava's bed the morning of Christmas Day.

"GAHHH!" Ava groaned. "*Get off!*"

Mac howled with laughter as he left her room, but not before ripping her blankets off her. Ava cursed him as she ran after him down the stairs.

Rays of radiant sunshine blasted through the windows above their front door, reflecting off the white tile of the front hall. It gave the illusion that the snow outside, which fell throughout the night, had invited itself in. The house seemed to sparkle, complete with the smell of cinnamon and cardamom wafting toward them from the kitchen.

"Merry Christmas!" Jacklyn shouted from the couch in the living room. Ava was surprised to see her mom already awake, a cup of actual steaming coffee in her hands.

"Merry Christmas!" Ava said. "I didn't know you'd be over so early."

"I'm off today!" Jacklyn answered. Her eyes were bright and cheery this morning, and Ava thought she was beginning to look like herself again. "Mei is staying open for carry-out only. I tried to tell her I could still help, but she wanted me to come be with you all. Plus, Aunt Brene said she'd have *quite* the Christmas feast for us."

Ava followed the glorious smells wafting in from the kitchen to find Aunt Brene at the stovetop, flipping bacon.

"Merry Christmas, love!" she shouted over the popping bacon grease. Ava wrapped an arm around her aunt, her eyes bulging at the sight of the countertop.

Two trays of plump cinnamon rolls frosted with a thick layer of icing sat cooling next to a basket of rolls sprinkled with cardamom seeds, along with a bowl of raspberry jam and pitcher of fresh-squeezed orange juice. Chocolate gravy simmered on the burner behind the bacon, and a cast-iron of breakfast potatoes lay waiting to be eaten to the left of it.

"Can you help me out here, hon?" Aunt Brene asked, pulling several bacon strips out of a pan and onto a plate with paper towels. "The table is set for the most part, but if you can start bringing all this food over, that would be mighty helpful!"

Ava carefully picked up a tray of cinnamon rolls and headed over to the dining room table. It was a beautiful sight, topped with a metallic light gold tablecloth and several white tapered candles in crystal holders.

After Ava's fifth trip to the table, Aunt Brene followed behind her, placing the bacon down last. She hugged Ava in close. "Thanks for helping me. I'm so grateful to be able to spend my favorite day of the year with you."

Aunt Brene left to call everybody into the dining room as Ava sniffled. As weird and different as this Christmas felt, she'd never been more excited for the holiday. There was something to being part of assembling the tree in the front room, helping with the decorations, and using her own saved up money to buy presents for the people she cared about.

When Mac and Jacklyn entered the room, gratitude swelled in her chest. Family meals had taken on a whole new meaning now that Aunt Brene was here. Even the silence of Mrs. Pierson didn't stop them from enjoying themselves; they were just glad to have her joining them at the table now.

"When do we open gifts?" Mac asked with his mouth still full from his last bite.

Aunt Brene snorted. "As soon as we get this table cleared and the dishes in the dishwasher!"

Mac shot up, stacking as many plates as he could muster. "Let's go, people!"

When the kitchen was restored to its former sparkling glory, they gathered around the Christmas tree in the front room. There was a moment of awkward pause where everyone looked around at one another; Mr. Pierson usually handed out gifts on Christmas morning.

Mac stepped forward without anyone having to say a word, and soon a small pile of presents formed in front of each of them. Ava sank down onto the ground first, followed by Jacklyn, Aunt Brene, and though she sat far away from everyone, Mrs. Pierson.

"Done!" Mac shouted, checking around the tree to make sure he got everything. "Can I open first?"

Without waiting for a response, he tore open the wrapping on his closest gift and held up a new video game.

"Ohhh, thanks, Sis! I've been wanting this one!" he said to Jacklyn.

When it was Ava's turn to open, she picked up a small box from Mac. She pulled out a dainty silver charm bracelet, a single ice cream cone dangling from a link in the middle.

"*Oh,*" Ava whispered.

"You hate it, don't you? I don't know what girls like!" Mac said, looking crestfallen. He fluffed his hair nervously.

"No, I . . . I love it," Ava said as she smiled over at Mac. She stood up and hugged him close, noting that it felt so good to show affection now that her dad wasn't around. When Ava sat back down, Jacklyn helped to clasp the bracelet around Ava's wrist.

They continued around the circle, Mac ecstatic about Ava's gift of another game controller so she could play more games with him. Jacklyn kissed Ava on the cheek when she opened her gift of a blanket that was the same color blue as Jacklyn's eyes. Ava put on Jacklyn's gift of a cashmere teal sweater immediately after opening it. The three siblings were very thankful for their present from Aunt Brene, a copy of her cookbook, which included all her favorite recipes.

"Now each of you can make something *other* than mac and cheese after I leave," she said, grinning at Mac.

When all the gifts had been opened, Mrs. Pierson cleared her throat. Everyone quieted immediately, shocked that she decided to break her silence.

"I have gifts for all of you," she said hoarsely. She stood up and walked to the closet, pulling out a large red gift bag. She took her time in taking smaller wrapped gifts out of the bag and handing them to each family member, shaking as she did so.

"For me, too?" Aunt Brene asked in a tone of surprise as Mrs. Pierson sat the last gift down in front of her.

Ava unwrapped the gift suspiciously, wondering what her mother could have gotten her. Jacklyn shot Ava a look of skepticism as she unwrapped hers.

Simultaneously, Jacklyn and Ava removed from their gift boxes two gold chain necklaces with a single diamond hanging from the centers. Their jaws dropped, admiring the size of the diamonds sparkling in the early morning sun.

"Th-those were a set of earrings gifted to me by your grandmother when I was about your age, Ava. I thought you girls might . . . ," Mrs. Pierson said, stopping herself short. She looked as if it was taking all the strength in her to speak.

"It's beautiful," Jacklyn answered, gently lowering the necklace to her palm.

"Y-yeah, Mom. Thank you," Ava stammered, unable to work through the many emotions stirring up in her.

Across the room, Mac held up a navy tie with thin gray stripes running diagonally across it.

"That . . . that was your grandfather's, my father's, favorite tie," Mrs. Pierson explained. "He passed away when you were just a baby, but he asked me to pass it along to you when you were old enough."

"Whoa," Mac said as he struggled to knot it around his neck. "Guess I should learn how to tie this thing."

"I-I-I can teach you, sometime, if you'd like," Mrs. Pierson whispered, dropping her gaze down to her hands.

"I would really like that, Mom," Mac said, smiling, his tie now jumbled comically around his throat.

Aunt Brene was the last to unwrap her gift from Mrs. Pierson. Jacklyn, Mac, and Ava all scooted in close as she held up what looked like a lump of cloth.

"*Oh, Amelia,*" Aunt Brene gasped, her hand shooting to her heart. "How did you . . . I thought I lost this forever."

Ava leaned in closer to find Aunt Brene was holding a small, ragged baby doll. Mac shot Ava a look of revulsion; the doll had certainly seen better days.

"I'm sorry," Mrs. Pierson's lower lip tremored, "I knew how much you loved it when we were kids. When you dropped it that day at the fair, I stashed it under my dress and kept it for myself. I'm, *I'm so sorry . . .*"

Mrs. Pierson gasped for air, her upper body shaking. "Y-you were always so much better at being happy, than I was. I thought if I could take this from you, you might become as miserable as I felt."

They all stared up at Mrs. Pierson, not sure if she would allow them to touch her. Aunt Brene stood up, but Mrs. Pierson held up a hand.

"I never stopped being jealous of you," Mrs. Pierson explained to Aunt Brene, her chest still heaving. "I thought having James would finally make us even, because then at least I had someone while you had no one. But now, *look at the mess I've made.*"

Aunt Brene threw her arms around her sister as she sobbed loudly.

"Most of us make a mess of things," Aunt Brene whispered. "I was jealous of you too, you know, but not because of James."

"What could you . . . what could you possibly be jealous of me for?" Amelia gasped between tears.

Jacklyn and Ava held each other's gaze, recognition passing between them. It was becoming clear to Ava that jealousy often didn't flow in one direction.

"Because you're intelligent, driven, and *strong*," Brene assured her. She reached up to stroke Mrs. Pierson's hair. "And you have these three amazing children who are *nothing* like their father. They are the best parts of you, Amelia. James is gone now, and I know, with every fiber of my being, that you're strong enough to make sure he stays gone."

Amelia sobbed harder. "I'm-I'm not even being a mother right now. I don't know how any of you will ever forgive me for how I've behaved."

They sat in silence, interrupted only by Mrs. Pierson's crying. Aunt Brene continued to console her, but none of the Pierson children moved. As much as Ava wanted to say it was all okay, for her, it wasn't. Forgiveness was something each of them would need to sit with and decide on in their own time.

When Mrs. Pierson quieted, Aunt Brene took Mrs. Pierson's hands into hers.

"It's never too late to become the parent your kids need you to be," Aunt Brene assured her. "Look at Dad! He didn't come around until the end of his life, but there was no doubt he adored his grandkids. And loved us. I know you love your children, Amelia. You always have. It's time to do the work to show them."

Mrs. Pierson didn't try to protect herself as Aunt Brene wrapped her arms around her this time. The two sisters held on to one another, unmoving as Mac, Jacklyn, and Ava gathered their gifts and left them alone to talk.

* * *

Later that evening, Mac, Jacklyn, Ava, Aunt Brene, and Mrs. Pierson gathered in the living room to watch Christmas movies. Aunt Brene had turned on the fireplace earlier; it warmed the room as it crackled behind the screen.

Jacklyn and Ava snuggled up close to one another under Jacklyn's new blanket. They spoke earlier that afternoon in Ava's bedroom, agreeing to work on what their new relationship might look like after everything that happened. They decided one thing was for sure; they didn't want to go months, or years, without speaking to one another again.

In the middle of their movie marathon, Ava's head drooped onto Jacklyn's shoulder. Minutes later, she was shaken awake as a loud knock issued from the front door.

"Are we expecting somebody?" Aunt Brene asked nervously, bolting upright. Mrs. Pierson gripped Aunt Brene's arm, her eyes wide with fear.

"You don't think it's . . . ," whispered Jacklyn, craning her neck to look at the door.

"I'll tell him to get the hell out of here!" Mac declared, squaring his shoulders, and striding confidently to the door.

However, the voice on the other side of the door wasn't the deep, threatening tone of Mr. Pierson's.

"Ava, it's for you!" Mac shouted, stepping back and gesturing the guest forward. Mac flashed a goofy smile at Ava before the unexpected visitor entered.

"Hello!" Penn said cheerily, waving at everyone in the living room with his free hand. His face was bright red from the cold, curls tamed under a navy ski cap. "I was just going to drop something off on the front step, but it's starting to snow again, and your lights looked so inviting . . . so, well, anyway. I'm here! Sorry for interrupting! I've been trying to call you, Ava. But you're busy, clearly, so I'll just leave this with you and get going—"

"No!" Ava shouted, scrambling up from the couch. She tried to tame her messy bun as she ran over to Penn in the entryway. "Don't go! You're not interrupting."

"Penn, it's so good to finally meet you!" Aunt Brene shouted on Ava's heels. "I've heard all about you!"

Ava's cheeks burned with embarrassment. Mac and Jacklyn had been teasing Ava about Penn all week.

"Good things, I hope?" Penn asked, smiling as he bounced up and down on his heels.

Aunt Brene beamed at him. "Only the nicest of things!"

"Do you want to join us?" Jacklyn shouted from the couch.

"No, but thank you!" Penn answered. "I don't want to stay too long, I just wanted to get your gift to you, Ava, before I head to Baltimore tomorrow for the rest of break."

"Wait," Ava said, noticing he didn't mention that Paola was waiting for him outside. "Did you bike over here? In the snow?"

"It wasn't a big deal or anything, it's not that . . . far," Penn lied, trailing off.

Ava followed his gaze around the room; Jacklyn and Mac weren't even trying to hide their raised eyebrows and wide grins. Then there was Mrs. Pierson, who stared at the TV, refusing to acknowledge Penn at all.

"Let's, uh, go to my room for a minute, will that work?" Ava asked.

Penn nodded enthusiastically. "Yeah, I think that'd be, that'd be best."

Ava led Penn up the stairs, her eyes shooting daggers over the railing at her family down below.

"Leave the door cracked!" shouted Jacklyn, sending Mac into a giggling fit.

Ava sighed as she shut her bedroom door behind her, relieved to be away from her siblings.

"Your house is—" Penn started to say as he took a seat on her desk chair.

"Way over decorated?" Ava guessed, plopping down onto her bed.

"No, it's just way bigger than I expected."

"Yikes," Ava said, biting her lower lip. "If you think that I'll make sure to never invite Kaysar over here. He'd never let me hear the end of it!"

Penn's gaze was surveying Ava's room, taking in old photos that had hung on the walls for years.

"I haven't changed my room since like the eighth grade; please don't judge me," Ava said, wishing he'd stop making her so nervous. Her palms were growing sweatier by the minute.

"Not judging," Penn said, finally bringing his eyes back to her face. "We should get you some new pictures, though. I'd, um, I'd like to be on your wall. *Damn it*, that sounded weird."

Ava laughed loudly, her nerves settling as she remembered it was just Penn sitting across from her. "No, not weird. I think I'd like that too."

Penn smiled, holding her gaze for a moment. "Anyways, I, uh, I got you something. It's not much but, I just, well, here."

He held out a package wrapped in silver wrapping paper, tied with a translucent white ribbon that glimmered as she moved it in the light.

"Th-thank you, I didn't expect . . . I mean you didn't have to . . . I didn't know you'd be coming over so I . . . ," Ava stuttered, wanting to bury her head in the snow accumulating outside.

"It's okay!" Penn shouted. "I didn't expect you to get me anything."

"I did get you something!" Ava exclaimed. "I just didn't wrap it yet."

"Go ahead and open your gift! You can give mine to me later."

Ava paused, observing him in his puffy coat, which he still hadn't removed. Her heart was pounding unusually fast in her chest. She wondered if his was too.

"Is your dad away on business tonight?" Penn asked.

Ava stared down at the half-unwrapped gift, unsure how to say it out loud. "He, um, he decided to . . . to move out."

Penn made a weird sound in his throat. "I really do ask *the worst* questions. I'm so sorry, Ava. That must be very hard for you."

Ava responded by ripping off the rest of the paper, escaping his invitation to talk about it. She pulled out a set of paintbrushes; their handles were long and delicate, stained a Tuscany red. She ran her fingers in the same direction as the wood grain.

"*These are beautiful,*" she marveled, looking up at Penn.

His attention was drawn to her back window as the snow began to fall quicker, each snowflake the size of a quarter. Olivia hopped up onto his lap and settled in. He patted her head gently as Ava looked back down to her gift.

Under the paintbrushes was a leather-encased journal with her name engraved on the front.

"I know you said you don't love poetry," Penn said, as she picked it up. "But you can write whatever you want in it! Anything at all. And there's some extra filler paper included when you fill up those pages. And the paintbrushes are you know, I'm sure you have some already, but Paola said these are the best."

"This is . . . it's all *perfect*, Penn. Really," Ava said, unsure how to properly thank him. She wanted to close the distance between them, but her legs felt heavy and useless.

"I'm so glad you—" Penn said.

"Let me find your gift! Hold on a second here . . ."

Ava stood and scrambled around her room, grateful to be able to do anything with her restlessness.

"Here it is!" she shouted from inside her closet. She handed it to Penn, her hand brushing his. "I'm sure you already, you know, have one of these for the new year but it looked like the one you have a-a-and there's a receipt you know, in case you want to return it."

"You got me a planner?" he asked, staring down at the plain black cover.

"W-well, yeah. Is that—" Ava sputtered.

"No! It's so thoughtful of you." Penn interrupted, flipping through the pages. "I hadn't bought a new one yet. Paola meant to, but, you know, she forgot about it so. It's exactly what I need!"

They smiled at one another, unsure what to do next.

"Do you want to talk about your dad?" Penn asked at the same time Ava blurted out, "Are you sure you don't want to stay?"

They laughed nervously.

"Well," Penn said. "I'll let you get back to your, uh, family and everything. Unless you do want to talk."

"No! You're right; I should get back downstairs," Ava answered, not wanting to talk about her father in the slightest. "But, really, you're welcome to watch movies with us and I can give you a ride later."

"No, no! I need to get back to Paola. We are getting up early tomorrow to visit the old neighborhood and see Kaysar and everything."

"Let me drive you home now then," Ava persisted.

"No, really. I enjoy riding my bike in the snow. I'll see you next Monday?"

Ava nodded. "Tell Kaysar I say hey?"

"You text him way more than I do now, but sure, I'll tell him."

Ava led Penn down the stairs, ignoring Mac and Jacklyn on the way out. She shut the door behind her and stood on the stoop, barefoot, the snow muffling the sounds around them.

"Hey, thanks again for my gifts," Ava said, her breath fogging in front of her.

Penn patted his hoodie pocket where he'd stashed his planner. "I'll use it every day!"

"Let me know that you get home safe, okay?" she asked, watching as he buckled his helmet.

"I will," he said, balancing himself on his bike. "See you in a little over a week!"

Ava smiled, watching him as he rode onto the street, disappearing into the snowy darkness. She exhaled into the night, enjoying the peacefulness of her neighborhood, trying to hold on to what she knew would be one of her favorite days for years to come.

"Oooooh, what did he get you?" Mac asked as soon as Ava stepped inside.

"Was the gift just a prop? Did he kiss you instead?" Jacklyn tagged on, puckering her lips.

"Leave her alone!" Aunt Brene shouted, pausing their movie. "He seems really nice Ava. And cute!"

"I'm going to bed," Ava said, long past the point of annoyance. She ran up the stairs as Jacklyn and Mac continued to pester her from the couch, Aunt Brene shushing them.

Alone in her room, Ava threw herself on her bed and opened the leather-bound journal from Penn. Before she clicked her pen, she stopped, noticing something written inside the front cover.

"*In case you need a safe place to hold your feelings. Or write your own pretentious poetry,*" it read in Penn's tiny scrawl.

Ava burst out laughing, rolling over to hold the journal close to her chest. She was interrupted by a quiet tapping on her door.

"Go away!" Ava yelled, not wanting to deal with Mac or Jacklyn anymore that evening.

"It's me," Mrs. Pierson said so softly Ava barely heard her.

"Oh, uh, come in," Ava said, stashing the journal under her covers.

Mrs. Pierson softly shut the door behind her. She sat at the foot of Ava's bed, her posture stiff and upright.

"He reminds me of someone," began Mrs. Pierson.

"Who? Penn?" Ava asked, jolting upward.

"Yes. He reminds me of someone I dated. Before your father."

"Really? I didn't know more than one of his kind existed," Ava said, trying to force her mom to lighten up.

"He was unique," she said in an even tone.

"Yeah . . . Penn is . . . well, he's Penn," Ava responded, trying to hide her smile.

"Mmm," Mrs. Pierson answered. "Be careful, okay?"

"Careful of, of what?" Ava asked, her forehead wrinkling.

"You remind me so much of myself when I was your age. Be careful that you start planning your own future, and don't get lost in someone else's."

Mrs. Pierson gently patted Ava's shoulder as she stood up. Ava tried to comprehend what her mother was saying.

"Wait, what happened?" Ava asked. "I mean obviously you married Dad, but what happened with that guy you say was like Penn?"

Mrs. Pierson hesitated, wringing her hands together. She looked up at Ava, her eyes the same piercing blue as Jacklyn's.

"He had bigger dreams than Westwood. But, I should say, at one point, so did I."

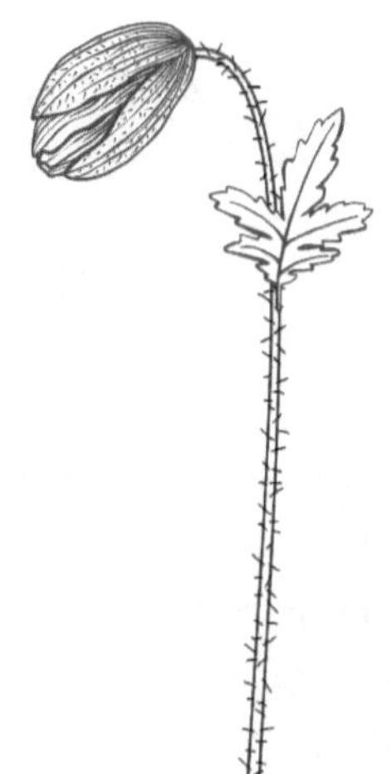

chapter twenty-five

Ava found Penn leaning against her locker, his nose buried deep in a book whose spine was held together by duct tape. Ava stood in front of him for several seconds before he noticed her. As soon as he did, he snapped his book shut, his face bright with excitement.

"Happy start of semester!" he exclaimed, unlatching his shoulder bag to put the book inside.

"It's a Monday," Ava groaned, fiddling with the combination on her locker as Penn stepped aside. "The first Monday back, at that. Why in the world are you so excited?"

"I love new semesters! So exciting! New classes, new possibilities."

"It truly is a miracle we became friends," Ava sighed, shoving books into her bag.

"AND," Penn shouted so that students passing by looked over at them funny. "It's my last semester at Westwood High! Can you believe it?!"

Ava's heart stopped. "I guess I . . . I didn't . . ."

"Only five more months 'til graduation!"

Ava slammed her locker door shut, but Penn wasn't paying any attention. His eyes were on the ceiling, his thoughts miles away from Westwood.

"Have you heard back from colleges yet?" Ava asked, trying to get him to land back in the present.

"Nah, too early. But hopefully soon!" Penn answered, striding down the hall. Ava hesitated before joining him, trying to think of what question to ask that would get some geographical clue as to where he thought he might end up.

"Are you coming?" Penn asked, stopping abruptly when he realized he was talking to himself. Ava jogged up beside him as he launched into updates about his trip to Baltimore. Although Ava opened her mouth several times to speak, Penn was all over the place this morning, jumping from topic to topic without stopping.

"See you in English?" Penn asked as they reached his classroom.

"Sure…see you," Ava responded, though Penn had already struck up a conversation with his teacher by the time she got any words out.

Ava was distracted for the rest of the morning, still unable to get a straight answer from Penn during English class about where he applied for college. When lunch arrived, Ava waited for him in their usual booth. She grew antsy as the minutes ticked by; Penn was never late. Surveying the lunchroom, anxiety pulsed through her. Without realizing it, she locked eyes with Trish, who waved warmly at her from across the room. Ava lifted her hand but quickly dropped it as Leona rolled her eyes.

"Sorry I'm late!" Penn gasped, out of breath. He sat down across from Ava and slid his lunch bag in her direction. "Had to meet with Mrs. P."

"About?"

"Oh yeah! I never got to tell you over break. The poetry reading competition Mrs. P mentioned to me before break is in March, so I've got to start preparing now! She wanted a few minutes to go over all the details and give me the registration papers."

"But you're already really good at performing, what do you have to prepare?"

"Everyone will be good at this thing! I've got to practice if I want a chance at placing. Anyway, enough about me. Have you had your new classes yet?"

"Not yet. I have Mr. Jenneman next—"

"Oh, he's awesome! You'll love him," Penn said, pulling out the forms Mrs. Papayanni had given to him.

"That's what Ms. Delic said," Ava said as Penn began to fill in his information.

"He's one of my favorite teachers! And your art class, you'll start that too?"

"Y-yeah," Ava said, a wave of nervousness rushing through her.

"I know you're worried about these new classes, but you will be great!" Penn assured her, glancing up from filling in his information.

"I know I just . . . *hate* being new to things. It's terrifying. What if I actually suck at art? What if—"

"Ava, I know it can be scary, but, I'm curious, have you thought about what if it all goes great? What if you end up loving your new classes?" Penn suggested, shifting his attention back to his forms.

Ava sighed heavily out of annoyance. Penn responded by scooting his lunch closer to her, knowing she hadn't eaten anything yet.

When the end of lunch bell rang, Ava felt extremely dissatisfied. She still hadn't managed to get anything out of Penn about his college options, and what little food she ate floated at the top of her stomach. When Penn left her side, Ava ran through the library to her favorite bathroom. She leaned against the tile wall near the sinks, trying to muster the strength to get through the rest of the school day.

The tardy bell rang, sending Ava into a panic and back into the hallway. She arrived in class as the bell rang, sinking into the last seat available, which happened to be directly in front of the teacher.

Mr. Jenneman leaned against the front of his desk, wearing an open flannel shirt with a faded sage-colored t-shirt underneath. His jeans were heavily worn and flecked with what looked like white paint. They stopped short at the ankle, revealing tall socks on his Birkenstock-laden feet.

He took his time in addressing the class, waiting as students settled into their unassigned seats. The class was rowdy, waiting for Mr. Jenneman to corral them, but he did nothing of the sort. It took several minutes before the students around Ava quieted on their own.

"Welcome," was all he said before beginning the roll call in a soothing, unassuming tone.

Ava turned around in her seat as Mr. Jenneman read out the names "Trish Sterling" and "Leila Zoet." She felt a small release of tension from her shoulders knowing two familiar faces sat behind her in class.

"Ava Pierson," Mr. Jenneman said, turning his spectacle-framed eyes toward her. "Are you Jacklyn Pierson's sister, by chance?"

"Y-yes," Ava answered, her face hot. She knew most teachers found her to be a disappointment in comparison to her sister.

When he finished taking attendance, Mr. Jenneman placed his pencil behind his ear and rolled up the attendance sheet. He stuck it in his front shirt pocket. Then he closed his eyes, and with the whole class watching, took a deep breath in and exhaled loudly, sighing out into the room. A couple students laughed, unsure how to react. Without opening his eyes, he did the same thing again, his exhale louder this time. After about the fifth round of this, the class grew impatient, nervous giggles issuing from around the room. Still, he continued to breathe.

"Join me," Mr. Jenneman eventually said, eyes still shut. "Inhale deeply, and exhale audibly."

Ava looked behind her left shoulder at Trish, who had a hand clapped over her mouth to keep herself from laughing. Leila, however, had closed her eyes and joined him.

"*Well, what the hell,*" Ava whispered to herself, joining him on the next round. Though her cheeks still burned in embarrassment, she joined him on the inhale, releasing her full breath on the exhale. After a few cycles, she found herself forgetting where she was, letting go of all the encroaching thoughts she'd had earlier in the bathroom.

"Now," Mr. Jenneman said after a few more minutes. "Open your eyes."

Ava blinked her eyelids open, noticing the classroom around her for the first time. She could hear the twitter of a bird outside and saw the room was bright as the sun bounced off the remaining snow outside and in through the windows. Her gaze returned to Mr. Jenneman, who was looking at her with curiosity.

"Ava, what were you feeling when you came into class today?" he asked nonchalantly.

Ava shifted in her seat, feeling several sets of eyes fall on her. "I . . . um . . . I guess . . . nervous?"

"And now?" he asked, tilting his head to one side.

Ava expected to still feel anxious and unsettled, as she did at the beginning of class. But something had shifted. "I-I-I think I feel . . . calmer?"

"That's wonderful, thank you for sharing. Leila, what about you?" he asked. "How do you feel right now?"

"I feel . . ."

Ava turned back toward Leila, whose blonde poofs had grown puffier since Ava had last seen her.

"*Grounded.*"

"Hmmm," was all Mr. Jenneman said. "And you, Xavier?" he asked, pointing to a boy Ava vaguely recognized in the back row.

"Awkward as hell, Mr. Jenneman," he answered, sending the rest of the class into a fit of laughter. Ava was surprised to see that Mr. Jenneman joined in on the laughter too.

"All very *valid* emotions, all of which are welcome here!" he exclaimed, crossing one sandal over the other. "Welcome to Psychology, my favorite subject in this whole weird wide world we live in.

"We'll start each class this way, taking a few minutes to breathe before we get started. I find it's important to check in with myself before opening my mind to others. I am, as you should know by now, Mr. Jenneman. I'll be your guide through the semester and hope to learn as much from you as you from me. I do, however, have a question before we begin. Let's see here, who would like to volunteer to answer before I ask it?"

Mr. Jenneman's eyes sparkled as he shifted his gaze around the room, nobody brave enough to respond.

"Trish, is it?" Mr. Jenneman asked after a while. Ava whipped her head around, surprised to find Trish's arm high up in the air. Trish nodded, her high ponytail springing up and down behind her. "Why did you decide to take this class?"

Trish half smiled, "Well, I heard it was an easy A for my senior year."

"I appreciate your honesty," Mr. Jenneman chuckled. "Here's the thing, I don't use scantron tests to determine your intelligence. But I do encourage you to participate in class as much as possible. If you're asking questions, I know you care. If you are filling up pages of your notebook as we go, I know you're learning. If you are struggling to understand a concept,

I want to know. Feel free to stop me during class to clarify. We all learn in our own way and at our own pace. I will warn you, however, if you think you can sit idly by until exams, that easy A is going to look more like a well-earned D."

Ava sat up straight in her seat, intrigued by Mr. Jenneman but also skeptical. She'd gotten by well enough in school by lying low during class and passing her exams. The thought of having to raise her hand every class period made her sick to her stomach.

"Let's see here, would anyone else like to answer why you decided to take this class?"

The class went quiet again, eyes darting everywhere to avoid Mr. Jenneman. When no one answered for several minutes, Ava felt her hand leave her desk and rise into the air. She stared at it, shocked to find it was attached to her.

"Yes, Ava?" Mr. Jenneman gestured toward her.

"Well . . . I, um . . . I was interested in . . . maybe studying . . ." Ava felt everyone's eyes on her again. She swallowed loudly. "Art therapy. So, Ms. Delic told me this would be a good class . . . for me."

"Interesting! Why art therapy?" Mr. Jenneman asked, leaning forward at the waist.

"I-I, um, well, I guess I really like art and think Ms. Delic's job is interesting, like helping people and stuff seems pretty cool."

"*Fascinating!* You see, already, these answers, the reasons you decided to take this class, vary among you!

"The Greek origin of the word 'psychology' translates to 'study of the soul' or 'science of the soul.' Psychology not only allows us to become more attuned to our inner selves, but it also helps us to understand and connect better with those around us. I know what some of you might be thinking, '*Mr. Jenneman is a hippy dippy weirdo who meditates at the beginning of class, and psychology is an easy-pass class*' . . . but here's the thing, people! Psychology is backed by science and research! This stuff *works*! This stuff, if you let it, can change the way you live and interact with the world. It's better than magic, kids. It's, well, *psychology*," he said, using his hands to fan out and up in the air.

"Each of you sitting in this classroom is so unique, not only physically, but behaviorally. You're made up of your own experiences as much as you are your DNA. Many different factors led you into this classroom, where it's my greatest honor to introduce you to, and hopefully captivate you through, the learning of this boundless subject area.

"This syllabus here," he pointed toward another rolled up paper in his jean pocket. "Is a guideline. If we need to spend an extra week on something, let's do it. If we cover several topics in one class period, so be it. We take our time here, we make our own choices, we each learn in our own ways, and we respect that. Are you all with me?"

Ava surveyed the classroom, catching Trish's eye again. Trish raised her eyebrows, causing Ava to break out into nervous giggles. With a half-hearted nod from the class, Mr. Jenneman continued explaining the topics they would cover over the semester.

At the end of class, Ava found she didn't want to leave. She'd never been more engaged in a class, and the fear of speaking up had already lessened after doing it twice in the past hour.

"Ava!" Mr. Jenneman called to her as she joined the wave of students exiting the classroom. "Come see me for a moment?"

Ava nodded, her heart racing as she approached his desk. It was rare a teacher noticed her at all.

"I apologize for asking if you are Jacklyn's sister. I bet you get that question a lot," Mr. Jenneman said, taking a seat behind his desk.

"Well yeah, but it's okay," Ava stuttered, caught off guard that he remembered.

"If it made you uncomfortable, it's not okay. I come from a family of six brothers, so I should know better than to ask that question. You are your own person, Ava, and I want you to know you are free to be whoever *you* are in this class."

"I, um, well, thank you, Mr. Jenneman, sir," Ava said, nervously shifting her feet back and forth.

"Sure thing! And Ava," he said, leaning back into his chair. "If you have any questions about the field of psychology, please ask. I know college can be a scary thing to think about. I don't know how you kids are expected to figure it out so soon but, if art therapy is something you are interested in, I'm here to help, alongside Ms. Delic."

"I, um . . . I . . . thank you, Mr. Jenneman. I'll try or, um, if I have any questions I'll try to ask."

"Even if you have to write them out first and hand them to me, that's okay too. I was an anxious kid when I was your age. Still am, in the right situation. Anxiety is funny like that. It took a long time for me to find coping skills to pursue what I love. I turned out alright though. I have no doubt you will too."

"Th-thanks, Mr. Jenneman. I'm just not really used to . . . I've never been good at speaking up in class."

"You did great today, Ava. Just as well as everybody else. I've found it's much easier to speak up in an environment that feels nonjudgmental. Unfortunately, the world doesn't give us enough of those. I hope to hear more from you! Let me know if I can do anything to make it easier. This class has been shaped over time by feedback from my students, and I hope it continues to be. Now, you might want to get going. You don't want to make your friends over there late for class."

Ava followed his gaze over to Trish and Leila, hovering right outside the door. Ava smiled at Mr. Jenneman in thanks, then walked gingerly toward the two girls.

"Hey!" Trish exclaimed. "It's like a volleyball team reunion!"

"Hi Ava!" Leila said. "We'll have to sit by each other tomorrow!"

"S-sure," Ava said, overcome with the kindness pouring in from all directions. "Sounds great, but I've really got to get going to my next class."

"Me too!" responded Leila. "See you tomorrow?"

Ava nodded, then turned down the hallway.

"Wait!" Trish yelled, following behind Ava. Ava stopped, hoping Trish wouldn't bring up Bradley or Leona. "Look, I know things are kind of weird, because of—"

"I've really got to get to class."

"Wait! I'm just trying to say, screw Leona! *Seriously!* Thank you for saying what you did at my house! I'm sick of how she treats me, and I have been for a long time. I just . . . I didn't know how to say it out loud. I'm so glad you did. And, like, just because you're not friends with Leona anymore doesn't mean you and I can't be friends."

"I . . . ," Ava struggled to respond; their relationship seemed too complex to discuss in between classes.

"We don't have to talk about Bradley or anything that happened if you don't want to! We can go get ice cream or something and talk about how weird but strangely attractive Mr. Jenneman is."

"*What?* You think he's cute?"

"I mean not in like a conventional way, or anything. But like in a 'respects-intelligent-women-and-doesn't-care-what-he-looks-like' kind of way."

"If you say so," Ava muttered, worried about Trish's taste in men.

"But really! Let's hang out!"

"Yeah, I guess we haven't really hung out, just you and I, have we?" Ava asked, considering it.

"No, but we should!" Trish said, her pink eyeshadow sparkling under the hallway light. "Actually, do you think it would . . . do you think I could . . ."

"Trish, really, I'd love to hang sometime, but I need to get going to my next class."

"Ah, me too! But, could I maybe sit with you and Penn at lunch from now on? I know you guys are kind of a thing—"

"Oh, y-yes. I mean, no! I mean, no we are definitely not a thing, but yes, of course you can sit with us."

Trish beamed at Ava, thanking her before running down the hall.

Ava took off, fighting the tardy bell as she made her way down to the basement for art class. She paused near the classroom door, taking a deep breath as students passed around her. The doubting, negative voices that usually swarmed in her mind like a colony of bees were nowhere to be found. Ava cursed Penn for being right as she stepped forward, curious to find what she might learn in her new class.

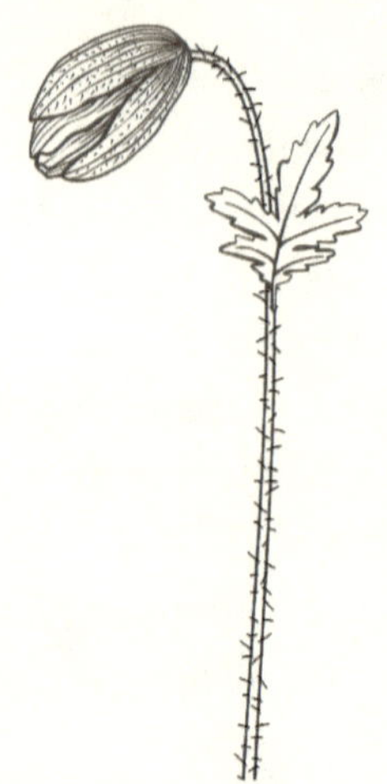

chapter twenty-six

January blew in and out of Westwood, leaving behind a gray slush that framed the roads on Ava's way to Baile Avenue. Stuck behind an ambling Oldsmobile, Ava's thoughts hovered on her mother. She had gone back to work last week full time and had even started helping Aunt Brene prep dinner in the evenings. Their household was unrecognizable now that it was full of so much warmth and laughter.

As the Oldsmobile turned left, Ava sped up, heading straight toward Penn's neighborhood. She smiled as she thought of Mr. Jenneman's class, how she'd spoken up several times over the past weeks, her voice growing more confident each time. Even lunch had become more enjoyable, with Trish and Leila joining Penn and Ava in their booth. Ava couldn't believe how long it had been since she'd wished to hide under her covers until high school was over.

Ava turned right, then parked in an open space across from Penn's house, keeping the driveway open as Paola requested. Inside the garage, Ava spotted two figures milling about. The melody of Kaysar's sarcastic tones interspersed with Paola's throaty laugh warmed Ava as she jogged through the cold to reach them.

"Ava!" Kaysar exclaimed. He embraced her, picking her up so that her feet dangled a few inches off the ground.

"Hey!" Paola yelled from beneath a rickety fold-out table as she tried to straighten a bent leg. "Thanks for coming!"

"Of course! Can I, um, help you?" Ava asked as Kaysar set her down.

"No, no! I got it," Paola shouted, hoisting herself up with the support of one of the metal chairs. The table still sloped down quite a bit on one side. Kaysar adjusted it further when Paola wasn't looking. "Can you guys help me set out the paint and drawing paper? I can't remember where I put it all."

"I think I can guess where it is," Kaysar answered, raising an eyebrow in Ava's direction. He motioned her inside the house. Ava followed him toward Paola's room, noting the smell of freshly brewed coffee that Penn must have enjoyed before leaving earlier that morning.

Kaysar led her into Paola's bedroom toward the closet. Ava's eyes traveled around the room, the true chaos of Paola's nature exploding around them. Her bed consisted of a lone full-sized mattress without a frame, sitting directly on the floor, with a mess of twisted white sheets and a feathery down comforter that hung off the side. The walls were covered with test strips of various paints, ranging in an array of brilliant colors. Ava knew it wasn't supposed to look like anything, but it had become a work of art all on its own.

"Shit!" Kaysar shouted from the closet as a mountain of junk cascaded onto his head. Ava ran to his side, helping to free him from a tangle of ribbon.

"I swear if she wasn't like a second mother to me," Kaysar complained, tossing aside a dried-up paint rag.

"Is it this stuff?" Ava asked, pointing to a tub of half-used paints, wrinkled paper, and packets of new paint brushes sitting on the bottom shelf next to cleaning supplies.

"I bet it is. Have mercy on us all," Kaysar muttered.

Ava pulled the tub out as Kaysar tried to organize the clutter back into Paola's closet. Together they walked back into the garage to find Paola frantically searching for something else.

"I swear I put it . . . Oh! I know where it is!" Paola said to herself, walking past Kaysar and Ava.

Kaysar waited until Paola was entirely out of earshot before asking, "How did Penn get out of this again?"

"He's checking out the stage he'll be performing on next month for his poetry competition," Ava answered. "But don't think I didn't notice the coincidence!"

Ava had asked Penn several times over the past week to reschedule, but Penn insisted he couldn't miss it. The competition was far more important to him than Ava had realized. Kaysar began to set the paint out on the tables as Ava did her best to smooth out the wrinkled drawing paper.

"Tell me why you thought it was a good idea to start this in the middle of February?" Kaysar demanded as Paola came back into the garage, balancing a tray of solo cups filled with water.

"Oh, Kaysar, stop; it's not that cold!" Paola said cheerily as a swift wind blew into the open garage, ruffling the paper and toppling over paint bottles. She ignored Kaysar's told-you-so expression. "It's good to get some fresh air in the winter months!"

Kaysar rolled his eyes and huddled near the small heater in the corner of the garage. Ava joined him to rub her own hands above the heat. Paola continued to hum in her thin sweater, content to freeze until a small group of people appeared at the bottom of the driveway.

"You brought everyone!?" Paola shouted at Mei and her boys as they drew near. "You didn't have to do that!"

Mei's oldest son wore a scowl similar to Kaysar's upon meeting Ava.

"Hi, Ava! Kaysar!" Mei said, beaming as she introduced the five boys.

"Boys, sit wherever you'd like!" Paola shouted as she turned to greet a handful of other neighborhood families who arrived after Mei, all bundled up in their winter gear.

"Damn it, we're going to need more seats," Kaysar noted, stepping away from the heater. Ava followed him into the house, her nerves spiking as she realized it would be a crowded class.

By the time everyone arrived, every space around the tables was occupied. The word had traveled fast, as it turned out many families were desperate for a way to get out of the house in February. Parents stood to the side, catching up with one another as Paola started the class.

"First things first!" Paola said, smiling warmly. "I have a couple of rules I like to tell my college students."

The garage grew quiet, eyes growing large on each child's face at the mention of rules.

"They aren't scary, I promise! Number one: it's okay to mess up. In fact, it's welcome. Number two: It's okay to have fun. In fact, it's encouraged. Number three: it's okay, in fact, it's a *beautiful* thing, to admire our neighbor's artwork, as long as we find something to admire about our work too. Sound good?"

A couple of kids giggled as they nodded their heads in agreement. Then Paola swept them away, encouraging everyone, including parents, to dive in. The hour flew by, with Ava and Kaysar helping to open difficult paint lids, mix colors, answer questions, and refill cups with fresh water. Ava found herself lost in the thrill of it, amazed at the breadth of imagination each child brought to their art. Mei's boys took to Kaysar especially, all refusing to leave at the end of the hour. Mei eventually bribed them away with promises of lunch somewhere other than the restaurant, but not before Kaysar gave several high fives to each of them.

"Well, I'll say that was a success!" Paola announced once the garage was clear except for the three of them again. "Even if it was a *tad* chilly."

"It is below freezing, Paola!" Kaysar argued, raising his hands in disbelief. Ava tried to hide her laughter as she cleaned up tables. "For the next one it better be in the forties, at least!"

"How did it go!?" Penn asked as he bounced happily up the driveway.

"Oh, *now* you show up, after we've done all the cleaning?" Kaysar accused, slapping Penn on the shoulder. "How'd your poetry thing go?"

"It went really well! I have some tough competition. There's this girl from Scranton who is reading "Still I Rise" by Maya Angelou, and I won't be surprised if she wins the whole thing."

Ava waved at Penn, noticing the gleam in his eye from what sounded like a great rehearsal. She screwed the cap on the last open bottle of paint.

"Hate to cut in here guys but could we maybe go inside and talk?" Ava asked. "My hands are numb."

"You know my answer to that!" answered Kaysar, grabbing the paint bottles from Ava before running inside the house.

"Oh hey, Ava, you have some . . . ," Penn leaned over the table that separated the two of them to wipe something off the top of her cheek. Ava glanced up and found herself reflected in his glasses, which he'd been wearing more often since Trish's party.

"Got it! Just some paint, it looks like." He held up his finger to show her. "How did it really go today?"

"It went . . . great, actually," Ava said, tightening her ponytail. "I had a lot of fun helping out and meeting your neighbors. It was so good to hang out with Kaysar for the first time since the party."

"I know he was so excited to see you! I mean, he never really shows his excitement, but I could just tell. You two didn't have too much fun without me though, right?" Penn asked, dropping his gaze to the top of his oxfords and shoving his hands deep into his pockets.

Ava furrowed her eyebrows, trying to figure out if Penn was joking. When he didn't look up, she cleared her throat. "We obviously wished you could have been here."

His head shot up instantly. "I was kidding!"

He laughed awkwardly, enough so that Ava knew he wasn't at all. She grinned in response before turning toward the door to head inside.

"Wait I, uh, I've been meaning to, uh, ask you something!" Penn stammered behind her.

Ava froze to the spot, her nervous system kicking into overdrive. "Do you want to maybe go to Mei's sometime. Just you and me? No offense to Paola or Kaysar or anything, but, I don't know, we haven't had much time to ourselves lately."

Ava's mind was racing, her back still turned to him.

"No pressure! Or anything," Penn said. Ava turned slowly. "It doesn't have to be formal. I just thought it might be nice, you know, to have a meal together that isn't in the Westwood High cafeteria."

Ava searched his face for clues as to what he was asking her to do. "I-I . . . um . . . s-sure. I mean, yeah. Yes."

"Great! Maybe next Friday night? Pick me up at six thirty?" Penn smiled as he said it, but Ava was spiraling, wondering what it would mean if their dynamic were to change. Even if she was learning to appreciate change, she didn't know if she was ready for it when it came to her and Penn's friendship.

"That seems pretty early for dinner."

"Well, that way we get a table before the rush!"

"You don't think Mei will save a table for us?" Ava asked, her voice harsher than she meant for it to sound.

"Oh gosh, you're right!" Penn said, swatting his own forehead with his hand. "I should make a reservation. Why didn't I think of that? Of course, you make a reservation when you take someone on a—"

"*HEY!*" Kaysar shouted, swinging open the door behind them. "What the hell are you two doing out here? If Paola asks me to dance with her one more time, I'll be honest, I'm going to lose my damn mind."

Penn held Ava's gaze for a moment before apologizing to Kaysar. He stepped around her, the smell of him filling her senses as he passed. Ava didn't move, listening as Penn and Kaysar's footsteps disappeared inside the house, the door cracked open for her.

Ava's eyes trailed down the drive, noticing the cracks in the concrete as small flakes of snow drifted lazily to the ground. The wind blew into the garage and whipped through her hair, shifting the present sharply into focus. With a rare spark of clarity, Ava knew it was time to be honest with herself, honest about something she'd been feeling for a long time. Though she knew it began with releasing the illusion that a friend is all Penn had ever been to her.

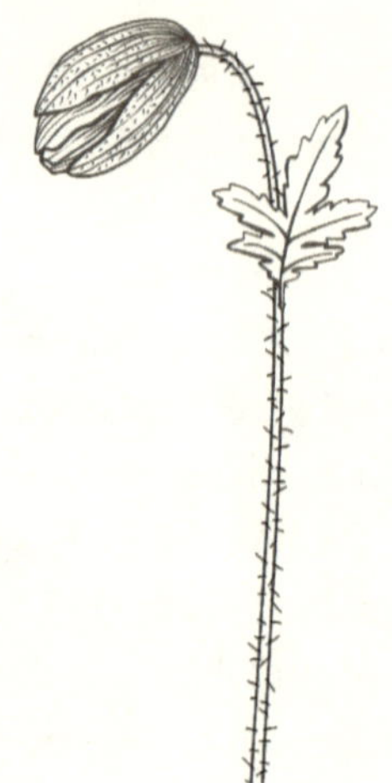

chapter twenty-seven

Though Paola tried to convince Ava to stay for dinner that evening, Ava found herself exhausted, albeit very fulfilled, after working with kids all afternoon. She drove home with the music off, yawning every few minutes. With hopes of hiding for the rest of the evening, Ava slipped in through the back door. Thinking the coast was clear, she snuck down the back hall and past the kitchen. She made it all the way to the bottom of the main stairs when Jacklyn shouted at her from the living room.

"And where have *you* been?" Jacklyn asked, pausing the video game she was playing with Mac.

"Come on!" Mac erupted from his side of the couch. "I was just about to pass you up!"

Ava exhaled in annoyance, missing, for a split second, the quiet of their home before Aunt Brene had moved in.

"Were you with Penn?" Jacklyn asked, smirking, her chin resting on the back of the couch.

"No, I had a, like, art class thing with Paola and Kaysar."

"Oh yeah! That's why it was just me serving lunch at Mei's today; I totally forgot! How did it go?"

Ava backed away from the stairs and came to sit on the couch arm nearest to Jacklyn.

"It was so much fun, actually. Way more fun than I thought it would be!"

"That's awesome, Sis!"

"Yeah, it was pretty great."

"That's wonderful, and all," Mac said, glaring at both of them. "But I was about to leave Jacklyn in the dust before you showed up, Ava."

"Mac, there are more important things than video games," Jacklyn said, popping a cheesy puff into her mouth from the bag in front of her.

"Jacklyn, STOP!" Mac yelled. "You're getting that gross cheese all over my controller!"

Jacklyn waved him off with her orange-stained fingertips. "So, you didn't see Penn at all then?"

"I mean, well, yeah, I did. It was weird," Ava hesitated, not sure she wanted anyone to make a big deal out of it. But Ava was still so confused, she couldn't help herself. "I don't know, I think he might have asked me . . . well, he asked me to go to dinner."

"WHAT!?!" Jacklyn jumped up, sending the game controller flying across the room.

"*Seriously, Jacklyn?*" shouted Mac, flying off the couch to make sure his precious controller was okay.

"Tell me everything!" Jacklyn demanded, grabbing Ava by the shoulders. Ava thought she would be annoyed by it, but it felt nice to talk to her sister about something that had nothing to do with their parents, Bradley, or Leona. She smiled as déjà vu hit her, remembering in eighth grade how she ran straight up to Jacklyn's room to tell her all the details of her first kiss.

"He invited me to Mei's on Friday night. Just him and me."

"THAT'S HUGE! That's definitely a date! How could it not be?"

"Well," Mac chimed in, calm now that he knew his controller wasn't damaged. "I do think he likes you, Ava, I always have. But he is seriously nice to *everyone*. He really could just want to take a friend to dinner."

"Mac!" Jacklyn's hands flew up in the air. "Are you kidding me?! You've always been with me on this!"

Mac shook his head. "If he was going to make a big move, I think he would've done it at Christmas. I kind of lost hope after that. Paint brushes are cool, and all, but if I really like somebody, I just come right out and say it."

"Don't listen to him," Jacklyn said, turning her back to Mac. "He's only thirteen. I think Penn knows you well enough to not spring it on you until you're ready to hear it. More importantly, what are you going to wear?"

"I don't know. I haven't even thought about it!" Ava felt stressed about the whole thing. "I may need you to bring me some options, unless I can come raid your things when Leona isn't around."

"Actually," Jacklyn shifted uncomfortably from side to side. "I found a new place to live."

"What?!" shouted Mac and Ava in unison.

"Yeah, it might sound a little crazy, but Mei has space over the restaurant. She offered it to me if I'd help fix it up and pay utilities. It will be a lot of work, but she said she'll let me live there as long as I need. I told her it's too generous, but you know Mei. She wants me to save up for my classes this summer."

"What classes?" Mac asked, sounding as dumbstruck as Ava felt.

"Oh, yeah, I'm starting classes at Everton Community College," Jacklyn said as if it were the most obvious thing in the world. "I'm going to pay for my classes with the money I earn at the restaurant."

"But can't you just, like, ask Mom to pay for school? Now that Dad's gone, I'm sure she would help."

"I could, but I'd rather do this on my own. They have this tutoring program I applied for that will help me get a discount on classes. This way I can complete my GenEds for relatively cheap and hopefully get a scholarship when it's time to go for my bachelor's."

Ava stared at her sister, stunned. "What do you think you would get your bachelor's in? I thought you hated your business classes?"

"Ugh, yeah, I did. I plan on majoring in Political Science this time around, actually."

"*Politics?*" Mac asked, repulsed. "Are you trying to become president or something?"

"Maybe someday," Jacklyn responded with full confidence. "But I'd really like to become the mayor of Westwood first."

"Why in the world would you want to do that?" Mac asked.

"That way, when there's corruption in this town, I might have the ability to do something about it."

Pangs of overwhelming love broke forth inside of Ava as it reaffirmed Jacklyn would never stop trying to protect those she cared about. It made perfect sense she would choose a career dedicated to keeping the people and the town she loved safe.

"Dang, that's pretty cool!" said Mac, breaking the silence. He threw the controller back over to Jacklyn and unpaused their video game. "Will you hire me as your bodyguard?"

"Boom! Take that!" Jacklyn shouted as her car passed Mac's on the screen again. "If you are a better bodyguard than driver, I'll consider it."

As Jacklyn and Mac continued to shout at one another, Ava left the couch and headed to her room, grateful for the opportunity to climb in bed. She nestled in beneath her covers, closing her eyes as Olivia settled in around her legs. Aunt Brene's voice carried up to her from the kitchen, calling her down for dinner. But Ava wasn't able to move, her body heavy. She drifted off to sleep, contentment draping itself over her as an extra layer of warmth.

* * *

Friday turned out to be the first warm day of the new year. It was one of those days where the world felt light and glorious. The birds twittered loudly outside, waking Ava up to a pounding heart. She ran to her window and threw open the blinds, inviting the sun to wake her sleepy face. Smiling into the light, Ava watched as a blue jay hopped from branch to branch.

"You decent?" shouted Mac as he flung the door open.

"Well, thank God I am, Mac, what in the—"

"It's the big day, isn't it! The big date!" Mac smiled at her as he flopped onto the bed, his hair growing shaggier by the day.

"*I thought you said it wasn't a date,*" Ava hissed, ripping her drawer open in search of a spring top under her bulky winter sweaters.

"I could ask him if it is, you know. I still have his number."

Ava jolted upright. "Absolutely not!"

Mac laughed hysterically as he stood back up. "Fine. I'll just have Jacklyn give me the play-by-play later tonight."

"Shit, I didn't even think about that. She better not tell you anything!"

Mac chuckled as he got up to leave but paused in the doorway. "I'm happy for you. You deserve someone like Penn."

Ava blinked a few times, Mac's words sinking in. She heard the door shut behind him and tried to wipe the silly smile spreading across her face. The smell of rising bread wafted up from the kitchen, snapping Ava back to the present. She threw herself together and ran down to see Aunt Brene.

"You don't have to make us breakfast every . . . ," Ava said, stepping out of the way as Aunt Brene came through with a hot pan of bacon.

"I know I don't have to, but I want to!"

"Is Mom up yet?" Ava asked, popping a fresh raspberry from a bowl on the counter into her mouth.

"Yes, actually," Aunt Brene said, coming back through to grab what Ava discovered were croissants fresh out of the oven. "She got up early to run some errands and is doing the grocery shopping today."

"Wow, that's good news. Has she, um . . . has she heard from . . ."

"James? No, but she seems to be taking it very well," Aunt Brene said, pausing as she took stock of all the food she'd made. She checked the oven and stovetop to make sure everything was turned off, then gave her full attention to Ava. "How are you dealing with all of this, darling? I've been so busy helping Amelia put things in order, I haven't checked in with you in a while."

"Oh, I don't know, he wasn't really around much anyway," Ava said hoarsely, snacking on the surrounding food to keep herself from having to be too honest with her aunt. "And when he was, it felt like we were all just kind of tiptoeing around him."

Aunt Brene clucked her tongue in her mouth as she motioned Ava over to the table to sit with her. "That's just no way to live . . . especially for you kids. I know your mom had her own reasons for staying with him, and

I can't judge her for it; heck, we had our own mess of a childhood. But you don't deserve this. She doesn't either. I wish he wouldn't have threatened Amelia to make me stay away all those years ago. But oh, Ava. I'm sorry. I need to watch what I say about him. He's still your father, even if he hasn't been, well, anyway. He's still your father and you can feel however you want to feel about all of this."

"I . . . I don't know what to feel. I feel like I am supposed to miss him, but honestly, I don't know if I do," Ava said, looking down at her plate, feeling guilty for saying it out loud.

"Oh, sweetheart," Aunt Brene whispered, reaching over to pat Ava's forearm. "That's completely valid. But if you do miss him, someday, that's okay too. I wish it were easier in these situations, to separate out what we know is healthy for us from emotions and memories and what we thought was love. Anyway, I didn't mean to air my grievances all over the kitchen. I just, I worry now that work is expecting me back soon and I don't want to leave you all . . ."

"We'll be okay, Aunt Brene, if you need to get back home," Ava assured her. As much as she didn't want her aunt to leave, she'd already done so much for them. "We're not little kids anymore. We understand you've got a life to go back to."

"I suppose you're right," Brene sighed. "Jacklyn said the same thing when I spoke with her. It looks like Amelia is going to all of her therapy appointments and she seems to be enjoying work again. And I forget you kids are growing up so fast; I hate how much of your childhood I missed. Anywho, I heard someone has a big date tonight?"

"Well, I . . . I don't know if it's . . ."

"Is it Penn, the boy that came over here for Christmas? He sure seemed nice!" Aunt Brene exclaimed.

"Yeah he's, he's . . ."

"Jacklyn did say he's a little nerdy."

"I wouldn't call him *nerdy*."

"Oh, nerdy is a good thing! She says he treats you with care and respect, and honey, that's the most important thing to look for in a partner."

"Yeah, well, I don't know if we'll ever be anything more than friends. It might just be dinner."

"Well, either way. It doesn't hurt to have a friend like that, now does it?"

Ava smiled, her face growing hot as she thought about picking up Penn later that evening. She shoveled food down her throat, hoping Aunt Brene didn't notice.

* * *

The school day passed in an insignificant manner, with Penn not mentioning much about dinner other than to solidify that she'd still pick him up at 6:30 on the dot. He seemed nervous and distracted through English and lunch, barely engaging with any of Ava's questions.

When Ava arrived later that evening at Penn's house, the sun was just beginning to set; brilliant streaks of fuchsia intermixed with gold spread vast across the sky. Paola stood on the lawn, barefoot, trying to capture it with her ancient Polaroid camera.

"Hey Paola!" Ava shouted as she made her way up the sidewalk.

"Hi there, beautiful! I brought this camera out here to take a picture of Penn and you, but do you see this sunset?"

"Ma, have you seen my—," Penn yelled to Paola, craning his head out the front door, shirtless. "Shit! Ava! You're here! Just, uh, just give me a second and I'll be right out!"

He slammed the door shut. Ava tried not to laugh at the whole scene, as Paola was too preoccupied with capturing the sunset to notice anything amiss. She joined Paola in the grass, crossing her arms across her chest as the setting sun took its warmth with it. A chill rose on her neck, but Ava wasn't sure if it was from the cold or from nerves. Seeing Penn outside of his usual context, especially without a shirt on, was kickstarting a whole new level of anxiety in her.

After what felt like an eternity, Penn burst forth through the front door and down the front steps. Wearing, to Ava's relief, a black t-shirt, a nice pair of jeans, and the same blazer he'd worn to Trish's party.

"Sorry I'm running late!" he said, jogging to meet them in the grass, his arms flying up in the air. "You know I hate being late, but I couldn't find this blazer and, wait, Ma, *what are you doing with the Polaroid?*"

"I got distracted by this marvelous view, but I want a picture of Ava and you."

Penn's face grew serious. "Ma, I told you, several times, we will not be making a big deal out of tonight. You promised you would *not* bring that antique out of your closet."

"It's not a big deal!" Paola argued. "It's just a picture! Please, please, please! Just one?"

Penn closed his eyes and raised his chin to the sky. Ava brought her hand to her mouth, not doing a good job of hiding her laughter.

"I'm totally okay with it," Ava said when Penn refused to budge. Paola's face lit up, but Penn's expression remained strained. Paola reached forward and shook Penn's shoulder in desperation.

"*Fine!*" he said, exasperated. "Just one!"

"Yay!" Paola shouted, doing a victory shake with her shoulders. "Okay, you two go right there in front of the house, in the middle of the sidewalk. Perfect!"

Ava could hear Penn's strangulated breathing as Paola took several minutes to line up the shot. They stood next to each other, not touching, both unsure of what to do with their bodies.

"Penn, put your arm around her or something!" Paola shouted, finally ready. "At least act like you like each other!"

"Is it okay if I put my arm around you?" he asked Ava. Ava nodded yes, though she wondered if he could sense how nervous she was. As Penn draped an arm over her shoulder, she looked up at him, and without over-thinking it, slid her arm around his waist. Ava thought she saw his eyes light up in response, but this was quickly erased as Paola continued to shout different cues at them.

"If you don't take the picture right now, we're leaving!" Penn threatened, but he pulled Ava closer to his side as he said it. He felt the cold on her skin as he did so.

"Here, take this," Penn said, taking off his blazer.

"No, I'm okay, it won't look right for the picture."

"Who cares about this stupid picture, please put it on. You're freezing."

Ava tried not to roll her eyes as she put it on but was relieved as the warmth spread over her. Penn pulled her back into him and shot his mom a thumb's up.

"Oh, it's even cuter with her wearing your jacket! On the count of three! One . . . two . . . three!" Paola snapped the picture right on three, at which Ava was pretty sure she blinked, but she knew better than to ask for a retake.

"Let's get out of here before she convinces us to take another," Penn said, releasing Ava and striding purposefully toward the Jeep. Ava waved goodbye to Paola, who was too busy fiddling with the camera to notice. Penn held her car door open for her, causing Ava's stomach to contort at the weirdness of being ushered into her own car.

"Thanks for picking me up! Did you have a good rest of your school day?" Penn asked once they were both inside, his knees bobbing up and down on the floorboard.

"Yeah, I guess so," Ava answered, backing out of the driveway, her hands clammy on the steering wheel. "I don't know how he does it, but Mr. Jenneman can make even the scientific method seem interesting."

"*Right!?* Love that guy, he's who urged me to look more into sociology as a major, and why I think I'll double major in English and sociology wherever I end up going. It may not be the best money-making combination, but, ah well, do what you love, isn't that what they say?"

"Right," Ava said, though she wasn't sure who "they" were. "What did your dad do, if you don't mind my asking? I know you said he was some type of professor."

"Yeah! He was an English Professor at Towson University."

"Is that what you want to be? A professor?" Ava asked, pulling onto Main Street. The road was lined bumper to bumper on either side with cars. She'd forgotten how everyone in Westwood flocked downtown on the first nice day of the year.

"Just park behind Mei's! She lets Ma do it all the time," Penn said, pointing in the direction of the hidden parking lot.

"I'm not sure if I'll end up being a professor like my dad was," Penn continued as Ava pulled into the lot. "I like sociology because it allows for better understanding of society and an opportunity to solve important human issues. I love English, as you know, because I think writers have this amazing gift of helping people feel less alone in the world. To me, the majors are more alike than you'd be led to believe. I think, whatever I do, if it involves helping people and learning more about the world around me, I'll be happy. If it's as a professor, I wouldn't be mad about it."

Ava tried to look interested, as she was very engaged with what Penn was saying. Still, as she parked in the last remaining spot behind Mei's, she thought she might have a heart attack from how fast her heart was beating in her chest.

"Shall we?" Penn asked, getting out of the car to open her door for her. He was bouncing so high on his heels, Ava thought he might take off in the night sky.

Ava tried to take in every detail as they walked through the small alley leading to the front of Mei's. Her eyes lingered on the small strip of neon orange sunlight still visible above the shops across the street. Penn stepped up to open the door wide for her when they reached it, his smile bordering on erratic. Ava braced herself as the loud noises of the restaurant met her full force.

Jacklyn stood behind the hostess stand, giggling at the sight of Penn and Ava framed in the doorway. If Ava felt nervous before, she was now falling face-first into mortification.

"Have you two dined with us before?" Jacklyn joked as they approached her, much to Ava's dismay. Mei waved at them from across the room as she took an order from a big party.

"We set up a special table, just for the two of you," Jacklyn said, winking. Ava thought she might die on the spot. She refused to make eye contact with Penn, afraid he might decide to cancel the night out and never talk about it again.

Jacklyn led them through the main dining area and toward a steel spiral staircase at the back of the restaurant. Ava followed directly behind Jacklyn, noticing how the noise grew quieter with each upward step. It was one of those rare times Ava wished to be hidden in the crowd rather than removed from it. The stairs opened up into a small landing at the top, big enough for a single table for two. They were so high up in the restaurant that they were level with the head of the dragon.

"Wow! This is great!" exclaimed Penn, leaning over the railing to look at the dining room below.

"I didn't even know this was here," Ava observed, trying to catch her breath. Penn's hand grazed hers, and she quickly moved away, happy to have Jacklyn there to interrupt the moment.

"It was for storage!" Jacklyn chimed in, beaming at the two of them. "But Mei and I thought it might be perfect for . . . special occasions. And we thought you two would be the perfect couple, or pair, whatever, to test it out first!"

The sight of the table, complete with a burning candle in the middle of it, sent Ava's stomach toppling over the railing and to the floor below. She thought Jacklyn might burst with happiness as Penn pulled out her chair for her. Ava widened her eyes at her sister, jerking her head to the stairs.

"I'll leave you two alone," Jacklyn said, getting the hint. But as soon as she left, Ava wished she would come back. The sight of Penn, eyes lit up from the burning flame, eliminated any control she had left of her nerves. She cringed as she scooted forward, her chair scraping loudly across the floor. Penn sat down across from her, somehow sending his dinner knife flying across the table and onto the floor.

"*Dang it,*" Penn said frantically, trying to pick up the knife but accidentally kicking it under Ava's chair. "You know what?" he said, sitting back into his seat, wiping his palms on the thighs of his jeans. "I am *incredibly* nervous right now. How are you doing over there?"

Ava took a deep breath, the first she'd taken of the night. She relaxed as she remembered it was only Penn who sat across from her. "You mean, aside from Jacklyn's embarrassing the hell out of me?"

Penn laughed loudly, shaking his head as he did so. "She was . . . a little much. But Paola was operating on a whole new level of humiliating tonight. Your sister, she looks really good—"

"What do you mean?" Ava interjected, jealousy taking hold of her before she could stop herself. She wanted to take the words back as soon as she saw Penn's face fall.

"Oh, no, Ava, I didn't . . . ," Penn stuttered. "I just meant she looks, she looks like she's, you know, healthy and curvy—"

"*Curvy?*" Ava asked, internally shouting at herself to shut up. She thought she'd grown past this, but here she was, fourteen all over again, in the shadow of her older sister.

"Oh man, I just don't think I'm good at this," Penn groaned.

"Good at what?" Ava asked, perplexed. Penn's usual air of confidence was receding before her.

"Dating. I've never, I don't really know what I'm doing."

They paused, both flustered, staring at one another. Jacklyn arrived back on the scene right on time, setting their waters down. They both picked up their glasses and started chugging.

"Just so you know," Jacklyn began, Ava watching as Penn tried to look up at the ceiling and anywhere but at Jacklyn's body. "Mei has a special menu prepared for the two of you tonight, so unless you have any special requests, we'll do all the work! We printed these out for you," she said, bending over the table to set the menus down. Penn's eyes didn't move from the ceiling. "So, take a look at what deliciousness you'll be enjoying tonight, and I'll be back when your apps are ready!"

Jacklyn noticed Penn's knife on the floor and bent to pick it up. Ava tried not to collapse in fits of giggles as Penn shifted uncomfortably in his seat, still staring upward.

"Everything okay?" Jacklyn asked, shooting Ava a look of concern.

"No, I mean, yes. Everything's great!" Ava blurted, holding it together the best she could as Jacklyn turned and headed back downstairs.

"I . . . ," Penn said as Ava sputtered out, "You . . ."

"You go," Penn said.

"No, you," Ava pleaded, laughing uncontrollably.

"Please say something?" Penn begged. "I'm not doing the best job of talking right now."

"Ugh, okay! I, um . . . I just . . . I'm sorry. I thought I was over being jealous of her. I thought I had evolved past it or something. *Clearly not.* She does look very healthy and way happier than I've seen her in a long time."

"You're glad she's home then? I know it's complicated."

Ava looked out onto the restaurant, spotting Jacklyn as she sent a table into uproarious laughter. "Yeah, I think I am. We're different, now. But different in a good way."

Penn nodded, a small smile on his lips. "Did she finally stop pestering you about Leona?"

"Yes, thankfully! That's what I mean! I missed her so much, but I don't know. I don't hate that our relationship has changed. Maybe that's weird."

"It's not weird at all. I think you just needed space to be yourself."

"That's, that's exactly it."

Mei greeted them this time as she set their appetizer down on the table.

"You two look so cozy up here!" she said, resting against the railing. "It was Jacklyn's idea to put a table up here, and I have to say, it's working! I've already had several couples ask to reserve this spot next time they come in. Thank goodness you two look so comfortable together; had this date gone wrong everyone would have a front row seat to your trainwreck!"

Mei laughed at her own joke before leaving them to share their appetizer. Penn waited for Ava to dig in before helping himself. As Penn took a bite, Ava thought about what he had said before Mei had arrived.

"So, is this really a date?" she asked.

Penn looked up from his plate, trying to chew the mouth full he'd just taken. Ava waited, wishing she could take it back. Penn struggled, gulping down water to try to answer her.

"I, well, I guess, well, yeah? Is that, did I not make that super clear?"

"You just never really said it was, so I-I don't know, I didn't want to assume."

Penn slapped himself on the forehead. "I'll say it again, I'm not good at this! This dating thing! Of course, I should have told you that's what this is or how would you know?!"

"It's okay!" Ava assured him. "Honestly, I've never been on a real date so I don't think I'm very good at this either."

"Really?" Penn asked, rolling his shoulders back after Ava's question had caused them to rise up to his ears.

"Really. Other guys just kind of met me at parties or whatever. This is kind of, well, my first real date."

They locked eyes for a moment, smiling at one another before settling into a comfortable silence.

"Have you heard anything? From your dad?" Penn asked after a while, pushing away his small plate.

"I think he's talking to my mom through lawyers. Funny how that works. Lawyers going through lawyers. But sadly, no. He sent a check for Christmas to us. Well, Mac and I, anyway. Mac ripped his up and threw it in the trash."

"I'm so sorry, Ava. That's terrible."

"It's . . . it is what it is. My mom is doing really well though. She's making dinner with Aunt Brene most nights now and is back to work full time. I haven't seen her drink anything for weeks now. Aunt Brene will probably go back to work soon, which sucks, but I really do think we will be okay."

Jacklyn arrived back upstairs, her hands full with their main course. She was in a hurry this time, since the dinner rush was hitting full force down below.

"Have you started thinking about colleges?" Penn asked as they waited for their food to cool.

"Ms. Delic and I have talked about it, but, I don't know."

"Yeah? What have you talked about?"

"Art therapy? But I don't know, saying it out loud sounds stupid."

"No way!" Penn shouted so that a table below looked up at them. "It sounds perfect for you!"

"I-I guess . . . it won't make much money, probably, but . . ."

"Maybe not, but success doesn't have to mean making a lot of money. What is that Maya Angelou quote? 'Success is liking yourself, liking what you do, and liking how you do it.' And who knows, you could wind up doing something completely different that utilizes the same skill set and does make money. Really, if you're pursuing something you love, that's true success in my book."

Ava smiled behind her water glass as she took a drink. "You sound like Ms. Delic."

"You know what? I'll take it, she's a smart one."

In between bites, they discussed Mrs. Papayanni's upcoming essay. Neither of them noticed anymore as Jacklyn and Mei came to refill their drinks and take away empty plates. They were so caught up in their conversation, it didn't even bother Ava that Jacklyn was so obviously eavesdropping.

As the final plates were cleared, Ava sat back in her chair with her hand resting on her stomach. "I am *stuffed*," she said.

Penn tugged at a curl near his left ear. "I guess this means you don't have any room left for Poppy's?"

"I *swear* the two times you have asked me to go to Poppy's are the *only* times I haven't wanted to go."

Penn chortled as he grabbed the bill in the middle of the table. Ava reached forward, then retracted her arm, remembering something Jacklyn said about letting him get the check.

"You can get the tip, if you want. But the rest is on me, deal?" he asked.

"Deal," Ava said with a grin.

"Of course," Penn sighed, looking over the receipt.

"Of course, what?"

"Half of this meal is comped, even though—"

Mei appeared at the top of the steps at the start of Penn's rant.

"Mei! There is no way—" Penn cried.

"Friends and family discount!" she said, tugging the bill out of his hand before he had a chance to refuse.

"Since when—" but Mei had already turned around and dashed back down the stairwell. Penn and Ava shared a frustrated eyeroll together. They let their food settle until Jacklyn returned with Penn's card.

"So is the tip going to you or to Mei?" Ava asked, wondering how the two of them seemed to read the other's mind as they served the entire restaurant together.

"Oh," Jacklyn said, craning her neck over the railing to spot where Mei was on the floor below. "We combine everything together at the end of the night and then Mei tries to give me more than half but I stash the extra into the cash register when she's not looking. It all evens out, in the end."

Ava and Penn looked at each other, eyebrows raised though neither one of them were surprised.

"Well," Jacklyn said, her eyes dancing between them. "How was everything?"

"It was ...," Penn started.

"Perfect, Jacklyn. Really," Ava finished. "Thank you for, well, thank you for taking care of us. Of me. Thank you for taking such good care of me."

Ava hadn't expected her eyes to become misty as she said it, but after talking about it with Penn, she was more than glad Jacklyn was home. Even though Ava had been trying to become more independent, it had been a great comfort to have her big sister around for her first actual date.

"Anytime, Sis," Jacklyn said, her sleeve flying to her face as she turned quickly toward the steps.

Penn handed the settled tab over to Ava. She opened her purse and took out the money she had cashed from her dad's check. She tried to discreetly place it into the book, but a couple of twenty-dollar bills floated out of her hand and onto the floor.

Penn bent down to pick them up for her. "I look like a cheap date! How much are you leaving?"

Ava gathered the cash together and organized it back into the server's book. "Let's just say it's the perfect way to piss off my dad and be the one to take care of my sister, for a change."

"And you say *I'm* the smart one," Penn said, beaming.

Penn waited for Ava to get her things together then stood up from the table first. Ava took her time in standing, not wanting the night to end. She surveyed the space slowly as she stood, then locked eyes with Penn, whose smile brightened at the sight of her. She drank him in: his glowing eyes, his wild curls, his long yet graceful neck. She placed the image of him deep in her consciousness, knowing that she'd need to come back to this memory on days where life didn't feel so light and easy.

Penn gestured toward the stairs, and Ava started the descent, searching for Jacklyn and Mei as she went. They both were running frantically from table to table, trying to close the many open tabs as the dinner hour ended. Penn and Ava waved goodbye to them as they exited, a cool breeze meeting them outside on the sidewalk.

Ava let Penn chatter on as she drove them home but was so lethargic from their meal she didn't contribute much to the conversation. Penn didn't seem to mind. When she pulled into his driveway, Ava left the car running, unsure what it meant to go into his house in the context of a date.

"D-do . . . ," Penn stammered. He cleared his throat and rubbed the back of his neck. "Do you want to come in? Paola might try to snap some more pictures, so, I don't blame you if you don't want to."

"Sure!" Ava surprised herself by saying.

She turned the car off promptly and hopped out of the car, cautiously walking around flowerpots, waiting at the top of the stoop for Penn to open the front door. Penn hesitated before unlocking it, turning toward Ava instead. Ava looked at him funny, wondering why he wasn't going inside when a thought dawned upon her. It was the end of a date. She'd watched enough rom coms to know what this meant. As Penn lowered his head toward hers, Ava closed her eyes, hoping he couldn't hear just how fast her heart was beating. She felt his breath on her face, then, suddenly, the porch light sprang to life.

"YOU GOT THE BIG ONE!" Paola yelled, swinging open the front door. She held up a large white envelope.

"Ma!" Penn scolded, exasperated. "Can this wait? I invited Ava in—"
"IT'S FROM STANFORD!"

Penn looked over at Ava, then back at the envelope.

"You should open it," Ava said, though she regretted it as soon as she said it. Penn lightly took the envelope from Paola, motioning Ava inside. Ava didn't budge.

"Maybe you should open it with, you know, just the two of you."

"No way! Don't be silly, Ava, come in!" Paola exclaimed, grabbing Ava's wrist and pulling her inside.

Penn immediately sank down into the small sofa, where Ava and Paola squeezed in on either side of him.

"Open it, open it!" Paola chanted while clapping her hands. Ava tried to force herself to smile, but all she managed was a pathetic-looking wince.

Penn carefully opened the envelope, taking his time to pull the stack of papers onto his lap. He scanned the letter in front, Ava watching as his expression changed.

"Is it, did you not get in?" asked Paola, looking down at the letter to read it for herself.

"No, I'm . . . I'm in and . . . I got the scholarship . . . a full ride."

"WHAT!?" Paola screamed, jumping up from the couch. "YOU GOT IN WITH A FULL RIDE! HOW? HOW!?"

"I-I had Mrs. Papayanni help me write essays to different scholarship funds. And I had quite a few teachers give me references and I guess, I guess it helped."

Paola bent over and squeezed Penn into a tight hug, tears of joy slipping from her eyes and streaming down her cheeks. Ava watched the scene unfold, finding herself wanting to edge toward the door as they embraced one another.

"Looks like we're moving to California!" Paola cheered. She released Penn and hugged Ava. "No way am I letting him go have all the fun without me along for the ride."

Paola let her go and ran to the kitchen to make celebratory phone calls.

Ava felt frozen halfway between the couch and the door, unsure where she belonged. Penn glanced up from his stack of papers at her. He immediately set them down at the sight of her face and, to her surprise, went to grab the stereo from the kitchen. He set it down on the floor next to the couch then squatted, taking his time to find a slow song. Once he did, he stood up and held his hand out to Ava. Though every piece of her felt numb, she watched as her hand reached out and clasped on to Penn's. He pulled her into him, pressing her against his chest as Paola's giddy laughter issued from the kitchen.

"*Congratulations,*" Ava whispered into Penn's ear.

Penn lowered his head so that their foreheads touched. He tucked a strand of hair behind her ear, not saying a word. He swayed with her around the room as the song played out, the colors of the walls blurring together behind them. When the song ended, Paola rushed back into the room, ripping Penn away to talk to someone on the phone.

Without a glance backward from Penn or Paola, Ava was left standing alone in the living room, staring at the big white envelope. Which, she couldn't help but notice, was in the same spot she'd sat before it was opened, in the space next to Penn.

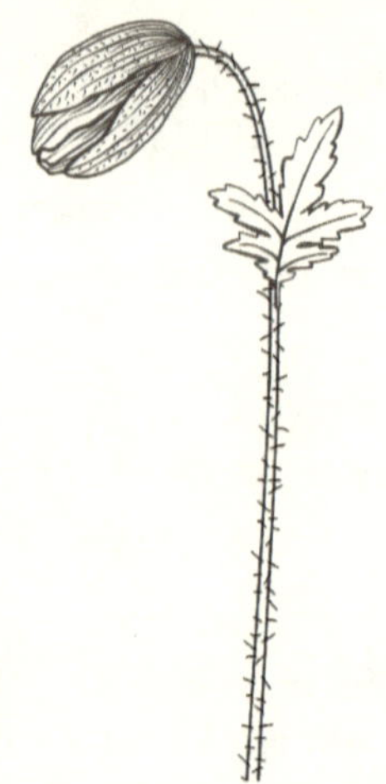

chapter twenty-eight

The following morning Ava woke up, and for the briefest second, forgot what had taken place the night before. For that small space in time everything was peaceful and everyone she loved had no intention of leaving Westwood. But as her brain chemicals sparked, signaling the start of the day, a pulsing dolefulness bled its way through her nervous system. Oliva jumped up from underneath the bed and burrowed herself into Ava's chest. Ava put her arm around her cat's soft belly, hoping Olivia's purrs would alleviate the sharp edges of her pain. Pain that she knew was only beginning to uncloak itself.

An array of knocks came at her door that morning, but she knew none belonged to the one person she wanted but also couldn't bear to see. Eventually, she fell back asleep, letting the comfort of sleep's darkness pull her back under.

Hours later, Ava awoke to a gentle hand on her shoulder. The same hand pulled her blanket down off her face. Ava winced as the bright afternoon sun sliced through the blinds, magnifying all the feelings she was trying to repress.

"Ava," said a voice. Ava rolled over, her forearm shielding her eyes, to find her mom staring concernedly down on her. "I'd like to speak with you downstairs."

There was a clarity in her mother's tone that Ava hadn't heard in quite some time. Ava waited for her to leave the room, listening as footsteps crossed over the hallway and down the stairs. Mac, Aunt Brene, and Jacklyn were chattering down below. Ava felt a sharp jab in her abdomen, not wanting to face their questions about how her date went last night.

As she rolled out of bed, every muscle in her body screamed at her to stop. Each ligament knew what this movement meant: life must go on, with or without Penn and Paola by her side. She sat on the edge of her bed, looking back at her pillow. As much as she wanted to believe placing her head back down would erase all the grief she felt, she knew it was a false promise. It only prolonged the agony she was bound to feel, and that she needed to feel.

She trudged to the bathroom, then gripped the edges of the sink to take a good look at herself. Her eye makeup from last night had fallen beneath her lower lashes, her hair knotted into a peculiar shape on the side of her head. It was written across her face: all the words and ways she felt for Penn that she could never tell him now. With a surge of anger, she turned on the cold water and dunked her head into the sink. Even though the water was freezing, she reveled in how terrifically it numbed her senses. In a haze, Ava dabbed off her face, ran a brush through her tangles, brushed her teeth, and somehow found herself descending the stairs to find her family in the living room.

Aunt Brene sat on the couch, with Jacklyn close on her left side, Mac to the right. Amelia stood at the front of the room, her hands folded professionally in front of her. She was back to wearing what Ava called her lawyer clothes: pressed black dress pants, sleek pumps, and an ivory silk blouse. The air of the room was austere; the chatter Ava heard moments before had ceased. Ava looked at her siblings, but they shrugged in response, unsure what the sudden family meeting was about.

Ava took a seat on the other side of the sectional, leaving a distance between herself and the rest of them. She pulled her knees into her chest, wishing the cushion she sat on would sink into the floor and drag her down with it. Amelia cleared her throat, then stood up straight, adjusting her posture. All eyes fell on her, the room silent except for the whir of the dishwasher behind them.

"I owe each of you my sincerest apologies," Amelia began.

"You don't have to do this," Aunt Brene interjected, sensing the tension rising in the room.

"No, I *need* to do this, Brene. I can no longer allow you to clean up my messes for me."

Aunt Brene's hand moved to her chest, bracing herself for whatever it was to come. Ava's eyes stay glued to her mother, daring her to add on to the shitstorm of emotions she already felt.

"I want to, I have to say," Amelia struggled to say, losing her composure. She closed her eyes, unable to look at them. "I am sorry. Not just for my behavior since your father left, but for letting my relationship with him affect my duty as a mother, and as a sister."

"Mom," Jacklyn interjected as she watched her mother shake like a leaf at the top of the room. "It's *okay*, we don't blame you for everything that's wrong with this family."

"Yeah," Mac piped up. "Dad's the one who left; that's not your fault."

They looked over at Ava, expecting her to join in, but Ava remained silent. Her emotional capacity was well past full.

"But it's," Amelia objected, opening her eyes again. "It's *not* okay. I believed that if I let myself get too close to you, to any of you, your father would find a way to use it against me. I thought if I could be everything for him, he would finally see me as enough. And when I was enough in his eyes, only *then* could I become a better mother and a better sister.

"I thought that's how love worked for so long. Yet no matter how much I tried or begged or sacrificed my own dreams for his, I was never enough. I wasn't enough for him, but worse, I was never enough for myself."

Ava watched, still behind a veil of depression, her mother's eyes, now rimmed in crimson and on the verge of pouring out long repressed tears.

"And I know this is a very awkward conversation to have," Amelia continued, doing her best to keep herself together. "But it's something my therapist and I have been working on, this vulnerability thing. I know I let you down. I let myself down, too. But I want to do better, for each of you. And for myself."

"Amelia," Aunt Brene said, scooting forward to sit on the edge of the couch. "You're putting a lot of this on your own shoulders. This kind of relationship between James and you, it's all we've ever known. It was only when Mom passed away that Dad saw a different way to live, and to love. You just can't blame yourself for all of this."

"I . . . I . . . ," Amelia struggled, wiping away a stray tear that had found its way down her cheek. "I don't blame myself for all of it, but I want to take responsibility for my role in it. I don't want you to feel like you need to protect me from myself anymore. Brene, I've watched as you've lived your life, pouring love into others and not letting our parent's relationship define who you are."

"I've had my struggles too, Amelia," Brene argued. "I just didn't let you see them. I've had to work really hard to get to a place where I'm not bitter toward them."

"That's exactly what I'm hoping to convey here, Brene. I'm choosing to do the work now, and you've got to let me do it for myself. I know I might let each of you down, but I want to try. I want to try to be here for all of you in all the ways," Amelia stopped herself as tears burst forth, swallowing loudly. "*In all the ways I couldn't before.*"

Ava watched as her mother cried openly at the front of the room. The words she'd said managed to claw their way through the wall Ava had built up around herself. She observed her family around her. At Aunt Brene, who had risen to wrap her arms around Amelia, the sisters holding one another up. Then at Jacklyn, who pulled Mac into her, both hiding their faces as they too began to cry. Ava remained seated, unable to reach out to them, still too overwhelmed to move.

When Amelia and Aunt Brene finished their hug, Amelia made her way over to sit by Ava. She grabbed Ava's slack hand and held it tight.

"I am honored to be a mother to each of you," she said, her gaze shifting from Jacklyn to Mac, and finally, at Ava. "And I hope you can each forgive me, but I understand if you can't. I promise, no matter how you feel toward me, from this day forward, I will do my best to care for you as I learn to care for myself."

Mac reached over for the tissues, then blew his nose obnoxiously loud, disrupting the moment. Everyone looked over at him, but he answered by doing it a second time, sending the room into laughter. Even Ava couldn't help herself from joining in. Mac passed the Kleenex around, each person taking a minute to wipe the tears and snot from their faces.

"I'd like to say a couple more things before we eat the lasagna Brene has worked so hard on for us," Amelia said, settling back into the couch still holding Ava's hand. While Ava hadn't shed a tear just yet, she held on to the Kleenexes in her lap.

"Everything you three are is not because of anything your father and I did right. I don't know how you did turn out so well," she said, turning to Jacklyn.

"The way you took over, so young, just like Brene, and became the parent your brother and sister needed. . . . you are an incredible young woman. And so much like your aunt it baffles me."

Jacklyn smiled, lowering her head onto Aunt Brene's shoulder.

Then she turned to face Mac. "You look just like your father. But you're different from him in all the best ways. Even as a thirteen year—"

"Fourteen next month!" Mac interjected.

Amelia laughed, then reached across to ruffle his shaggy hair. "Yes, excuse me. Even as a near fourteen-year-old, you are more dedicated to this family and capable of love than he could hope to be."

Mac blushed and lowered his eyes to his hands on his lap. Then Amelia faced Ava, squeezing her hand as she did so.

"And Ava. You remind me so much of myself at your age, but already you're making better choices than I've ever been able to make on my own. Watching you become your own person has encouraged me in more ways than you might ever understand."

Ava didn't want to feel anything, didn't expect to feel anything, didn't think she could feel anything. Before she could comprehend what she was doing, she threw herself into her mother's arms and let herself be held. Amelia hesitated at first, not sure what to do with her arms, but, after a moment, Ava felt a hand rubbing gentle circles on her back. Amelia was pacifying Ava as she had never allowed herself to. It was, Ava thought, everything they had both needed for so long. Like quenching a deep, excruciating thirst to find the water had been there within reach all along, just waiting for them to drink it.

Ava kept her head in her mother's lap as she continued to speak, Ava's tears soaking through her expensive suit fabric.

"One other important announcement," Amelia said in her most professional tone, her hand now in Ava's hair. "I filed for a divorce from your father this past week. It's something I should have done a long, long time ago, but with Aunt Brene's help, I've been able to go through with it this time. I was hoping he would be here today, to talk through what it might look like going forward, but he . . . he wasn't able to make it."

Jacklyn let out a hiss and string of cuss words that nobody bothered to object to.

"Whatever kind of relationship you choose to have with your father is completely up to each of you," Amelia continued. "But if he ever, ever tries to manipulate or control you in any way you feel you can't handle, know I am here for you and support you in breaking ties with him. I will do my best to not say negative things about him, and let you have your own relationship with him. But I'm also a mother who wants to do a better job of protecting her children."

"I can handle him, Mom. Don't you worry!" Jacklyn said proudly.

"*Don't I know it*," Amelia whispered, smiling. "And one last thing—"

"There's more? How can there be more? I feel like we've just covered the past fifty years!" Mac shouted.

"Well, after speaking with Jacklyn, who has decided she doesn't want to move back into this house—"

"Mom, I'm sorry I just . . . ," Jacklyn said, but Amelia waved her off.

"And with Brene leaving soon to go back to her own life, though I'd love for her to stay with us . . ."

"You know I would love to, but I have to go back to work sometime," Aunt Brene interjected.

"And with Ava finishing high school soon, I think this house is too big for just Mac and me. This house was designed by James, but I've been dreaming of living in a house that fits more of who we are as a family now. I'd like to ask all of you, how do you feel about moving?"

They looked around at one another, no one sure how to respond.

"I think…," Ava whispered, surprised to find herself speaking up after not saying a word all morning. "I think it never feels like the right time to leave behind a place that feels like home. But I also think we have to trust that home will find us again, wherever we choose to go."

The room fell silent, and without thinking or looking at anyone, Ava shot up and ran upstairs to her bedroom. She powered on her phone, her screen filled with texts from Kaysar, Jacklyn, Mac, Trish, even one from Leila. She scrolled until she found his name and ran her finger across it.

While her sadness didn't lift, and her anger didn't fade, she knew there was no stopping Penn from going after the future he dreamed of, and the one she knew he deserved. What she wanted, with all her being, was to support the person who'd believed in her when no one else did. Even if the next several months would be excruciating, it was time to show up for Penn in all the beautiful ways he'd shown up for her since October.

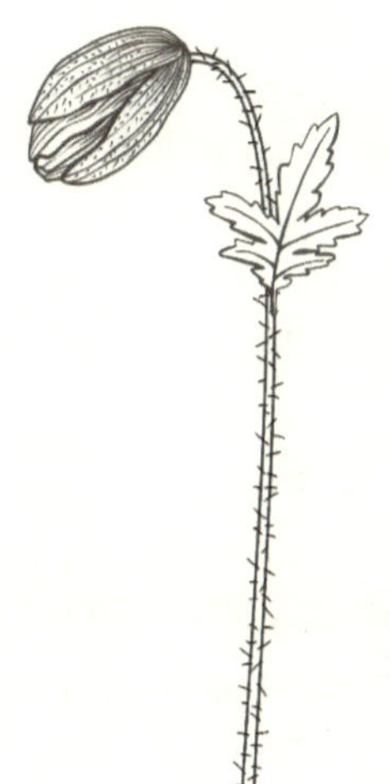

chapter twenty-nine

Trish reached over to stop Ava's paper from flying across the classroom. Mr. Jenneman had decided to leave the windows open during class. It was delightful other than the strong wind gusts that sent their assignment flying across the room on several occasions. Leila secured her papers down with various items, including her *Star Wars* lunch box. Still, it made it difficult for her to write notes between the obstacles. They listened together in the top right corner of the class as Mr. Jenneman introduced something called the "Personal Bill of Rights."

As interesting as the assignment was, Ava's mind drifted, ruminating over the past week. She couldn't help but sense a gap already forming between her and Penn. Neither of them had brought up the events that happened last Friday, and the cheerier she acted around him, the more he seemed to pull away. She was more grateful than ever that Trish and Leila joined them at lunch, as Penn was distracted or missing entirely in preparation for his upcoming competition.

"Now it's your turn!" Mr. Jenneman exclaimed, bursting Ava's daydream. Ava dropped back into reality to find Leila and Trish scribbling away in their notebooks. She glanced up at Mr. Jenneman to see he was smiling politely at her, leaning against the front of his desk. Knowing she hadn't listened, he motioned at her to join him at the top of the room.

"*Sorry!*" Ava whispered when she reached him.

"No need to apologize! I struggle to pay attention when the world is outside waiting for me, too. The assignment is simple: write your own Personal Bill of Rights."

"I, um, I may have missed when you said what that was." Ava wanted to kick herself for disappointing her favorite teacher.

"Read through the handout I gave, if it hasn't flown off your desk yet," he said, adjusting the round spectacles up the bridge of his nose. "There are twenty-five statements on there, all about what you have a right to in your life. It's in line with what we've been discussing this past week about learning to assert yourself and asking for what you need. You don't have to write a full twenty-five statements, but write at least five you feel confident in, and share at least one of those with your small group. Does that make sense?"

Ava nodded, wringing her hands together. She sat back in her seat, then bent over the handout sitting on her desk, now weighed down by Leila's glasses case. She read through each of the statements, none of them sinking in much on the first read-through. She glanced over at Trish, who had now written close to twenty of her own statements. Ava blew out hot air, feeling her pulse begin to quicken. She felt the sudden urge to run out of the classroom and escape all of the emotions coming up as she read through the statements a second time.

"*I have the right to change my mind . . . I have the right to say no to anything when I feel I am not ready . . . I have the right to be angry . . . I have the right to my own needs for personal space and time . . . I have the right to change and grow . . .*"

Ava tried to gulp down air, feeling like she couldn't get enough oxygen into her lungs. She hadn't written down a single word when Trish and Leila set down their pencils. Mr. Jenneman announced it was time to share with their group. Ava doodled in her notebook then slapped her handout down on top of it, hoping to make it appear like she too had written her statements.

"I'll go first!" Trish volunteered. Ava breathed a sigh of relief. "I couldn't stop writing these! But I think my favorite one is my number eight: I have the right to stand up against those who have harmed me."

Ava looked toward the door, wondering how fast she could get out to her car. Everything in her was squirming, begging her to stop thinking what she was thinking.

"Wow, that's so powerful, Trish," Leila commented. Trish smiled, her eyes downcast. "The one I'm sharing is a little different. It's, I have the right to choose friends who don't make fun of me."

Trish reached out and squeezed Leila's forearm. "I'm so sorry I did that to you, Leila. Especially when it has happened to me too."

Leila smiled sadly, patting Trish's hand with her own. After a minute or two, they looked over at Ava.

"Did you want to share, Ava?" Trish asked, her lips extra pink and glossy this afternoon. "You've been a little quiet today."

"Oh, y-yeah, I . . ." Ava looked around the classroom, searching for the wall clock. She couldn't believe her luck as the bell rang, sending the class scrambling toward the door. Trish and Leila packed up slowly, but Ava shot up, running into the hall. She hid in the sophomore locker bay around the corner of the class, watching as Trish and Leila left Mr. Jenneman's classroom together. When she knew the class was empty, she snuck back in as Mr. Jenneman sat down behind his desk.

"Yes, Ava?" he asked. "Did you have more questions on the assignment? I won't collect them until Monday, it's okay if you didn't—"

"No, I, um, I had a different question for you," she said in a rush.

Mr. Jenneman sat up straighter in his chair, leaning toward Ava, eyebrows raised.

"Do you think . . . well, what happens when, you know, people start being less passive, and start being more assertive? Those rights, or whatever, what happens when you believe they are true?"

"What do you think happens?" Mr. Jenneman asked with kindness in his voice. Ava heaved a sigh, frustrated he wouldn't give her a straight answer.

"Well, I think, like something you said on Tuesday, people start putting their own needs first. Which would mean instead of pushing down all these thoughts and feelings that I, I mean, that *people* have . . . they start asking for what they really need, instead of tiptoeing around it, I guess?"

"Mmhmm, and what do you think that means, for people, as you so put it?"

Ava hesitated, staring out at the tall oak trees that lined the walkway outside. "I think it means people start living their own lives and stop waiting, or letting, other people run it for them."

"I think you're onto something," Mr. Jenneman responded softly, watching as Ava's face changed. She nodded blankly, turning away. Then she whipped back around when she got to the doorway.

"Is it normal? To feel like this?"

"Feel like what, Ava?"

"Like I'm feeling everything at once. Confused. Wanting to run. But more than anything, angry."

"It is completely valid, Ava. Anger is a part of healing, too. And if you listen to it, instead of fighting against it, it might tell you exactly what you need to do."

Ava felt herself nodding again but didn't quite comprehend his words. She floated out of his room and through the throng of students, heading in the opposite direction of her art class. Several minutes later, she was surprised to find her fist raised, about to knock on a door.

"Ava!" Ms. Delic said from behind her. "I just got back from lunch, sorry about that! Come on in!"

Ava staggered in behind her, taking her usual spot on the couch. She barely registered much of Ms. Delic at all, only noticing her lipstick was the color of mulberries.

"How are you doing?" Ms. Delic asked from what seemed like miles away. Ava wasn't even sure that she processed the question as words began to fall out of her.

"Penn is leaving," she heard herself say.

"Oh, Ava, he told me earlier this week he got into Stanford. *I'm so sorry—*"

"My mom filed for divorce from my dad. My dad who hasn't bothered to reach out to me since he left, outside of a Christmas check."

"Let's slow down, talk about some of this—"

"I was raped last summer," Ava blurted out over her. The word "rape" felt harsh and heavy on her tongue. "I've talked about what he did and how I felt but I've never said it. Not out loud like this. Bradley raped me."

"You've got so much going on, Ava; let's unpack this one thing at a time."

"I'm ready."

"Great! Let's start back at the beginning. Let's start with Penn."

"No, Ms. Delic. *I'm ready to report Bradley.*"

"Oh! Well, I-I mean, that's, that's a huge step, Ava. It is really, really brave of you. But can I ask, why are you feeling so motivated to do this now?"

"I . . . ," Ava trailed off, finding the poster to help with grounding on the wall. She counted her breath until she was finally able to focus. "I have the right to decide, on my own, when I'm ready to report someone who has harmed me."

"You are absolutely right, Ava. I am so proud of you for deciding this in your own time. You tell me where you want to go with all of this."

"Can you help me? I think I know what I want to do, but I'm not sure how to do it."

"Of course, I can help you, but can I just say before we continue, that I hope you can take some time to acknowledge just how far you've come. Let's pause, for a minute, and appreciate all the progress you've made in just a few short months before we rush into this."

Ava stared down at her knees, thinking back to the emptiness she felt after Bradley rolled off of her last summer. Her gaze lowered to her feet that had carried her to Ms. Delic's office today. It was these same feet that led her down Trish's steps, away from Bradley, delivering her to safety. She had taken those first steps, all on her own. There wasn't Penn or anyone else around to save her back then. Ava braced herself as an immense wave of grief and gratitude washed over her. It was truly remarkable how far she had come since that night. And how far she was still willing to go.

* * *

The bedroom door stood ajar. Ava knocked gently anyway; it still felt weird to enter the master bedroom freely.

"Yes?" Amelia answered, looking over her readers. Her bed was covered with documents and folders.

"Hey Mom, okay if I come in?" Ava asked. "I can come back later."

"No, no, I can stop here."

Amelia made space for Ava on the bed, shifting a stack of papers to her nightstand. Ava sat lightly in what used to be her father's side of the bed, trying to silence the voices that screamed at her to retreat.

"Did you want to talk to me about moving?" Amelia asked, removing her readers completely. Ava shook her head.

"Is it about the divorce? I know it's a lot to take in, all of this. And I know it was so sudden."

"No, I think that's a good thing, actually."

"Okay," Amelia said, sitting up straighter on the bed, crossing her legs beneath her. "Are you upset with me?"

"No, Mom. I don't think so, anyway. I ...," Ava struggled. She thought she'd worked through this with Ms. Delic, but it was much more difficult face-to-face than she'd anticipated. "I need your help with something."

"I'll do whatever I can, Ava; just let me know what you need."

Ava felt her stomach tighten, her throat constrict. Everything in her told her to stop, to remain small, to not speak another word. Her mom scooted closer to place a hand on Ava's knee. The simple gesture quieted the voices enough for Ava to continue.

"I need you to help me bring a case against someone. His name is Bradley Gerken."

"Didn't your sister date a Bradley last year?" she asked, confused.

"Yeah, it's the same person."

"Okay, what kind of case?"

"He, um, he-he assaulted, no, he raped me, last summer. And Trish, around the same time."

Ava could barely stand to look over at her mother as she struggled to find the right words. Her fingers dug into Ava's knee, her face pale. "I'm so sorry this happened to you, Ava. We should go to the police with this immediately."

"Trish did already. It turns out Bradley's uncle works at the force, so nothing ever happened with it."

"You're not serious?!" Amelia shouted, jumping up from the bed and sending a stack of folders flying across the room.

"I know we probably don't have much to go on," Ava said, feeling very stupid for saying anything at all. She wasn't sure anymore why she thought this was such a good idea.

"No, you *misunderstand* me, Ava. I have managed some very corrupt cases in this town over the years, but this is . . . this is . . . can you call Trish? Can you get her over here?"

Ava's eyes widened. "I-I guess I can . . . are we, are we going to do it? Bring a case or whatever, against Bradley?"

Amelia drew herself up to full height. She straightened out her dress pants, her jaw set. She fastened her hair into a tight bun at the base of her neck as she set her fiery eyes on Ava.

"Yes, Ava, we are going to bring a case against him. But not just him. You better get up and give Trish a call. *Right now.* We've got a lot of work to do if we're going to sue the Westwood Police Department."

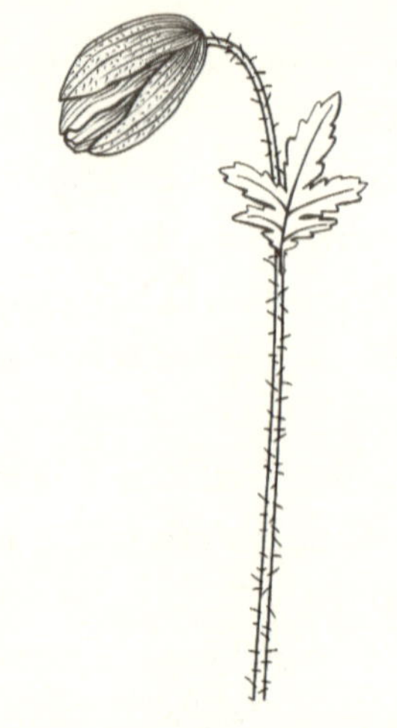

chapter thirty

Ava rushed to get ready, not wanting to be late for Penn's big day. She raced down the steps, screeching to a halt at the sight of bags piled by the front door. Following the scent of frying bacon, Ava found Aunt Brene in front of the stove.

"Um, good morning?" Ava asked.

"Good morning, sweetheart!" Aunt Brene answered with a large smile. She flipped the front burner off, transferring the last strips of bacon onto a plate. "Get on in here and eat up! I made plenty and your mom and brother aren't even moving yet."

"Are those your bags by the door?"

Aunt Brene's smile faltered.

"Join me at the table, love. No point in having this conversation on an empty stomach."

Ava grabbed a plate from the clean stack on the counter, filling it lightly, since she was aware of the time. She joined her aunt at the kitchen table, bracing herself for what she knew was coming.

"No easy way to say this," Aunt Brene said between bites. "Work has been generous, allowing me so much time off. But it's time for me to head back home."

Ava shoved bacon into her mouth to keep it busy, not wanting to face the inevitable sadness rising up in her.

"You're welcome to come visit me in Pittsburgh anytime!" Aunt Brene pressed on, not looking directly at Ava. "It's not too far, you know. You can even drive there yourself now! And you can bring Mac with you, and Jacklyn, if she's off work. It'll be fun!"

Ava chugged down her orange juice in response. Aunt Brene reached out and placed her hand on top of Ava's.

"I'm going to . . . ," Ava tried to get out, but the words backed up in her throat, preventing her from saying anything meaningful.

"Oh honey!" Aunt Brene sprang from her seat and wrapped Ava in a hug. "Oh, *damn it*, I knew this wasn't going to be easy on you kids. I told your Mom—"

"N-no," Ava sputtered. "We're going to be f-f-fine! Thank you for *everything*, Aunt Brene."

Ava held on to Aunt Brene as long as she could before noticing the time. She stood up, untangling herself from her aunt's arms.

"Do you need help with your bags?" Ava asked before leaving.

"No, love, you get going! Mac and your mom can help me, if they ever wake up. Please tell Penn I say good luck!"

Ava stole one more quick hug from her aunt, inhaling her sweet and now bacon-tinged scent. Her eyes prickled as she let go. She raced toward the front door before her aunt could notice her tears.

"Wait, Ava!" Aunt Brene shouted after her. Ava turned, her hand gripping the doorknob. She looked at her aunt, whose eyes were unmistakably glistening as the sun streamed into the foyer.

"I wanted to say before you go, those shoes I bought you, they sure look like they are a part of you now, don't you think?"

Ava glanced downward, forgetting that she'd thrown on her high tops earlier that morning. No longer were they sparkling white with newness as they were the day she dared to wear them back in October. Now they were stained, scuffed, and best of all, broken-in from wearing them nearly every day since then.

"More than you know," Ava answered, breaking out into a wide smile as she opened the door and rushed out into the fresh spring air.

* * *

On her way out of town, Ava stopped to get gas. She bit her lower lip, impatiently waiting as her tank filled. When she got back into her car, she found her phone blown up with calls from Kaysar. She rolled her eyes as she called him back, assuming he was calling to complain about how boring the competition was already.

"Ava!" he answered, panicked. "Are you with Penn?"

"What do you mean?" Ava answered, thinking he was joking. "Of course not. He said he was going with you guys."

"He told us he was coming with Mrs. Papayanni, but she's already here. He even said goodbye when he left early this morning."

Ava's mind was racing. "Did he seem nervous last night?"

"No! He was excited, you know?! He was going on about all the other participants, how good they all were. Wait, do you think he's okay? Should Paola and I come back and look for him? What if he's hurt, or something worse?"

Ava could hear her heart beating in her eardrums.

"I'll look for him here; stay there with Paola. I'll look everywhere I can think of and get back to you as soon as I can, okay?"

"If you can't find him anywhere, let us know immediately, got it?"

Ava reassured Kaysar before hanging up, already trying to think of every place in Westwood Penn might be. She sped immediately over to his house to see if he'd gone back. She knocked on the door for several minutes to no answer, then peeked through his window around back. As creepy as she felt, she was too worried to care. With no sign of him or his bike, Ava drove to Westwood High. She checked the perimeter and all the doors, but they were all locked. Still no trace of Penn, she raced downtown, finding a space on the street near Mei's.

Since the restaurant wasn't open yet, Ava banged on the front door, hoping someone would hear her.

Jacklyn poked her head out, annoyed.

"Ava?" she asked, confused.

"*Have-you-seen-Penn?*"

"Penn? No. I thought today was his big poetry thing? He came in here last night with Kaysar and Paola."

"You haven't seen him since?"

"No. What's going on? Is he okay?"

"I don't know!"

"Okay! Okay," Jacklyn cooed, stepping outside. She placed a hand on Ava's shoulder. "Let's breathe and think through this, okay?"

Ava tried to take deep breaths but couldn't calm down. Penn had never been anything less than dependable and always on time. What if something really was wrong?

"Does Penn have a spot he likes to go to alone? One that he's told you about?"

Ava shook her head back and forth. "No! He's always in the same places: Mei's, school, home."

"Is there a place the two of you like to go?"

"The Lookout…but he's only got a bike and it's way too steep for him to get up there. I don't want him to miss this stupid competition! It's the only thing he's been talking about for months! I don't get it!"

"I know this is scary, Ava. But you used to disappear on me all the time when you were little, remember? I'd turn around and you'd have wandered off somewhere. But I'd always find you, or you'd always wander back to me. Anywhere else, anywhere at all you could think of where he might be?"

Ava squeezed her eyes shut. Poppy's wasn't open yet, and she hoped with all her might he hadn't taken a train out of town. She thought back to when she was little and why she'd wandered off. It was always when she'd needed space, space to think when the world felt like it was closing in around her.

She threw her arms around Jacklyn, knowing just where he might be.

"I'm so glad you came back here!" Ava cried, then she took off back toward her Jeep.

"Let me know when you find him, okay?!" Jacklyn shouted behind her.

Ava threaded through Westwood, praying she was right about this. She pulled into the gravel parking lot and ran into Blackbranch Park, searching the vast surroundings for him. She ran further and further in the park, no sign of him anywhere.

After sprinting for what felt like miles, Ava bent over her knees, steadying herself on a tree trunk. She heard footsteps to the right and glanced up only to find a woman walking her dog. Ava waved, then sank down on the tree roots sticking up from the ground.

A twig snapped behind her, and Ava jumped to alert. She pulled her keychain with mace attached out in front of her.

"It's just me!" Penn shouted, holding his hands up.

"*Where have you been?*" Ava shouted, alarming herself with the fear in her voice. "I've been looking everywhere for you! You have us worried as hell!"

"I'm sorry!" Penn said, taking a cautious step backward from Ava, who still hadn't lowered the mace. "I just—"

"It doesn't matter right now! We've got to get you to this thing—"

"No. I don't think I can do it."

"*What?*" Ava lowered her arm, taking in his appearance. Penn was sweating profusely, dripping from his hair and down his face. His complexion was ghostly, and his eyes were undeniably bloodshot.

"What's going on with you?" she asked, her voice softer this time.

"N-nothing! I just don't feel prepared for today, that's all. I should have practiced more, but I didn't, so, I just won't do it."

Ava stared at him in disbelief.

"You have never underprepared for *anything, ever,* in the *history of time.* What is really going on?"

Penn wiped a bead of sweat dripping into his eye.

"This is all too much, too fast."

"What is too much?" Ava asked. She took a step closer, closing the gap between them.

"Don't!" Penn said again, holding up his arms. "I smell, and I don't like you seeing me like this."

"What, all sweaty? You've seen me look worse."

"No, just, not like *this*."

Ava searched his face, trying to find the answers he wasn't giving. Penn shifted his gaze toward the front of the park. Ava assumed he was plotting the quickest route away from her.

"What aren't you ready for?" she asked him. "I know it's not the poetry competition, so what is it? College?"

"It's not just college, Ava, it's *Stanford*."

"So what?"

"It's the college my dad dreamed I would go to someday. I never thought I'd actually get in! I applied to ten other places as backups, believing I wouldn't. And I didn't just get in . . . *they want to pay me to go*."

"I know! It's incredible! You worked so hard for something you really, really wanted, and it paid off. You deserve this, Penn. You deserve it!"

"You don't, you don't understand."

"What don't I understand?" Ava grew more frustrated by the minute, trying her best to be the supportive friend she told herself she should be.

"It's too much!" he insisted.

"Why is it too much?!" Ava shouted, losing her patience.

Penn clasped his hands behind his neck, his elbows meeting in front of him.

"*What if I fuck this all up?* What if I've worked hard for nothing. What if I get there, and like Jacklyn, I realize it's not for me? What if I followed my dad's dream and not my own? Or worse, what if it is my dream and I end up failing? What do I do then?"

Ava looked him dead in his face, finally piecing it together.

"You're scared."

Penn scoffed. "I'm not scared. That's just, no way. I'm eighteen years old, not six!"

"Adults get scared too, Penn. My mom was scared throughout her entire marriage. And until yesterday, I was scared to ask anyone for help when I needed it."

"I'm telling you, I'm not scared. Wait, what happened yesterday?" Penn asked, confusion etched on his face.

"I told my mom about Bradley last night."

"What!? Ava! That's huge!" Penn momentarily forgot he was upset. "Are you bringing a case against him?"

"Well, my mom is doing all of the work, but yeah. She's also going to help Trish sue the Westwood Police Department."

Penn's arms shot up in the air, then he stepped forward and squeezed her into him.

"I'm so proud of you!" he exclaimed.

"Woof, you do smell!" Ava joked; Penn wasn't lying about his stench.

"Oh, gross, I'm sorry," he said, pulling away. They both readjusted as they remembered why they were in the park in the first place.

"Look, Penn, I'm all too familiar with being scared of change. I know it's new to you, this fear thing."

"I guess," he said shaking his head. "Whatever it is, it sucks! I hate it! It's terrible!"

"It really, really is," Ava laughed. "But running from it doesn't work, I've found. It just makes it worse."

"Running from it was working great for me. Until you showed up."

Ava giggled, then snorted, then couldn't stop herself from laughing hysterically.

"What did I say?" Penn asked.

"*The irony of it all, I can't take it*," Ava said as she tried to catch her breath.

"What are you—"

"You're the reason I stopped running. From everything. You showed up, rather abruptly, into my life, and now I have this very annoying voice in my head that tells me to never settle for less than I deserve."

"Should I be sorry? You sound annoyed with me," Penn said, tugging at his sweat-soaked t-shirt.

"No. But you are about to become very annoyed with me. We're going to your competition. I'm going to drive you to your house so you can get cleaned up first. If we leave now, we can still get there before it ends."

"Ava, it's done, I'm not going."

"It's not done. Not yet. You didn't give up on me, and I'm not letting you give up on yourself."

"What if—"

"You already have everything inside of you that you need to do this, Penn. We don't have time for what ifs. We need to go. *Now.*"

Ava began walking with fierce determination toward her car, hoping Penn was behind her. She didn't look back until she reached her driver's side door. Thankfully, Penn was right behind her, walking alongside his bike. He signaled to her to unlock the back of the Jeep. Ava texted Kaysar to let him know they were on their way as Penn hopped in, bracing himself as she sped out of the park.

* * *

Ava dropped Penn off at the auditorium door, shouting at him to hurry as he tried to thank her. She parked around the corner and jogged inside, spotting Paola and Kaysar seated near the front of the stage. She took a seat at the end of the row nearest Kaysar as the final contestant began to recite.

"Is he okay?" Kaysar and Paola asked, their faces panicked.

"He's doing alright," Ava whispered, but people around them shushed her as she tried to say more.

Mrs. Papayanni rushed in from a side door and sat in front of them.

"I begged them to allow Penn to perform," Mrs. Papayanni whispered, much to the annoyance of the people sitting around them. "Some of the participants wanted to disqualify him for being late. He's up after this."

Paola reached over and grabbed Ava's hand, squeezing it in thanks. She then got her Polaroid ready as the student on stage spoke the last line of his poem.

"I knew you'd be able to get him here today," Kaysar said to Ava, the audience breaking out into applause as the contestant left the stage.

"Why? What do you mean?" Ava asked, but Kaysar didn't answer, turning to watch Penn take center stage.

Penn blinked uncomfortably, raising an arm to shield his eyes from the overhead lighting. He searched around the auditorium, trying to get his bearings. The crowd murmured in complaint, confused another student was performing. Ava felt nervous for him. If he was scared before in the park, now he appeared petrified.

Someone in the audience cleared their throat as Penn continued to search the crowd. Paola waved her hands up in the air and Penn's attention snapped in her direction. He visibly exhaled at the sight of his mom, then stood up straighter as he waved at Kaysar. He caught sight of Mrs. Papayanni and smiled. When his eyes landed on Ava, he lifted his hands up and took a wider stance, ready to begin.

"*Thank you,*" he mouthed. Ava tried to suppress the smile plastered across her face.

"That's why!" Kaysar said, catching them. "I told him to take you out on that date, you know."

"You?!" Ava asked.

"Shh!" Kaysar said, putting a finger to his sly lips. "He's starting!"

"I'm, I'm Penn Abrams," he said, his voice cracking into the microphone. A girl in the audience giggled. "Ex-excuse me. I'd like to dedicate this performance to my dad, who is no longer here . . . with us."

Penn paused to adjust his glasses as the audience grew silent.

"He read this poem out loud every night in hopes to instill in me the critical lessons of manhood. I have this weird gut feeling he knew, even then, he wouldn't be able to see me grow up into the man he knew I could be.

"And I, I want to apologize for my tardiness today. For a moment, I have to admit, I lost my will to hold on. I forgot, somewhere along the line, that my father's heart and nerve and sinew, as Rudyard so wonderfully describes in this poem, lives on in me. I needed a uh, a good friend to remind me of who I am, and who I'm capable of becoming. This is 'If—' by Rudyard Kipling."

Penn's voice crack was soon forgotten as he launched into the poem. Ava couldn't believe how much he'd improved since reciting in class. He crossed the stage with ease, inviting the audience to walk with him through the stanzas. Paola snapped photo after photo, but Penn was far too captivating for anyone around them to notice.

As Penn entered the final lines, Paola handed one of the photos over to Ava. Ava didn't look as it developed, hanging on to Penn's every word as he drew out the final sentence. When he finished, the audience fell into a respectful silence before breaking out into thunderous applause.

Paola stood up, photos falling from her lap as tears streamed down her cheeks. Kaysar and Ava rose beside her, not wanting her to stand alone. But soon, everyone in the packed auditorium had risen too, giving Penn the standing ovation he deserved.

Penn exited the stage, a hand to his heart in humble gratitude. When they sat back down, Ava looked down at the photo she clung to in her hand. At first glance, she thought it was Mr. Abrams himself. She did a double take, wondering how she'd missed how much he was beginning to look like his dad.

"Hey, you okay?" Kaysar asked, noticing the odd look on her face.

"Oh, oh yeah," Ava answered, unsettled. "Just, you know, glad Penn was able to get up there today."

"Man, me too! No wonder those kids were glad he didn't show up. It's actually quite annoying how talented he is, isn't it?"

"It is," Ava smiled, looking back down at the photo. "It really, *really* is."

* * *

They waited for Penn outside on the lawn as he posed for pictures alongside the other winners. He ran over to them as soon as he could, corralling them into a group hug. Ava thought it would be weird to be squashed close to Mrs. Papayanni, but it turned out it wasn't at all.

"Awesome job, man!" Kaysar shouted, slapping him on the back.

"Excellent performance, Penn. You included every little gesture we worked on!" Mrs. Papayanni complimented.

"Amazing, as always," Ava said, smiling.

Ava stepped back with Kaysar and Mrs. Papayanni to allow Paola time for just her and Penn. Paola reached up, placing her hands on the sides of his face.

"Your father would be, you know what, your father *is* so proud of you," she said.

"*Ma . . .*"

"No, I mean it! A full ride to Stanford and now winning a poetry competition with his favorite poem!"

"Well, I didn't win, I placed second. It seems to be my sweet spot."

"Oh, whatever! It still counts!" she said. "We need a few photos before we go, everyone get in together!"

Ignoring Penn's objections, Paola grabbed a stranger to take a photo of the five of them.

"Now just one with Penn and Ava! To celebrate getting Penn here today!"

Penn groaned but pulled Ava in toward him. Ava leaned into him, feeling much more comfortable than she had the last time Paola forced them to take a picture together. Penn allowed Paola to take a few this time, much to her excitement. Afterward, Paola slipped one into Ava's hand. Though Ava didn't say a word out loud, Paola winked, knowing how much it meant to Ava to have it.

"Well," Kaysar said as they walked toward their cars and waved good-bye to Mrs. Papayanni. "It's your big day, man. What do you want to do now?"

Penn tilted his head in Ava's direction. "I owe someone Poppy's, if she doesn't mind a couple of extra people joining us."

"I think ice cream sounds … perfect," Ava said, holding the two photos from Paola close to her chest. She already knew just the spot on her wall where she was going to hang them.

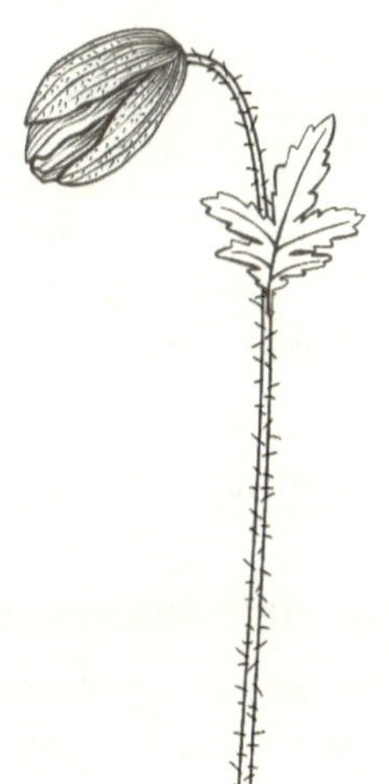

chapter thirty-one

The days sped forward, no matter how much Ava tried to catch them in her arms and slow them down. Between preparing for trial, taking on extra readings suggested by Mr. Jenneman, keeping up with assignments for Mrs. Papayanni, and spending every spare moment she had with Penn, spring arrived in full bloom.

It was on a particularly brilliant April afternoon that Penn and Ava sat atop The Lookout. The red blanket underneath them was damp from a sprinkle of rain that passed earlier in the day. Ava held a hand across her brow to block aggressive rays of sunshine as the sun began to set, which didn't seem to bother Penn as he jabbered on about California. Ava listened quietly, staring out at Westwood, trying to picture it without him and Paola in it. As supportive as she'd been, her patience was waning. Penn had not once spoken about how much he would miss Westwood. Or anyone who would reside there after he left.

When the sun began to sink behind the town, Ava jumped to her feet, cutting Penn off midsentence.

"Welp, I need to get going. I think Mac and my mom are making a special dinner tonight," Ava lied, heading toward her Jeep.

"You should have said something!" Penn exclaimed, grabbing the blanket as he ran after her.

Ava didn't speak a word to him as she drove him home. When he asked a question, she turned the volume up on the stereo to drown him out.

"Do you want to come in and say hi to Paola?" Penn asked once Ava parked in his driveway.

"Nope, I'm good," she answered, jaw clenched, wishing her Jeep had an eject button.

"Just for a minute? She's all excited; she is talking with a lady near Stanford who owns one of those paint and wine studios or whatever they are called. This way she might have some part-time work while she looks for something more permanent. I know she'd love to tell you about it!"

If Ava had to hear one more thing about Stanford she thought she might detonate, taking everyone in the vicinity down with her. She pictured Paola and Penn in Palo Alto, happily living their lives on the West Coast, forgetting they ever knew her. It made her sick to her stomach to think of the first college girl Penn would invite to his new house.

"I really need to get going," Ava said, staring straight ahead, her tone definite.

Penn hesitated, opening the door to get out. Then he slammed it shut again.

"What's going on, exactly? This feels a little passive aggressive," he said.

Ava whipped around in her seat, unable to hold it in any longer.

"You're not just going away for college! You're leaving Westwood!" Ava cried, waving her arms around to try to get him to see her clearly. "You're leaving . . . *you're leaving me behind when you go!*"

Penn's face changed, the soft edges of his mouth hardening at her words. His eyes narrowed as a familiar fire ignited behind them.

"You know it's not like that. You know how much this means to Paola. And to me. And to my dad, even. You know I—"

"*I know!*" Ava shouted, ripping off her seatbelt. "*I GET IT!* Don't think for a second I don't understand how much it means to you, and how much you deserve it, and how much I want it for you! But you haven't even thought about how it might make me feel! I can't . . . I can't."

Ava's tears ran thick, her throat strangled by all the pain she felt since she saw him open the envelope after their date. Their date, which neither of them had talked about since that night. Penn reached over the center console, but Ava jolted backward as if he could burn her. A touch from him was too much. She knew, now, exactly how he felt before his poetry competition. It was all too much. She suddenly needed to be anywhere else.

Ava threw open her door and started running. She ran down Penn's block, and then another, and another, until she found herself on a street she'd never been on before. The night was growing chilly, the sky almost black. The neighborhood was empty and quiet now that everyone had gone inside for the night.

Stopping when her legs could no longer carry her, Ava collapsed into a stranger's front yard. Lying flat on the grass, she looked up to find the stars flickering back at her. They told her what she already knew: Penn was leaving, and there was no stopping it. There was no changing his mind. No pausing time. Even beneath the sprawling sky she felt claustrophobic. Powerless. There was nothing she could do. She pulled her knees tight into her chest, cradling her head in her arm.

After a while, she heard steady footsteps walking toward her.

"Can I join you?" Penn asked from the sidewalk, his hands stuffed in his pockets. Ava couldn't stand to look at him. She uncurled herself and sat up on her elbows, eyes still angled upward.

"I'll take that as a yes," he said. He sat down beside her but left space between them. Ava resented how calming his presence felt.

"I want you to know something, Ava. You weren't part of the plan, you know. This is something I've worked hard for, well, for most of my life. And I can't pretend that I'm not happy about it."

"Is this supposed to make me feel better?" Ava spat. Even to her own ears, her voice sounded bitter and childish.

"No," Penn answered. "But this might. I am going to miss you, more than you know. *More than I should.* You have changed me for the better. You taught me things I couldn't learn from any book, and you know me," he said, scooting close in beside her. "I've read most of them."

"Like what? How to skip class and quit stuff?" Ava asked, sniffling.

"Well, yeah, but also how to be brave. And I don't mean, excuse my French, bullshit superhero brave. I mean dance in the face of your trauma brave. Defy expectations of others brave. Trust a new friend after yours abandoned you brave. Maybe even, let a boy you barely know cry on your shoulder brave."

He nudged her arm, and Ava hated that it made her smile.

"You're going to do great things without me around. You're one of the most resilient people I know. And it's different, now, than it was back in October. You have people around who really, truly care about you. Hell, you've got more friends than I do now!"

They sat still as Ava contemplated his words.

"I don't think you ever needed me as much as you thought you did," he continued. "You already had everything inside of you that you needed to get where you are. *See?* I'm basically quoting lines from you now. But I'm so, so glad you let me be your partner that day in English class. It was me who needed you, you know."

Ava finally lowered her eyes from the sky to look at him. It was Penn that shifted his gaze away.

"You're why Westwood has felt like a home for me," he said, his voice catching. "You're why it's going to be so hard to leave."

Ava wanted to pull him close and scream up at the stars all at the same time. She settled for reaching out and placing her hand on top of his. She wished she could tell him everything he meant to her, but it was too much to put into words. She only had a few, and she knew they were insufficient.

"You've been . . . home . . . for me, too," Ava whispered.

Penn turned his hand over and spread open his palm. Ava intertwined her fingers with his.

"Write to me," Penn asked, squeezing her hand. "After I move? I don't mean texting. You never let me read the poem you wrote, but, if you change your mind, or write anything you'd like to share with me at all, write to me?"

Ava gave a slight nod but didn't want to think of any point in the future just now.

They sat together long after the stranger's porch light went out, gazing up at the night sky, holding on to what little time they had left.

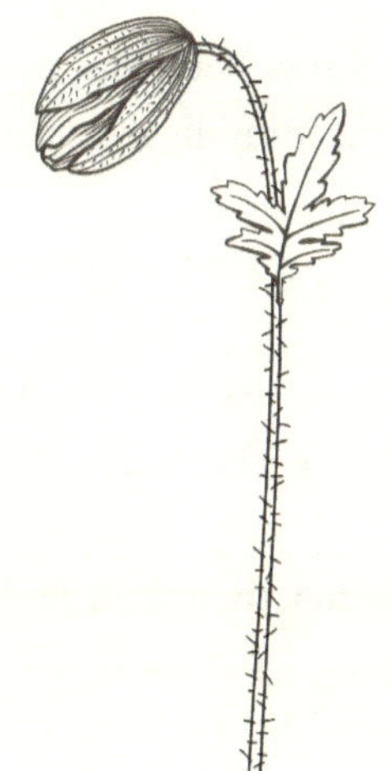

chapter thirty-two

Ava stood alone in the middle of the senior locker bay, where Penn asked her to wait for him after school. She heaved out an audible sigh, arms crossed over her chest. She couldn't believe the school year was over. While she'd tried to grip on to every second of the past few months, the ending arrived all the same.

A familiar shriek of laughter filled the empty locker bay, sending Ava into high alert. She turned toward the hall to find Leona rounding the corner, Liam by her side.

"Oh, hey, Ava!" Liam called, stuffing a hand full of chips into his mouth as he headed to his locker. "I haven't seen you around lately."

"She's probably waiting for her little boyfriend," Leona sneered, leaning against the locker next to Liam's.

"You know perfectly well he's not my boyfriend, Leona," Ava shot back.

The sound of footsteps running toward them broke through the tension.

"Leona, I didn't know you'd be here," Trish shouted as she stepped, out of breath, into the bay. "Ava! You're who I was looking for!"

Trish ran forward and threw her arms around Ava's neck. She'd applied glitter hairspray on her tumbling mass of curls in celebration of school ending.

"Congratulations, Trish! Just a few more months and you'll be at Parsons!" Ava exclaimed.

"Thank you! I wanted to make sure I got a picture with you before I left! Penn said you'd be waiting back here. I passed him in the hallway talking to Ms. Delic."

Trish glanced over at Leona, then thought better of it.

"Liam, do you mind taking a picture of us?" Trish asked.

"Anything for you ladies," he said, crumpling up his chip bag and throwing it into his locker. He took Trish's phone from her, oblivious to Leona's death stare.

"Parsons, that's like, fashion design, right?" Liam asked.

"Yep!" Trish said, glowing. "It's always been a dream of mine to move to New York City and start a fashion line of my own!"

Trish turned toward Ava, taking her hands in hers.

"I know we still have a lot of work to do this summer to prepare for the trial, before I move to the city. You know I'll come back as often as I need to. And you can call me, anytime, to talk."

"I know," Ava said, looking down at their hands. She didn't want to think about school next year without Trish. "But we can be sad later. Today is a day to celebrate!"

Trish beamed and hugged Ava tight, posing cheek to cheek as Liam took their picture.

"I gotta get going!" Trish said, taking her phone back before skipping away. "I'll see you in a couple of days, Ava! Bye, Liam!"

"Oh," Trish stopped in the hallway, then pivoted back around. "Congratulations, Leona. On getting into Clemson. I bet your parents are proud you're continuing the family tradition."

Leona stared at Trish, wide-eyed.

"Yeah, uh, thanks," Leona said after a long pause. "Congrats, or whatever, to you, too."

Trish gave her a small smile and ran back down the hall, her sparkling hair streaming behind her.

"I gotta run too," Liam said, shutting his locker. "See you at graduation, Leona?"

Leona shrugged, uninterested.

"Uh, okay? Hope you have a good senior year, Ava!"

"Bye, Liam, enjoy Penn State next year!" she said, waving as Liam left her alone with Leona.

Ava hoped Penn would come hurtling around the corner any second now. As Leona opened her mouth, Ava closed her eyes, bracing for impact.

"I . . . ," Leona began. Ava squinted her eyes open to find Leona shuffling her feet. "I think it's really cool that you and Trish are suing Bradley and the police department. I didn't think either of you had it in you, to do something like that."

Ava grunt-laughed, impressed with Leona's ability to turn any compliment into an insult.

"I mean," Leona struggled. "I never meant to make you two feel bad about yourselves, or whatever. I just, I missed Jacklyn. I wanted you to be bold and stand for something, like she does. You both seemed so—"

"Cardboard?" Ava asked, drawing herself up to full height, which was a couple inches taller than Leona.

"Yeah, I guess. But I know, like now, that you're not."

Ava narrowed her eyes, trying to figure out if she was genuine.

"I guess I'm trying to say I am sorry, okay? I misjudged the two of you. And I know you'll be busy this summer with everything going on. But if you ever want to come over and lie by the pool with Jacklyn and me . . . well, you can."

Ava glanced up to find Penn near the mouth of the bay, leaning against a pillar. His eyebrows were raised high, stunned at what he'd just witnessed. Ava knew her face must mirror his same surprise.

As Ava brought her gaze back to Leona, she couldn't help but notice how small she was without her heels on. Her makeup today was subdued, her outfit unusually casual. It was hard to believe, seeing her like this, that Ava had so long been terrified of her.

"I appreciate your apology, Leona. I'll keep your offer in mind. Congratulations, on Clemson, and on graduation. And I did want to thank you."

"Thank me? For what?" Leona asked.

"For teaching me what I will and won't accept from people. You'll never know how much you motivated me to find friends," Ava glanced over at Penn. "And a life of my own."

Leona followed Ava's gaze, realizing she was in the middle of something that had nothing to do with her anymore. She scanned Ava up and down before giving one last brilliant hair toss, strutting past Penn on her way out.

"Ready to go?" Ava asked as Penn walked toward her.

"One more thing," he said, pulling Ava by the arm down the stairs and through the library, taking the shortcut she had shown him.

She was panting by the time they arrived at his locker. When he opened it up, only two items remained at the bottom.

"That's it? I know you, you already cleaned this out," Ava accused.

"Hold on, will you!" he demanded, bending down to retrieve one of the books. "*Here.*" He shoved it into her hands.

"I don't collect books, Penn, I'm not you," she said, stopping abruptly as she saw what it was.

"I know you have your own copy, but I thought you might want to keep mine, too. Maybe it's dumb."

"It's not dumb," Ava said, running her fingers over the battered cover.

Penn blushed as he tried to explain why it was so beat up.

"Wait, what is the other thing in there?" Ava asked, pointing to the bottom of his locker.

"Oh, just my old planner. I use the one you got me now, but I like to keep the old ones," he said, bending down to pick it up.

"What for?"

"I do this goofy thing where I write down the details of my day, alongside my plans. Anytime something I want to remember happens, I jot it down."

"So, you aren't *quite* as obsessed with your schedule as I thought you were?" Ava asked.

"Oh no, still very much obsessed with my schedule. But I like to keep track of little things, just to remind me how each day is new and different, and that there's always something to be grateful for."

Ava studied him for a moment, wondering how much there was still to know about him. She smiled as he took one last look at his empty locker then shut it, twirling the combination lock.

"Ready?" he asked, beginning to lead the way down the hall.

Ava hesitated, her brain sparking with a memory. "Wait, do you write stuff about me in there?"

Penn stopped in his tracks.

"Why do you want to know?" he asked, not turning to meet her eyes.

"No reason," she said, delight washing over her as she jogged to catch up with him.

Together they strode through the doors of Westwood High and into the May afternoon sunshine. The back of their hands met as they descended the steps, Penn holding on to his planner and Ava to his copy of *Death of a Salesman.*

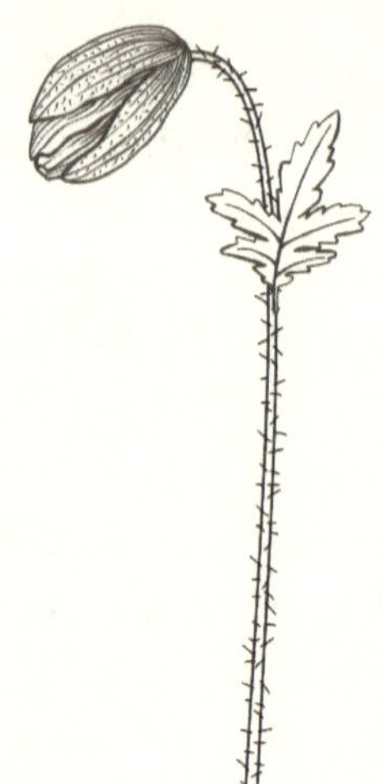

chapter thirty-three

It had been a hot and muggy June, and the first day of July was no different. Kaysar and Ava stood on Penn and Paola's front lawn, holding on to their sides, trying not to split apart from laughter.

"You should have packed this in the moving truck that's already *halfway to California* by now!" Penn yelled. He removed metal scraps from the backseat that Paola tried to sneak into their overpacked car.

"But I might need them for a project!" Paola cried, finagling a small piece back behind the front seat.

It seemed surreal that they were leaving today. Kaysar stepped in beside Ava and placed his hand on her shoulder. To Ava's bemusement, he still wore all black, even as temperatures hovered around ninety degrees.

Penn wiped sweat off his forehead as Paola broke out her Polaroid camera.

"*Ma! Come on!*" he shouted as she began taking pictures of the house.

"Just a few more! Don't you want one with Kaysar and Ava?"

Kaysar and Ava failed to keep straight faces as Penn slunk across the yard.

"ONE picture, Ma. ONE! Then we are leaving! We're already way behind schedule!"

"Wait!" Paola said. Ava felt Penn tense up beside her. "Turn so your backs are to the house, I want it in the background!"

They turned together as a unit, Penn grumbling complaints beneath his breath. Paola took several pictures before Penn tore away, demanding she hand him the camera.

"We're leaving now!" he said once she gave it to him.

"Okay, okay!" Paola agreed. "*Wait!*"

"MA!"

"No really! I have something I need to give Ava! Hold on a second!"

Paola ran toward the house, her flowy turquoise skirt and waves of dark hair rippling behind her.

"I swear I'll be lucky if I make it to California before September," Penn sighed. He turned toward Kaysar, his hands on his hips.

"Well, man, this is it."

"Let's not make this a whole thing," Kaysar said, stopping him. He held out his hand to shake Penn's. Penn knocked it aside and encompassed Kaysar in a big bear hug. They held on for several seconds before Kaysar stepped aside, turning his back to Ava to hide his face.

Penn turned next to Ava. She was grateful he didn't say anything as he pulled her into a hug, allowing her to hide her tears in his chest.

When he released her, they did their best to collect themselves as Paola ran back toward them on the lawn.

"This is for you!" she said, thrusting a canvas into Ava's arms.

"But I didn't . . . ," Ava began, confused as she looked down.

The painting, although somewhat abstract, was unmistakably of Ava. She was leaning over Mei's boys, helping the youngest with his drawing. The background consisted of Paola's signature jewel-toned swirls, but a unique stroke of black created depth against the vibrancy of the rest of the painting.

"It's the painting you thought you messed up!" Paola exclaimed. "I took a break from it for a while because it wasn't sure what it wanted to be yet. Then I saw the way you lit up around kiddos during our art classes, and I just had to capture it for you."

"Th-this, this is . . . ," Ava tried to thank Paola, but her voice broke off. There was no way to convey how much her relationship with Paola had changed the course of her life. Now that Paola had welcomed her into a world of curiosity and possibility, Ava couldn't help but feel hopeful for what her own future might bring. Even if it meant saying goodbye to her mentor first.

"Oh, Ava! I didn't mean to make you cry," Paola said as she hugged Ava and kissed her on the cheek. "I just wanted you to have something to remember that no matter how imperfect something may seem at first, it can wind up being—"

"*Beautiful,*" Ava finished for her. She leaned the painting against her leg and hugged Paola in closer, hating to think she'd be all the way across the country from now on instead of a short drive away.

"Keep the art classes going for me?" Paola asked. "Mei offered to host in her driveway!"

"Who knows," Ava answered. "My mom has been looking for houses near this neighborhood, I might be able to host them at my place."

"And I'll be there to help!" Kaysar piped up. "On the weekends when I'm not teaching them in my own neighborhood, that is."

Paola beamed at him, pulling him into her hug with Ava.

"We really do need to get going," Penn said, though he made no movement toward the car. Instead, he joined in on the hug, wrapping his arms around all of them.

Eventually, they broke apart, Penn stepping back first. Then Paola snaked her arm around Penn's waist. They turned away and walked in sync toward the driveway. Before opening the car doors, they waved once more to Kaysar and Ava. Ava threaded her arm through Kaysar's, watching as they buckled in and backed down the driveway.

Neither Kaysar nor Ava spoke a word as they watched the car disappear down Baile Avenue. They stood together long after they left, listening as crickets broke out in chorus around them.

"They asked me to do a final walkthrough and lock up the house. Want to join me?" Kaysar asked.

Ava followed behind him as he meandered toward the house. While the front garden was bursting to life with herbs and wildflowers, Paola had taken her collection of pots with her. It felt wrong to walk the path to the front door unencumbered.

Once inside, Ava was shocked to find the walls stripped of all their color. They had been painted a stark white, not a hint of Paola's mural present. Ava walked beneath the curved doorway into the kitchen to find each surface unnaturally shiny. The smell of cleaning agents offended Ava's nostrils; she craved the scent of Paola's simmering mystery concoctions. The countertop where the stereo once sat seemed abandoned, confused as to why it had been left behind.

Ava trailed her finger along the white wall in the hallway, lost without the guidance of shape and color. She peeked into Paola's bedroom. It looked now as if it had never belonged to her. She turned away and crossed over into Penn's room, where Kaysar stood looking out the back window into the woods.

"I can't believe they are really gone," Ava said, joining beside him.

"I can't believe they put me through this, *twice*," Kaysar said, half joking, though Ava could tell he was serious by the pain in his voice.

Ava turned, moving toward the space that Penn's bed had occupied. She could still make out the indents where the legs of his bed left their mark. She set down Paola's painting and put her back to the wall, sliding down onto the floor.

Kaysar sank down next to her. Ava rested her head on his shoulder, crumbling as she let the beginning stages of grief crash down on her. Kaysar angled his head to rest on hers. Ava felt warm tears drop into her hair.

She tried to bring the details of Penn's face to mind, but they were already fading fast. A full, deep belly laugh of a neighbor met her ears, and Ava wondered when she'd be able to do that again. Or if going forward, she'd be able to look at the world in quite the same way without Penn there to point little things out for her.

As her tears cleared enough for her to see again, Ava found herself staring at what was Penn's bookshelf. She thought of the book he had gifted her, unsure when she'd be able to open it. But it gave the slightest solace to know Penn would be there, in the margins. It reminded her of his ability to appreciate every character in a story, no matter how flawed they may be.

Ava glanced up at Kaysar, smiling slightly as she nestled her head further into his shoulder. Somehow, she knew Penn would still find ways to open her mind, even as he crossed over the edge of town and into the world beyond Westwood.

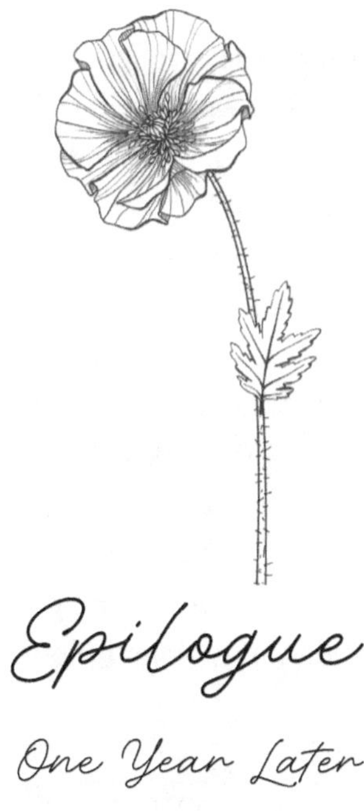

Epilogue

One Year Later

"Ava Juliet Pierson!" Mr. Tully called into the microphone. Ava walked down the center aisle toward the stage. Mr. Jenneman held up his hand, and Ava high-fived him as she passed. Ms. Delic sat beside him, giving her two thumbs-ups. Even Mrs. Papayanni, though maintaining her professionalism, let out an audible whoop as Ava climbed the stairs toward the podium. A loud wolf whistle issued from somewhere in the auditorium as she was handed her diploma.

Cameras flashed as Ava sat back down. She let out a long exhale as she listened to her fellow classmates' names being called. She couldn't believe her high school career was officially over. For so long, she couldn't wait for it to end, but now that it was here, the horizon of possibility loomed large and intimidating in front of her.

When the ceremony ended, Ava was swept outside in a wave of graduates to the soccer field. She searched the sea of faces, trying to find any belonging to those she most wanted to see. For a second, she thought she saw someone in the distance, but the clouds shifted above, sending a ray of sun to block her vision. She reached up, shielding her eyes, but he was gone. Ava shook her head. It was stupid to think he'd be here today.

"Congratulations, Ava!" someone shouted to her left.

"Coach Arruda!" Ava answered when she spotted her favorite coach. She ran forward to hug her. "Congrats on the state championship! I didn't make it to watch the game because of, you know, court stuff, but Leila gave me the play-by-play of the big win!"

"Thank you! The best of luck to you at the University of Michigan, Ava. You deserve everything you've worked for. It's amazing what you, your mom, and Trish have done for women in this town, even if things didn't—"

"Ava! Honey! Over here!" Aunt Brene called, beckoning Ava over to the circle of friends and family formed near a goal post.

Ava gave Coach Arruda an apologetic look. "Thanks, Coach, I, uh, gotta go."

"Of course, go celebrate!"

She waved goodbye to Coach Arruda, tucking her kind comments away.

Mac rushed over to Ava first and threw his arms around her neck. He was almost a whole foot taller than she was now.

"Congrats, Sis! I don't know what I'm going to do without you here next year. Who is going to eat lunch with me now?"

"Like that will be an issue, Mr. Popular," Ava said, aware of the many girls around them that hoped Mac would glance in their direction. Mac, however, was far too occupied enjoying time with his family to notice.

"Move over!" Jacklyn demanded, taking Ava into her arms. "So proud of you, sister!"

"*Proud of you, too,*" Ava said into her ear.

Jacklyn had finished her first full year of classes at Everton just a couple of days before. She was as beautiful as ever today, but Ava felt secure enough in her skin these days to no longer feel jealous of her. Jacklyn had even gone with Ava to the hair salon last week, cheering as Ava chopped her long locks to her chin.

"My turn, my turn!" Aunt Brene sang as she wove herself into the mix. Ava let herself rest into her aunt's comforting embrace, gratitude flowing through her as she recognized how many people had shown up for her today.

Aunt Brene released Ava as her mom moved in to hug her next. Ava hugged her the hardest. Her mom had been there for her in every way over the past year. The thought of parting from her in a few months had already caused Ava a few sleepless nights.

"I'm so proud of you, Ava. And I'm sorry your father isn't here," she said hoarsely.

"You don't have to apologize for him anymore, Mom," Ava said, pulling her closer. "It's best for all of us that he stays gone."

"Can I get in on this one?" Trish asked after several moments. Amelia opened up her arms, and the three women embraced, recreating the circle of trust that had solidified between them over the past year.

"Alright, *alright*, I've waited patiently enough, damn it," Kaysar complained.

Ava laughed, wiping her eyes with the sleeve of her robe. Kaysar picked her up and swung her around in a circle. They'd been teaching art classes together twice a month, one Saturday in Baltimore and one in Westwood. Kaysar had even received a grant to create an art-based after-school program in his neighborhood. He told Ava it was something Mr. Abrams and Paola had always dreamed of doing together. Paola was beyond thrilled when Kaysar told her he was working to make it come true.

"Are we ready to go to Mei's? Leila said she'll meet us there," Ava said to everyone as Kaysar set her down.

Everyone stared back at her, a mysterious silence settling over them.

"What? Did I forget about someone?" Ava asked, looking around at the group that had gathered around her.

"Pardon me, uh, miss?" an all-too-familiar voice said behind her.

Ava spun around, not believing her ears.

His hair was cropped short and was now much lighter than Ava remembered it. She thought he'd even grown a few inches taller. His clothes were far more stylish than before: a fitted navy t-shirt flecked with crimson red and burnt orange, paired with dark blue jeans. Even his glasses were sleeker. But he still wore oxfords, and his eyes remained precisely the same shade of bronze.

"What are . . . *what are you doing here?!*" Ava squealed, failing to hide her excitement.

Penn laughed nervously, lifting a hand to tug at his phantom curls.

"Kaysar told me the date, got me a ticket, and threatened to drive all the way to California and throw me in the car if I didn't agree to—"

"You've kept this a secret from me!" Ava shouted, whipping back around.

"Oh, get over it," Mac said, rolling his eyes from beside Kaysar. "We all know you're ridiculously happy to see him."

Ava tried to swat at him, but he hid behind Jacklyn, who wore a very smug look on her face.

"I heard Mei's is up next?" Penn asked, rubbing his hands together. "Paola insists I give Mei as many hugs as days we've been away. We better get going; it could take all night."

Mei's had become such a staple of Westwood that she'd expanded the restaurant into the building next door. When they arrived, Mei cried out at the sight of Penn. Ava was glad she wasn't the only one surprised by his visit. After their long and teary embrace, Mei tried to grab the menus, but Jacklyn stopped her.

"You have a hostess and a whole serving staff now! You're here to manage, not serve!" Jacklyn argued, handing the menus over to the hostess.

"You know this is hard for me!" Mei said while smiling, stepping in beside Ava to congratulate her.

"*California looks good on him,*" Jacklyn whispered to Ava as Mei moved over to ask Penn questions about his first year of college. Ava rolled her eyes at her sister, though she didn't disagree.

Leila waved excitedly when they got to the table on the new side of the restaurant. Mac rushed in to sit beside her. It appeared he'd still have a lunch buddy when Ava left, after all. Ava chose to sit between her mom and Aunt Brene, avoiding close contact with Penn, who sat on the opposite end of the table.

As Jacklyn and Kaysar argued over the best appetizers to order, Ava slipped away. She wound through the main restaurant, which was packed to the max. She felt relief wash over her as she entered the bathroom and locked herself in an empty stall. As happy as it made her to see Penn, it was equally as unsettling. She hadn't expected him to look so different. And she hadn't expected to feel what she told herself she was no longer allowed to feel.

Trying to collect herself, she stepped out of the bathroom, not paying attention as she walked back toward their table.

"Shit I'm—" she said, smacking into someone.

"Ow, sorry I—"

Penn and Ava stepped back, laughing once they realized they'd collided with each other. Then Ava quieted immediately, looking up to find they were under the stairs that led to the table where they sat together on their date. Ava rubbed her lips together, looking away as she crossed her arms over her chest.

"Hey, can I ask you something?" Penn questioned.

"Oh, this is never good," Ava said, trying her best to sound sarcastic.

"After we finish eating, do you want to ditch this place and go somewhere? I'm only here for the night. I have to leave tomorrow morning to start my internship."

Ava's gut twisted at the thought of him leaving again so soon after he'd arrived.

"I, um," Ava considered saying no, fearful of what being alone with Penn might bring up for her. It was a relief, without him here, to hide her feelings before she was ready to share them. "I think I know the perfect place we can go."

Penn's eyes lit up, flashing with the same intensity they'd had for her when they sat at the table above them. She broke away, afraid of what she saw there.

When Ava got back to the table, her palms felt sweaty. She took her time looking at each person, savoring how the people she cared about were in one place at the same time. She had a sinking feeling these types of gatherings wouldn't happen often going forward. Change was coming, and Ava knew from experience, she needed to grab hold of the present moment before it slipped away.

When Penn returned to his seat, Ava waved Mei over from another table, asking her to stay for a moment. Fighting against her anxiety, Ava reached forward and grabbed her water glass. She stood up, lifting it as she cleared her throat.

"I, um," the table quieted in surprise as Ava addressed them. "I just wanted, I wanted to say . . ."

The words were there in her head, but as everyone stared up at her, Ava lost them. She thought she'd worked through this, but like Mr. Jenneman had taught her, anxiety wasn't something that ever went away completely. She lifted her eyes, and they settled on Penn, who didn't have to say anything. His presence was enough to remind her she had already spoken up in the face of much worse than this.

"Thank you all for being here," Ava continued. "Each of you has shown up today because you care about me, and I mean me as I am, not someone you think I should be."

Penn lowered his eyes, recognizing his words.

"Soon I'll leave for college, and as excited as I am, I know it's going to be really hard to leave Westwood. But it's because of all of you that I know now what it means to belong. It gives me this small hope that wherever I go, college and beyond, I can be a piece of home like you all have been for me. If you'll join me in raising a glass . . ."

Ava lifted her glass, scanning the faces around her, which were all in various stages of sniffling, crumbling, and full-out sobbing.

"Here's to being home for others," Ava said, trying to hold back the flood gate of tears about to burst.

"To being home for others," they said in unison, clinking their glasses together.

Ava tried to smile at them, but her eyes were watering, overcome with the emotions of a very long day. And a very long year, at that. Thankfully their meals arrived, distracting everyone from Ava's ugly-cry and sending the table back into a frenzied chatter.

After consuming a masterful dessert creation provided free, of course, by Mei, Ava soon found herself standing outside hugging everyone good-bye. A cool breeze rippled through the late afternoon air as Penn and Ava were left standing alone on the sidewalk. They watched as cars disappeared down the street.

"Ready?" Ava asked, jiggling her keys.

"Actually, I rented a car, so I'll meet you up there," Penn said on the sly.

"You got your license?! *Who did California turn you into?*"

Penn smiled sheepishly. "I'll see you on The Lookout?"

"See you there," Ava answered, walking away toward her Jeep.

The drive up to The Lookout felt longer than usual. She hadn't been up here since Penn left, though Jacklyn had invited her multiple times. Ava felt an internal resistance when she saw Penn waiting near the trail as she pulled in behind his rental.

"You know," he said as she joined him. "I don't get car sick when I'm the driver, which does make me wonder."

"Wonder what?" Ava asked.

"Maybe you weren't the best driver, after all?"

Ava shoved him lightly. "You have no right to complain after all the rides I gave you!"

"Yeah, but you had to notice I took my bike as often as I could."

"Do you still ride your bike? Now that you drive, I mean?" Ava asked as they made their way up the steep trail.

"Every once in a while, but I get all gross and sweaty. It's so . . . sunny in California."

Ava wasn't sure what to make of his comment. When they got to the top of the trail, Ava pulled aside the branches for him, allowing him to step into the clearing first.

The Lookout hadn't changed one bit, but the sunset tonight was a striking marigold, streaked with deep plum. Threatening clouds were rolling in, creating a sharp contrast between dark and light.

"It's still pretty incredible," Penn said, whistling as he sat down on the grass.

"Yeah, it really is," Ava marveled, settling in beside him.

"I did want to say a proper congratulations, to you, without everyone around. You're like Biff, you know?"

Ava gave him the side-eye. "A sexist asshole who slightly redeems themselves in the end? Thanks, Penn, that means a lot!"

"No, well, yeah, he totally is, but I mean, *you know who you are, kid.*"

Ava bumped his arm with hers. "You didn't stop being a nerd in college, I guess."

"No, it's actually cool to be a nerd in college. You just wait," Penn joked. Ava shook her head at him. "So, University of Michigan, huh? Kaysar told me you're double majoring in art and psychology?"

"Yeah, the double major was inspired by you. Mr. Jenneman and Ms. Delic helped me apply for some scholarships since my dad isn't financially supporting us anymore."

"I'm so sorry, Ava."

"No, it's really okay. It's a relief actually, not having to rely on him for anything. It's just been extra tight because my mom obviously took on my case pro bono."

"Yeah, I'm sorry that didn't go the way you wished it would. I followed the whole thing. I don't know how in the world they got off without charges! But I did see that the Chief of Police and Bradley's uncle got fired. Not to mention Bradley's reputation is beyond ruined. I tried to call you about it, you know. Several times, in fact."

Ava stared straight ahead, guilt filling her senses.

"I know. I'm sorry, Penn. After you left, I just couldn't. And when the not-guilty verdicts were announced, I wished you were here, I guess. But you weren't."

Penn and Ava looked out over Westwood, neither sure what to say.

"I know it wasn't the outcome you hoped for," Penn said eventually, his voice soft, "but it was still a groundbreaking case for the town. Watching you, your mom, and Trish on the news, it was inspiring, really. I'm sure you've heard about the record number of abuse victims coming forward in Westwood now. And there's a new Police Chief that actually listens to assault victims! *You* did that."

"I mean my mom did all the work," Ava said, a weight starting to lift that had clung to her since the trial ended. "And Trish had way more to handle with the police department—"

"Ava, you always, *always* sell yourself short. You are the one who went to your mom about it. *You* helped make this town a safer place to live. It isn't small, what you've done."

Ava dropped her head down to her knees. Even after a year of not speaking much to him, she hated how he still knew exactly what she needed to hear. She felt his eyes on her, but he didn't move in to comfort her. As much as she wished he would, she knew he kept a space between them for a reason.

"What do you think, now that you're getting out of this place?" Penn asked.

Ava looked up from her knees, watching as the ominous clouds drew closer.

"It's funny," she answered after a while. "I used to think I'd give anything to get away from here. Now that I'm about to leave, I don't know how to feel. It will always be the place where I grew up, and I think that might really mean something to me someday. What about you? You haven't said much about life in California. I bet this place looks like a joke compared to Palo Alto."

Penn smiled, but there was hardness at the edges.

"I know I wasn't here in Westwood long, but it feels like nothing has changed and at the same time everything has. It's like I belong less and less here and more and more somewhere else. I'm not sure if that somewhere else is California. Even sitting here with you, it's so wonderful to be with you, Ava. I couldn't wait to see you again. But you've changed too. And I don't just mean your hair. Which I love short, by the way. You've become this beautiful and confident version of yourself."

Ava's heart beat wildly in her chest as their eyes met.

"But it's just not the same," he said, finality in his tone. He tore his eyes away from hers.

They let the silence settle upon them, the ache of growing apart as strong as the incoming storm. A rumble of thunder sounded in the distance.

"Was that?" Penn asked, standing up.

"I think it was," Ava said as a bolt of lightning flashed across the sky.

The patter of rain sounded on the topmost tree branches. They ran for the trail, racing back the way they'd come.

"Wait!" Ava shouted when they reached their cars. "I've got something for you!"

Penn squinted near his car door as raindrops broke across his forehead. Ava rifled through her glove department, throwing things around until she found what she was looking for. She ran back to him, the rain picking up around them.

"You told me to write to you. And I know I didn't send it to you, but read it, sometime. Okay?"

Penn looked down at the moleskin, opening the cover to find his inscription on it. "But this was a gift for you. I don't—"

"I want it back, the next time we see each other. Keep it with you until then."

The sky ripped open, drenching Ava's poppy-red sundress.

Penn placed the moleskin in his front shirt pocket and tapped it with care. He held his arms out, hesitating. Ava threw herself around him, holding him close to her as water dripped into her hair and down her back.

"Drive safe, have a good flight, and text me when you get home? I promise I'll text you back!" Ava shouted over the rain.

"I will," he shouted back. "Let's not go so long without seeing each other, deal? Michigan isn't as far from California as Pennsylvania is, you know!"

Ava nodded as she released him, running back to her Jeep before he could figure out it wasn't just rain falling down her face.

Penn followed close behind as she backed out, cautiously making their way down the slick winding road. When she reached the bottom, Ava adjusted her rearview mirror. Between wiper blades clearing the rear windshield, she saw Penn reach up and wipe his face with his sleeve. She turned her left signal on as he turned on his right. Their eyes caught in the mirror, gray meeting bronze, before heading their separate ways.

Minutes later, Ava pulled into the driveway of her new house on the other side of town. She turned her Jeep off in the drive and planted her elbows on her steering wheel. Staring straight ahead at the one-car garage, she wiped away tears as they fell freely down her face. Ava wondered if some future version of herself might be brave enough to tell Penn how much he still meant to her. Until then, a poem would have to do.

It wasn't my first kiss—
    The one in the field behind Westwood Middle
It wasn't my first boyfriend—
    The one who smelled like pepperoni
It wasn't my first crush—
    The one who dyed his hair tips blonde
It wasn't my worst nightmare—
    The one I thought I could erase

It wasn't reddest of roses
    or the palest, softest of pinks
It wasn't symphonies
    or a Magnum Opus
        (you taught me what that means)

It was rain when I was wilting
It was ice cream on an otherwise forgettable day
It was a door held open to see the world through
It was walking side by side, day by day

  We were hands held under starlight,
    legs running wild to escape
      We were dancing, laughing, growing—
      We were friends,
          and love,
            and fate.